Arthur Paterson

Cromwell's Own

A Story of the Great Civil War

Arthur Paterson

Cromwell's Own
A Story of the Great Civil War

ISBN/EAN: 9783337400958

Printed in Europe, USA, Canada, Australia, Japan

Cover: Foto ©Andreas Hilbeck / pixelio.de

More available books at **www.hansebooks.com**

CROMWELL'S OWN

A Story of the Great Civil War
By ARTHUR PATERSON
Author of "The Gospel Writ in Steel"
"For Freedom's Sake" etc., etc.

NEW YORK AND LONDON
HARPER & BROTHERS PUBLISHERS
1899

CROMWELL'S OWN

CHAPTER I

A CLOSE, sultry evening in June, 1640. The day
had been cloudy and threatening, the sun had set
in fiery splendour, and the weather-wise predicted rain.
But the farmers who knew best and needed the rain most,
shook their heads gloomily, and said it would not come
yet, and when it did would be a deluge, and do more
harm than good.

In the court of Sidney Sussex College, Cambridge, the
bees hummed drowsily, heavily laden and homeward
bound. The master was fond of flowers, and from the
trim beds, arranged in exact order among the rows of
poplars which bordered the college lawns from gate to
lodge, stole the scent of roses, wallflowers, and mignon-
ette, filling with their sweet fragrance the students'
studies and chambers above.

"Sidney" of that day was, in outward appearance, very
different from "Sidney" of this. Now we only see a
building which, though fine in outline and conception, is
of a cold grey, smooth and uninteresting as the stone-
work of a modern cathedral. In those days it was in all
the glory of a mellowed red brick, rich and deep in colouring and tone. The restorer's work had not begun.

Sidney held at that time 120 students. Space was limited, and four men slept in one room — generally about
twelve feet square; and though each undergraduate had

a separate study in communication with the common sleeping chamber, it was seldom more than six feet by five, sometimes less. Here the student sported his oak and worked, when he had an inclination, which was even less often than his descendent of to-day.

In one of these studies this evening, at about seven of the clock — that is, an hour after supper — an undergraduate was sitting alone, his face in his hands, staring at the wall. He had some writing-paper before him, and a quill pen, which he had dipped into the ink three times. But he had written nothing; he only bit the end of the pen with a determined savage crunch, and stared at the wall.

He was a lad of seventeen, and had been in residence twelve months, so young did our ancestors begin their 'Varsity course in the seventeenth century. A spare, well-knit figure, muscular of limb, though not broad enough yet for its height of six feet. His head was square, with a short chin, a delicately-shaped nose wide at the nostrils, and bright brown eyes. It was a handsome face, full of force, vitality, and expression, but it had serious faults. There was passion and self-will in the tightly-drawn under lip, a twist and wrinkle between the brows which did not speak well for patience or temper — the face of one who from youth to age would strive for what he wanted, and say what he thought fit, though the whole world forbade him; a nature which only the battle of life, if that were hard enough, would tame. His taste in dress was simple, but his clothes were fashionably cut — doublet and hose of claret-coloured silk, loose sleeves slashed with satin, and a collar of point lace. There were no tassels on sword-sash or garters, no jewels on his shoe-buckles, not even a ring on his finger. His hair fell to his shoulders, but was too curly for elegance, and just now looked like a rumpled mane, and added to the paleness of his face. His cap and gown hung in a closet behind the door. They were seldom worn.

"What can I say? How can I write it down?" he cried aloud, dashing his pen on the table with a splutter, and making two more blots. "It will nigh kill him with grief. If I'd but told him last home-coming, when there was only fifty pounds to pay! He would have grieved — grieved sore, and spent a night, maybe, in prayer, dear heart! But then it would have been over. I would have sworn never to play again, and kept my word. I have always done that at least. I would have worked heart and soul this term to make up for lost time, and even pleased Master Ward and made him smile, if a tutor ever smiles. Now! Oh, I cannot tell him!"

He writhed in his chair, and bit his nails to the quick. "Why did I do it? I never cared overmuch. I disliked all I met but Charlton. Yet night after night I played with them because — because he played. And losing, I played on to win the money back. Fool! spendthrift! liar! thief! I am that, naught less, and I will tell the dear dad so and the master; then skulk away discredited and beggared, and list as a common soldier over seas. I will! God's life I will."

He brought his clenched fist down upon the table with a bang that made the ink-pot dance, and sent the paper flying. Then he looked round with a conscious start, for he heard a step in the doorway. A man stood there looking at him. The blood rushed back to the pale face, and the brows drew together.

"Curse you, Charlton, you have played spy upon me. I'll tell you this much, then, you are a worse devil than I by twenty times."

The visitor shrugged his shoulders with a cynical smile.

"Gadzooks, dear boy, that's true. But what ails you? Faith! you look bitter as sour wine. What is wrong?"

He lounged into the tiny room, past its indignant tenant, and sat down leisurely upon the table.

A large, fair man, with regular features, inclined to coarseness, and merry blue eyes. He was dressed in the extreme of fashion. The buckles of his shoes were set with precious stones; his stockings were of the finest silk, matching his doublet of grey satin, edged with silver braid. There were jewels upon his rapier hilt and dagger, and the sash which carried his sword was of scarlet, worked with golden thread. He wore a castor and feather instead of the college cap, and in place of his gown a short cloak, lined with silk, flung over his left shoulder.

Viscount Charlton was the richest young nobleman at the university, and was one of those men whose most serious occupation in life was the procuring of every pleasure that money could buy. A bad friend for the son of a poor gentleman, with an income of five hundred pounds a year.

"Ralph Dangerfield," he said in a tone of authority, "you are in trouble. Sit ye down and give me the news of it." His smile had vanished. The full, sensual lips were closed and firm, the eyes sympathetic and tender. He stretched out a heavy hand and laid it on his companion's shoulder. "Do ye hear me, man? Sit down and tell this devil, as you call him, that is worse than you, and knows it, by gad, but who loves you very dear, what has gone amiss to-day."

Their eyes met, and Ralph sat down and heaved a bitter sigh.

"Tell you? What good lies in that? You know it already. I owe money I cannot pay; I have dishonoured my father's name; I am ruined for life."

Lord Charlton looked relieved.

"That all? A devil take me, man. I thought —— Well, never mind. But this? Psha, what are your debts? Five hundred pound or so. A flea-bite. Your father, if he begins by being angered at you, will end by blaming himself for keeping a lad of spirit on such short allowance."

But Dangerfield stopped him.

4

"My lord, I beg your silence; you intend well, but your talk is foolish. You do not know my father. Angered with me? God is my witness, I'd desire nothing better. But he is never angry, just the gentlest, sweetest-natured man that lives. He will not say one reproachful word; he will pay the money to a penny, then go away to mourn over it alone, and when I am absent starve and pinch himself and live on crusts to save what I have squandered. Charlton, I am a villain, and you have made me one. But, God knows, I don't excuse myself."

He picked up the paper from the floor, took his pen again, and settled down to write.

"That to your father?" Charlton said, a curious look of uneasiness in his eyes.

"Aye, it is," was the sharp answer.

"Is he in London?"

"That is where he lives, and where I was born, as I have told you oftentimes;" and Ralph, scowling, began his letter in earnest. Charlton watched him, rubbing his chin and playing with his rapier in a nervous, abstracted manner, which Ralph would have remarked at another time, for his lordship was not a nervous man. But Ralph saw nothing, nor, in his preoccupation of mind, did he remember how strange a thing it was for Charlton to be anywhere at that time of an evening outside of "The Three Tuns."

For some minutes Ralph's pen scratched busily. Then Charlton asked a sudden question.

"What is your father's Christian name?"

"John."

"My God!"

The words were spoken as though he had been stabbed, and Ralph's pen dropped from his hand.

"A strange chance indeed," and his lordship began to whistle — very much out of tune; "naught but a mere coincidence."

"What have you in your mind?"

5

They had changed places. Ralph was in authority now.

"Tell me, man," he added impatiently.

His lordship yawned. "Time enough when your work is done. 'Tis but a snip of news — no concern to you. There are many Dangerfields, I suppose, in England."

"None beside my father and myself. The family has died out elsewhere. Well?"

There was a knock at the door, and Ralph's servant entered, saluted my lord, and handed his master a letter.

"A groom awaits your answer, sir."

"What groom?"

"I do not know him, but he's in the doctor's livery. He's rid from London." The words came jerkily, and the man's hand trembled so that he dropped the letter before Ralph could take it.

Ralph frowned at him.

"Barnaby, you've been drinking again. I will not have this."

The man turned away without answer, and covered his eyes with his hand. Ralph was about to question him when Charlton cried out, his face as white as the servant's:—

"Open and read — quick! He is not drunk."

It was a very short note:—

"RALPH,—There is trouble. Take horse and ride to my house. Ask no questions. But haste — haste!
"SYDNEY TAUNTON."

Ralph read the note twice with drawn lips, then handed it to Charlton.

"If you know what that means tell me." Then to his servant, "I'll bear the answer myself. See that the messenger be well refreshed."

As the door closed behind the man Ralph sprang from his chair and grasped Lord Charlton's arm in feverish impatience

"Now — what can it be? Taunton is my father's oldest friend."

There was no reply. His lordship had turned his back, and was studying the letter intently. Ralph, after a quick glance at him, went into the sleeping-chamber and hastily put on his riding-boots, a doublet of thick cloth, buckled his sword, and drew on his gloves.

Then he called out:—

"Charlton, wilt lend me your best horse? I will be careful of him."

No answer still.

Ralph came back into the study, laid his hand upon the letter, and said roughly:—

"I can wait no longer. Give me this an' I will hire a hack as you will not oblige me."

But Charlton turned with a heavy oath, and then Ralph saw that there were tears in his eyes.

"Curse you and your hack! The horse! Take him — take twenty. Oh, if I were but of full age and at Court! Curse those bishops! They be cruel as death and as merciless, and my reverend godfather be the worst of them all."

Ralph's grip upon his friend's shoulder tightened, but he spoke quietly still.

"Before I go you will tell me what you mean."

His lordship considered a moment, then turned away.

"No; there may be a mistake. Come to the stables."

He would have left the room, but Ralph stepped before him.

"Tell me," he gasped, "for God's sake!"

They looked into one another's eyes, down into one another's soul, and read what was written here. Charlton yielded.

"Well, then, I am godson, you may know, to the Archbishop of Canterbury; the worst he has, but no matter. I gave some money the other day for one of his favourite churches, and this so pleased His Grace that he writ an acknowledgment with his own hand. This came to-day, and in it are these words."

Lord Charlton drew a letter from his pocket and read aloud from it:—

"I am weary after many hours of labour, but it was the work of the Lord. A Socinian book, the most damnable I have yet seen, full of infinite blasphemy and vilest heresy, hath been written by one John Dangerfield. This wretch was tried to-day by the Star Chamber, and a severe and most righteous sentence delivered upon him."

"There," Charlton said looking up, "that is all I know. What make you of it?"

Ralph laughed a hard, bitter laugh.

"I was wrong, you right. This is some unknown namesake. My father deny the Godhead of Christ! Even the Star Chamber, which they do say will swear that white is black, could not make that good. Taunton's letter means a sudden sickness. Father was never strong. You have my thanks. Now for the horse."

It is fifty miles from Cambridge to London as the crow flies, sixty by road and the roads of those days were bad; but Ralph was a superb rider, and upon a beast that would go at its best without whip or spur until it dropped from exhaustion. He left Cambridge at nine o'clock; by five the next morning he was clattering over the ill-paved thoroughfares of Westminster. Doctor Taunton lived near the abbey in a red-brick Elizabethan house, shut in from the clang of the busy world by a large garden and high walls. A groom was waiting to take Ralph's horse, and a maidservant, evidently on the look-out, ushered him at once into the doctor's surgery, and said that her master would be with him in a few minutes.

A sombre room, malodorous with the fumes of stale chemicals; close from want of air. It was panelled from floor to ceiling with black oak, and there being but one small window, seemed dark as a tomb to those coming in from the daylight. The window, however, faced east,

and to-day a fugitive ray of sun had struck a shaft of light
through the diamond panes upon a niche in the opposite
wall, where stood an ebony crucifix, the Christ of marble
carved by a master hand. To Ralph, in the overstrung
state of his nerves, a horrible realism seemed to cling to
this figure. The sunlight warmed the cold marble into a
likeness of human flesh; he could have imagined he saw
it move. The face was turned towards him, calm, yet
terrible in its expression of divine patience under mortal
agony. He turned away with a shudder, and strode to
the window: but he could feel the face behind him still.
Was it an omen? He had laughed at Charlton's news;
but it had been with his lips, not with his heart. No man
could tell at that time whom the Star Chamber might
seize for its next victim. The power of the bishops, so
soon to sink to nothingness, was at its height. Spies
of the most infamous kind abounded, ready to catch at
any straw of worthless evidence to earn reward and countenance from the archbishop. And Laud, though himself anxious to be just — a better man than his enemies
knew — was credulous and cruel where heresy was whispered in his ear.

"Merciful God!" Ralph exclaimed aloud. "If it were
true — but it cannot be."

A hand touched his, a bony chilly hand. He started
violently, and turned to find the doctor at his elbow.

"Oh, is it you, sir?" he began apologetically. "I did
not hear your step ——" but the doctor cut him short.

"You rode fast. I expected you later. Nay, no words
now — no questions — until your breakfast comes. It
will be ready soon."

He sat down and made Ralph do the same, then cross-
ing one leg over the other, and clasping his hands over
that, peered at him like an inquisitive bird. Doctor
Sydney Taunton was not unlike a bird. He was a little
shrivelled old man, with a withered, wrinkled face. His
head was round and perfectly bald, set like an apple

between narrow, high shoulders; his nose was long and pointed; his lips thin and drawn inwards, for he had no teeth; his chin was pointed, too, and nearly as prominent as his nose. It was a keen, clever face, but not an amiable one. He had black eyes, very round and bright — quick, vigilant eyes that saw much and told nothing. At this moment they were devouring Ralph from spurs to love-locks; but the doctor did not speak, and only waved his hand impatiently when Ralph tried to do so — a most irritating man. At last the maid arrived with a breakfast of meat and wheat cakes steaming hot and a tankard of ale.

"Eat," the doctor cried, darting from his chair and trotting to one of the many cabinets filled with bottles. "Here, drink this first. Drink, I say," and he handed Ralph a glass of cognac.

Ralph drank it at a draught, then attacked his breakfast with a determination. He was not hungry, but he knew his man. No one who refused Doctor Taunton's prescriptions ever gained anything by it.

"There, sir," he cried, laying down the empty tankard with relief. "Now your news."

"What have you heard?" was all the doctor said.

"Nothing — concerning my father."

"Touching whom, then?"

"I was told yesternight that someone of our name was tried by the Star Chamber, but ——"

"The Star Chamber!" interjected the doctor. "What of the Star Chamber?"

"They sentenced some Dangerfield for — for Socinianism. But what of it? 'Tis no concern of mine."

Doctor Taunton's head twitched and his eyelids quivered. He bent forward until his face was within a foot of Ralph's, and whispered: —

"Why, lad, why? Who told you it was no concern of yours?"

Ralph's heart seemed as though it would burst. He

would have given the world to cry out, but the doctor's
eyes were upon him, and he felt as if he were under a
spell. Beads of perspiration stood upon his brow, and
he could not say a word for a minute. At last he muttered hoarsely: —

"Speak not in riddles; tell me the worst. What! God
have mercy! That man is my father!"

Taunton nodded, and again there was silence. When
Ralph broke it his voice was steady but very cold.

"The punishment — what is it to be?"

"A heavy fine — five thousand pounds."

"What else?"

"The pillory."

"What else?"

Taunton's lips closed like a trap.

"No more, I understand."

Ralph observed him a moment.

"That is not true. What else?"

A pause. Ralph repeated his question sharply.

"Mutilation."

"And — what else?"

The words were hissed now from between his teeth.

"Naught; I swear it before God."

Another silence, then Ralph slowly and deliberately
drew his sword.

"Doctor, you are my oldest friend, the dearest my
father hath. You are a Catholic, but you are a Christian. Listen then to me. I swear to you on my sword
by God the Father, God the Son, and God the Holy
Ghost, that I will take no more pleasures in this world,
but will labour heart and soul and hand to compass the
undoing of that damned tribunal; aye, from the meanest
member of it to the king himself. I swear it by all I
hold sacred in the world — so help me God!"

He sheathed his sword at the last words, sat down
quietly, and for a space there was no sound but the
breathing of two men. Presently Ralph looked up.

" When was it? "

" This morning at rise of sun."

" Then it is not ended yet." Ralph sprang to his feet. Taunton went swiftly before him to the door, locked it, and thrust the key in his doublet.

" Hold, son. Thou must not leave this room."

" Must not — must not go to my father! God's life, sir, let me pass! Out with that key, or I will burst the door! "

The doctor peered at him, groaned, then slowly opened it.

" Wait till I get my cloak," was all he said, bustling into the hall.

Ralph stared, and the doctor chuckled grimly as he took his arm.

" Sooth, my young friend, I'd not trust thee alone in Palace Yard this day with that sword; no, not for a king's ransom. We go together; come."

CHAPTER II

A SURGING crowd of people, numbering many hundreds, clustering round a wooden platform, where three men stood, cramped and confined between heavy beams, sweltering bareheaded under the summer sun. As a background the rugged walls of Westminster Palace. They were well used to such scenes, these old walls. Yet there was a difference in the spectacle to-day from most if its predecessors. The crowds about the sufferers were usually the scourings from the slums, creatures who flocked with stores of missiles in their pouches, too filthy to mention, to pelt the unhappy victims, and jeer at their pain. To-day, though there were a few such persons, prudence forbade the least expression of their natural sentiments. The bulk of the crowd was composed of grave citizens and their sharp-faced 'prentices; sturdy artisans, and bronzed sailors from the wharves; while here and there a portly city father, protected by a body-guard of serving-men, lent a gravity and importance to the gathering which those in authority did not fail to note. Indeed, the officers charged with the conduct of affairs did not at all like the look of things, and doubled the guard of halberdiers about the pillories. Well for them that this had been done, for when the executioner came to do his work a shout of anger, deep and ominous, swept the crowd from end to end, threats were delivered, and swords drawn. But the halberdiers held manfully to their weapons, and no blood was spilt. This was before Ralph arrived upon the scene. As an additional hardship the usual order of punishments — two hours in pillory, followed by mutilation — was

13

reversed, and the sufferers, with some rough-and-ready stanching of their wounds, were obliged to do their penance after they had lost their ears. They were persons of no influence and little known. Two were ministers, a Brownist and an Independent; and the third, condemned as a Socinian, had not a friendly face to look upon. These facts made the demonstrations of the crowd very significant, and bore witness to the popular hatred of the prelates and the Star Chamber. The ministers were no sooner in the pillory than they began to preach, soon losing all consciousness of pain in their excitement, shouting denunciations of prelacy and popery at the utmost pitch of their voices, and calling upon all "God-fearing" Christians to "cast out Antichrist," by whom they meant Archbishop Laud, as all men knew well. Their speech was rude and bombastic, garnished with coarse epithets and violent abuse; but no one dissented from their opinions, and every allusion to the bishops was received with marked approval.

John Dangerfield did not preach. His face, quiet and refined — the face of a scholar — contrasted sharply with those of his companions. He said nothing to anyone except to thank the attendant who stanched the flow of blood, and answered courteously in the negative an enquiry of the executioner whether he had dealt hardly with him. "I would not an' I knew it, sir. 'Struth, 'tis a fact," he said, softened by the gentle patience of his victim. "But now all is done now, and the rest will soon be over; wish ye well."

Mr. Dangerfield was very different from his son in appearance; so different, that few ever saw any likeness between them. He was of slight build, with oval face, pronounced features and high forehead. The lower part of the face was small and feminine, and was covered by a long white beard which made him look many years older than he really was. He had an abundance of silvery hair which a kindly touch from an attendant brought over the sides of his face, concealing all signs of mutilation. When Ralph, an hour after the execution of the sentence forced his way to the front of the crowd, he could only see a few streaks of blood. But it was enough, and more than enough. He saw the skin quivering with pain and the sweat dripping from the forehead; and while he waited for his father to see him — for Mr. Dangerfield's eyes were closed, his lips moving in silent prayer — he felt, through sheer force of sympathy, the throb and smart of wounds, a deadly faintness made his knees tremble beneath him, and his throat became so parched with thirst that when he tried to speak no sound would come, only the dry whisper of a name. It was then that the iron entered into Ralph's soul, and the blind passion of his furious anger hardened, and took form and shape as molten lead when it is dropped into a mould. He looked about him, saw the stern faces, and heard the angry hum of many voices. They braced his nerves and gave him hope. Others shared his feelings. His father was not the only one who had suffered martyrdom.

At last Mr. Dangerfield saw him and called him by name, and the spell was broken.

" Ralph, dear son, you here! Bless you, boy! bless you, Taunton, too! Ah, now I guess who planned it. Nay, I do not suffer," answering the mute questioning of the upturned face, " nothing to mention. This good fellow," smiling benignly upon his attendant, " hath been kindness itself. Now it is such a happiness to see your face that I feel naught. I shall soon be with you, dear one. Cheer up, cheer up! "

He spoke in strong, bright tones, and for the hour that remained of his penance talked at intervals, now to Ralph, now to the doctor, whose presence seemed to have a great effect upon the keepers of the pillory, the men being assiduous in their ministrations, bathing the sufferer's forehead with vinegar, and giving him wine and water, trying in all ways to assuage the pain. But in spite of all this care, the prisoner became rapidly weaker, and when the penance came to an end at last he fainted in Doctor Taunton's arms. Nothing was wanting now that knowledge could suggest or money procure. A litter was brought into the yard, and Mr. Dangerfield borne quickly away to his friend's house. Upon their arrival the doctor peremptorily dismissed Ralph.

"You will not see him for two days at least," he said. "I know you both. Together your tongues would not cease wagging until you had worn him out. He must be quiet. Go, get you a horse and ride; or better, still, take this twenty pound, and spend it on the pleasures of the town. You will not! Pish! then I know not what to recommend. Take your own course, as you ever would and will. I wash my hands of ye. But come not near your father. He is in no danger yet."

Ralph went away disconsolate enough, but upon going down into the hall his face brightened. A man had just dismounted in the courtyard begrimed with dust — Lord Charlton.

"Ha! run to earth," he cried. "Well, you have found refuge in an old fox's hole, dear boy, in very truth. But, never mind, get me a mouthful of food, and tell me all your news, and send word to your good doctor that I have come to stay awhile. He and I have met before."

Charlton remained a week. Acting on a hint from Taunton, he never left Ralph, but listened patiently to his friend's outbursts of invective against the Government and the Star Chamber, and his dark forebodings concerning his father's condition. In the intervals he made him ride and fence with him, and take all kinds of violent exercise, and thereby probably saved his reason. Ralph was not allowed to see his father for seven days, and though each day Taunton said there was no danger, a presentiment of evil weighed upon Ralph's soul. He did not believe the doctor. At last, on the eighth day, Charlton returned to his protesting University, and the father and son met.

Ralph's first glance at the white and transparent face confirmed his worst fears. His father was dying. The shock to his system and the loss of blood had been too much for his constitution, enfeebled by thirty years of sedentary life. The end was but a matter of time. Yet Ralph, though he saw all this, was outwardly calm, and Mr. Dangerfield, who had expected an outburst of grief and anger, looked up with anxious surprise.

" Give me your hand, son. Why, it is quite cold."

And then, thrusting aside the lassitude which oppressed him, and made even the exertion of speaking a positive torture, he took Ralph to task.

" My boy, this silence pains me grievously. I see that you are suffering, and I know that it is on my account. Utter your thoughts as you ever have done. Have I lost my son too?"

There was a pathetic quaver and suggestion in his voice that completely unmanned Ralph.

" Those accursed villains, they have killed you!" he burst out. But Mr. Dangerfield stopped him.

" Nay, that is not true; it is my weak body. Others would have withstood with ease what crushes me. They could not know how frail I was. Be not unjust."

" Unjust!" Ralph cried. " 'Fore God, sir, no! That could not be unless I were to forgive, and that I never will."

A sharp sigh of pain escaped Mr. Dangerfield, but he said nothing, and Ralph went on, his passion rising within him like an angry sea. " Oh for the day to come when I have them by the throat! It will come. I could see it in the faces of the crowd, and it comforted me mightily. It comforts me even yet. Deem me not bloodthirsty, father. Why, if they had done it to me I would say little. But that you should suffer, you who never harmed a soul, who have done good all your life; that they should hunt you down and crush you upon some black-mouthed devil's lie. I say they are worse than beasts. God curse them all!"

"Stay!"

Ralph paused, arrested by a strange sternness in his father's tone.

"Son, you have gone too far. No one has lied. Even these 'priests' as the bishops call themselves, even Laud himself, spake the truth so far as they could see it."

"But, father, they called you a Socinian, one who denies Christ."

"They accused me of two things," Mr. Dangerfield rejoined, his eyes kindling, his voice stronger than it had been since Ralph entered the room. "The first, that I was a Socinian by faith and practice; the second, that I had writ a book attempting to prove that my faith was based upon the words of our dear Lord Himself. Now this was true; nay, more for I have proved it. These lords of the Star Chamber, son, thought I would be halting in my speech and feeble in my arguments because I was a weakling in body. I promise thee, I made them pipe another tune before I had done with them. Never was I so roused. Well," suddenly pausing and lowering his voice to its former weary tone, "I should not dwell upon this. Perchance I was uplifted by vanity more than by earnestness of faith. It is nearly always thus with disputations in religion. The blood heated by controversy carries the tongue away; but, indeed, if I sinned in such a manner I have been punished for it. Taunton tells me the worst rigour of my sentence was due to the castigation God enabled me to inflict upon my judges, and Taunton knows all Court secrets. Be that as it may, no witnesses other than their own ears, which I trust did tingle mightily, were needed to prove the breach of their canon law; wherefore they punished me. God forgive them for their cruelty to an old man. But of injustice, as they construe the word, there was none. I grant them that."

He ceased, panting, and observed his son intently. Ralph was staring at him with horror-struck eyes and parted lips.

"A Socinian!" he cried at last. "You! Father, what does it mean? Why — why did you keep me ignorant of your faith? I would have denied it, I have denied it, with my life."

A spasm of pain passed over Mr. Dangerfield's face, and he closed his eyes.

"My poor lad," Ralph heard him murmur, "I should have known — yet I did not — how harshly it would sound unto thee. Heavenly Father, be merciful to him in this most bitter trial. Let me suffer still, but spare my boy. Ralph," he said aloud, "listen, before you judge me — listen to what I have to tell. Your mother was of the English Church, and when her last illness came upon her she begged that you should be brought up in her faith, and that until you reached manhood no word should be spoken that might lead you into doubts. I made the promise. In keeping it I had to conceal my faith from you, and hand over your religious education to our rector. He was a good and worthy man, but it was hard. God knows it has been the penance of my life. Now, looking back, I do not know that I was wrong. It is my belief that whatsoever doctrine appeals most strongly to the heart and understanding of a man that doctrine he should embrace, and so that his life be pure and upright, he will be acceptable to God. Truly it must be so, else God would be unjust to the creatures He hath made. The time hath come now when you should know. You are a man, matured by what has passed, and I thank God for His goodness in permitting me to tell you so much. I can say no more. I have no strength to expound or argue, were that judicious or desirable, and this I doubt. But there is my book. The

bishops, in their vanity, think they have destroyed my
life's work. This is not so. Two copies still exist. One
hath been sent abroad, where it will be printed when
better times arrive by men of my faith and issued in
this country; the other is in this house — for you. It
has been the work of thirty years; I can die content now
it is finished. Thy will, O God, not mine, be done."

He was talking to himself again, and Ralph, with an
intensity of grief which cast all other thoughts, saw that
a grey, leaden tinge was creeping over the worn face,
and that the hand which held his own was growing chill.
A wave of passionate misery swept over his heart. He
threw himself upon his knees and kissed the cold fingers
again and again.

"Daddy, hear me. Can you hear?" a ghastly fear
striking him that never again might his words reach his
father's understanding. But of this he was reassured.

"Speak distinctly, and not too fast. Go on, tell me
what you will."

"I only want you to know how I love you, dearest,
dearest." And then his voice broke, and he sobbed
aloud. "That whatever your faith may be or mine, you
have all the love and reverence that ever father had from
son. Is there no hope? Don't leave me yet, when I
need you most. Father, you must know how weak I
am, how wicked. I have gambled, I am in debt, I have
lied to you. It is I who should have been tortured. I
am bad; not worthy to be your son, not worthy of your
love."

"Hush, Ralph, hush. Thou art my dearest. Nay, I
am not so simple as you think. I knew there were some
debts; I have saved money to pay them. The
doctor holds it. Peace, dear, let me speak on graver
matters while I have the strength. Our good doctor said
this morning, he swore by the Blessed Virgin, that at
my death he will cherish you as his son and make you
his heir. I am glad, for he has much wealth, and none

on whom he might bestow it; and he truly loves you. I
trust that through the goodness of God your life may be
bright and happy when this cloud has passed away.
But you must promise me this: when I have been laid
to rest, follow our friend's counsel and go abroad. He
is willing, should you seriously desire it, to buy you a
commission in the army of the States General in Holland. I dread that you should learn the trade of war,
but I know your fiery nature, and should be content.
In time I know a wish to see your native land will bring
you home, and then you will be to the dear doctor what
you would have been to me — a loving, loyal son. Now,
tell me, Ralph, will you promise this? I cannot give you
time to think, for I know not, moment by moment, when
my call may come."

He paused to cough, a dry, choking cough, which
alarmed Ralph.

"Tell me, dear," he whispered. "Do not be too long."

Ralph sighed heavily. It would be a bitter thing to
leave England with storm-clouds in the air, and the
people awakening as a strong man from sleep to the
injustice and cruelty in high places. The thought was
not to be endured, yet could he deny his father? But
Mr. Dangerfield, who in spite of his suffering was watching his son's face keenly, saw what was passing in his
mind, and with an effort spoke again, this time with
greater strength.

"Do not think that I would prevent you from doing
your part, dear, when, if ever, the people of England are
forced to take strenuous measures to win their rights.
God forbid! But as yet pressure from Parliament may
do all that is needed. The king wants money; very
soon he must appeal to the Commons for it, and then
the nation's grievances will be displayed and redress
called for in a tone no monarch may disregard. Yet, if
the king doth not yield, or, yielding, doth not keep his
word — he hath not in the past — then the future is

dark. But this I see, freedom will come, though it be by the sword, and if you would bear a fitting part in such a struggle you should put yourself under some training. The idea grows upon me. I welcome Taunton's thought of a commission. Though war is hateful to me, you, true to your blood, love action, strife, and arms. God's finger may be in this. I dare not dispute His will. Yet you are very young, too young, to trace your way alone amid this civil strife which I now foresee is hastening upon us. Before long the country will be divided into parties; men now obscure will come to the front, drawn thither by their strength of character. I would I could feel that you were with such a one. A man who loves true freedom, but not anarchy, who fears nothing, and when his mind is set, will never rest, but go steadily on to the goal he hath set himself to win — a man faithful to his country and his friends. My son, bring pen and paper to me. I would write a letter. Yes, I am strong enough. Fear not for that. When God puts such a purpose into a man's heart as He hath placed in mine He will give the power to carry it through."

A wonderful change had come over Mr. Dangerfield's face, the change often seen just before death in those whose minds have largely dominated their bodies. His eyes were bright, his face full of animation. With a little assistance from Ralph he sat up in bed, propped by pillows, and wrote rapidly for several minutes. Then he sealed the letter down with his own hand, and directed it in bold, clear characters: —

"To Oliver Cromwell, of Ely, sometime Member of Parliament for Cambridge, Esquire."

The work was barely accomplished, and he still held the letter in his hand, when Doctor Taunton entered the room.

"Writing, indeed! Truly, John, you are cozening us, and are not sick at all."

Mr. Dangerfield smiled at the abruptness of the words

and the inquisitive glance shot by the doctor at the letter.

"I had work to do, but, thank God, have got well through with it. Ralph, the man to whom this letter is addressed is an old and valued friend of mine. If trouble ever comes such as I mentioned, seek him out, and give him this, and he will treat you well. Remember you Cromwell at college, Taunton? Now, good chicurgeon, out with thy instruments of torture; I defy thee and thy works. My mind is at peace with all the world. Son, leave the room a space."

They kissed one another, and Mr. Dangerfield smiled and nodded brightly. But when Ralph was gone he sank back upon the pillows.

"Let me alone, old friend," he whispered, "my time is almost come. I would be at rest."

· Taunton's only answer was to feel his pulse and listen to his breathing. Then he quietly put his bandages away, and sat down beside the bed.

"It will be in an hour, John, or less."

"Then call Ralph back — but stay. Taunton, thou hast been my truest friend, and I trust thee with all that is precious to me — Ralph."

The doctor twitched his head.

"Why did you write to Cromwell?"

"Because"— he hesitated with a look of pain, then his mouth grew firm —"because, dear friend, thou art, and ever wilt remain, a supporter of the king, even though he put England into chains, and that Ralph can never be. I know your principles, even as I know your heart. That heart I trust, it is the best I know; thy principles be the worst."

"Because I am a Catholic."

"No such thing, indeed! You mock me. Man, it is your religion which will save your soul."

"Why trust you this Cromwell?"

"Because I know him. He hath grave faults, but

they will not harm my boy. I am well aware," he added, as Taunton significantly shrugged his shoulders, "that he is but a country squire, and that mayhap he will never be more. But I know this, any who are in trouble go to him; he fights, and fights roughly, but it is on behalf of the poor and oppressed. That is the man I wish Ralph to be with when his country is in need. Now send him to me. I feel to grow weaker every minute. The end comes fast. God bless you, friend."

Taunton rose to obey, then bent over the bed and kissed the cold forehead twice. He had gone before Mr. Dangerfield could speak, and hastening from the room, called Ralph to his father's side.

CHAPTER III

RALPH went abroad in accordance with his father's wish, but he did not go alone. Three days after Mr. Dangerfield died Lord Charlton, dressed in deep mourning, called at the doctor's house and asked to be allowed to attend the funeral. Ralph was greatly touched at such a mark of respect, and gave an eager consent; but Taunton, the worldly-wise, shook his head and drew the young man aside.

"Do not venture it, my lord. I know your motive, but think! 'Twill be a scandal that will cling to you like a bloodstain. All his friends but me hold back afraid, as well they may. A Socinian is worse than an infidel in the eyes of the bishops. I am tough and too prickly even for his grace to touch. But you — his godson — as all the world knows ——"

"Therefore," his lordship interrupted, "I go. Waste not your breath, worthy doctor. He sent for me yesterday, hearing that I had been with Ralph. My audience lasted half an hour, and I warrant you that I was not the one who wearied first. 'Slife, doctor! my blood, which in usual is much too cool, was hot for once — boiling! I might have been Ralph himself! I fairly put his grace agape with horror; I ended by telling him I'd go to-morrow in my best coach with full array of servants. Deny me not, my heart is set upon it."

The doctor made no answer, scanning Charlton with curious, searching eyes. Then he held out both hands.

"My faith, young sir, but you are the best friend that boy of mine hath made. Command me always!"

So Lord Charlton had his way, and in consequence

the authorities of Sidney refused to readmit him to his college. But his lordship only laughed, and, fired by Ralph's example, made up his mind to accompany him abroad. They joined the same regiment. From the day, however, that the friends entered upon this new life they began to see less and less of one another. The change came gradually, and it said much for the quality of their friendship that to the end their intimacy and affection never wavered. It was but the natural, inevitable drifting apart of natures set in different moulds. In the army, as at college, Charlton did as little work as circumstances permitted, and devoted his best energies to amusing himself; while Ralph, possessed now by a purpose which grew ever stronger as time passed, worked with all the energy and strength that was in him, and found his chief pleasure in the things which his lordship particularly loathed — the daily drill and military exercises. Ralph seemed to have found his vocation. On active service he was the most zealous officer in the regiment. Hardship, coarse food, and lack of sleep he took like a veteran, without complaint, almost without notice. In camp he spent one-half of his time learning the art of handling cavalry, the other half in studying gunnery and fortification under his colonel, who had been a soldier for forty years. Cards, dice, horse-racing he gave up absolutely. Charlton taxed him with Puritanism; Ralph replied that he had not time.

"I liked them at college," he said, smiling. "Now I like soldiering better. Perchance I shall be tired of that soon, and take to something else."

And then he would knit his brows thoughtfully, and fall into an abstracted silence that greatly puzzled his lordship.

When twelve months had gone Charlton noticed another change in Ralph. He was getting restless and homesick. Not a day passed but he would be found asking for news from England. Yet he had little need to make enquiry, for he was better supplied than anyone else. Doctor Taunton was not only a very faithful chronicler of events, but he had exceptionally accurate knowledge of what was passing both at Court and in Parliament. He stood at the head of his profession for diseases of the nerves and brain, and was consulted by the greatest men in the land; he belonged to a powerful Catholic family, and was medical attendant to the queen.

Yet, though Taunton was in all the secrets of the Court, and had even been consulted, it was said, by her majesty in delicate affairs of State, it would have passed the ingenuity of an Italian Jesuit to discover his politics by his letters to Ralph. He found fault with everyone alike — king, Parliament, and people. The first, he said, was weak; the second, self-seeking; the third, noisy and impudent. As time went on, however, though Taunton's comments upon the king's blunders, his vacillation, his betrayal of Strafford, and his ignorance of the temper of his people, were caustic enough to have landed him in the Tower had they been read by the authorities, Ralph noticed that the chief bitterness of his criticism was directed against the leaders in the Commons.

" Hampden may be honest," he wrote. " He hath a fine presence and a polished tongue. He is a gentleman. But God help him! He is the most popular man in England, and will come to a violent end. Pym and the rest behave like men who, having tasted strong liquors, to which they be unaccustomed, are determined to continue drinking until they see the bottom of the cask, though it bring them to the gutter. Oliver Cromwell, member for Cambridge, is the worst of these. I went to the House the other day to hear him speak. He is not greatly changed since college days, except in bulk of body. Unmannerly, as he was then, without respect for any but himself, saying roundly what he thinks, or pretends to think, spite of all authority. A plague upon such mushroom men. All they ask for his majesty hath granted; yet they are not content. No, do not come home yet. England, with this stink-pot of a Parliament and its foolish king, is no place for honest men at present. Wait! "

At last, in July, 1642, Ralph received all unexpectedly a summons which sent him in haste to his commander-in-chief. The letter was a mere scrap: —

"The time has come. I await you here.

SYDNEY TAUNTON.

"P. S.— The cask is dry."

When Ralph went to seek an audience with his general he found Charlton bound on the same errand. Whom his lordship had heard from, or what he had heard, Ralph never knew; but they resigned their commissions together, and travelled to England by the same ship. The air was full of rumours. One said war had been declared by the king upon the rebel Parliament; another that Westminster was already surrounded by troops, and there would be a score of members beheaded; a third that the king's life was in danger, and so it went on. Charlton was in a feverish state of excitement, cursed the slow pace of the ship, and burned to throw himself at the feet of the king.

"It is not the bishops he upholds," he said to Ralph as they paced the deck together. "When my godfather was clapped into the Tower the sun went down, and I for one said Amen to it. But for these Commons to ruffle it in the face of his majesty! God's truth! 'tis past all patience. Nay, the king has been too patient, too gentle, with the knaves. Thank God, he's turned on them at last. We'll rally to him, as all true men must, and put the rascals down."

He turned to Ralph for sympathy, but Ralph was grimly silent. Yet he made no attempt to defend the men who had defied the king. He simply kept his own counsel and said nothing at all. Charlton was amazed and hurt, as well as vaguely uneasy; but feeling that there were depths here he had better leave unfathomed, he did not press too far, and their friendship came forth even from this ordeal as strong and true as ever. They parted at the river-side, and Ralph went straight to Doctor Taunton's house. It was again early in the morning of a summer's day when Ralph found himself alone in the surgery waiting for the doctor, as he had waited two years ago. He looked about him curiously. All was the same, even to the glint of sunlight glancing on the crucifix against the wall. He alone was changed. He went to the figure on the cross and gravely kissed it.

"As Thou suffered," he murmured, "so did he. And now the time has come when, please God, I shall keep my vow. But, oh, the loneliness — the loneliness of life. Two years! It seems a score. I feel old. I have nigh worked myself into a dry bone of a man. Thank God, it is over."

The door opened, and the doctor came in. They shook hands in silence, and then Taunton said shortly: —

"I should not have known ye. Broader by a hand's breadth, but that is not it. Tanned by sun and wind to a red brick-brown; but that is naught. It is the shape of thy face, the cast of thy features, the mouth, the chin. H'm — come to breakfast."

The doctor had not altered a bit. The same dry, inscrutable face; the same keen, restless eyes; the same quick, alert movements. Yet Ralph could have fancied he was a little smaller than he used to be.

"There will be no rest, lad, for you!" he said, after he had asked a few questions about life in the Low Countries. "Time presses for all, but most particularly for those who would serve the king."

He paused, and looked Ralph in the face, but receiving no reply, he went on rapidly: "There are not any who have kept their senses in the Commons; but I know one. We will call on him to-day. To-morrow I will take you to the king."

"Not to-morrow, doctor."

Taunton wiped his mouth with a napkin, and slowly drank half a glass of ale.

"Why not?"

Ralph pushed his plate away.

"I have other business. To-morrow, by rise of sun, or an hour before an' the day be warm, I start for Ely. I understand Master Cromwell dwells there still."

"You have kept that letter?"

For answer Ralph took it from an inner pocket of his doublet, kissed it reverently, and thrust it back again.

"It has been there, doctor, since he gave it me."

"This Cromwell," the doctor said, with peculiar dryness and distinctness, "is a very bloody-minded rebel. Your father was never that. To-day he would stand with us."

"Think you so? I do not." Ralph spoke with a bluntness that was almost rude. Then, controlling himself, "Forgive me, doctor dear. I am a soldier, and my manners are grown rough. I will not talk politics with you."

"A soldier are you?" Taunton said, paying no attention to the last words. "Then you must believe in discipline. Where'er Cromwell goes, they say, a hungry rabble follows at his heels to rob or plunder. He and his friends would overturn the throne and govern England with a mob. But, say you, Charles is a tyrant, and you like not tyrants. Why, boy, this Parliament will prove a greater tyrant than any king — two hundred tyrants in the place of one. Know you that they have passed a law that they should not be dissolved without their own consent? What does that mean? But I waste breath upon you. Is your mind quite made up? I see it is. How youth rushes at life, never weighing bad with good, but running headlong upon impulse. Well, well, I'd thought your brain had cooled when I saw your face an hour since; but it is the same mad, hasty Ralph as of old."

"Nay, sir," the young man answered quickly, "not hasty this time."

"How so? You said your mind was set."

"And so it hath been for full two years. I pray you,

doctor, let us talk of something else." His tone was beseeching, but Taunton shrugged his shoulders.

"No, for our minds are full of this. You go to offer yourself to Cromwell?"

"I go to keep my promise; nothing more. I know not how I shall like Master Cromwell, nor whether he will take to me. From all I hear I do not expect to remain long with him."

Taunton's face brightened.

"Why not?"

"I am, as you have said, a soldier. That he hath never been. Then he is a very pious man, they say. As my father's son — a Socinian's son — I may not be welcome. But no more of this, sir. I will not speak another word about my plans."

It was very early indeed when Ralph started for Ely, but he found the doctor on the steps to see him off. At sight of the traveller's dress Taunton threw up his hands in affected horror.

"Good lord, boy, what is this? Black riding-cloak, boots like a train-band trooper, a castor featherless, doublet of leather. You are a Puritan, indeed! Clip your hair, and you'd be the worst Roundhead of them all."

Ralph laughed, and shook his love-locks in vigorous protest.

"Not yet. I am but an old campaigner preparing for rough travel. My armour's in my trunk; but I keep that for the day I meet the king," and his eyes gleamed curiously.

"Do ye mean battle?" snapped Taunton scornfully.

"In battle, sir!" Ralph said, flushing; "and then"— he drew a deep breath and knit his heavy brows — "may God give me strength to drive my sword well home."

The doctor shuddered, then his eyes blazed, and he drew himself up.

"What!" he thundered. "Boy, thou'rt mad. Lay

thy hand upon the Lord's anointed! It would wither at the wrist!"

"That is as God wills," was the cool reply. "I know this: the king signed the warrant against father, and for that, were he lord of all the earth, I'd kill him, an' I get fair opportunity. Doctor, fare you well."

He set spurs to his horse, and the animal, fresh from the stable, bounded gaily off.

Taunton wiped his brow.

"My God! what a fool I was to think two years might tame him; two hundred, if he lived, would not wipe out the memory of that day. Changed did I say? Aye, as green wood you may bend turns to the oak you cannot break. He will never change."

Ralph rode leisurely. He knew by bitter experience what happens to the rider that spares not his beast on a hot day. It was, therefore, late when he approached his destination. The ride from London to Ely was nowhere very interesting or picturesque in those days. The country was bare, marshy, and treeless, and when Cambridge was passed there was nothing to right or left but one long stretch of fen. The road from Cambridge to Ely was good, for it had been raised artificially above the level of the green, oozy marsh around it; but it was monotonous and dreary to the last degree, and Ralph, who was tired and hot and very thirsty, became exceedingly depressed. Here and there rows of willows and poplars broke the horizon line, and at intervals he passed a rude and weather-beaten hamlet; but he did not meet a soul, and had nothing to occupy his attention but his own thoughts. At last before him, rising as it were from space, he saw the great square tower of the cathedral, and was comforted, as so many generations of travellers must have been, by the prospect of a speedy arrival at his journey's end. Distances, however, on a clear day are sometimes illusory in the fens, and Ralph found that though he plodded steadily on the cathedral seemed to get no nearer. But the nature of the road was changing. High walls lined the roadside; he was approaching a village. This was cheering; a village meant an inn, and an inn refreshments. Ralph's horse was apparently struck by this fact at the same moment as his master, for he quickened his pace. Then they turned a corner where the road curved sharply to the left, and then to his amazement Ralph found himself surrounded by armed men, two of whom caught his bridle and called on him to halt.

Now Ralph was exactly in the mood when a quarrel is most grateful to the feelings, and he had not been a soldier for two years for nothing. He reined in sharply as if in obedience to the order, noted that there were but half a dozen troopers, and plunging in the spur, caused his horse to bound forward against one man, while at the same moment he drew his pistol from his holster and fired point-blank at the other. Such a manœuvre as this was totally unexpected, and though Ralph's pistol missed fire, the men were thrown violently backwards, and Ralph dashed on; but just as he thought himself free he received a blow on the back of his head which knocked him off his horse and stunned him. When he came to himself it was nearly dark. He was lying on the grass, a cloak rolled beneath his head, and a murmur of voices about him. A light flashed in his eyes; someone had lit a lantern and placed it near his face.

"Quartermaster's struck home!" he heard a voice say. "I' fackins, Sanctify, but it's near settled him!"

"It's a joyful mercy, then," another replied solemnly. "He meant death unto you, corporal. It is plain, anyway, that he be a bloody malignant."

"How know you that, you dreaping fool?" broke in a deeper voice — the quartermaster's Ralph felt by instinct. "Lift the light higher. See, the young man is coming to sense again. Now, sir, who be you and

what's your errand in the fens? Speak up, we mean ye
no harm!"

Ralph waited a minute before answering. He was
fully conscious now, but wished to get some idea of the
situation before he committed himself.

"By what warrant do you question me? You are
a soldier. Is there war in the fens?"

While he was speaking he heard the sound of
approaching hoofs along the road, and now by the dim
lantern-light saw a man dismount and the quartermaster
straighten himself with a salute.

"A prisoner, Reuben? Wounded? What is this?"
The voice was harsh and strong.

"No wound, captain," growled the quartermaster.
"'Twas but a stroke I lent him from my pike's end when
he fired upon Sanctify there. We had stopped him —
according to orders."

"Tush, man!" the officer ejaculated impatiently.
"Naught I said justified violence. Who is this
gentleman?"

"That he'd best answer for himself," and the quartermaster drew back offended.

The newcomer was standing over Ralph now, observing him closely, and Ralph saw that he was a squarely-
made man of middle age, dressed in plain riding-clothes.
He looked like a country farmer, with something military in his bearing.

"Art hurt?" he said, his tone curt and business-like.
"Methinks the stroke of pike was a shrewd one."

"I should not be here else," Ralph said, smiling at the
frankness of the admission.

"Ah, say you so? What did you to deserve it?"

"All that I could. But they took me in ambuscade."

"Then they acted foolishly," was the prompt reply.
"Whither are you bound?"

Ralph returned his questioner's keen stare with
interest.

" What may be your reason for asking? "

" The safety of the nation, friend. I hold warrant from Parliament to enquire into the business of all riders to the north. Now, I pray you, your errand? "

" I am journeying to Ely, to the house of one Oliver Cromwell. Perchance you can direct me."

The man frowned.

" Mean you Sir Oliver, the worshipful knight? "

" He may be a knight," Ralph said doubtfully. " But that is not likely. I mean the member of Parliament for Cambridge town."

There was a sudden uneasy movement among the men, who had clustered round the group in a very unmilitary manner, and the quartermaster was heard to mutter curious words. The officer, meanwhile, caught up the lantern and held it close to Ralph's face.

" What d'ye want with him? "

" Take me to his house, and if it be his pleasure I will tell you."

The other laughed — a short, rough laugh.

" That need hardly be, man. I am Oliver Cromwell."

Ralph drew a long breath of surprise. So great was his astonishment that he forgot his giddiness and faintness, sprang from the ground, and stared blankly at his questioner for several moments. He had pictured to himself these two years what his father's old friend would be like, and had always seen a tall, dignified person, a man who in manner and speech would be cold, formal, and prim, with the high-crowned hat and closely-cut hair already affected by the Puritans of the stricter sort. This man, the real Cromwell, was the reverse of all these things. He wore his hair moderately long, he was two inches shorter than Ralph himself, and in face, as in figure, he was broad, massive, and strong. His lips were full, his eyes steel-grey, very large and deeply set, his nose heavy, his chin long and deep — an ugly face, yet remarkable even at first glance by reason of its power and dignity of expression. Ralph could not take his eyes away.

"I have a letter to deliver unto you," he said at last. "I think it will make my business clear."

Cromwell glanced at the superscription, dropped on one knee, and read it by the lantern-light; while Ralph stood over him, clenching his hands, conscious of an uncomfortable dryness at the back of his throat and an irritation round the eyes. His father's words were ringing in his ears. It seemed as if they had been spoken yesterday.

Cromwell read the letter slowly from end to end, folded it up with reverent care, and then, to Ralph's extreme surprise, laid both hands upon his shoulders.

"Welcome — welcome, John Dangerfield's son. Let me look at thee. Is there a likeness? I cannot see it — except a trace, perchance, in the expression of your eyes. John's son! It brings back old, old days to hear his name — the days he would sit talking to my mother with the quiet and gentle deference she loved, and used to wish I would imitate. Ah! have I pained thee, lad? That is not well. Nay, be not ashamed of tears. Truly, a man who did not weep for the loss of such a father would be without a heart. I heard of his punishment — so ill deserved. I grieved much that he had not writ to me for aid. But it was his nature never to complain. And he sends thee — but, tut, how I prate, whilst thou art fainting. Reuben, hither!"

He wheeled round and dropped back into his customary curt speech. The quartermaster, Reuben Sweetlove, a grizzled veteran of the Thirty Years' War, came forward with slow precision, and, because he expected a severe reprimand, stood peculiarly erect, towering above his captain some four inches, a pillar of protesting self-righteousness.

"You have heard me," was all Cromwell said. "Give orders to two men to escort this gentleman to my house.

Canst ride now?" turning to Ralph again, his voice soft-
ening. "Reuben, though he meant no harm, is not
light-handed when in haste."

Ralph laughed and tenderly felt the place.

"My brain sings still," he said. "But it is nothing.
I trust the man my horse knocked over is in no worse
plight. My pistol, by good fortune, missed its fire."

"You failed then to look at your priming when you
set forth to-day," Cromwell said gruffly. "Fie on your
carelessness. Here is your horse. I have business in
this village, but will follow soon. Is that you, Sanctify
Jordan? Then I charge you to give Mistress Cromwell
this letter, and tell her from me that Master Dangerfield
will sup and remain with us the night. Your name,
Ralph, will be your welcome. Now, my men, mount
you quickly. Reuben, ride with me."

CHAPTER IV

THE task of the men who first took upon themselves the responsibility and expense of raising an army for the service of the Parliament was a very laborious and difficult one. Affairs were in a strangely chaotic state at this time. Reliable news from London travelled slowly, and the number of men outside Parliament in the early part of the summer of 1642 who knew the precise significance of the deadlock between the king and the Commons was very few.

On May 26th Parliament resolved to take "measures of defence" against the king, and in August the Royal Standard was raised at Nottingham; but during the intervening months it was only in certain counties that any systematic preparations were even begun, most men hoping against hope that a compromise would be made which would prevent actual bloodshed. Here and there, however, were men who had lost all hope of a peaceful settlement. Cromwell was one of these, and early in July he set to work to enlist and equip a troop of horse with characteristic energy. The recruiting of the rank and file he accomplished with comparative ease, for he had a strong personal influence in the fens. Moreover, he was fortunate in procuring in Reuben Sweetlove a first-rate quartermaster.

Reuben had originally been groom to Cromwell's uncle, Sir Oliver, in the days of his glory as the Knight of Hinchinbrook; but early in youth, finding service uncongenial, he had gone abroad, and enlisted under Gustavus Adolphus. As a soldier he not only earned some distinction, but laid by a goodly store of savings; and

38

leaving the army after the battle of Lutzen, at the death
of the King of Sweden, he returned to his native land
and country to settle down. Here he rented a farm from
Cromwell, and it was not long before a close friendship
sprang up between the men. Cromwell, indeed, in this
instance as in others, scandalized his aristocratic relations by the degree of intimacy he allowed, and even
encouraged, between his family and his uncle's old servant. Not only did he take counsel with Reuben on
many farming matters, especially horses, of which the
old cavalry man had a profound knowledge, but he
invited him to sup at his house, and would listen by the
hour to his stories of the prowess of his beloved commander "the Lion of the North," and to circumstantial
accounts of his campaigns.

When the war clouds began to gather, it was to Reuben
that Cromwell first went for aid to mould his troop. He
found the old veteran eager for action, and ready not only
to serve himself, but to add his mite to the subscription
for arms, which Cromwell had headed with a gift of five
hundred pounds.

The day that Ralph arrived at Ely thirty men had been
enrolled, and were already acquainted with the rudi-
ments of drill. Cromwell could have had twice this
number, but he was hampered by want of officers. Ely
and the immediate neighbourhood was a hot-bed of Royalists; and Cromwell had obtained a warrant from Parliament to watch "suspects," and arrest them if need
be, search suspicious houses for stores of plate and arms,
and intercept messengers to the king. Such work as
this demanded a discretion on the part of the officer in
command — a quickness of judgment, firmness, and self-
restraint which it was not easy to find. The exceptional
quality of the troopers, and the superiority of Sweetlove
to most quartermasters, made the choice of cornet and
lieutenant peculiarly difficult, and so far Cromwell had
found no one to his mind. It was not his way to be

easily satisfied with men. The work required of his troop was done and, so far, done well; but this was due to his own energy and Sweetlove's, and meant a constant wearing activity for them both, night and day, which could not last.

The business which Cromwell had on hand when he sent Ralph on to his house was a visit to the principal mansion in the village of Stretham, in which a hundred pikes and muskets were said to have been collected for the use of the royal army. The inspection of this place took him half an hour. The family were away, and an aged housekeeper was the only person to be seen. Courteously detaining the woman in the hall, Cromwell, with an apology for the necessities of the time, distributed his men in different directions, and presently discovered the arms in a closet. He removed them, gravely handed a formal receipt in the name of the Parliament to the protesting servant, and departed, not so much as a pasty taken from the larder or a pennyworth of plunder from the house. The troop now turned homewards, Reuben and his captain riding ahead.

"What think you of that youth Dangerfield?" Cromwell said suddenly.

The quartermaster winced as if a wasp had stung him.

"Too big for his boots," he growled, "too proud i' the stomach; wilful and sharp-tongued — that's what I think."

"What else?"

"I will see him in daylight first."

"Nonsense! Your eyes need no daylight to read character. Play not with me. Has the shield another side?"

Sweetlove wriggled in his saddle, and swore a deep Dutch oath. Swearing was strictly forbidden in the troop, but in Reuben's opinion the interdict only applied to English. Cromwell was never heard to contradict him.

"You knew his father, captain," he said; "'tis you should answer that." Then after a pause, Cromwell keeping silence, knowing the man with whom he had to deal, he continued in a voice suggestive of water pumped from a deep well: —

"I don't say he's a laggard, and he rides pretty. Fear don't come anigh him, and I could fancy you will find that he's commanded men."

"How know you that?"

"Know it?" exclaimed the quartermaster testily. "Did I say I knew it? I know this, he's as froward a cockerel as ever I've seen, with just a soft enough tip to his tongue to cozen his father's friend, while I warrant he drank the king's health this morning with his own."

He gave a hoarse laugh, and prepared himself for an unpleasant rejoinder; but Cromwell said nothing, nor did he speak again until he briefly dismissed his men for the night.

It was now nine o'clock, a late hour in those days, and Cromwell entered his house quietly, expecting to find his family in bed.

This house, which still stands, was an unpretentious dwelling of two stories facing the Cambridge road. On the right was St. Mary's Church; to the left the great tithe barn of Ely, long since pulled down. The house was of grey stone, with a roof of brown tiles, from which the windows of the second storey peeped out upon the side road and a little spread of green sward common, a cluster of small houses, St. Mary's Church, and the cathedral. So high and so steep was the roof, that the upper rooms were more lofty than those below, though all were spacious. The front entrance opened into a large, square hall, with a great fire-place, cold and empty now, in winter a mass of glowing embers and roaring logs. At the further end of the hall was a passage which led with many a twist and turn to the rest of the house: first, the staircase on the left, narrow and winding; then round a corner, and on the right Cromwell's library and study, with an outer door, through which the farmers came to pay their tithes; another turn, and there was the kitchen with its mighty beams, countless nooks, and huge chimney-corner; at the end of the passage the garden, stretching seventy yards and more by the churchyard, walled in, with good turf and well-kept flower-beds. A modest, unassuming little house, dwarfed to insignificance by that imposing pile the deanery, frowned upon by the cathedral, yet holding within it a greater human interest than them all as the home for many years of one of England's greatest sons.

The living-room was a square, plainly-furnished apartment, the largest in the house, opening out of the hall, close by the front door, and here Cromwell found his family. A lady of middle age and three girls were seated at a table laid for supper, and at the further end of the room were two men who had not yet taken their places — Ralph and a tall, spare personage, dressed in the Geneva gown of a Presbyterian minister. The man had a remarkable face. His forehead was high, but narrow and flat at the sides; the eyes prominent, with overhanging brows, which stood out in sharp distinctness from a mass of short, bristling hair. He had the appearance of a man of superabundant energy of mind — one who wore away his bodily strength in a continual fever and fret. At the moment of Cromwell's entrance he was speaking in a tone of severe rebuke.

"Young man, your language is abominable. It is beyond endurance. Retire immediately to your chamber. Indeed, I mean this, and can command obedience, having some authority in this house. The heresy you mouth so glibly is a foul and horrible thing, unfit to pollute the ears of these innocent women. Think you that a God-fearing household will break bread with the son of an accursed ——"

"Silence!"

Ralph stamped his foot, and the glasses on the table rattled. One of the ladies screamed.

"Repeat not that word," he thundered, "or, aged though you be, I will drive it down your throat! Understand that I allow no man, though it were the king himself, to insult my father's name. He led a pure and sinless life, and, whate'er his faith, he died a martyr to it. Now let me pass. I leave this house to-night. I'll not trouble its master for his hospitality."

He turned with proudly-lifted head, and came face to face with Cromwell.

"Stay, friend! Nay "— as Ralph would have pushed past him with scant ceremony —" I will not have it! I'll hold you though I tie you to your bed with ropes. Tush! have you forgotten all I said? This is my house. Come, I insist."

He had grasped Ralph's arm with one hand; now he laid the other on his shoulder.

"Master Hepworth, you are under some strange mistake. This young gentleman is the son of a dear friend. Ralph, I would introduce you to the Reverend Isaac Hepworth, a most godly minister. Peace now, sirs, both! We must to prayers and a chapter, and then to our supper. The hour is late."

With great gentleness, but with a firmness there was no resisting, Cromwell drew Ralph with him to the table; and then, as if nothing had happened, he took up a Bible that lay there and sat quietly down.

The minister and Ralph looked at one another, and Ralph bit his lip.

"I crave your pardon, sir," he said, drawing a quick breath. "My speech was hasty, but "— with another breath —" I cannot withdraw my words."

"Let them pass," the minister rejoined, with a grave inclination of the head. "Truly, this is not my dwelling, but Master Cromwell's. My friends, let us pray."

They all knelt down, Ralph between Cromwell and

the minister. The prayer was long and eloquent — there were no short prayers in those days — but the pith of it lay in the last sentence.

"We ask Thy blessing, O Lord, upon this house and all who dwell therein, even upon the guest arrived this night within its gates. We crave Thy mercy and consideration for his sad case in fullest measure for Christ's sake."

Cromwell then read a chapter from the Psalms, and then at last all took their places at the table. The conclusion of the meal was the signal for the ladies to retire. When they rose Ralph, according to the usage he had learnt abroad, hastened to open the door, greeting each as she passed him with a courteous obeisance. The attention was evidently unexpected. The first of the ladies, Mistress Cromwell, acknowledged the salutation with a stiff little bow; the next, a tall girl, her eldest daughter, tried to respond with grace, but spoilt the effect by a giggle; the third, a little maiden of thirteen, shook a roguish face and a head of yellow curls at him, and laughed outright; but the fourth, a damsel who seemed older than the rest, curtsied back with a composure that was both dignified and modest. Ralph wondered who she was.

As Ralph closed the door, the minister raised his brows at Cromwell and coughed significantly, as a hint that some emphatic expression of opinion concerning such demeanour — considered highly incorrect in Puritan households of the time — would be seasonable. But Cromwell only filled a goblet with wine.

"Drink this, young friend, and then to your bed. You must be aweary. A ride from London, with my quartermaster's pike-end against your skull at the close, maketh a hard day's work. To-morrow I shall ask you certain questions. You have seen military service?"

"Two years in Holland, sir."

"What commission held you?"

" Cornet of horse, afterwards lieutenant."

" I thought so.   Now to rest — to rest."

There was a gleam of satisfaction in Cromwell's eye as he ushered his guest to his chamber which puzzled Ralph, and the grasp of his hand as they parted was almost paternal in its warmth.   Ralph pondered over this, then upon the harsh bigotry of the minister, upon the Cromwell family and their homely ways, lastly on that maiden. Who was she — another daughter?   Then he fell asleep.

CHAPTER V

WHEN Cromwell came downstairs after seeing Ralph to his room, he found his wife waiting for him in the hall. She was walking restlessly to and fro — after the manner of nervous people when they are tired and out of sorts — pushing the furniture into unaccustomed places, and thrusting into cupboards articles which were generally left out.

Mistress Cromwell was a pale woman of forty, with a round face and small, regular features. In girlhood she had been pretty, but her face was spoilt by a querulous, dissatisfied expression, due partly to temperament, partly to ill-health. Mistress Cromwell, it was said, seldom found the world to her taste, or the people in it. She greeted her husband now in a tone of fretful protest.

" Past eleven o'clock, and you up at five this morning! Not one fair sleep, or even rest for your limbs, have you taken these two weeks past. It is a most grievous matter, if you could but see it. Even a young man should not play so rashly with himself, and you are not young."

" Wherefore, dear heart, I know my own capacities full well. Strength of body! Pooh! I have enough and to spare. I would my mind and brain were quicker, but it rests with God. He made me. Thou'rt tired, wife. Follow the rest at once. I have work, a matter of some writing. I should be in the library now, not spoiling your sleep."

He bent down and kissed her on the forehead, but she turned fretfully away.

" The library is locked up. Yes, Susan lit the candles, but I snuffed them out, and awaited you here.

46

Now hearken to me, if but for once, and go to bed. It will be sinful if you work again to-night. An' you love me and the children you will not. But we are seldom in your thoughts, methinks, these days."

Cromwell sighed.

"My dear wife," he said very gently, "speak not vain words; God hath given me this work to do, and His will must be fulfilled. I shall not sleep to-night. In a few hours we start for Cambridge on an errand of the urgentest importance. Till then I must write with all the speed I may. Do not again, an' it please you, my dear, undo what I have ordered to be done. It wastes my time and wears my patience. Now — good-night."

He kissed her again, walked into the library and closed the door.

It was one of the trials of Cromwell's life that he rarely received support or sympathy from his wife in his public work. Mrs. Cromwell was a conscientious woman, a careful mother, a thrifty housewife; but she found it hard to understand why her husband, with the many claims upon his time at home, should expend so much energy upon other people. When honours came, and a great position, she accepted them with resignation, and struggled hard to do her duty according to her lights. But she was not happy. Mrs. Cromwell was emphatically one of those people who believe that charity should begin and end at home.

There is an evil fate about interrupted work. No sooner had Cromwell relighted his candles and sorted out the mass of correspondence which had been pouring in all day, than a knock came at his door, and he was delayed again. The culprit was his second daughter, the curly-headed maiden of thirteen. She came in without waiting for an answer to her knock, and rushing impetuously to him, planted herself upon his knee.

"Nay, scold me not, daddy, dear heart," she cried, as her father laid his pen down with a grave shake of the head. "I ought to be in bed, I know. Yes, but so ought you; I heard mother say so. Well, I would have been long since, but I could not let Rachel go alone to the kitchen, she might have had a fright; and then — and this is the *real* reason — I was just going to say my prayers, when I found I must ask you something first — a most urgent thing. But oh, daddy, why look you so very, very tired?"

All this came in a breath and a half, her soft cheek pressed against his, her hand smoothing back the locks of iron-grey from the careworn forehead.

Cromwell tried to look severe.

"Elizabeth," he began, but she put her hand to his mouth.

"Oh, don't," she cried, "Elizabeth means you are angered with me. You must not be. It is a matter of great importance I've to ask you concerning my prayers."

She spoke in so solemn a tone that Cromwell became curious.

"It is a long time in the asking, Betty. Out with it, then, and scamper back again. Thine aunts would say it was my duty to whip thee well for such a midnight freak. Tell me, and be off."

"I did not think to come," the child said, flushing and smiling, "till Bridget said I was afeared. I had to then. Father, it's — it's about that gentleman, Mr. Ralph. I do not remember his other name. I want to pray for him. May I? Bridget said it was not right for me to pray for a stranger when he was a man, but when I asked her why she could not tell. I may, an' I wish to, may I not?"

Cromwell looked keenly down into the earnest little face.

"Why dost wish to pray for our guest, pussy?"

"Because he hath been used so ill," she cried, tossing back her curls and sitting erect. "If you had heard what

Master Hepworth said you would believe it. When
mother brought Mr.— Mr. Ralph in where we were waiting supper, no sooner did Master Hepworth hear his
name — Dangerfield, that was it — than he made a horrid gruff noise in his throat. 'What!' he cried out "—
and here Miss Betty deepened her own little voice into
a comical likeness of the minister's —"'are you the son
of that Socinian Schismatic whose book hath been so
great a detriment to all true believers and an encouragement to the vilest heretics? Stand back, sir'— Mr.
Dangerfield had bowed to him —'I will not touch your
hand.' At this Mr. Ralph did stand back, as indeed he
well might, and a look came into his face of such hot
anger that I trembled.

"'Sir!' he said in sharp tones, 'I am John Dangerfield's son — and proud of it.'

"He was very quiet and scornful, but for all that he
looked like one hurt; and I was not the only one to see
it. Rachel did, for when I squeezed her hand under
the table she squeezed mine back. As for Master Hepworth, he seemed to lose himself in anger, and while we
sighed sorely for our supper, he began accusing Mr.
Dangerfield's father of every wicked thought and deed
there is — all because he had writ this book. And I
think it was very cruel of him, and unjust; for that Mr.
Dangerfield is dead, and this one had naught to do with
the book. I watched his face close. It looked like —
oh, I do not know what. His eyes were fierce and his
mouth bitter; but his lips trembled, as I saw yours tremble when you whipped Dick once for telling lies. At
last he broke in, and said such things must not be said
about his father, and that the book was a beautiful and
sacred book. This sent Master Hepworth into a high
passion, and when you came he had just ordered Mr.
Dangerfield to leave the room — *your* room! We were
so glad you came — Rachel and I. Rachel was crying.
She felt her uncle's words to be as unjust as I did. I

could have danced with joy to see your face, and how
you brought Ralph — I mean Mr. Dangerfield — back.
I have cried since, because I knew he felt very badly.
I do so want to pray for him. You will let me, won't
you, daddy dear? Say yes, and I will run straight away
to bed. I want to ask God to keep Master Hepworth
from ever saying such things again."

The child had slipped from her father's knee in the
excitement of the moment, and now she stood with
demurely-folded hands, but eager eyes, searching his
face. She could not read its expression. He seemed
displeased, yet when he spoke it was with his customary
tenderness.

"Child, thy little brain is a sadly active and inquisitive
one. Thou art too prone to pry into what thy elders do
and say, the rights of which thou canst not judge and
should not question. Still, I would not discourage thee
in prayer. Pray for our young friend, and especially
ask God to give him patience, he will need it sorely all
his life. Why, Rachel!"

The door had opened again, and the damsel who had
curtsied to Ralph came in with a tray in her hands, bearing a steaming tumbler of cognac, a beaten egg, and
milk.

"The house is 'witched to-night," Cromwell went on,
as Betty, having got her wish, kissed him and vanished.
"What have you here, wicked adopted daughter of
mine? Where have you been? Fie, fie!"

"Mistress Cromwell gave me the flask," she answered,
stooping over the chair to kiss him, "I have but heated
the milk and beat the egg. Must you take no rest
to-night?"

"It is a conspiracy," Cromwell said laughing, "and
this, I believe, be a drug. Yet the flesh is weak, for I
cannot resist the taste. 'Tis good indeed. Rest, say
you? My child, I have twenty letters to write, and I
start for Cambridge in four hours. Would you then tell

me to rest? Daughter of Thomas Fullerton, what mean you?"

"I did not know that," the girl said hastily, "or I would not have asked so useless a question. But I long to help you. I cannot bear to see your face grow wearier day by day, and sit by idle and useless. These are times when it is hard to be a woman."

Cromwell turned in his chair and held her at arm's length.

"Worse and worse. Upon my faith thou'rt no less a child than little Betty, for all thy knowledge and thy grave deportment. I must preach thee a homily, I see. Listen! It is a man's business to strike down evil and uphold the right. A man that doeth this, if he strike but hard enough, doeth the will of the Lord. But God's most perfect work is a woman — such as my mother hath been and is now, such as thou wilt be. Men do the fighting, but women hold the power if they but choose. Let them see they use it aright. Your time hath not come yet, but it will some day. And now to thy bed, daughter Rachel."

He kissed her, then turned his back upon her and took up his pen.

The girl slowly retired, looking over her shoulder as she went at the weary head bent over the heap of papers. Before she reached the door an idea occurred to her, and she came back again.

"I can help you," she cried, with a decision that made Cromwell look up in surprise, "and I must. These letters, I could write them to your dictation if you would let me. I can spell, father taught me, and I writ much for him to his agent in foreign parts. Oh, try me, sir!"

Her eyes — quiet sober ones — shone with a mute but eloquent appeal; then, seeing him shake his head, she caught his hand between both of hers.

"I know these fingers are tired, strong though they be. Mine have done no work to-day. Besides, you can dictate much speedier than write. Father used to say I could be a swift scribe when I tried. It would be a great happiness to me to do it. My life is empty oftentimes just for want of the work I used to do. You are all good to me — too good — but I miss that work. Then these," touching the letters, " are sacred. If I am worthy to help you how father would rejoice. He ever promised that I should do my share — when the time came. It has come now."

There was a deep silence for a minute. Then Cromwell rose from his chair and paced the room and Rachel had to wait two minutes more before he answered her.

" Yet, why not? " he said suddenly, as if he were communing with himself. " I say, Why not? This cause is not mine or that of any man. It is God's. We are His instruments, set here to tear down the evils that the devil hath built up. Let all help, then — women and children, old men and maids. Yes, my daughter, you shall have your way, and shall begin to-night. What thy Uncle Hepworth will say — but it shall be. Sit there, then! Take up thy pen and write! "

CHAPTER VI

CROMWELL dictated and Rachel wrote for two hours. He began slowly, and when the first letter was written took it up and read it through. He made no comment, but the succeeding ones were dictated much more rapidly. And now Rachel had no respite, for Cromwell's mind was concentrated upon his work. The girl soon became extremely weary, for early hours were kept in those days, and she had risen at five that morning; but she showed no sign of faltering, nor thought of it, and was only distressed because of an increasing difficulty she felt to keep pace with the sharply-spoken sentences — sometimes long, involved, and bristling with parentheses, at others crisp and brief and telling. At last the harsh voice stopped, and Cromwell kissed her on the forehead.

"All are finished. Twenty letters in two hours! Truly, while you live with me — which will not be for long if I work you so — I shall be in little trouble with my letter-writing. Thou hast done well. Away with you — secretary."

The correcting and signing of the correspondence occupied Cromwell half an hour; then he got up and slowly paced the room in deep thought.

"Shall I put that test upon him?" he mused. "It will be rash, yet worth a risk. If blood doth count for anything in these matters he should be of the best. His father was strong in thought though weak in body, audacious even to sinfulness in his independence of authority. His grandfather was Francis Drake's best captain — one who spoke blunt truth to Queen Eliza-

beth, and was imprisoned for it. But, stay, there was
the mother — a woman, I remember, much on her dignity. H'm! He gets his handsome face from her,
maybe his nature too. Then he must have lived these
two years among malignants. Yet he comes to me; he
hath kept that letter warm in his bosom and his love
for his father fresh and green. He respects no person
when his blood is up. Witness Hepworth. I am
tempted sore. Wait, 'Not the king himself,' he said.
Why should he name Charles Stuart an' he was not to
him his 'great and sacred majesty,' as they term the
man? The scales are weighted here. Perhaps in time,
but for this expedition, no — he will not do."

He paused in his stride, and snuffed out one of the
two candles standing on the table and put away the
papers on his desk; then, taking the other candle, held
it up to a picture on the wall. It was a drawing of a
boy's head, crudely executed and of sickly colouring, yet
touched with a certain power, a likeness, not a daub.
Beneath it, in Cromwell's hand, was written, " Robert.
Aged 14."

He had been the eldest, his parents' joy and pride.
His death, three years before, was the severest wrench of
his father's life, and had nearly broken his mother's
heart. A bright, strong face, wide-open, eager eyes, and
firm-set mouth; the lips just parted with a smile.
To-night the character of this son, serious beyond his
years, impulsive, forcible, came into Cromwell's memory
with a curious insistence; tears fell from his eyes and
rolled down his cheeks, and he muttered aloud:

"Robin, Robin, if I had but thee at my side. Oliver
poor lad, will do his best, but thou! O God, Thy ways
are indeed inscrutable! Why didst Thou take him whom
we needed so? That face — how I remember it! There
was no other like it, nor ever will be. I never — but,
hold; that is strange! strange! "

He held the candle close. " Where is the likeness?

He is dark; Robin was fair. He is tall, which Robin never would have been. Neither in feature nor in form can I see any resemblance at all. And yet — it was that defiance to the minister, the flash of eye, the ringing tone of voice, the righteous anger in defence of one he loved. Aye, this reminded me of Robin. Was it for naught — a passing fancy of the brain, or a message from the Almighty sent to guide my action now?"

He stood some moments buried in thought. "And I was not the only one whose heart he touched," he muttered again; "Betty trusted him. A child gifted with the unerring instinct of a child. It shall guide me."

He left the room and mounted the stairs to Ralph's room. Ralph was sleeping peacefully and soundly; but at Cromwell's entrance he roused at once, true to his military training, with all his wits about him.

"I have disturbed you, friend," Cromwell began, "because I have matters that require your close attention. First, I require your promise that naught which passes my lips shall be repeated elsewhere."

"You have it."

"How long have you been in England?"

"Not two days."

"Why did you return?"

Ralph did not answer. There was a peremptoriness of tone, a rough sternness now about this man — old friend of his father's though he was — against which Ralph's soul rebelled.

Cromwell, seeing his hesitation, misunderstood the cause.

"Whom would you serve," he added, "that is what I wish to learn — the country or the king?"

"You mean the Parliament!"

"I mean the people. Came you here to aid them — to succour the oppressed, raise the downtrodden, and humble the house of Stuart? or to abase yourself, and join the rest of the gallants in their cuckoo cry, 'God

save the king?' Answer me that question, and quickly.
Time presses. Give me your mind."

Ralph hesitated still. There was a desperate earnestness in the heavy face which made his heart beat quickly.
Yet the tone of authority in the voice still jarred against
his pride.

"I came, in the first instance," he said slowly, "to
deliver into your hands my father's letter. As to my
politics — well, all my friends, sir, be stout Royalists."

Cromwell turned away.

"Tell me no more. Nay, not another word. You
shall go as you came, in peace, being John's son. But
what I did intend to say hath died upon my lips. I had
imagined that his precepts — though, God knows, I am
no Socinian — might so have weighed with you that we
should be at one in this. But I will leave you to your
rest."

He had taken up the light and crossed the room, when
he saw Ralph leap out of bed and go to the window.

"My faith!" he cried, "I thought I could not be mistaken. There be the ring of bridles and hoofs in the
road; a troop, I'll swear. Is it yours?"

Ralph's face was clear now, his tone one of eager
enquiry.

"There be thirty men," he went on, "with pots and
backs and breastplates, all complete, by gad! Well
horsed, too, and disciplined. The man that drilled those
lads, sir, knew his business."

He was all excitement and animation. The night was
fine, a full moon was shining, and the troop stood in
rank across the road — a motionless mass of steel.

"Whither be they bound?"

"Cambridge, to seize supplies garnered there for the
king."

"Let me ride with you."

Cromwell came slowly back to him across the room.

"Against the king?"

56

"Against the king."

"Know you Cambridge?"

"I was at college there."

"Which?"

"Sidney."

"Your father's and my own. How long ago?"

"Two years."

"Hast been there since? You have friends in the college. Are they well affected?"

Ralph shook his head. Doctor Taunton had told him that the Fellows of Sidney, headed by the present master, his old tutor, were declaring for the king.

Cromwell heard him sigh.

"Mark you," he said, "the issue lies there. But I must to my men. If you desire to come, be ready when I return. Search your heart and bare your thoughts to God. 'Tis your friends or — your father!"

He said the last two words as he went out of the door, and then Ralph heard his heavy step descending the stair and the creak of the front door. He went to the window again, and saw the swords of the troopers flash to the salute, and the quartermaster dismount and enter the house.

Some fifteen minutes later Cromwell's step was upon the stair again. He found Ralph fully dressed.

"Have you decided, then?"

"I will go with you. Let me get my horse."

"We have one waiting. Is your mind quite clear?"

"It has been, sir, for long enough. But you touched my pride, and I played with words. That is over. I'll serve you faithfully as trooper."

Cromwell smiled.

"We welcome thee, my son, but not in the ranks. For this day and the work thereof thou'lt be my second in command."

CHAPTER VII

THE dawn was breaking when the troop set forth for Cambridge. It was fair day, and at the outskirts of the town, on a piece of waste common land, were a busy crowd of merry-jacks, gipsy fortune-tellers, and booth-keepers, with grotesque caricatures painted on their tents of the dwarfs, giants, strong men, and fat women to be found inside. The morning was cloudless, and the people were already collecting to enjoy their holiday, as eager over it as though the miseries of civil war were a century away. Even Cromwell's troopers wondered where they would quarter to-night, and pondered upon what excuses they might make to get leave for a few hours' pleasuring.

The journey was nearly over. To the left were the windings of the Cam, and just visible among the trees the brown roofs of houses, church spires, and college towers. To the right, on rising ground, a massive stone building — the castle. This was their destination. It was used as an arsenal and storehouse for the college plate in times of trouble, and here the loyal Fellows had sent silver to the value of ten thousand pounds, arms, and a magazine of gunpowder for the service of the king.

Ralph and Cromwell were riding together. As they turned off the main road and faced the castle Cromwell said abruptly: —

"Think you it would stand a siege?"

Ralph scanned the building with swift, practised eye and laughed.

"Aye, sir, were there no gunpowder. But to-day — give me two drakes, a dozen rounds of ammunition, a gunner of parts, and a score or two of resolute men to follow when the breach was made, and I would account for that place before noon."

Cromwell nodded.

"Such business is familiar to you. That is well, but to-day there will be no need of your skill; I have a friend within. Yet I may require hard words of you. Will they be forthcoming against your friends?"

Their eyes met — Ralph's surprised and half indignant, Cromwell's with a steady, measuring glance, cool, deliberate, calculating.

"I have passed my word," Ralph answered shortly. "You will find that I do not break promises."

"I doubt you not, man," was the sharp answer. "But have you heart for such work?"

"I would rather it were fighting an enemy."

Cromwell frowned.

"The same story — ever the same. This king and his father before him and their creatures oppressed, robbed, and murdered honest men. The nation cries out upon them. Yet the moment a sword is raised it is, 'Our friends and brothers, touch them not.' But I say no more. Keep your promise to-day. To-morrow do what your conscience and your heart may prompt. March!"

He touched his horse with the spur, and the troop quickened its pace and swept at a round trot up the road which led to the main entrance of the castle. The grounds were of considerable extent, and at intervals a trooper was detached to follow a by-path which might lead to other entrances. His orders were to stop all vehicles coming to or from the castle and examine their contents. The castle was of Norman origin, but the old building had disappeared, and that which had been erected in its place — since crumbled away in its turn — was hardly more than a fortified house, its chief protection a wall ten feet in height surrounding it on all sides, and of immense thickness and strength. There was a moat beyond the wall, but it was half full of rubbish and securely bridged over.

The gates were closed and barred, and when Cromwell demanded admittance the porter sharply asked his business.

"Friend," Cromwell replied, levelling a pistol at the man's head, "that is not your affair. Open, or I fire."

The man, frightened at the grim array of armed men, hurriedly did his bidding, and the troop rode into a spacious courtyard.

"Secure him, Reuben," Cromwell said. Then, turning to Ralph, "I go to the governor. I shall need but two men. Dispose the rest as you deem fit. Close the gates and let no one leave. Keep watch on all approaches. Our danger lies from without."

He crossed the courtyard and went boldly in, while Ralph rapidly explored the place and sent scouts to ride round the walls outside. They returned shortly to report that there was no other entrance, and that no one seemed stirring. Half an hour passed by. Then one of the troopers who had accompanied Cromwell appeared at a side door and beckoned.

"The captain craves your presence, sir."

Ralph followed the man along a dark and narrow passage to where the other trooper, carbine in hand, stood on guard at the door of the governor's private apartments. In the first of these rooms Ralph found Cromwell sipping a glass of wine and conversing amicably with an elderly man of bibulous appearance, in a ruff that had seen better days and ill-fitting clothes fashioned a generation ago. This was Sir Joseph Strangford, the governor of the castle, an old acquaintance of the Cromwell family. Ralph was formally introduced, and then Cromwell said in brief, curt tones: —

"We require your services. The treasure is here, but the key of the strong-room containing it is held by one

Doctor Samuel Ward, master of Sidney College. I desire you to take the quartermaster and ten picked men and demand that key of Doctor Ward. Doubtless you are acquainted with him, and may be able to persuade him to yield it to you civilly. Make your request in Sir Joseph's name. But whatever betides"—Cromwell spoke slowly and distinctly —"return with the key. There is gunpowder in this chamber; therefore to blow the door open would be but wanton destruction. Be as speedy as you can; I await you here."

Ralph withdrew without reply, and retraced his steps slowly to the courtyard. He felt as if a weight had been placed upon his shoulders that was almost more than he could bear. Doctor Ward had been a severe disciplinarian and an unsympathetic teacher, yet kind in his way when Ralph was ill once, and a friend of his father's. He was a staunch Royalist, and would resist to the death such a demand as this. A horrid vision of being obliged to draw his sword upon the master haunted Ralph's imagination, and he shuddered as he strode through the gloomy passage. But once in the courtyard he regained his balance and nerve. The men were selected, the gates thrown back, and with Reuben Sweetlove at his side, he started briskly off to do his duty. Their way lay downhill, through narrow, crooked streets, littered with evil-smelling rubbish shot from the house windows with blissful disregard for all laws of sanitation. These windows were filled with curious faces as the steel-clad men clattered past; and though they were but ten minutes on their journey, an excited rabble of boys and idlers collected in their wake, following them to the gates of Sidney; but the men heeded them not. Ralph was in grim earnest now, and his troopers caught his spirit. He smiled as he rode down the well-remembered street, over the familiar cobble stones, past the overhanging houses, past Magdalene, past the round church, and so to the red buildings and grey walls of Sidney.

Within the gateway, then in the centre of the main court opposite the master's lodge, lounged the porter, round-faced and rubicund, an old ally of Ralph's. He stared hard at the cavalcade, but recognised Ralph with a broad grin.

"Blessed if it ain't Master Dangerfield! 'Slid! but it's like old times, sir, to see your face. You have come betimes, too, for my Lord Charlton is here, back from the wars over sea."

Ralph's teeth closed upon his under lip.

"I want the master, Popham. He is within?"

"Aye, surely, i' the lodge. His lordship's still in bed, for he'd a gay carouse last night. Wil't breakfast with him?"

"Not till I have seen the master. Open the gate, good Popham. I am on matters of urgent public concern. Delay is dangerous. Open!"

The porter scratched his head dubiously. He did not like the look of these men in buff and steel. Yet he could not do wrong to open to Lord Charlton's friend. There must be some rebel plot afoot. These troopers were the king's. So he obeyed, and then closed them smartly in the face of the gaping crowd. Ralph turned to Sweetlove.

"Leave half the men here on guard. The rest must come with us. No, Popham," as the porter would have preceded him to the lodge, "I need you not. Keep to the gate. Now, my men."

They crossed the court, and from the windows of the students' rooms eager faces peered down upon them, and the word was passed through the college that soldiers were within the gates and something untoward was on foot. In front of the master's house Ralph halted and dismounted his men, and prepared to go in alone.

"Hold the passage and staircase, quartermaster, I'll be with you in a short space."

But this was so unprofessional that Reuben entered a protest.

"Nay, nay, take us, or even Sanctify, if you'll not have more, he be the biggest. Go not by yourself into such a wasp's nest. That is too rash."

Ralph cut him short.

"Wait, I say, and let no one pass. Keep the way to the gates."

He ran up the narrow, winding stair, every turn of which he knew by heart and knocked at the master's door.

"Come you in," cried a well-remembered voice, sharp and incisive, and Ralph was in the room.

The master was a short, stout man, with a strong, ruddy face — a man of determined character and quick temper. There was probably no one more respected in the University.

"Who is this?" he said sharply. "Nay, speak not; I see it is Ralph Dangerfield. I was a little slow to know you. Your dress is somewhat different from the college gown, and the years have changed you, but no man I have once seen ever passed me by unrecognised. I am glad to see you in this guise. At college you were idle, like your friend the viscount; but, like him, you can fight though you'll not work, and we need fighters. Sit thee down. Tell me what you have been doing these two years past."

Ralph greeted him respectfully.

"Had I time nothing would be more pleasant, master; but now I am here on public service. I must request, in the name of Sir Joseph Strangford, that you hand to me the key of that chamber in the castle containing treasure for the king."

Ralph said the words as if he were repeating a lesson. His heart was at his throat, his nerves on edge. Doctor Ward had always inspired awe among the undergraduates, and Ralph, do what he would, found it impossible to speak with the confidence which in such cases is half the battle.

As for the master, after staring a moment in blank astonishment, he burst out laughing.

"What say you? You want — *what?* My Certes, youth, but your life abroad hath not mended your manners or your sense, whatever it may have done for your body. You want the key? For whom? Sir Joseph. Really! Where be your warrant? And think you that I am likely to do your will? Not so. No, though Sir Joseph came himself and asked me on his bended knee. Once he had that key, but we removed it into safer custody. There it will remain."

He laughed so disagreeably that the blood came surging back into Ralph's face with a vengeance, and his spirits rose.

"It is a matter of extreme urgency, or I'd not have troubled you," he began, when the master interrupted him.

"Nay, nay, most gallant sir, stoop not to apologise to me, nor even to explain. Urgent, is it? My faith, delay not then an instant. Back to Sir Joseph and present my compliments. Tell him that I, Samuel Ward, his most humble servant to command, do refuse now, and at any time, to give to him or any messenger of his, with or without a written letter, that key entrusted to my care by his superiors. So bear him that message, and God keep you, Ralph, for a pretty-looking fellow and a blockhead. Fare you well."

He waved his hand contemptuously, and took up a pen as if to continue a letter he had been writing. Ralph stepped close to his side.

"The key, master, and quickly, or I take it. I pray you, spare me the need of violence."

He watched the old man's eyes. It had suddenly occurred to him that the identification of the key might be difficult. At that moment, however, Doctor Ward made a snatch at a bunch that was hanging from his desk and thrust it into his gown.

"Stand back! Leave my room!" he cried. "What art thou, then, some vile emissary from the rebel Parliament? Aye, I see it from your eye. Get you hence, or I will have ye thrust in prison."

He spoke in loud tones, glancing at a door opposite to the one by which Ralph had entered, as if he expected assistance there. No time was to be lost, and Ralph closed with him, caught the hand which held the keys, wrenched them from him, and tripping the old gentleman up, laid him as gently as he could upon the floor. All this was easy, for the master was but a child in Ralph's powerful hands; yet he struggled so gallantly, and Ralph was so anxious not to hurt him, that it was some minutes before he could dispose of him, and ere he had time to retreat to the outer door three men rushed in from the inner one with drawn swords.

"Seize him! kill him!" panted the master. "A spy from the Parliament! Bring him down in the king's name!"

It was three to one, and Ralph's assailants were strong and active; moreover, one at least was a soldier, for as Ralph drew his sword and faced them, backing towards the door, this man said quietly: —

"Round that table, Vavasour, and cut him off. Greville, advance briskly. We have him in a clutch. Now, you crop-eared rebel —— Good God! 'tis Ralph!"

It was Lord Charlton. As he recognised his friend he lowered the point of his sword and laughed.

"Master, you are under some mistake. Gad, comrade Ralph, what game are you playing upon him? You should be past such jokes at your age, the times are too serious. Come along and breakfast with me, and leave the doctor to his books."

He made a motion as if to sheath his sword, but there was an anxious look in his eyes which belied the confidence of his words. Ralph winced, his mouth drawn with pain.

"Nay, Charlton, the master is under no mistake respecting my politics; I am for the Parliament."

He made an advance toward the door, while Charlton breathed hard, and looked into his eyes as men gaze into the face of one who is dead.

"Then, by God, man," he cried in a thick, strained voice, "stay where you are! Thrust upon him, Greville, if he stirs a step. No rebel leaves this chamber without the master's leave."

Ralph's reply was to spring forward, and with a quick and skilful twist of the wrist send the sword of the man nearest to him flying from his hand, wounding him in the arm. The second man he struck over the shoulder and hurled aside, and then he was face to face with Charlton.

One instant they stood almost motionless, watching; and then they closed, and the others looked on calmly. It was too well matched a strife for interference the young men thought, and Doctor Ward, a man of peace, cowered and kept still. But it was deadly. With the flash of steel the devil of the men awoke, and both had plenty of it. One minute passed, two, and Charlton's neck was bleeding from a deep and ugly dash. In three minutes Ralph's doublet was torn, and there were red stains upon his shirt. Four — a hand on the door outside now, a heavy, masterful hand. It had been locked within. Crash! A man's shoulder came against it, and the lock gave way. In a moment the room was full of troopers, and Charlton's sword was struck to the ground by Sweetlove. The quartermaster raised his weapon to strike again, for he saw the blood upon Ralph's breast; but Ralph stopped him.

"Do him no harm, on your life; he is my friend."

"A lie!" exclaimed Charlton, folding his arms, as he saw that resistance was useless. "The man I loved was a loyal subject of the king. You are a traitor. I would have killed you, so help me God!"

Sweetlove laughed loudly. His blood had risen too.

"Would ye now! Ye would? Then curse you for a whelp who'd bite the hand that 'ud free ye from the chain your master buckled on. Ye're both whelps, flinching from blood as wenches run from mice. Bah, lieutenant, ye've not cut your milk-teeth yet; ye must have slept in Deuschland. Let me take this cockerel at his word and rip him up. He bears you no goodwill."

Ralph made an impatient movement with his hand.

"Hold your peace, quartermaster, and obey my order. Disarm these gentlemen, then leave them in this room. We take no prisoners, and make no delay."

Ralph was pale and collected now, and took no apparent notice of Charlton's words. In a few minutes they were in the court, passing down the path between the rows of poplars. A score of students had gathered in the court, and hooted the soldiers vigorously, but there was an ugly look about these grim men in steel caps that discouraged any attack. Besides, no one knew precisely what they had done. So they were allowed to depart without opposition, and to Reuben's unspeakable disgust regained the castle without adventure. Cromwell was in the courtyard, and Ralph's sore heart, sorer than he knew at the time, found comfort in his greeting.

"Your work done? Then you have saved many a hundred lives. I hear there are arms and munition eno' to equip a regiment of musketeers. Now to load our prize in carts and waggons, and then to London with it."

CHAPTER VIII

THE Cromwell household rose late the day the troop went to Cambridge, and breakfast was not until seven, an hour after the usual time.

The Reverend Isaac Hepworth read the Scriptures and offered up prayers, and Rachel Fullerton, in the absence of Mrs. Cromwell, who was unwell, presided at table.

Rachel looked old for her eighteen years. She was slightly made, with brown eyes, and a great deal of soft, dark hair, brushed severely back, according to the prevailing Puritan fashion, showing to advantage a square, white forehead. Her features were irregular, her complexion inclined to freckles; but her figure, though below the usual height of women, was well formed and graceful — a girl of quiet manner and of unobtrusive ways, much inclined to silence, whom most people thought rather insignificant, especially when compared to Bridget Cromwell, the eldest daughter. A few, and those who knew her best, said that this quietude was deceptive, and that Rachel could turn the whole family round the smallest of her fingers when she chose to try. Even her admirers, however, were fain to own that few things were more difficult than to find out what Rachel thought or felt.

This had always been so. In her childhood Rachel had been a solemn little creature, with great melancholy eyes and quaint, grown-up manners, shrinking from caresses and notice, rarely naughty, always quiet and still, an enigma to her nurse and a severe trial to her mother. Mrs. Fullerton was a well-meaning woman, extremely energetic and outspoken, but unsympathetic and lacking in perception. This silent little daughter, so different from ordinary children, was beyond her ken. She came very early to the conclusion that the child had no heart, and after more or less spasmodic attempts to gain her confidence, gave it up, and let her go her own way. This was a mistake. Rachel's doll — a dreadful piece of wood, heavy as a club, with round, grinning head splashed with red paint, and insufficiently clothed in a rag of blue calico — could have told her things which would have astounded her. Many a time, after a day during which she had scarcely spoken a word to her mother, Rachel had cried herself to sleep with Dorothea in her arms, kissing its ugly face with passionate affection, and telling it between her sobs that no one else loved her, or would ever love her, in the whole world.

The life of an only child in a strict Puritan household — Thomas Fullerton was an elder of a Presbyterian church — was dreary and monotonous to a degree difficult to realise at the present time. Lessons — very dull ones — sewing, and housework filled the whole day. Rachel's only exercise was a daily walk with her governess — a poor relation of her father's — a sour old maid; her only pleasure playing with her doll. It was Dorothea, she used to say, when in happier days she displayed it to children of her own, which kept her alive. All her griefs and troubles and difficulties were told to the doll, discussed with it, and submitted to its judgment, which, like many a human being's, reflected another's, and was, perhaps, none the worse for that. All the wealth of lovingness that was in her the child poured upon Dorothea. To her mother she was, on the whole, dutiful and obedient; and she gave her governess little trouble, being naturally quick at learning; but her love was for Dorothea, and Dorothea alone. She seldom saw her father. He was a taciturn, reserved man, very conscientious, very strict, very cold in manner. A London merchant, by hard work and shrewdness he had made a large fortune, a considerable portion of which he spent upon his church, and still more, anonymously, among the poor, living himself in plainest fashion. He was widely respected, but loved by few and feared by many, his wife amongst others.

As Rachel began life so she grew up until her fifteenth year. Then came a change. Mrs. Fullerton fell sick and died after a short illness. It was feared that the disease was infectious, and Rachel was only allowed to see her mother once just before her death. The dying woman blessed her, and then gave a hopeless sigh as she looked in vain for tears on the set, white face.

"Be good," she cried hoarsely, "and oh, child, child, be loving! Cherish thy father, he has only thee."

She ended with a burst of hysterical sobs, and Rachel was hurried away and not allowed to enter the sick chamber again. When all was over Mr. Fullerton went himself to break the news, and the sight of his haggard, stricken face, the sound of his voice, tender and gentle for the first time, swept away all the reserve and awe which the long years of repression had wrought in his daughter's heart, and with a low, inarticulate cry Rachel ran to him and sobbed her heart out upon his breast.

It was the beginning of a new life for both of them, for Thomas Fullerton, too, had a heart under his reserve. All his leisure hours were spent in his daughter's company, while Rachel, from a timid, retiring girl, in a few months quietly emancipated herself from governess control, and, young as she was, became mistress of her father's house. Two years passed — happy, peaceful years — and then came the darkest hours of Rachel's life. To the last she could not bear to speak of that terrible time. Wealth was a dangerous possession for a determined man, bound by the strongest ties to a persecuted religious sect and a political party which the reigning powers spared no pains to crush. It was the time

of " ship-moneys," and monopolies, and the hundred and
one miserable subterfuges by which Charles raised sub-
sidies behind his people's back. Every class of the community suffered, but the London poor suffered the most,
and in the welfare of his workpeople Thomas Fullerton's
heart was bound up. At first, like John Hampden, he
disputed in his own person the illegal taxes. He lost
his case and was heavily fined. He refused to pay the
fine, and was sentenced to imprisonment. He served his
time, but upon his release deliberately broke the law
again; a warrant was then issued for his immediate
arrest, but he could not be found. His house had been
given up, his effects sold, and his daughter sent to her
uncle, Isaac Hepworth, then living in Kensington village. It was reported that Mr. Fullerton had gone
abroad, and the chase ceased. Soon after this, however,
the custom-house officers discovered that large quantities of soap and salt and other necessaries upon which a
heavy tax had been placed — to fill the pockets of the
queen's favourites, it was said — were being imported
secretly from abroad and sold at cheap rates to the poor
of London. Spies were set to work, rewards offered
and at last treachery did the rest. Thomas Fullerton
was found to be the culprit, and was taken by the sheriff's
officers in Hepworth's house. He was warned at the last
moment, sprang through a window, and mounted his
horse, but was shot through the spine, and brought in
mortally wounded. It was a sign of the respect that was
felt for him that the man who had shot him was the first
to go for a chirurgeon, and that afterwards a large
portion of his fortune was saved for Rachel. To the
girl herself these things were of no importance at the
time. At one blow the chief joy of her life was crushed,
the only friend she had — father, mother, brother, and
sister all in one — was taken from her. She was scarcely
herself for many weeks. By an extraordinary effort of
control she preserved a calm appearance before her

uncle, with whom she was to live in future; but alone in her chamber she gave way to passionate outbursts of hopeless grief, and prayed earnestly that she might die.

Her father's will, duly executed, left the whole of his property to her, and appointed as her guardians " My brother, Isaac Hepworth, and my trusty friend, Oliver Cromwell." Until she was two-and-twenty years of age her guardians were to possess full control over her person, and she was not to marry without their full consent. Her uncle was sole executor — to receive the interest of her fortune until she was of age, and to be responsible for her maintenance. Surprise was expressed by many, and deeply felt by Hepworth, that a second guardian should have been appointed at all; but the lawyers told him that the will was carefully and exactly worded, and admitted of no dispute. To Rachel it was a matter of complete indifference; she had never seen Mr. Cromwell, and he readily agreed to leave her with her uncle. A year went by, and then one day this Mr. Cromwell appeared unexpectedly at Kensington, and was closeted for some hours alone with Isaac Hepworth. Cromwell came in answer to a letter he had received from an old family friend, who in blunt terms informed him that the loneliness of the girl's life was destroying her health, and that she was in the first stage of a decline. The same thing had been said still more forcibly to Isaac Hepworth; but that good man, who had found Rachel a very patient listener to his sermons, and a model house-keeper, had refused to believe it. The appeal to Cromwell was not in vain. What passed between him and her uncle Rachel never knew; but when he returned to Ely she went with him, and never saw her uncle's house again.

At Ely Rachel entered upon a new world. She had never before seen family life, and never mixed, except on rare intervals, with young people of her own age. All was changed now. The Cromwells were a lively, energetic brood. There was Oliver, a youth of eighteen, with arms and legs too long for him, and a propensity for teasing, not in the gentlest manner, which caused Rachel much inward annoyance, and even trepidation, yet a good-natured, honest lad, with a ringing laugh, and merry word for all. Bridget came next, three months Rachel's junior — a clever, handsome girl, twice Rachel's size, talkative, and full of self-assertion, sharp-tongued when she did not giggle, and inclined to put on airs in the presence of men. Rachel did not find Bridget easy to get on with. The boys came next — Dick and Henry. In their holidays — for they were at a boarding-school in Felstead, Essex — Rachel was a second mother to them. She mended their clothes when they burst at awkward times and in awkward places, as boys' clothes will; she lent them pocket-money, which Henry repaid and Dick did not; and when they got into scrapes, she acted as mediator between them and their father. But it was Betty, the thirteen-year-old, who loved Rachel best. Betty was what Oliver called the family scourge until Rachel came to Ely. As a little thing she had been the youngest, and as such was over-petted and caressed by her mother; and being a precocious child, with a masterful will, had been very much spoiled. But at eight years old she was dethroned by a baby sister, and then trouble began; and the model daughter, who Mrs. Cromwell had assured all her friends was of the sweetest disposition and most perfect temper, suddenly developed almost every sin known to childhood. She was jealous, she was violent, she was cruel; she slapped and pinched the baby which had ousted her from power, she defied the nurse to whose care she was now left, she stole the dainties which used to be hers by right, she fought like a small tiger with Bridget when that young person began to assert the privileges of superior age; she became mischievous and cross beyond endurance, driving the servants to despair, and causing the more superstitious of them to shake their heads and mutter "change-ling," and tell gruesome stories of the fairies of the fens. In her father's presence alone was Betty her old self, and threats of a punishment from him was the only effective check upon her the household possessed. But when the times became anxious, and Cromwell's parliamentary labours more severe, even that remedy failed, and then they were at their wits' end.

Into this confusion and chaos Rachel brought order and peace. Betty fell in love with the white-faced girl with her large, sad eyes.

"You be so different from Bridget," the child said confidentially. "You are so quiet and gentle, while she is always talking — of herself. You are a dear, and you will not preach me sermons, will you? Nurse said you would do little else, because your uncle was a Presbyter. But nurse would love to make me afeared of you if she only could."

Rachel did not preach sermons, but from the first she began to correct Miss Betty's wilfulness and slap-dash ways. Rachel was of well-ordered mind and dainty nature, and Betty's habits — frocks and stockings always in holes, hands seldom clean, hair never brushed — shocked her terribly, and with the unmercifulness of youth she criticised Mrs. Cromwell severely in her own mind for neglect. Later on she recognised the multi-plicity of cares and duties which weigh upon a mother with a large family of children of all ages, especially when she is far from strong, and from the first day Rachel set quickly to work to lighten the load. An improvement in Betty began almost immediately. Like most wilful peo-ple, when taken the right way she was docility itself, and could be led by a thread of silk where ropes would not have dragged her. Nor was the advantage all on one side. Betty's outspokenness and, to put it mildly, absence of awe of her elders were a revelation to Rachel, and drew her out of the reserve which the grief at her

father's death and the companionship of her uncle had
brought again into her nature; while the effort of will
and thought necessary to control and manage the unruly
little personage roused her from the lassitude of mind
and body into which she had been sinking; and slowly
but surely her health improved, the natural activity of
her brain reasserted itself, and all danger of a decline
passed away.

Rachel led a busy life, full of other people's business.
If anyone was ill she nursed them. Thanks to her father,
she had received a sound education, and by Cromwell's
special request undertook the duties of governess to
Betty. She taught Bridget fine sewing, gave an eye
to the babies when Mrs. Cromwell was unwell, and last,
but not least by any means, spent a part of each day as
companion to Madam Cromwell — Cromwell's mother.
This old lady lived with her son in rooms especially
reserved for her use. Once a day, when dinner was
served, she appeared at the family table, at her son's
right hand. At other times she kept to her own apartments, receiving there any of the household who required
her counsel or chose to bear her company. Rachel soon
became a regular visitor, and as time went on spent all
her leisure hours there, until it became a habit of everyone in the house to run at once to Madam Cromwell's
room when they wanted Rachel. If she were not there
the old lady generally knew where she could be found.
It was Rachel's custom to go up directly after breakfast
and read aloud the Scriptures for half an hour. Madam
Cromwell said it was an act of mercy, as reading tried
her eyes. Perhaps the sound of the fresh young voice
— for Rachel had a very sweet one — and the company
of youth had more to do with it than failing sight.
Madam Cromwell's life, though she never allowed it, was
a very lonely one.

The day after Ralph's arrival the old lady awaited
Rachel's morning visit with even more than her usual

75

anticipation, and Rachel noticed that the Bible was not upon the table.

"Ah, my girlie," the old lady cried, " late to-day — late a full hour, and just when I had wished you should be early. Nay, nay, do not answer. I know without telling that thou hast good reason. Now, before thou gettest the book, tell me where is the young man?"

Madam Cromwell had a large, pleasant face, set in firm, strong lines. Her son inherited from her his massive chin and broad forehead, the grey eyes and the slight pout of the under lip; but her features were finer than his, and the eyes smaller and more animated. Even in her severest moods — and as all the family knew to their cost she could be terribly severe — there was ever the suggestion of a humorous gleam in those searching eyes. An old lady of great presence, upright as a dart, dressed with the severe simplicity of an earlier generation, a black kerchief of net-point around her head, a chemisette of spotless linen falling to the shoulders, and a grey dress of serviceable woollen material.

"He has gone," Rachel began, in answer to her question, when Madam Cromwell interrupted her in a tone of keen disappointment.

"Gone! Did thy uncle's words bite so shrewdly, then?"

"No, no. I mean he has gone with the troop to Cambridge."

Madam Cromwell gave a sigh of relief.

"That is good news. I was afraid it might be otherwise. I remember, when he was a little fellow, his father telling me he was the image of the captain, his grandfather, and he, like all the Dangerfields, was a man of very warm temper and high spirit. I shall see the lad, then, presently. Now tell me what he is like. Didst note his looks? Tell me, little one."

Rachel smiled, for the old lady's tone was as eager as a girl's.

"He is handsome, granny, dark-complexioned, with bright eyes, and he carries his head high — a gentleman of very fine appearance; I should think — you will chide me for vain thoughts — he is one who has been more used to ruffle it at Court than among quiet folk. Yet I liked him," Rachel went on reflectively. "His eyes are honest, though a little proud; but his mouth — I do not like his mouth. It is of fierce expression, the corners of the lips turned downwards, and when he spoke to my uncle he set his teeth like an angry ban-dog, and the words came from between them as if he would have bitten him."

"Thou hast a quick eye, Rachel mine, and a power of expressing thy thoughts which give me quite a picture of the youth. They did well to name him Ralph. His grandfather had just such a habit of speech. Truly, when I see the lad, I shall feel quite young again. But be not too hasty in thy judgments. A man had better be too hard than too soft. A ban-dog you said? Well, a ban-dog is a trusty brute — savage with his foes, but of noble nature when well bred. So you like him not?"

"I did not say so much as that. I have taken little thought of him as yet. You should ask Betty,"— Rachel laughed —"she can talk of nothing else."

"A very froward puss," Madam Cromwell said severely. "Thou must discourage her, Rachel. It is not becoming that any girl, even though young, should express such thoughts. In my day she would be severely trounced and put on bread and water for a day had she dared to mention the young man's name familiarly. But, child, what hast been doing with thyself? Now that the light falls upon thy face I see pale cheeks and tired eyes. Is it lack of sleep last night — or what? Why should it be?"

At this sharp personal question Rachel blushed scarlet, fearing that in Madam Cromwell's present mood she would receive a severe reproof for her midnight labours, and she hesitated a moment before she answered, at which the old lady muttered beneath her breath, " What, can it be that the handsome face hath touched her heart? Heaven forfend!" Then Rachel found her tongue, and Madam Cromwell's fears were allayed, and to the girl's infinite relief the old lady gave the incident her heartiest approval.

" Thou art a noble child. But, indeed, thou'rt highly honoured, though I, his mother, say it. I know no other woman, young or old, he would have treated with such confidence; but there, we all trust thee, aye, and lean on thy young shoulders. When thy time comes, as come it must, though I trust the day be far distant, when thou are sought in marriage, what wealth thy husband will find in thee! He should be no ordinary man. See to it thou choosest wisely."

Rachel gave a merry laugh.

" I will not choose at all, granny. I shall send the gentleman to you when he comes, then to my guardian. If you both approve him then I will be his wife, not otherwise."

Madam Cromwell shook her head.

" What, still a child? Yet there is a woman in thy face. Nay, nay, no one, not even my own son, with all his powerful will, shall take thy heart and give it where he lists. The choice will be thine own, little one. God grant it be worthy. No one I have seen yet —— Betty, what means this? "

The door had opened suddenly without the ordinary preliminary knock, and Betty, flushed and excited, peeped in with an anxious face.

" Is Rachel here? Oh, Rachel, come with me. I have been looking everywhere for you; do not delay. I promised him many minutes since; he is in the hall. Hark! you can hear the jangle of his spurs — such big ones; and such beautiful armour hath he, bought only yesterday. But I must not stay. Grandmamma — oh!

— yes — I — I crave your pardon; but you see, I wanted Rachel, and I forgot, indeed I did."

"Grandchild Elizabeth," the old lady said in an awful voice, though Rachel saw the keen eyes twinkling, "how shall I make thee understand that before thou comest into my apartment thou must knock for admittance?"

She paused, then in a tone deeper still: —

"Who is below?"

"Oliver, an' it please you, ma'am."

"He is asking for Rachel?"

"He is indeed, and — *please*, may we go? He is so impatient, and will be so wroth with me. You see, I promised, and — I am very sorry. I will never, never so offend again."

She spoke in soft, entreating tones, and tears came into her eyes. Yet she did not move. No one, not even Betty, disobeyed Madam Cromwell in her own room. The old lady softened.

"Go, children," she said, smiling. "Betty, you must return presently; I shall require you to read to me this morning for an hour. Be not long away."

The girls left the room demurely, but Madam Cromwell heard them run downstairs like kittens. She smiled, then sighed.

"Was it in answer to my thoughts — Oliver? Perhaps. He is a good lad; not worthy yet, but young, and the times that are upon us will be like to make a man of him."

CHAPTER IX

A S the girls appeared at the top of the stairs a young man swung up to meet them.

"Have you come at last, then, Rachel? Faith, I began to wonder whether Betsy Bunting was cozening me when she said you were in the house. But save us! What is this? Hoity-toity! how we are changed!"

He had held out his arms to receive Rachel in her descent with a laugh that echoed round the house, and Rachel had drawn back hastily with a grave little curtsey. She now stood still, uncertain whether or not to beat a retreat, for Master Oliver was a notoriously determined person in such matters. That young man, however settled the point by retreating himself to the foot of the stairs and making her a sweeping bow — as graceful as the stiffness of his new armour permitted.

"*Mistress* Rachel Fullerton, I be your very humble servant."

Then Betty seized her hand.

"Oh come, come to him," she cried. "Why may he not kiss you as of old? You liked it when he went away, and that is but six months ago!"

Miss Betty, it may be remarked, had not quite recovered from the effect of her grandmother's reproof.

Rachel descended with her head in the air.

"We are too old for such things, Oliver. But you should know that I am glad to see you," and she gave him her hand. He kissed it with a flourish, and Betty, the malicious, clapped her hands and danced about them.

"Oh, fie, fie, the cavalier! See the cavalier and his lady-love!"

Oliver laughed good-humouredly, though he went very red in the face.

"Chut! Be quiet, thou baggage. Thou'rt jealous as an angry kitten. Well, Mistress Rachel, I could wish for better evidence of your friendship than your hand, but I must be content, I suppose, for the present. Truly, it is hard to believe when I look at you that only six months have gone since our parting. You are quite plump, and your cheeks — i' faith, they are like roses. What, may I not even look at you, then? Nay, that is too bad."

She had shrunk a little from his gaze, but at his last words she gave him her hand again with a frank smile.

"Indeed, you may look if you please. So will I. Surely I am not so changed as you. Why, you are two inches taller at the least. Have you seen Bridget? She was so anxious for your coming. Your mother is abed, but will be up at noon. Your father is away with the troop."

"Aye, I know. And rarely put out I was until this moment. Heigho! how hot it is in the house. Let us take a walk down the garden. Betsy, my kitten, thou canst go to thy lessons now, d'ye see?"

Betty began to pout.

"But I want to be with you. I did not intend Rachel to turn me out. Oh, let me come. I must go to granny in a little space."

"Sister mine, you will go now. Come, be off, or I'll show thee how they tickle stubborn horses over sea. Nay, I mean it earnest. I want Rachel; I do not want thee."

He made a grab at her, half threatening, half playful, and Betty fled. On the stairway above she met Bridget.

"Did I not hear Oliver's voice?"

"You well might, for he is here. But you cannot see him."

"And why not, Miss Impudence? Indeed, I will."

"Then look to yourself. He has sent me packing. All he wants and all he cares for in this house is Rachel, Rachel, Rachel!"

She shouted the name at the top of her voice, laughed spitefully in Bridget's face, and ran away. The elder girl paid no attention to her, but ran downstairs. She was in time to see the pair disappear into the garden.

"Oh, oh, Miss Prim Face," she said to herself, "so this is what you have waited for, when we thought you so modest and so cold! Lucky for you, my madam, that he's my brother. But I will pay him out for this."

Oliver and Rachel meanwhile, unconscious of this sisterly benison, strolled placidly and slowly down the garden path toward a summer-house at the lower end of it. The sun gleamed on his breastplate, and a light breeze, heavy with the scent of flowers, stirred the folds of her dress. Oliver was talking, describing his life abroad, or some of it. He had been in Holland for a few months, soldiering, after a year at college, and had now returned post-haste to find a place in the Parliament army. He was a strong, well-built young fellow, with his father's features, his father's voice, and something of his father's strength; yet not his father, as Rachel, watching him with quiet observance, thought to-day. The difference, she decided, lay in the size of the face: it was not so massive, the eyes much smaller, the chin of less depth, the lips fuller, and not often closed. But it was an honest face, and Rachel liked it well. The mouth was pleasant and good-tempered, much more amiable in expression than Mr. Ralph Dangerfield's.

Oliver, for his part, though airing his opinions on public affairs in the intervals of talk about himself, was scanning Rachel closely. Before he went abroad he had thought her to be rather a plain girl, with expressive eyes. Now — well, she might not be exactly beautiful, but there was a charm and grace in her movements, an unconscious dignity and a perfect sweetness in her face, that grew upon him moment by moment as they walked together, until he swore to himself that he had never seen so fair a maiden in his life.

All this time they were approaching the arbour, which Oliver intended to appropriate as soon as possible. At present they were under inspection of the maids at half the windows of the house. Suddenly Oliver said: —

"How I do envy that Dangerfield! Had I but returned a few hours earlier I'd have been in his place to-day. There is no saying what sport I may have missed. Rumour has it that £20,000 worth of plate is lying at Cambridge Castle for the king, and a magazine of powder besides. The malignants will not, forsooth, part with such treasure easily, which is why my father mustered all the troop. There will be some shrewd blows struck; a rare scrimmage like enough, and here I am idle — a lady's carpet-knight. And though truly 'tis most pleasant to be with thee, Rachel, Ralph Dangerfield is greatly to be envied."

Oliver had a loud voice, and on this still morning it carried far, rousing from deep meditation, or, to be quite truthful, a little morning nap, someone who had already taken possession of the summer-house — the Reverend Isaac Hepworth. He had not heard all that was said, but quite enough to rouse his irritable nerves; and sallying forth from his retreat, he confronted the young people with brows drawn ominously down and eyes aflame. Oliver, at sight of him, uttered an exclamation under his breath and whispered to Rachel:—

"Thy reverend uncle! By my faith, I am more unlucky than I knew."

Then he saluted, and gave the minister a most respectful greeting, which Hepworth scarcely seemed to hear.

"Did my ears deceive me," he said, "looking from

one to the other, " or did I understand you to say, young sir, that you looked upon that — that youth as one deserving of your envy? "

He spoke in a low voice, but Rachel trembled. She detected an ominous vibration in the tone, and knew Oliver's hasty temper. Oliver coughed and reddened a little.

" Well, I suppose — that is, perchance I did say words somewhat to that effect. You see, good sir —— "

But Hepworth would hear no more.

" Then listen; but first, hast ever met him in thy travels? I know thou hast been in godless countries, among godless men. Dost know him? "

" I do not. Nay, I assure you that I do not."

" Then I will give you warning, friend, which I trust will bear fruit in your behaviour."

He spoke to Oliver, but he looked at Rachel, and she felt that the words which followed were aimed at her.

" Know, young sir, thou speakest in ignorance and fatuity. He may excite thy pity — the meanest of God's creatures should do that. But, for the rest, avoid him as thou wouldst a leper. His father, whom I knew, was a serpent, meek and gentle to the outward sense, but nourishing within his brain the blackest, foulest poison. He was a Socinian of Socinians, a veritable Antichrist. When he begot this boy, through shame at his own belief, or from a deep and devilish cunning — I incline myself to the latter view — he had him brought up by an Arminian rector, and at the age of sixteen sent him to Cambridge University. Here the youth, as might have been expected from such parentage, lived among the flesh-pots of Egypt, and fell into the hands of the priests of Baal. He mixed with debauched malignants and men of the worst appetites and lewdest minds. I speak of what I know," he added, glaring at Rachel, who had opened her lips as if to protest. " The young man's tutor now turned malignant, was once my friend; he told me.

From such pursuits the youth was torn by the news
that the prelates had seized his father, and were about
to deal with him according to their canon law. And
let it be said that for once Laud and his myrmidons
meted out bare justice. The youth saw it all — the pillory, the mutilation, the subsequent death of his father
— and from a debauchee he became a bitter fanatic. He
went beyond seas, and for these two years has been
devoted heart and soul to the art of killing men. Now
he has returned, like a vulture who scents carnage from
afar. Your father, too lenient where his compassion is
aroused, hath stretched forth his hand and brought him
within this fold. God grant he has not let in a wolf
among his sheep. Such is the youth's history. And now
mark you this: spite of teachings in orthodoxy by the
rector, I suspect this youth to be a Socinian at heart.
He will doubtless keep his heresy secret, even as his
father did. But it is there, or he would not have glori-
fied his father, or defied me in such language as he used
last night. Avoid him, then, Oliver. His father was
full of evil, and out of evil only evil comes. He is a thing
unclean. Not that I would be unjust, even to a Socinian," the minister continued; "the young man hath a
courage, and maybe skill in arms, that may do the cause
good service by-and-by. But for thee — son of a God-
fearing man, and thyself brought up in the true faith —
to talk as thou didst of this scoffer, this schismatical outcast, that I cannot endure. Nor will I for one instant.
Now, answer me. Hath my word taken root in thy
mind? Dost believe me? It is not meet that I should
speak if thine ears are deaf to what I say. I might as
profitably prate to stones. Drive thy thoughts forth, do
not hesitate."

Isaac Hepworth folded his arms, drew himself up, and
gazed questioningly into Oliver's face, a tower of conscious rectitude and authority.

Rachel also waited anxiously for Oliver to reply. Her

uncle's words, spoken in his harshest tones, had jarred her through and through. She hoped to hear Oliver give a blunt and forcible contradiction in what terms he chose to such a sweeping denunciation of an absent man. But she waited in vain. All Oliver did was to say feebly:—

"My thoughts, Master Hepworth — well, for sure I know not what to think, you are the better judge, far better than I. Socinian is he? Why, that is bad indeed. But I knew naught of his religion, nor even that he had a father. All I meant by my words was a desire to be with the troop — in his place there. I was rash to say it, doubtless I was. It is my way. Truly I will remember all that you have said."

He spoke awkwardly, but with so much apparent earnestness that Hepworth was pleased.

"It is well, my son," he said, turning towards the house; "I ask no more than that. Thy sense and discretion will do the rest. I must now to my studies."

He waved his hand to them both with a paternal gesture, and walked briskly away. As soon as he was out of hearing, Oliver heaved a deep sigh of relief.

"Merciful gods! what a coil of words. I ask your pardon — he is your uncle. But ugh! he sets my teeth on edge. What right hath he, either, to preach to me in my father's house about my father's guest. Faith! I had more than two minds to tell him so," and he gave a short laugh.

"Why then, did you not?"

Rachel spoke very quietly, but there was enough suggestion in her voice to make him uneasy.

"Why? We—ell, I thought of you, sweet friend, and then — gad! to say truth I cannot argue with a Presbyter. He'd beat down my guard and thrust in on me six times while I lunged once. I have no strength in words."

There was a short, uneasy silence.

"My uncle was in great anger," Rachel said kindly; "when he feels thus no argument avails, and opposition only puts him in a fury. Yet, indeed, he should not speak so. Oh, when I hear such cruel, bitter words I want to cry 'shame' aloud."

Oliver kicked a stone from the path.

"This youth, then, Socinian or whatever he be, hath gained your favour?"

"I was not thinking of Mr. Dangerfield in especial," Rachel said. "We have not spoken — I know nothing of him. It is my uncle's want of charity toward a stranger — one who hath never harmed him. I should not judge my elders, but I could wish that someone would tell him roundly how wrong and cruel it be to say those things. It would be a righteous deed."

Oliver hung his head, then said impetuously:—

"Nay, but you are right. I should have done it. Well, it is not too late. When they come home I will take this Dangerfield by the hand. My faith I will, under your uncle's very eye. And if he rebuke me, then will I tell him that he is — what you have said. But a truce to the whole business. The summer-house looks cool and cosy, eh? Come in. Now tell me what you have been doing these six months. My tongue has wagged enough. Oh! this is a dear home. The war must be, and I trust will bring good times when the godly party triumphs. Yet 'twill be a blessed day when we hang our swords up — England free — and settle to our own firesides again. Sit in this corner, sweet friend, you will be comfortable there, and tell me everything about yourself."

CHAPTER X

WHEN Isaac Hepworth left the young people he went to Cromwell's library to resume the consideration of a sermon he had intended to write that morning. But though the text he had chosen — " The stone which the builders rejected, the same is become the head of the corner " — was a familiar one, on which he had preached before with striking success, he could not fix his mind upon it to-day; he was too much concerned with fears and anxiety closely touching his own life.

Isaac Hepworth had been brought up in a narrow school, a school that maintained on principle an attitude of unbending antagonism towards all other beliefs. Intolerance was far from being the exclusive possession of any sect; but at this period, until after the Restoration, the Presbyterian divines were perhaps the bitterest and most implacable opposers of anything approaching latitude in religious belief. It was a Presbyterian who wrote:—

" A toleration is the grand design of the devil; it is his master-piece, and the chief engine he works by at this time to uphold his tottering kingdom. . . . As original sin is the most fundamental sin, so a toleration hath all errors in it and all evils."

In such a creed as this Hepworth had believed from the time he began to think at all; and his vehement nature, which saw and felt all things in extremes, carried him to the furthest point that a man could go, who, as far as he could see it did what was right for right's sake, and lived a pure and self-denying life. He was wedded,

body and soul and mind to his ministerial work; it was
the staff of life to him, his sole nourishment and stimu-
lant. In the dark days of the war he was one of the
originators of a service which lasted from nine in the
morning to five in the evening. After preaching himself
to an immense congregation for two hours he listened to
another sermon of an hour, a prayer of two hours, a second sermon lasting another hour, and a second prayer of
two hours more.

He was a bachelor, and until past middle life had taken
no interest, except as a minister, in any human being. It
was only when, upon the death of Rachel's father, his
duties as guardian to the orphan began that he knew the
real meaning of personal responsibility, and realised that
he had anything to live for but his church; but he realised
it then, and appreciated the blessing of it. In spite of her
depression of mind, Rachel brightened his house and
brought comfort into his formerly erratic, dismal mode
of existence. Alas for him that it came so late in life that
he was unable to respond to the timid advances she made
from time to time to give him the love he so sorely
needed, and to receive from him support, guidance, and
sympathy in her bitter loneliness of heart. He did care,
he did sympathise, but he could not show it; and thus,
when Cromwell came and Rachel was snatched away to
save her life, she left her uncle in his solitude without a
pang, and was unconscious at the time of the blank she
left behind, and what a large space she had occupied in
the heart of this morose and irritable man. Hepworth
himself knew it well; and though, when Rachel lived with
him, he rarely noticed whether she were well or ill, and to
the last resented the doctor's visits, no sooner had she
taken her departure than he thought constantly of her,
and was for ever making excuses to visit Cromwell at
Ely, while her welfare, spiritual and temporal, became one
of the chief objects of his life. As time went on Rachel's
two guardians, at first almost strangers to one another,

began to form a close friendship, partly from the active part both were taking in the struggle of the people against the Crown, but chiefly through the love they shared for their ward; and so it came about that before a year had passed the minister was a frequent guest at Ely, and it was not without justice he had made his boast that he possessed authority in the house. His great ally was Mrs. Cromwell, who was a devout woman, of simple and rather narrow mind. In her opinion a Presbyter could do no wrong.

Hepworth's mode of expressing his affection for his niece was characteristic. His knowledge of women was of the slightest, and in his opinion they were all influenced by the same motives and equally liable to the same temptations. Thus, though he had never found Rachel in the least inclined to desire the company of young men, no sooner did Ralph appear upon the scene and receive from her that unlucky curtsey, than her uncle began to torture himself with every imaginable foreboding, and could neither eat nor work nor take his rest by night for thinking of the dark, handsome face of the Socinian's son, and the danger to his loved one's peace.

This morning, while Oliver and Rachel chatted in the summer-house, while Ralph obeyed Cromwell's order at Cambridge, Hepworth turned over the question in his mind for the twentieth time, and came to the conclusion that, whatever might happen, Rachel and the stranger should not meet again. He had not been blind to her resentment of his words to Oliver. These words had been spoken as much to induce her to betray the partiality for Ralph which Hepworth was sure she felt as to warn Oliver. And the minister, in his simplicity, hugged himself, and thought how well he had succeeded. The only question that remained was the best way of getting rid of this man. Hepworth pondered over various plans for an hour, and then, unable to endure inaction and suspense, he bethought himself of the advantage of securing a powerful friend, and went to pay his respects to Madam Cromwell.

The old lady received him kindly, but with a reserve of manner which most people would have remarked at once. Perception, however, was not Isaac Hepworth's strong point.

"My grandson, Oliver, has returned home they tell me," Madam Cromwell said, for the sake of something to say, as the minister, after greetings, sat down in silence.

He smiled good-humouredly.

"I have just met him — with my niece. A fine young man, madam, hasty in speech, yet respectful to age, and sensible, I trust, to reproof and warning. A worthy son of his good father. He has my full approval."

Madam Cromwell raised her eyebrows and coughed. "For what reason," she thought to herself, "should this good man patronise our house?" Then an idea occurred to her, and her eyes gleamed with mischief.

"It is hard upon an old dame like me, reverend sir, to find her place taken by the young, even though the usurper be one she loves well. Never before hath Oliver failed to greet me within an hour of his home-coming; yet to-day I have not seen his face, Rachel hath charmed him away."

The minister smiled again.

"Say you so, madam. It is not well; yet they are young, and the sun shines. We must forgive them."

He sighed, and his stern face softened for a moment. Madam Cromwell looked at him in wonder. Had even this man been young?

"You are right, reverend friend," she rejoined; "and if Oliver be drawn to Rachel, and she incline toward him as time goes on, there could be naught but deep thankfulness in our hearts. It was this, perhaps, you came to converse upon this morning?"

A home thrust. The minister started, then collected himself.

"No, no," he answered, at least — well — in part, perchance. I could have no objection — that is, I should be pleased to discuss such a business with my worthy friend. The future of the child troubles me and weighs upon my mind. The times are troubled. The head of a young girl is easily turned with vanity. Devourers of the innocent are everywhere. Schismatics, heretics, atheists, Anabaptists, Socinians abound and flourish like foul weeds; no household is safe from their presence. Why, madam —" He paused to take breath before plunging into a tirade which would have lasted half an hour. Madam Cromwell hastened to interrupt him.

"Sir," she exclaimed, her tone cold and measured, but emphatic as his own, "this be all true, but I fail to understand its application to Rachel. My son protects her. Is this not enough?"

"Aye, aye," the minister replied with an impatient shake of the head, such as a horse gives when checked in a gallop on turf, "I deny not his strength. Yet, madam, I confess myself in doubt touching his perception of the danger. Yea, I fear that blindness overtakes him when public matters occupy his mind. Else — nay, I will be precise with you. This is the case. Last night a youth arrived, invited by your son, treated by him with, I had almost said a fatherly affection. To-day I understand the youth marcheth as his lieutenant to Cambridge, to-morrow he will return here. This young man," he raised his voice to the tone of solemn denunciation he had used to Oliver, "this youth is godless. You must know his parentage, and I fear that as the father was so the son will be. I am sorely ill at ease. It is not right that one who reviles and even dares to threaten a servant of the Lord should be an inmate of this house. You may tell me I am but a guest myself, and that my words, therefore savour of undue interference. Madam, I deny that. While my niece is here I have a right to watch every man who tarries in this place; I hold that in such company as this her soul's welfare is in danger. What is to be done? I ask you that. There is but one answer possible. Either he must depart forthwith, or I shall be constrained to withdraw Rachel from Master Cromwell's care. I must find some godly roof where no long-haired, slashing dare-devil may enter and tempt her with the fripperies and trickeries that catch the eye and sense, and which Satan ever bestows upon his dearest sons. That, madam," changing his tone and bowing gravely, "is the message I come to bear to you this morning, and which I must communicate to my friend upon his return. I would now know your thoughts touching the matter. May I possess them?"

It was not often that the minister made such a request to anyone. It was an honest tribute of respect to Madam Cromwell, and a sign of his desire to gain her goodwill.

The old lady, however, did not seem much affected by the honour. She was quite calm, but looked perplexed, with a tinge of mild surprise in her face.

"Truly, sir, I am at a loss to understand you. How and in what manner is Rachel's soul, the purest that I know, in danger through this youth? A few minutes since we spake of Oliver."

"The youth is handsomer," snapped the minister rudely, "of braver carriage and more courtly bearing."

"And these," she said mildly, "are in your eyes deadly sins."

"They are the sleekness and the smoothness of a tiger's skin. I would not trust him an instant out of sight. His father ——"

"And what of him?" There was a ring in the old lady's voice Rachel would have loved to hear. "Good sir, I knew this man. I may grieve at his falling off in faith. I have read his book." She paused an instant to enjoy Mr. Hepworth's look of horror. "He is mistaken. His premises are based on falsities; his arguments touching our Lord are a tissue of fine-spun sophistries. But even so, I found much that was good in the work, much that expressed the gentle soul of one who was my son's dearest friend until life's responsibilities drew their lives apart. I say this," she added hastily, for the minister's face was purple with the passionate protest boiling within him, " not to commence an argument upon Socinianism — we are agreed upon that, nor to tear asunder the cobwebs these poor creatures spin within their brains. But I would have you understand, and from my lips, which are less hasty than my son's, that we in this house deem the name of Dangerfield worthy of all respect, and that I think that those who dwell with us would be wise to remember this in their conversation."

She bowed as she spoke, as a queen might to a courtier who had said something indiscreet about the heir-apparent. And Hepworth, proud and confident as he was, could find no words in which to answer her. But he was neither conquered nor convinced; it only made him angry.

" Assuredly, madam," he said in withering tones, " I am, then, fully confirmed in my resolution. A house where a Socinian's book is belauded and a Socinian's son embraced is no fit home for Rachel. I had better at once prepare her for her departure. It will not, I promise you, be any fault of mine if it is delayed."

He bowed frigidly, and stalked out of the room. Until he had gone Madam Cromwell preserved an impressive dignity, only acknowledging his salute with the slightest possible inclination of the head; but when the door closed her face changed.

" Will he really carry this matter through? He hath the power, for by the Will the child was to be with him, and this Presbyter is as obstinate as any mule, and greatly roused. Alas! my reproof hath not softened him, I fear; but I cannot live without my sweet daughter. God grant that son Oliver find a way of bringing the man to reason. But he will, he will! All depends on his speedy return.

As for this Ralph, I desire to see him greatly; my curiosity hath not been so put on tip-toe concerning anyone for many years."

The old lady had her desire gratified before she slept, for Cromwell and Ralph returned in time for the evening meal. To the astonishment of the family, Madam Cromwell broke through her rule and appeared at table, and little Betty nearly danced out of her chair when Ralph went forward at Cromwell's introduction and, bowing low, kissed the old lady's hand.

"Thy grandfather to the life," was all Madam Cromwell said, in a curiously sharp, strained voice, "even as I saw him just before he went to sea. We never met again." Then speaking with an emphasis which at least one of the company understood, she said, as she went slowly to her place, "He was a brave and honourable man, young sir, beloved by all who knew him. God grant that thou art as like him in nature as thou art in face."

Madam Cromwell had called Hepworth an obstinate man. She was right. No sooner did he see that not a person in the household, except, perhaps, Mistress Cromwell, shared his distrust of Ralph, than his intention to be rid of him, or remove Rachel, became a fixed resolve, and he spent the greater part of the night rehearsing the speech which he should make to Cromwell the next day. It is a practice common to self-conscious men, and has the advantage of relieving the mind and familiarising it with the subject in hand, but otherwise it is usually waste of effort. In nine cases out of ten the opponent says exactly the opposite of what he was expected to say.

The interview took place directly after breakfast in the library.

"You have somewhat to say to me touching our ward," Cromwell began before the minister had time to speak. "Speak freely; hold nothing back. That child is dear to me as one of my own; I have no wish but for her welfare."

He sat down and motioned the minister to do the same, but Hepworth kept his feet.

"I shall indeed speak," he replied; "but it must be in the form of a question. What are your intentions regarding the disposal of this youth Dangerfield, the son of — of your old friend?"

"A strange question," Cromwell replied coldly, "but I will answer it. Yesterday I put him to a test. He stood it well; and as I find that he is wishful to serve with me I shall enroll him as cornet in the troop. Indeed, had I not promised the lieutenancy to that Geoffrey Capell, whom you are acquainted with, and whom I approved last time I was in London, I should judge this Dangerfield to be well fitted for the post."

The minister's face darkened. "Where will he reside?"

"Wheresoever the troop is quartered. At the present in this house."

"Have you considered what this means? Nay, but you cannot." His tone was full of earnestness and pain, almost supplicating. "I desire not to speak harshly of the youth. He is, doubtless, what his father made him; but he is not, cannot be, a fit member of a godly household."

"What!" Cromwell's voice was like the first growl of thunder in a storm. "What say you? You go too far, sir, and speak in ignorance and prejudice. I tell you, I have tried the lad. I know him; you do not. He is hot-brained and hasty-tongued; he ever champs the bit as blood-colts will. But he is of serious mind, full of good purpose and of military knowledge; a rare youth; a weapon made to my hand, sent by God Himself! The need we have for just such men as he is desperate. Let me tell you that the success of the godly cause hangs upon it, and in my belief upon naught else. There are honest soldiers enough and to spare if we but drill, arm, and pay them; but officers, where are they? Generals we may find, belike, and even a few colonels to pass muster; but of captains, good captains, I know few here-abouts, and of subordinate officers none, or good as none. Our younger gentry are malignant to a man. At the University of Cambridge the students are one and all for the king. I tell you, an army to win victory must have as leaders of the rank and file men full of courage, full of the love of truth and the noble spirit that is born of an upright life — such men only. Dangerfield is one of these. Wherefore, be his views touching religion what they may — Arminian, Socinian, Anabaptist even — I shall appoint him this day, and no man or men, under-stand me, shall in this matter set my will aside or reverse what I have judged fit to do."

He had been walking up and down the room accord-ing to his habit, and now turned short round opposite the minister, and, thrusting his fingers in his sword-belt, stood with feet apart and head thrown back waiting for his reply. This was speedily forthcoming. Hepworth's eyes were gleaming; his nostrils dilated like those of a horse awaiting the word to charge.

"You have answered me. It is not needful that I say another word about this youth. I leave him will-ingly, and turn to that which concerns myself and thy-self, Cromwell, as private men. My sister's child is under thy roof. Is it to be permitted that a man who, in pres-ence of thy wife and others, deliberately affirmed that a scandalous work, containing the most shocking blasphe-mies against our Lord, was a sacred book, whose father, by whom his mind was formed, was — I must say it — a damnable schismatic — is it to be permitted, I ask you, that such an one shall have access to the company of this our ewe lamb? Rid thy mind of politics; think first of the trust that hath been laid upon us. He is a goodly youth to look upon; she fair and winsome, and a jewel in mind and heart. Who knows what Satan may not do here, drawing these two together by every wile of devil-ish cunning, until neither you nor I nor God Himself

7

can part them? Think of this, and pause before it is too late. But if thou wilt not " — Cromwell's face was as hard and expressionless as stone — "then I tell thee I will withdraw her from this house — aye, this very night — and never shall she be under thy roof again."

Still Cromwell stood unmoved. " Where can you take her? You have no home fit for a young gentlewoman. London will not do; these are not the times to take our young girls pleasuring to town. But enough — I say we have talked enough." His face reddened, and his voice grew harsh and stern. "The day is drawing on, and I have much to do. Hearken! You will not take Rachel from this house. I forbid it, and, if needful, will retain her by force. But I would not that we quarrelled. How like you this: the child to remain, with your full consent, and I to promise — to swear, if it please you, pledge my word to God — that should he prove to be of his father's faith, and any love-leaning appear between them, be it ever so little, in so far as it be real and mutual, I would separate their lives as with a sword? Will this content you? If so, then I will pass my word. If not, go your way. Rouse against me the thunder of your pulpits, appeal to the authority of Parliament; only remember that neither thou nor they will move me one handsbreadth to right or left from the path I elect to follow. Now, make your choice, and make it quickly, for the day wears on."

They faced each other — minister and laymen — equal in courage and obstinacy, men who had rarely known the meaning of the word " submit." Hepworth glared back into Cromwell's eyes a moment, then slowly bowed his head in silent prayer. When he raised it, after a short interval, the fire in his eyes had gone.

" I accept thy word, Cromwell," he replied. " I do not need an oath, for thou art an honourable man. It is understood between us, then, that thou wilt watch over our child as thine own, and prevent with all thy might and with all thy strength any possibility of union between this youth and her."

Cromwell crossed the room, and laid his hand upon a Bible.

"Brother, if Ralph Dangerfield share his father's unbelief, I swear that I will spare no means to prevent such union. I swear it on this holy Book. Let God be judge between us if I break my word."

CHAPTER XI

THE train of waggons with its valuable freight was despatched to London with an escort of twenty men under Ralph's command. It was a sign of the uncertainty of men's minds, and the want of preparation on the part of the Royalists, that treasure of immense value could be safely conveyed sixty miles under such slight protection. But to Ralph it was a very anxious business, and he allowed his men little rest, and took none himself, until the money was lodged in the Tower. He despatched a messenger to Ely to acquaint Cromwell with the arrival of the treasure, and then went to see Doctor Taunton. He was prepared for a cool or even a harsh reception, but after careful thought determined that the estrangement, if it must come, should not arise from any neglect of his. The doctor's manner, however, was unchanged. He held Ralph's hand a moment longer than usual, and pressed it warmly as he said:—

"I knew I'd see you; it is not in your nature to forget your friends. Nay, I know all," as Ralph was going to speak. "Charlton has been here. You are a rebel in arms against the king. By rights, now that I have you in safe keeping, I should convey ye to a loyal stronghold, there to be tried and condemned. I shall not. I bear no malice against you, neither against Noll Cromwell. It was a shrewd blow, well delivered, and has opened the eyes of our party. But bah! away with politics, lad, between us now and for evermore. While I live and these walls hold together you will find a home and a refuge here, let the times be what they may. And when the country has done tearing and worrying itself, what money I have left is yours, whoever wins. How long can you remain? This night? Good. Then we'll have a bottle of the best, if you are not turned water-drinker. Tell me of these Cromwells. Are there daughters? Mistress Cromwell was fair eno' before she married. They do not all, I trust, favour their father."

At Ely, even in his absence, Ralph was still a disturbing element. Madam Cromwell, indeed, thought of little else, and all day long after the interview between her son and Hepworth she sat in her room listening for Cromwell, waiting to hear the news. At last, when it was growing dark, she heard the brisk, firm step, and he came in, took her hand, and kissed it.

"Thou art a-weary, son," she said tenderly, returning his salute. "Has the day gone hard with thee? Alas! the burden of thy public work bears heavily upon thy shoulders. Shall we be at war, think you, or will this misguided king see the error of his ways?"

"Charles will not do that, mother, until God hath given the godly party such advantage that he dare not raise his hand without our leave. At least, this is my view, as I told John Hampden but a week ago."

"What thinks he?"

"The same. Oh, we see eye to eye. He is one of ten thousand, a thorough man, yet with a nicety of manner, speech, and bearing that charms the most particular; a lion's courage, too, and a heart of tempered steel. All love him and all trust him. A true king of men; but he stands alone, and is vexed beyond expression at the backwardness and laxness of those who command the army. But now, touching Rachel."

Madam Cromwell bent anxiously forward.

"What is resolved upon?"

"She stays with us."

"Thank God!"

Cromwell was silent, and his mother became uneasy.

"There is something on thy mind."

He frowned.

" My patience is nigh worn out, that is all. A little more, and I will turn and rend him, smite him hip and thigh with his own weapons, and make him blush for the Church he holds so dear. Ye Presbyters! ye Presbyters! God have mercy on this distracted country if some of you ever get its throat within your grasp. Have ye not closed your ears even against the words of the apostle in your unchristian zeal? How runs it, mother? ' Though I speak with the tongues of angels, and have not charity, I am become as sounding brass, and a tinkling cymbal. . . . Though I have all faith, so that I could remove mountains, and have not charity, I am nothing. Charity suffereth long, and is kind; . . . she is not easily provoked, thinketh no evil; . . . hopeth all things, endureth all things.' Well," stopping short and resuming his usual tone, " such thoughts as these were on my lips this morning as Hepworth spoke. I gave them no expression. Indeed, he was wondrous moderate in what he said. You tamed him, mother." He took her hand, smiling, " Hast not tamed me so when my head was full of blind unreason? It is a great power, and only given to women. So, I kept my tongue within my teeth for once — to a point; but upon one thing I enlightened him, and that was touching Ralph Dangerfield. That lad stays with the troop, and Master Hepworth knows it."

" Ah, you told him that! It was like thee, Oliver. What did he answer? "

" That Rachel should leave this house to-night."

" I feared he would."

" Upon which," Cromwell went on quietly, " I spoke somewhat to the point."

His mother laughed softly.

" I laid down terms to which he agreed," Cromwell continued. " Nay, the man is worthy, mother. If I said otherwise I should myself be wanting in the charity he lacks. When I gave my word that we'd keep watch over the child, he accepted it with readiness. The matter will not trouble us again."

Madam Cromwell looked puzzled. Her son noticed it, and added with some emphasis:—

"It was a simple thing enough; the Presbyter is haunted by the thought that Rachel and Ralph might make a match of it, and, looking upon the lad as a Socinian, he would rather she should die. My answer was that should this danger arise I would see to it myself. In short, that it should not be. This contented him."

Cromwell spoke in the tone of a man who has done all that is necessary and is perfectly satisfied with himself. But he watched his mother narrowly, and a few moments later remarked:—

"Madam mother, what have I said that should make you look so troubled? Dost wish for a Socinian grandson because his grandfather was thy playfellow?"

"God forbid, son."

"And yet — what is it, then?"

"My dear," she replied slowly, "thou, not I, must be the judge of this; thou art her guardian and his friend, I am a foolish old woman; I have thoughts, but they are of little worth."

"Pish!" he exclaimed roughly; "mother, that is foolish talk. Come now, reprove me as if I were again the boy that sat upon your knee. What have I done?"

The old lady sighed.

"I will speak, then. Thou hast passed thy word that this shall never be?"

Cromwell nodded.

"Thou hast promised too much."

"How should that be?"

Madam Cromwell was silent for a moment, then in a musing tone she answered:—

"I judge by what I see and know. I do not prophesy, but the words of an old woman, who hath watched and

loved and wept over many children, are not to be lightly
set aside. I see a man, young in years, but headstrong,
knowing no fear, and whose father and father's father
knew no fear, a youth who may now be guided, checked,
and admonished by such an one as thee, but who, when
he loveth a woman will be held by none. Then I see a
girl, as yet a child in many things, who hath all her life
been of a docile temper and gentle disposition. There
are many who would say, As she hath been so she will
ever be. Believe them not. Behind this meekness there
be courage, steadfastness, nay, obstinacy, which, once
roused by love, will never be subdued. All this may
never be. They may never care the least; indeed, there
are signs which lead quite another way with her. But
if God doth incline their hearts towards one another,
well, my dear, I would thou hadst not pledged thy word."

"I have done more," Cromwell said quietly. "I have
sworn it before God, and I would do it again. You know
I reverence your words, but as you have said, I alone
must be judge of this. I confess, mother, I love the
youth, he mindeth me of Robin; and though we have
been acquaint so short a time, yet I would lay any trust
upon him. He is honest, he fears God, and naught else;
he brooks not hard speech, but he knows when to obey;
he is gracious to the men, but they do his bidding on
the instant. Why, even Reuben, hard old soldier though
he be, disputes him not, and, I can see, loves him. So
whether he be Socinian, Episcopalian, or Presbyterian,
my heart is, and will be, so soft toward him that if I have
not a care I could deny him nothing later on. This
must not be. I will press no man's confidence. In God's
good time, but not before, we shall know Ralph Dangerfield's religion. If his father's unbelief hath gripped him,
which, I own I fear may be the case, then must he keep
away from Rachel. 'Twas for this I took an oath, and
now I am at rest. As to his will or hers, or both, against
my own, tush! it is not will alone that lovers need. I

could find an hundred ways of compassing my ends. It is of myself that I am afraid, or was; but I must leave ye, and to my letters until bed-time. Fear not, dearest mother " — he bent and kissed her hand — " God will put us in the right path. I pray nightly for His guidance in this as in all things, but I know my wilfulness, and that where my affections take possession of me I must use the strongest curb upon myself. Good night."

CHAPTER XII

OLIVER CROMWELL the younger was nineteen years old. It is generally an awkward age for a man, and Oliver was no exception to the rule. In stature he was fully developed, and in bodily strength above the average of men. He was intelligent, and he had plenty of common sense. But for all this he was still very young. He knew little of the world, and was under the impression that he knew everything; he had only a rudimentary knowledge of things military, yet felt equal to taking a regiment into action. With men of his own age he was inclined to be overbearing, with older men argumentative. He had courage and enthusiasm in plenty, but not much patience or self-control, and no discretion at all.

Cromwell understood his son perfectly, and to Oliver's disgust had procured him a cornetcy in a troop of horse that a friend was about to raise in the north of England, instead of following the usual custom of the time and drafting him into his own. Cromwell knew too well that for the work of the troop at Ely and Cambridge Oliver would be worse than useless. Therefore, upon the lad's return from abroad, his father only told him to amuse himself and be in readiness to obey a summons from his commander.

A young man in a quiet country-place in the seventeenth century spent his time much as he spends it in the nineteenth, except that in the fens hawking and fishing were the only forms of sport. Oliver was a keen lover of falconry, of which art his father had been a past-master in younger days, and for the first week or two after he

reached home he was at it from dawn to dark. Very
soon, however, another interest more engrossing than
sport claimed his sole attention, and falconry and fishing,
and even the welfare of a favourite mare who had just
foaled, fell into the background and became of little
moment, and in this quiet time at home before the war
Oliver's love for Rachel became the absorbing passion
of his life. When this really happened it is hard to say.
Oliver himself always declared that it began when she
first came to Ely, a year ago, but at this his family scoffed.
Yet, as Betty could testify, his eagerness to see Rachel
upon his return from abroad was considerable, and the
long talk in the garden afterwards suspicious. Be this
as it may, a very short time passed after that before he
set himself with all the strength and ardour of his growing manhood to attract her notice and regard.

He had not a very easy time of it. His sisters, as soon
as they saw what had happened, threw themselves into
vigorous opposition. Bridget did not approve of a man,
though he was her brother, seeking anyone's society but
her own. Men were a necessity to Bridget, not to flirt
with — though compliments and polite attentions never
came amiss — but from the glimpses she snatched
through them of public affairs and of matters outside the
dull routine of house and home. She had been looking
forward to Oliver's return from foreign parts with much
eagerness, and when she found herself neglected for
Rachel she became extremely disagreeable. Rachel she
left alone, for after that first day even Bridget found no
cause to complain that Oliver was monopolised by her.
It was upon Oliver himself that his sister's ill-nature
vented itself. She twitted him with awkwardness and
clownishness in Rachel's presence, compared him invidi-
ously with Ralph — whom in her heart she cordially disliked — and finally threw every obstacle in the way of
tête-a-tête meetings that she could invent. But, like many
another clever person. Bridget overreached herself.

Rachel would have thought much more seriously of Oliver's little weaknesses had Bridget left her alone to find them out. Bridget's cutting remarks made her rally to his defence, while the artifices to prevent or spoil the interviews which Oliver had planned were so obvious, that he saw through them at once, and swept them into space as a maid sweeps a cobweb from the wall.

Betty, child as she was, proved more difficult to deal with. Her jealousy was deeper than Bridget's, and she suffered acutely, for until Oliver came Rachel had been Betty's especial property. So the girl, with a pertinacity for which Oliver longed to beat her, was always getting in the way, and drove her brother nearly frantic by the number of excuses she invented to spend Rachel's time unprofitably. Betty, however, was not always in a contrary mood. She was very fond of Oliver, and he had only to smile upon her and coax a little beforehand to make her his devoted slave for the day.

In this manner July and the first three weeks of August passed away, and Oliver, in spite of Bridget's barbed arrows and Betty's jealousy, made good progress. Rachel liked his company, as well she might, for he taught her to ride, and with Betty took her a-hawking and fishing, both of which sports her soul delighted in. Rachel as well as Bridget sometimes became tired enough of housework and the babies. Oliver hoped that a deeper feeling was growing by degrees, and his only complaint was the extreme difficulty of seeing enough of her. Rachel was Cromwell's secretary now in practice as in title, and some hours each day were spent in the library, and no attraction that Oliver could offer was allowed to interfere with this duty. There were certain times, too, when Oliver suffered acute twinges of jealousy. Ralph had returned from London to be Cromwell's right hand until the arrival of the new lieutenant; and though this kept him hard at work with the troop — drilling recruits, breaking in horses for cavalry service, and searching suspected houses for arms — he was present at many consultations, in all of which Rachel had her place. Oliver did not like this, and as the day drew near when he was likely to receive the summons from his captain he began to turn over in his mind the advisability of bringing matters to a climax. Not that Ralph's presence seriously troubled Oliver: the young men were on excellent terms, and Oliver spent much fruitless breath trying to persuade the cornet to practice fencing and wrestling with him, exercises of which he was devotedly fond.

Matters were in this position when on the morning of August 24th, as the family were leaving the breakfast-table, messengers arrived in hot haste with news that the Royal Standard had been raised at Nottingham, and war declared.

Cromwell read the letter containing the intelligence with a quiet exclamation of satisfaction, handed to Oliver a summons to join his troop, and then sent word to all the members of his household to meet him in the dining-room.

They filed in, the men flushed and excited, the women pale and anxious, the younger maids whimpering and trembling, until they saw their master's face. When they had taken their places Cromwell raised his hand, and all fell silent. Everyone was there: Madam Cromwell, Mrs. Cromwell, Rachel, Bridget, and little Betty, Oliver and Ralph standing together, the old nurse who had held Cromwell in her arms in his babyhood, the maids, the gardener and his boy, the grooms from the stables, and lastly Reuben Sweetlove, a grim, appropriate figure in armour and buff coat leaning on his sword.

" Friends and dear ones," Cromwell said, speaking in a quiet, even tone, " the storm threatening long hath broke at last. From this day forward every man who loveth freedom and the right, who believeth that the law of God is higher than a king's prerogative will be branded as a traitor and a rebel and stand in danger of his life. Well, let this be. I say, let it be! We will throw back their words in their teeth, not with tongues but with the edge of the sword; we will gird up our loins, and go forth rejoicing to do the will of God. I have no fears of any of you," looking round upon the men. "Ye have all given sacred pledges of your loyalty to the Parliament and the people; ye will do your parts, and that right manfully, unto the end. God bless you! Yet I would say a word, and this to the women."

He took his mother's hand, and his voice was full of deep feeling. "Tender hearts and loving ones, 'tis ye will suffer most in the dark days that are coming upon us. I beseech you, stand not on one side to weaken us by tears and bewailings; rather clothe your faces with cheerful smiles, and give us your strong and womanly support. If we fall on the field of battle, and lie torn and wounded, who but ye will care and tend us? if we be vanquished it is your faith that must cheer our failing hearts; if victory crown our arms, anoint us with your tenderness and patience, so that we temper our just anger with mercy. Women! God created ye for such work. Let none, however lowly her estate or few her years, think to withhold herself from a due share in this godly strife. Then indeed will the Lord preserve us from all evil; and whether our enemies flee before us, or take us in chains to prison and death, He will preserve our going out and our coming in from this time forth, for ever and for evermore." He knelt and raised his hands in prayer.

"Almighty God, deal with us as we deal with Thee. Though it be with our own brethren that we dispute, forget not that it is for Thy sake. Give us strength, Lord, to smite them heavily, for then will their agony be short. Grant that our commanders be faithful and single in heart, skilful in strategy, courageous and mighty in battle. Give to our soldiers the godliness — not of lip service, but of pure lives. Let them fear no evil — nay, nor do it; obey their leaders, and never turn their backs upon their foe. Almighty God, cause the hearts of our enemies to fail within them, bring their counsels to confusion, turn them one against another, until, by their own corrupt and evil ways, they are utterly destroyed. Purge this poor country of its humours and corruptions, strike down the proud and wicked, raise up the humble and the godly to rule the land and keep Thy holy Word. We ask this for Thy Son's sake. In His name we put our hands unto this work, never to yield, never to cease the strife until the fight be won. Amen." He rose from his knees. "This day, friends, no work will be done in my house; let it be as a Sabbath. Cleanse your hearts of selfish or vain-glorious thoughts, and brace your minds for what is upon us. God bless you all!"

The gathering of servants now dispersed, and Cromwell drew Oliver aside. "Canst make a holiday, son, for Ralph here? He works too hard. Take Rachel with you and the puss Betty, and all of ye make a pleasure-day of it. Neither you nor he will have many more until the war be done."

Oliver promised with eagerness and Ralph was not hard to persuade, and they presently set off on horseback, with food in their pockets, to make a picnic to Denny Abbey, an old ruined nunnery eight miles out on the Cambridge road. Oliver was in a state of intense, ill-repressed excitement. Upon receiving the letter from his commander he had determined that he would speak his mind to Rachel without delay. This ride seemed like a stroke of fate. A little management soon disposed of Ralph and Betty, for the child was proud of being escorted by Master Dangerfield, and Ralph saw from Oliver's flushed face that something was in the wind, so he spurred on briskly with his chattering companion, and the other two were soon left some distance behind.

The instant that they were alone Oliver unburdened his soul. It was much less difficult at that time for a young man to propose than some of us find it to-day. Parents or guardians had to decide the matter ultimately, and it was often but a mere question of breeding and good taste to make the request to the lady herself at all. Oliver was aware of this; but, nevertheless, he was as keenly anxious for Rachel's own consent as the most exacting maiden could desire, and no modern lover could have spoken more earnestly.

"Thou hast been all things to me since I saw thee first. Before, I ne'er looked in a maiden's face with pleasure; since, I've not beheld one so fair. Rachel, thou'rt my first love and my last. What sayest thou? What think'st of me? Don't turn away so, as if I'd angered thee. God's truth, sweet, look up, look up with those true eyes of thine and tell me my fate."

He spoke breathlessly, and bent over his horse's neck to look into her averted eyes. Slowly she turned and faced him, her cheeks aglow, but her voice steady and controlled.

"I cannot tell you; I have never thought of such a thing in seriousness. But why"— with a shiver as of pain —"did you speak to-day? How can you think of me or anything so small after your father's words? Oh, it is sacrilege!"

He laughed at this — actually laughed a ringing, masterful laugh. "Sacrilege, dearest of hearts! Not that. Oh, I will fight! I have not told thee that in a few days I shall be with my troop. Indeed, that is why I speak, for who knows when we may meet again. But sacrilege, I will not have the word. Thou art as sacred as the cause itself; an' I fight for one — I want to fight for both. That is, if thou wilt give me leave, sweetheart. But if thou hatest me, Rachel — Dost hate me? Tell me that."

She had turned her head away, and he could see her hands trembling so much that she could scarcely hold the reins. Now she glanced up half smiling.

"Why should I hate you? It is not likely; but, Oliver ——"

"Psha," he broke in, "no buts. I will have none, I say," and he laughed again. "Phew, but my heart is lightened of a load of care. Thou dost not hate, then must thou like me — a little. And if there be liking now, my faith, but very soon I will make it something more. I'll be in London to-night."

"In London!" she said faintly. "Why London?"

"To see thine uncle, sweet. Who else? What he will say God knows. But I will wrestle with him as never I wrestled in argument yet. If I gain his consent I gain all. There be but my father then. Ha! see the baggage Betty waiting for us with her gallant esquire. Gad, how that man sits his horse. I'd give — what would I not give to ride like Ralph Dangerfield."

He quickened his pace, and they joined the others. All rode together now — Oliver in the highest spirits, Rachel pale and absent-minded. Her face was as calm as usual, thanks to her self-control, but her brain was in a whirl, and she spoke to no one. Ralph noticed this, and with his previous suspicions to aid him, began to put two and two together; for Ralph, in common with the rest of the younger members of the family, had been well aware of Oliver's state of mind, and he knew that marching orders had arrived that morning. Had Oliver been successful? Probably. He was Cromwell's eldest son, and, on the whole, a fine fellow. Rachel had known him since childhood, probably. Ralph was unacquainted with her history. Oliver would have money and a comfortable estate by-and-by. It was a very suitable match. Ralph told himself this several times — every time, indeed, that he glanced at Rachel's face. But for all this he did not convince himself. Then he threw off the thought with an effort and joined in the conversation with the rest. Soon after this the abbey was reached and the picnic held. When they turned homewards Oliver, who was still in high spirits, but in a state of intense restlessness, exclaimed:—

"Betsy Bunting, what say to a race? Thy pony is small, but thou'rt a mere feather-weight. Let us put the beasts to speed to yonder tree; a mile I judge it by the eye. You people," nodding at Ralph, "follow as ye list. Now, Betsy, off!"

He gave his horse the spur, and Betty, with a shriek of delight, cut her mettlesome pony smartly over the shoulder, and away they flew, leaving Ralph and Rachel pacing leisurely after them.

It was the first time these two had ever been alone together; their previous meetings had taken place in Cromwell's presence, and their conversation had been limited to a few words on public business. Now, as their horses ambled homewards, both felt that in some subtle way their relationship had altered. They were friends — had been friends for a long time. Rachel gave expression to the thought by saying:—

"Did Madam Cromwell ever give you invitation to visit her? Pardon the question; but she hath so often spoken of you and wished to see you, that I determined I would ask when I had the opportunity."

Ralph looked up with a pleased smile. It might be but a little thing that an old lady who had known his grandfather wished to see him, but to one so lonely it seemed a great deal.

"She hath not directly, or you may be sure I would have waited on her long ago. Something, indeed, was dropped; but I did not wish"— he looked a little grim, and Rachel wondered whether he was thinking of her uncle —"I did not wish to run the least risk of an intrusion. I will go to-night if you advise it."

"I do. She loved your father as a son."

His face lighted up again, and Rachel saw she had struck the right note.

"It might well be; father was the most lovable of men,

though I say so. I wish you had known him, Mistress Rachel."

He spoke with frank impetuosity.

"I would I had, indeed. I know what you must have felt at his death. My father was killed, and he was everything to me!"

"Your father?" Ralph spoke in a tone of genuine interest. "What was he? What did he suffer for? Nay, then," as he saw his companion wince, "I sincerely beg your pardon if I hurt you; but it is surely a strange coincidence. Some time," he spoke now in his gentlest and most persuasive tone, "perchance, I may be so far favoured as to hear of him. Now, I trust you will grant me forgiveness for the question."

"You are very kind. It does not hurt me to speak of it — at least, it will not to tell you, who have suffered also. I ought not to be so sensitive, but it is my nature to shrink from pain. It all came about in this wise."

And then she told him the whole story, and afterwards, from questions which naturally arose out of the narrative, he heard much about her life; and so engrossed were they both in the conversation, that they were surprised to find the journey over, and to see Oliver waiting on the doorstep to lift Rachel from her horse.

CHAPTER XIII

THE weather was hot and the roads were dusty and Oliver weighed twelve stone; but neither thirst nor heat nor the sufferings of his horse kept him to a moderate pace; and two days after he spoke to Rachel he rode back from London just before the party met at supper, covered with dust, very tired, and hugely hungry, but so radiant that those not in the secret wondered what had happened to him. Ralph found a curious fascination in watching the young man and his beaming glances at Rachel. Success was written on his face, and his laugh — as he told comical stories of the terror of certain London citizens at the news from Nottingham — never had Ralph heard so joyous a laugh. A fortunate youth this, with such a father as few men possessed and mother and sisters to love him. Ralph now began to look at Rachel out of the corners of his eyes. What a sweet face it was. Did she really love this man? He was honest and well-intentioned, but how rough — rude as any farmer. Then Ralph bit his lip and frowned at himself. "Am I jealous? That must not be. Love and marriage, even were they in my grasp, would be impossible until this war were done with — the war that hath not begun. Nay, may the fellow have good fortune. He hath a true heart. Whatever betide, I will be no dog-in-the-manger."

And then he devoted himself to his supper, and looked neither to right nor left until all rose from the table, when, as his habit was, he retired to the garden and walked up and down the paths alone. He had not taken more than two or three turns before he met Cromwell and Oliver arm-in-arm.

" You Ralph!" the elder man said as they passed. " A wonted run of yours, this place. A right good place, too, these hot nights. Come, son, to the arbour and have thy say out there."

He drew his hand from Oliver's arm and leant affectionately upon his shoulder, and Ralph saw them disappear in the summer-house, and heard Oliver begin to speak in tense, earnest tones. Then he turned resolutely away and went to bed.

In the arbour the father and son had seated themselves, and Oliver, leaning his arms on a table in the centre, plunged into his subject as a bold swimmer leaps into the sea.

" It is this, father. I am in love, and want thy consent to my betrothal before I joint my troop. Faith! 'tis a match after thine own heart." He paused with a happy laugh, then tried hard to make out the expression of his father's face. But this he could not do. Cromwell was sitting with his back to the west, and the light was failing fast.

" Thy news is startling, son. Who is the maiden?"

" Why, Rachel!" He threw back his head to laugh again, when Cromwell brought his hand down upon the table with a blow that made it quiver.

" Thou'rt fooling me. Rachel betrothed to *thee?*"

Oliver went cold all over, and forgot his manners.

" Who else? Zounds, sir, what mean you?"

A momentary pause. Then Cromwell said slowly:—

" Naught, lad. I am but taken by surprise. Thy mother is right, my mind is too far from home these days. But thou hast been uncommon speedy in thy wooing. Hast spoken to the maid herself?"

" I did that first."

" When?"

" Two days since."

"The answer, then?"

Oliver cleared his throat. "Well, there was none to be called an answer. She hates me not"—this was said slowly, with great complacency—"nay, she likes me, so straightway I rode to her uncle and put the question to him."

"What said he?"

There was a coolness, not to say indifference, in the way that this question was asked which Oliver noted with surprise.

"Gave consent, thank God! I was to speak to you, of course, and"—Oliver coughed again—"a final confirmation was to wait until the matter of settlement and dowry was arranged, but nothing more. Truly, sir, I think the worthy gentleman was something pleased. He spake me very kind, indeed he did."

He stopped, and there was a long silence. This was terrible to Oliver.

"Father, have I angered you? Say something! 'Slife, I can't endure this."

Cromwell started as if he had been roused from deep thought.

"Angry, boy! Tush, how could I be? I am praying for guidance. Thou hast placed me in a strange position. As thy father I might say 'Yea' freely. Rachel is one in a thousand—a pearl beyond price. Wait"—as Oliver gave a joyful assent—"I say wait and hearken." His voice was now stern and harsh. "Though I am thy father, I am her guardian first—forget not that."

"Master Hepworth consents," Oliver began vehemently.

"That is his affair," his father rejoined in the same tone. "You deal not with him now. Be not so froward with me, I must have time to consider the matter. I shall see the maid to-morrow, and then you and I will have further speech together. Meantime you must hold yourself aloof, and neither see nor speak to her. It will be best, perhaps, if you take breakfast in your chamber."

Oliver gasped.

" Good Lord, sir," he groaned, " must we wait so long? See, it is not late. She knows my mind; let me bring her to you. It is hard measure to make me wait another night."

He spoke now in a tone few sons of that time dared to use toward their parents; but it had been Cromwell's principle to encourage in his children the utmost freedom of speech, as in later days he did with his soldiers. He valued the knowledge this gave him far more than the most respectful form of address. There were times, however, when he was not in the mood for it.

" Enough," he said; " would you dictate to me, then, in this matter? Be silent, and go to your chamber. Think you that I have naught to consider but this fancy of yours — the fancy of a week? Love, quotha? Before the passion for a woman deserves that sacred name there must be trial — prayers to God, great searchings of the heart. Dost think thy sudden humour a worthy bargain for a woman's life?"

" 'Tis no humour," Oliver muttered; " I have loved her from our first acquaintance."

" You say so. I reply that must be proved by deeds. Come in."

They walked down the garden slowly, Oliver's head sunk between his shoulders, his fingers fumbling with the buckle of his sword-belt, and his feet dragging despondently. His father accompanied him to his room, saying as he bid him good night:—

" Thou'rt a very foolish fellow, on my life. Is thy back so weak that the first weight breaks it? I'd not have thought thee such a faint heart."

" My back be tough enough," Oliver retorted; " but it is hard to miss your sympathy when I'd been most sure of it."

Cromwell laid a hand upon his arm and shook it.

"I protest I have no patience with thee. Know'st me so little? Nay, lad, I've no lack of sympathy. I loved and lost once. I was young as you, but I do not forget the pain of it. Go, lay thy head upon thy pillow and dream of her, to-morrow thou shalt know my mind; but hold to this room till I see you. Take your Bible, methinks you do not often study it; read and ponder well, it is the best comforter for a sore heart. When thou art as old as I am mayhap it will be thine only one."

He sighed, patted Oliver's shoulder affectionately, and walked away. In the library he found Rachel waiting with a pile of letters. He took them from her and pretended to read, studying her face the while. She was pale, he noticed, and more silent than usual, but he could not detect either nervousness or self-consciousness in her manner. By-and-by he threw himself into his work, dictating some letters and sending Rachel to the kitchen to arrange for their immediate despatch. When the girl returned she found him studying the portrait of his dead son. He was so lost in meditation that he did not hear her enter, and in his face, though he was frowning as if from some disagreeable thought, there was a sadness and a yearning that touched her to the heart.

"It is a beautiful portrait," she said softly, slipping her hand into his. "I used to wonder, when I first came, whether I would ever see him. When I heard the truth I wept; 'twas as if I had lost a friend."

Cromwell pressed her hand, and his brow became smooth again.

"That was strange, little one, was it not, for thou'rt not given to tears."

"I should not be so foolish now," Rachel said hastily. "It was months ago, when I was lonely and longed for a brother. There was something in Robert's face which has always stirred me; had he lived I would have loved him with my whole heart."

Cromwell gave a slight start, and the fancied likeness he had once traced between Robert and Ralph came back to him with some force. He said drily:—

"What see you in this face to love in particular?"

"Earnestness and courage," she cried, with an emphasis which made Cromwell wince again. "He would have done the right, and would ever think it. If he heard or saw aught that was unjust to others he would not have passed it by, but have fought it to the death."

"See you that in the portrait? It was there truly in the boy. Hast ever seen a face that reminded you of his?"

Rachel shook her head.

"None — unless," she smiled, and Cromwell bit his lip —"unless it be your own."

"Pish! what other?"

"Not one that I could call to mind; no one."

"Not Oliver's?"

He put the question brusquely, and Rachel blushed to the tip of her ears, yet she faced him bravely.

"No," she said in a low voice, "not Oliver's, dear sir."

Cromwell led her to a chair and drew another up to it.

"Rest you there, child. Now grant me, if thou canst, a true insight into your mind; cloak not your feelings with any simperings or modest silences; there is naught in honest love for man or maid to be ashamed; dost know that Oliver has been both to your uncle and to me to declare his love for you?"

"I do know it, sir."

"When did he speak to you?"

"Two days ago."

"And your answer?"

Rachel hesitated a moment.

Cromwell frowned. "Hath played the coquette with him then?"

The girl opened her eyes in amazement. "Indeed, I know not what you mean."

"Then, little one, what answer did you make the lad?"

Rachel looked perplexed. "He got none that I remember; there was no time. I was so startled that my breath forsook me, and before it returned we were not alone, nor have we been since. He left me saying he would speak to you and my uncle."

Cromwell took her hand. "Then answer me. It is much to ask, for I am rude and harsh; but you know I love you. Tell me, dost care for the lad? Wouldst be his wife?"

Rachel looked up without hesitation and said: "I do not know. He has been my friend a great while. He is dear to me, and — and he is your son. Yet I have not thought of him in such a way. I have thought of no one. But, then, it would not be meet, I suppose, for me to judge such things. Your wishes and my uncle's must guide me. What, dear sir, do you wish me to do?"

She spoke quite frankly — no blushes, no confusion. Cromwell was rather taken aback.

"What age are you?"

"Eighteen and six months."

"Young," he muttered. "Yet not so young."

"Tell me," he said aloud, "tell me this: Were neither myself nor thy uncle concerned here, and thou free to follow thy inclination, what answer would Master Oliver receive?"

Rachel considered. "I would tell him," she said thoughtfully, "that he would do ill to have me for a wife, that he should seek a maid who loves him ten times more."

"And if he would not give you up, what then?"

"Then — then — well, I would insist that he should wait until he had seen others. He said he knew none but me."

. "And if after absence he presently returned loving thee more than ever, what then?"

" Then "—- very gravely —" I would marry him. That would be naught but fair."

Cromwell rose and kissed her. " I thank thee, sweet daughter; thou hast taken a burden from my mind. Now we will go to our rest. It is late."

CHAPTER XIV

CROMWELL did not find Oliver reading his Bible next morning, but sitting on his bed, with bare arms, vigorously polishing a rapier. So intent was he upon his occupation, that, at his father's entrance, he only waved it in the air by way of greeting, and let the sunlight glitter on the burnished steel.

"What think'st of this, sir? Six shillings was the price; 'i faith, a bargain! Look at its temper; see when I breathe upon it. A genuine Toledo, as I live."

" A pretty weapon," Cromwell said critically, " but no more use these times, son, than thy mother's bodkin."

"Say you so? See here, then," and Oliver sprang from the bed, and pinked in the centre a round pad of leather he had nailed to the wall. " Sa — sa — methinks a malignant had need of jointless armour and visor closed were he to challenge me without danger to his skin. Even then, sooth, I'd find a way to his brain, an' he had one, between the bars. No, no, I'll grant you that in the push and moil of battle the heavy broadsword is the fitter weapon; but on foot give me a rapier if I have room. Faith! an' we but lived in the days when a war was often left to single combat, I'd challenge the king's best knight, and, so that Rachel's eyes were upon me, 'twould go hard indeed if the godly cause went down — sa — sa."

He made another pass, recovered himself with a flourish, and threw the rapier upon the bed.

" I am out of training, sure. If your cornet was not so occupied we'd have some rare turns together. He

hath a pretty skill by all accounts. I'd give much to
measure swords with him. Eh — hark to that! Father,
hast spoken?"

The window was open, and now the sound of voices,
Rachel's and Betty's, came from the garden, and fencing
was forgotten.

Cromwell closed the window.

"Aye; but the fruit is not ripe yet, boy, for thee or
any man. The flower's i' the bud at present — the
woman's but a child. You must wait."

"I cannot wait."

"I tell thee," Cromwell said very gently, while upon
his face there came a sternness that his children seldom
saw, "thou must wait and pray. Her heart is younger
than her mind. I'd not have believed, had I not seen, that
a woman of her years and wit could be so simple; but this
is so. Wherefore, what sayest thou?" Oliver had cast
himself down upon the bed with an exclamation very like
a curse. "Tell me your thought," his father said sternly;
"out with it."

"Willingly, sir," and the young man sprang up, his
face red with passion. "I said to myself that if her
simplicity be the check, I'd soon remove it; and I will,
be sure of that."

Cromwell's face darkened.

"Wouldst play the braggart, then, and with me?"
He spoke slowly and contemptuously. "Thou art indeed
a fool!"

Oliver writhed.

"And thou a tyrant!" he cried defiantly. "I love
the maid, and honestly. At cost of sweat and trouble,
an' a good horse, I obtained consent from her uncle;
yet when I come to you — my father — I am received
with black looks and a refusal! Zounds, sir, be there
another suitor more favoured in your sight than me?
God's life, I do believe it! Thy cornet, perchance,
Dangerfield — this Socinian devil!"

"Hold thy peace!" Cromwell's face was white. "Another word," he said in a dry, strained tone, "and the Lord have mercy on us both." He paused, while Oliver hung his head, abashed. "Son," continued Cromwell, "what mean you by such insinuations? Hath life in Holland — a few months out i' the world — sowed such corruption in thy nature, that at the first cross to thy wishes thou wouldst rend like a wolf-cub thine own father! What have I done ever to deserve this from thee? That first — answer!"

Oliver lowered his eyes. The gust of passion had passed. "I was distraught," he muttered; "I knew not what I said. But you tried me very sore."

"I told you the truth. Now, hearken. Take thy case and hold it to the light. The Presbyter gave consent, and you argue that Rachel and I must needs bend the knee without question to thy midsummer madness and his weak and selfish fears. Is this indeed true? Well, I knew thy spirit to be ever impatient and self-willed, but I did not until now expect conduct so ungenerous from thee."

Oliver winced. "You lash me unjustly, father. How is it ungenerous to offer all I have? Faith, no man can offer more."

"A *man*," was the stern rejoinder, "should scorn to seek a woman's hand unless he gain her whole heart in return."

"I will gain it."

"In what manner?"

"My love will compel return."

"Love! Have I not told thee that is not the word to use. Choose some meaner one. Love is humble. Thou'rt arrogant, nay, impudent. This maiden, quotha, must bind herself to thee, promise to give herself into thy keeping, because thou desirest her. She hath no wish to call thee husband, mind you that! How then? Wilt

force a cold, unwilling hand into your own and say,
'This is mine'?"

"I want — I want to win her love, I say."

"That is better. Those words ring true. But, an'
you mean them, think you that this is like to bring your
suit to a successful issue? Nay, lad," his voice was earnest now, and tender, "put aside the hunger of thy heart.
Think but of her, then answer."

Oliver's face worked.

"I — I'll obey thy wish."

"That I believe. But my question is not answered.
How wouldst thou, my wish apart, win this maiden's
love. Believe me, it is not to be lightly won."

Oliver sighed, and sat slowly down upon his bed
again.

"I will be patient, then. Aye, I see now it is the
only way. I want no promise from her. But she must
know beyond mistake that I truly love her, and intend,
God willing, to make her my wife some day — if she will
have me. That is all I would say. Every word could
be spoken in your presence."

Cromwell was touched. He clapped his son on the
shoulder and his brow cleared.

"Go, then, and fetch her. Nay, I mean it," as Oliver
stared; "bring her to the library. Speak thy mind
there."

No second bidding was needed. Oliver left the bed
at a bound and had reached the door, when a laugh
from his father made him suddenly recollect his bare
arms and ungartered hose.

"My faith, good cornet of Nat Walton's horse,
prithee be more careful. If thy namesake uncle, the
knight, were to hear thou wert starting forth in such
guise to court a maiden he would die in a fit. Fie on
thy want of gallantry! Yet, indeed, I like it," Cromwell added to himself after Oliver had left the room.
"He is as simple in his way as the maiden is in hers.

Pure in heart and strong of arm. Knights, quotha!
Set him and Ralph yonder side by side, and I warrant
those gallants round the king would be put to it to find
their match. Now to see them together."

Down the garden-walk strode Oliver, and his father
smiled at the sweeping bow with which he greeted Rachel
as she stood with Betty gathering flowers, and the
unwonted deference in his attitude when he delivered his
message.

"I should chide him by rights," Cromwell muttered.
"Hepworth would say 'twas aping the cavaliers. Pish,
how these godly men do prate! I love to see the manner of a lusty lad to a dainty maid. Here they come.
My word, how he ruffles it! How he'd love a duello in
her defence. Ah! love — when the man is young and
the maid be fair and 'tis summer-time — no joy upon
God's earth can equal it; none."

He sighed, and for a moment there was an unwonted
softness in his face. An instant later his eyes were watchful again. He strode to the window and looked out, resting his chin reflectively upon his hand.

The girls had been plucking flowers from a bed at the
lower end of the garden, and as Rachel obeyed Oliver's
summons, Betty was left behind disconsolate and jealous.
Suddenly she brightened and ran towards someone who
had entered the garden by the back gate — Ralph.

"Greet ye, greet ye," she cried joyfully. "You have
come just in time to be my company. Here am I set to
gather a heap of posies for grandmamma, while this
Rachel, who should help me, follows Oliver. Do not say
now that you will desert me too. I need your help here."

Ralph smiled at this imperative hint, but his eyes followed the two figures with an anxious glance.

"I fear I cannot stay, little mistress; I seek your
father. Is he in the house?"

"Yes; but, oh, do not follow them!" as Ralph turned
away. "I heard Oliver tell Rachel that father wished to

see her. He said not why, but he was so solemn and she blushed so that I know there is something brewing. You cannot see him yet. Now, pray lift that flower-pot for me, 'tis too heavy for my wrist." The command was not to be evaded, and Ralph obeyed. But he looked after the retreating couple wistfully until they disappeared into the house, and Betty wondered why he looked so grave. As the young people entered the passage Cromwell left the window.

"Turn his thoughts toward the maid, then?" he thought. "It may well be so. Pity! What a pity! God have mercy upon his father's soul!"

CHAPTER XV

THOUGH Oliver had declared in the fulness of his heart that all he wished to say to Rachel could be told in the presence of a third person, when it came to the point he devoutly wished his father at the other side of the library door.

"This son of mine," Cromwell said, taking Rachel by the hand, "hath somewhat to say touching yourself which I desired him to say before me. Make such answer as your inclination prompts. Oliver, speak thy mind."

Oliver blushed and coughed. Then he blurted out:—

"I wish, Mistress Rachel, that is, I would fain inquire — Lord! but I am making a sorry mess of this. Dearest of hearts, dost love me? There's the point. I only ask a little love. I have so much for thee! Wilt be betrothed, and one day have me for a husband? I gave you Master Hepworth's letter; my father hath spoken to you; you know my heart. All that is left for me is to learn your feelings. God grant they be favourable."

His voice became more and more vehement as he went on, and at the end he approached her with eager invitation, but Rachel drew back.

"I cannot — I cannot," she said in a low voice, looking at him at the same time so wistfully that he fairly groaned with a desire to clasp her in his arms, kiss away the gathering tears, and laugh her doubts to scorn. "It grieves me sorely to say aught to give you pain. But — oh! how shall I express my meaning aright? — though I love you, it is but as a brother. I know it be no more now. I have never thought of lovers; I cannot give my heart as you give yours, for I have none to give."

The tears welled over, for Oliver's face was the picture of despair. In a moment he would have been at her side, but a restraining hand grasped him firmly.

"Be a man, son," his father said, "or thou'lt lose thy chance for life. Whatsoever she may say now, I'll not give my consent. Courage, Rachel, thou speakest with sense and judgment. Give him no promises."

She looked up gratefully.

"You make my way easy, sir. But, Oliver, I would not have you think — I would you should understand that I feel deeply all you have said. Do you catch my meaning? Alas! how can I make it clear? I need your friendship, but I cannot take your love."

Again she turned to him appealingly, and this time all that was best in his nature responded.

"Dear mistress," he said slowly and gravely, "I beg your forgiveness. 'Deed, I am rude and blundering. Let me wait, then, and serve thee as a friend. If thou canst allow that I'll be happy, or at least content. I ask no more now."

Her face brightened. "That is what I wish — just what I wish, if "— turning to Cromwell —" it meets with your consent."

"Yes," he answered after a pause. "See thou keep thy compact, son. And remember, friendship be not love."

Oliver sighed.

"That, indeed, I am not like to forget. Anyway, I depart to-morrow at dawn. Heigho! But, Rachel, I would like thy company to-day. Wilt have a ride, if we take Betty? Grandmamma will spare you this morning, I'll be sworn — my last day."

Rachel looked at her guardian, and she saw there was pleasure in his face. He laughed.

"Nay, I have no fears. Betty is good company. Tell Ralph, if you see him, that I have matters requiring his attention here. Now be off, young people, and get to your saddles."

They were soon upon their way — Oliver and Rachel rather quieter than usual, Betty in the highest spirits. Of a sudden the child paused in her merry chatter and heaved a portentous sigh.

"Mercy! What ails the baggage?" Oliver exclaimed, laughing.

Betty sighed again.

"We are on the path I rode with Ralph three days ago. I wish he were with us."

"Say you so? 'Pon my honour, I had better gallop home, then, and tell him to follow. But to be serious, methinks, chit, you are somewhat too free with the cornet's Christian name."

"I see not why," was the tart rejoinder. "Rachel hath called him so. Yes, ma'am, I heard you once. Master Dangerfield is far too big a mouthful. Besides, I knew him first. I pray for him — father gave me leave. And, oh, when I heard what the minister said afterwards I have wished to tell Ralph that, whatever his religion, he was very dear to me. I will tell him some day."

"Nay, tell Master Hepworth," Oliver cried with a chuckle; "it would make him so glad."

"An' I had a mind to I would," the child cried, tossing her head. "But it might cause him to do Ralph another mischief."

"Why speak you so bitterly?" Rachel said, looking at her. "There have been no words between them since that night."

Betty pursed her lips.

"I heard — but it was said to father. Yet, if I choose, I could tell what would astonish you."

Oliver laid his hand upon her bridle.

"Puss-cat, what are you hiding? I know there is something a-buzz in your little pate. Hearts! Let us

hear it. What said the minister to father? Speak, kitten, or I will shake you off your pony."

At this sharp questioning Betty looked guilty, but she
pouted obstinately and shook her head.

" I will not. No, you may beat me, an' I will not. I
did not mean to listen, but the window was open, and I
dared not move, fearing they'd hear me. Nay, I *cannot*
tell you. Rachel, make him let me go. I will tell *you*
some day."

" Elizabeth, if thou dost not speak ——" Oliver began,
when Rachel intervened.

" Force her not. We have no right to hear what
cannot concern us. See, a stretch of turf! I am going
to gallop."

She loosened her rein and sped away. Oliver dashed
after her, and Betty brought up the rear breathless but
radiant.

" I will tell you everything," she whispered to Rachel.
" I know you'll not betray me. I've longed to tell someone for weeks, but I dared not. It's *all* about you."

They returned home at dinner-time, and the rest of
the day Oliver spent with his mother and Madam Cromwell. When the farewells were said it was noticed by
Ralph that Oliver was very pale, and that Rachel's
eyes were wet. Oliver said good-bye quietly enough,
but after a glance at her face he took her hand and
kissed it before them all. Rachel was much startled,
but recovered herself instantly.

" God bless you," she said in a voice which trembled
a little, " and keep you safe from harm, dear friend, and
bring you home."

The young men sat up late that night. Cromwell
had invited them both to take a glass of wine in the
library.

" We have a toast to drink," he said, filling their
glasses and his own. " 'Tis a custom I seldom approve,
but there are times and seasons. Ralph, a man whom

you know hath wooed a maid this day. He hath not won her yet, but if he learneth patience and is of constant mind all may be well. I ask you to drink success to him with me."

They rose, glasses in hand — a strange sight in a Puritan household when such ceremonies were held to savour of the worst malignancy; but Cromwell's ways, as friends and foes acknowledged, were his own. The glasses chinked, and Ralph chimed in, "Success to you, Oliver, and a long life." As for Oliver, he knew not where to look and hardly what to say. He held out a hand to each. "Father, I thank you. Dangerfield, thou'rt my friend and comrade from to-day. Now, I'll drink back your health and Rachel's. God bless her, and if I die may a man who is worthier than I am win her love."

"Amen," said his father gravely, and then they fell into talk about the times — the probable strength of the Parliament army in Yorkshire under Lord Fairfax, whom Oliver was to join; the quality of the main force in the south, now assembling under the Earl of Essex. Nothing was known of the movements of the king. Oliver had heard that he had few followers, and prophesied, with the lusty confidence of youth, that he would never have more, and would presently be a prisoner in their hands; but his father checked him.

"Tut! Believe that when ye see the warrant which commits him to the Tower, not earlier. Mark me, friends, there be at present hardly a man in England who'd dare lay a finger on his person — I could name them all; the time for that is not yet ripe. We must watch and pray and fight; the rest is God's. Now I must away for a little space. Stay you here and finish the bottle between you; I will soon return."

For some minutes the young men sipped their wine in silence. Both were grave and thoughtful.

"Oliver," said Ralph at last, "why are you not betrothed to Mistress Rachel?"

The words were spoken so sharply, that Oliver looked up in surprise; Ralph's mouth was stern, but his eyes were absent and dreamy.

"I ought to be," he answered with a huge sigh, "but father was set against it because the maid was coy — that is the reason. It's hard, i' faith," he continued, lowering his voice and moving nearer to his companion. "S'truth, Ralph, if I'd been left to take my own course with her she would have yielded, she must! But he held me; I was like a hound in the leash with hare in view; in a minute puss was beyond me. 'Twill come right though in the end, I doubt not that. She knows I care with all my soul, and that is half the battle with a woman when there is no one else. What think you?"

Ralph held his glass up to the light, and appeared to be studying the quality of the wine.

"You may be right; I know not, I have not had experience."

Oliver laughed loudly — the wine had excited him.

"I' fackins! don't tell me that; keep it for the French! Have I not been in the Low Countries? Why you, you were there with the cream — Charlton and Spencer and Henry Verney, fine gentlemen every one, blades of high temper, bloods of the hottest. Psha! I could tell a score of tales of their adventures, but not within father's hearing. Thou had no experience! Fie on thee for a hypocrite. Nay, get not warm," as Ralph's face darkened suddenly, "I love thee too well to quarrel. But be not so proud with me. Tell me thy secret; I'll swear thou hast one somewhere. Thou knowest mine, and I'm glad; never have I seen a man I'd trust as soon as thee. But confidence should beget confidence; return my openness, and let us beat our friendship into shape. Come, friend, I mean it heart and soul — confess." He stretched his hand across the table, and Ralph grasped it. Oliver's speech might be wanting in delicacy, but it was as honest as his open face, and to-night Ralph felt hungry for friendship.

"I would, truly, were there aught to tell, but I was a dull dog. Charlton I knew at college, the rest I scarce spoke to; I worked while they were playing. I liked it," he added hastily, "'twas inclination, not virtue; the shadow of my father's death was upon my life. It is there still."

He sighed, and Oliver wrung his hand.

"Soft, good Ralph, think not of it. Oh, throw it off your mind; thou'rt too young for such a trouble. Keep it away till battle comes. S'blood, comrade, I would you and I could deal together with those who did the deed. Truly you have had a bitter life; I am sorry that I jeered. But you'll forgive me. I've had easy times; though now, if the cavaliers fight, I'll get my share of knocks. Heigho! what a difference the women make in that though. Faith! Rachel has near made a coward of me. A month ago I'd given an ear for the war to begin at once; now I'd not mind if the king ran away without a blow, so that I might get back the quicker. 'Tis hard to go away uncertain. You take me in this? Why should she not know? Hearts! how queerly made these women be. I am like a man in a fever — one minute all hot with hope, the next shaking with despair. I could endure all if I *knew*. But to go away thus, be killed, belike, and never know at all — s'truth it's too much. Dear Ralph, give me thy counsel, I am very low."

He pushed his wine glass away and leant his head drearily upon his hand. Ralph drew his chair close to him, and moved by a sudden sympathy, threw his arm over the broad shoulder.

"Come, come," he said cheerily, "this is not like you, Oliver. Heart up! You who be on the ladder of glory and happiness should not sit and weep. You go forth to win laurels, and return to grasp your father's hand and take your reward from your lady's eyes. Why, I

know none so fortunate. 'Fore heaven, I do envy thee
with all my heart. Think what might be. Think of
those with no mother, father, sweetheart, not even a dog
to love them. You asked my confidence, you shall have
it then. I am worse off than you. I've naught in the
world — nobody to care for, nothing to think upon but
the memory of my father's death. All my friends be
Royalists. If I meet them again they will be at my
throat and I at theirs. There is but one man in the
world I care for — your father, and I am naught to him."

He stopped abruptly, for the door had opened, and
Cromwell came in. But Oliver, with tears in his eyes,
sprang up and went to him.

"Father, speak to this man. He says you be his best
friend, but care nothing in return."

Cromwell looked from one flushed face to the other,
and laid a hand upon the shoulder of each.

"He lies then, Oliver, and he knows it. I plucked
him from the jaws of malignancy and brought him into
the heart of my household. I did this against fierce
opposition. I have not regretted it, and shall not. Did
I do right, think you? Canst rely upon him as a friend
— as a brother?"

Oliver laughed aloud and turned upon Ralph in
triumph.

"There, what say'st to that? Indeed I can, and do,
father. He hath given me sweet comfort when most I
needed it. Some day, please God, I'll do the same by
him."

"Amen to that," Cromwell rejoined. Then he said
very tenderly, " Ralph, thou'rt tired out; you too, Oliver.
Go ye to bed — both."

When the young men had departed he paced the
room with knitted brow.

"The seed is uprooted, the flower nipped in the bud,"
he said aloud. "I should be well content. And yet —
and yet, my heart is sore."

CHAPTER XVI

WHAT think ye of the new lieutenant, Sanctify?"
"I've seen but one."
"I mean the man who came a week since."
"Where's the other?"
"'Slid! our cornet. He's done the work of two. Noll will lose by the change."
"Nay, he should mightily rejoice."

The words were spoken with a slight unction of tone which made the other man grunt impatiently.

"Grammercy for thy opinion, then — if it be thine, which I doubt."

"Jeremiah Micklejohn," said his companion solemnly, "thou'rt a blind and impious worm of the flesh. Canst not comprehend that a man of religion ——"

"Ouns, comrade, I am a soldier and thy corporal, and comprehend my business. But away with this word-play. Who and what is Lieutenant Capell?"

The men were trotting homewards along the high-road from Cambridge, the setting sun splashing the long stretch of fen with red and orange. It was the close of an October day. Micklejohn had to repeat his question before he received an answer.

"If thou be a corporal," the other said at last, "thou knowest more of officers than me, a poor trooper."

"Now a curse be on ye, man, for a surly knave. An' the captain's orders were less strict, I'd lend thee a buffet that might mend thy manners and relieve my temper. I've but seen the man at drill; thou wast bred in Huntingdon, his birthplace, and hast known him more years than I have days. What's he made of — good steel or sounding brass?"

"There be little sound in him," the other replied, a gleam in his sombre eyes; "if he speak ten words in a day beyond his business, 'tis a wonder. Nay, I tell thee, Jem, he's one whom the ministers love, being full of religion. Yet he's no shirker of the carnal duties. His father was a glover in our town, and died in the lieutenant's boyhood, leaving him poor i' the world's goods, but rich in an example of godliness. It is said that he trounced the lieutenant when a child a half-hour daily for a week because he spoke a scoffing word of a Presbyter. Assuredly he was brought up under firm and proper discipline. At his father's death the boy — he was but fifteen — went to London, and through the grace of the Lord that was in him; the patronage of Presbyter Hepworth, and an exceeding thriftiness, he prospered, and was pursuing a study of the law, when the country's troubles began, upon which he enlisted in the train-bands of London, and rose to a captaincy."

"Pooh; he be no soldier, then."

"That thou'st may affirm and I may not contradict thee," was the dry rejoinder; "nevertheless, he hath given satisfaction to soldiers in the ranks above him, and is thought well of in all quarters. It is surely an abundant mercy for us that we have him as our second in command."

"You say so. But what do you think? I stand by Cornet Dangerfield."

The trooper pursed his lips and raised his eyebrows. "Dost know his religion? Be it not true that he is tainted with that heresy they call Socinianism?"

The corporal laughed.

"Witherskins! Then by all that is true in Gospel I'll turn Socinian myself. Ralph Dangerfield is the properest lad a-horse or a-foot, in council or in camp, that I've seen since I was old enough to swing a sword or throw a leg across a gelding; and that was before thou wast born, most worshipful, godly Sanctify Sopstick! And now, old comrade, we must prate no more, but haste to quarters, or Reuben's tongue will rain and hail upon us until our suppers nigh turn sour."

The speaker suited his action to the word, and, spurring his horse, they clattered through the village of Stretham, scattering geese, dogs, and children right and left.

They were a great contrast in appearance these men of Cromwell's troop. The corporal was small and squarely made, a tough little pippin of a man, fresh-coloured, with a button of a nose very much turned up. He had been in the wars with Sweetlove, through whom he had joined the troop. But he had saved no money, and was a typical specimen of the better sort of mercenary of the time — careless and thriftless, yet of fairly sober life, genuinely fond of his profession, and a skilled man at arms. The other man, Sanctify Jordan, was as tall as the corporal was short. His face was thin and lank, melancholy, and saturnine. He was long-necked, long-backed, long-limbed, and sat his horse like a figure of wood. Everything about the man was stiff and angular; yet, owing partly to a gravity of speech and manner and partly to a reputation for austere piety, Sanctify's opinion, when he expressed it, possessed more weight with his comrades than anyone else's, except the quartermaster's. One thing about him, however, puzzled everybody, even Cromwell it was said; this was his intimate friendship with Corporal Micklejohn, whose morals were matters of grave suspicion, who had been more than once fined for scandalous language, and who steadily refused to become a member of any religious community. That Micklejohn was a corporal of the troop he owed solely to his military experience and the friendship of Reuben Sweetlove.

The men were silent for a time, and then the corporal broke out afresh: —

"I will tell ye my opinion of this younker lieutenant, and thou shalt gainsay it if thou canst. I like him not. Every day, when taking orders from him, I says to myself, 'Ye've a dreaping, surly look about ye, my master. Your face is heavy and hard, your eyes dull — the eyes of a fish — and ne'er look straight into mine. Yet I'll warrant they see if there is a spot in my armour, though it be no bigger than a pin's head. I'd not trust ye, nay, no further than a sword's thrust off.' That's what I says to myself, comrade, and I says it now to thee. 'Slife, this Capell be here for no good either to us or the cornet. Ain't he a friend of the Presbyter's? And don't they say the reverend man would oust our lad from Cromwell's favour by any means in his power, being so feared lest young Mistress Rachel may fancy him? They do say it," as Sanctify looked incredulous, "and thou knowest they do, old fox! Well, he's failed, as he deserved. First he tried a bully with Noll himself; but that went up like a French petard. Then he put Oliver the younger upon the chase; but that miscarried I've heard. Now he twists in Lieutenant Capell; and this, mark you, is going to be the worst blow of all for the cornet. The old Oliver was too strong, the young one too simple; but Capell is supple and cautious and deep — one of the waiting kind. Mayhap he'll take time to get hold, but his grip'll be hard to loose. What thinkst ye of it all thyself? Speak!"

The tall man gave his head an impressive jerk.

"Nay, nay, master corporal, not I. What need for my halting words. Thy mind is made up. Thou hast dubbed the man a knave and hypocrite, and no cleansing by me would take the stain out of him. Yet I would repeat in other words that which I have already set forth. This man, though no shedder of blood at the present, is skilled in his work. He hath the full confidence of

Cromwell and the strenuous support of many members of Parliament. Before long he will command the minds of our troop. His designs I know not. So far he be complaisant toward the cornet I have observed; at least, he listens with much attention while the youth speaketh. Let us do the like and watch the outcome. Some day the Lord will bring forth the reckonings of these two men. We may then strike a balance, and if it be not a fair one, perchance we might give our humble services to make it so."

The corporal laughed.

" 'Twas a vain and foolish attempt of mine to try drawing thee, old iron-head. Let it pass. I know thy heart. So we march to-morrow for Worcester — work, real work, will soon begin. Good lack! how I thirst for it."

"Thou'lt get a throttle-full, Jim, if report speaks truly."

"Aye, the king hath collected a fine army since he raised his standard. Some say twice my Lord Essex's. The very troopers are gentlemen, mounted on blood horses, their armour worth a ransom."

Sanctify gave a quiet chuckle.

"Doubtless the devil hath equipped his own. Yet will we cast them under our feet and scatter them like straw on a threshing-floor. But this will not be without slaughter and blood, good comrade, and the rending of hearts in twain, sore loss of godly lives, and the sending of souls to judgment to suffer the tortures of hell. So thou thinkst that Mistress Rachel favours the Socinian?"

The question came so suddenly and unexpectedly that Micklejohn had answered it before he could collect his wits.

"Marry, yes." Then he stopped and twisted in his saddle. "Hey, but my thoughts are going too cheap. What think you?"

"My mind on such matters is a waste. Yet I know

that Lieutenant Capell, in the minds of most females, be a very godly man."

"A curse upon his godliness!" snarled the corporal. "But soft! yonder is he ahead, and the cornet also. Haste ye — spur thy slow beast, man! If they be in Ely before us Cromwell will hear of it."

The officers were riding leisurely, and the troopers soon overtook them and passed them with a silent salute, which Ralph alone acknowledged.

"There is mischief there," his companion said in an undertone. "They have been wandering."

"Very likely. But I have no fear for either; both are tried men."

The lieutenant coughed.

"I'd trust none of the rogues were I you, friend. Nay, night and day I would watch them. It is the only way to preserve true discipline, and keep them in their place."

Ralph did not reply, and the conversation languished.

Lieutenant Capell had been a week at Ely, and Ralph had never spent a longer seven days in his life. He did not dislike the man, and would have said with justice that Corporal Micklejohn's description of him was exaggerated; but he did not find much pleasure in his company. Capell was not handsome. In figure he was stout and clumsily made. His features were roughly cut, with fleshy nose, and small eyes. It was a face which lacked expression, and he had a habit when talking of looking over the shoulder of the person he addressed, which made it extremely difficult for that person to guess his thoughts; yet the face was neither hard nor treacherous, and those who knew Capell best trusted him the most. He had the reputation everywhere for sound sense and judgment, a discretion that could always be depended upon, steadiness of conduct, energy in his work, and extraordinary industry. Cromwell, who made strict inquiry about the man before he received him at Ely upon Isaac Hepworth's recommendation, was well satisfied with all that he heard, and more than satisfied with the efficiency of the train-band of which Capell had been captain. The only point about the man which puzzled Cromwell was his willingness to give up his commission in London and serve him at Ely as lieutenant; but that was his own affair. It was a difficult position for Capell. He was a stranger to the Cromwell family and to the men under him. His manners with the ladies were awkward; with the troop he was stiff and cold; but there was a quiet deference to Cromwell and an absence of any assumption of authority towards Ralph that kept them on excellent terms. In spite of this, however, Capell's presence was a severe trial to Ralph — a trial which did not grow less as time went on. The young men, though at one in their desire to promote the efficiency of the troop, soon found that they differed upon every other subject. Capell was a strict Puritan, even to his dress. His doublet was of coarse, black cloth; his cloak of the same material, worn long and drawn close round his shoulders; his headgear was a high-crowned hat with narrow brim, and he cut his hair close to his head. Ralph, on the other hand, though he had removed the feathers from his castor still wore it a little on one side; and over a short white collar of linen — for he had discarded the lace — his love-locks fell as luxuriantly as ever; while his cloak and doublet, though of a sombre hue, were still jauntily cut. In temperament and in experience of life also they differed as much as in their views upon dress. But, after all, the real difficulty lay in another direction. Ralph was jealous. Though it was true that Capell did not exert his authority in a way likely to be galling to his junior, yet he was tenacious of one privilege, which to Ralph had been the most precious of all, the first place at Cromwell's side. Until Capell came Ralph had worked with his captain early and late. Before Capell's arrival Cromwell had taken no step, either in recruiting new men, buying horses, arms, and accoutrements, or any matter concerning the well-being of the troop, without consulting Ralph; now he consulted Capell. There was nothing to complain of in this, Ralph told himself. The lieutenant was an older man by five years; and though he had not seen foreign service, he was quite up to his work; while his standing in the army, as Cromwell more than once remarked, was a very high one for a subordinate officer. Nevertheless, Ralph was sore. He was scrupulously careful not to give the least expression to his feelings; but he felt that he had been slighted for a stranger, and this wounded him in a very tender place. Life at the best was a very dreary business, and now that the stimulus of Cromwell's companionship was withdrawn it became desperately lonely. Ralph was one of those people who can never be happy unless they feel themselves to be indispensable to somebody. It is a weakness chiefly belonging to women, but is much more common among men than they are generally willing to acknowledge.

On this particular evening, the last which the troop was to spend at Ely, Ralph felt as miserable as a neglected child. The preparations for the march were complete. There was nothing to take his attention from himself, and he was alone. Cromwell was as usual engaged with Capell; Betty, Bridget, and Rachel were with Mrs. Cromwell. It was true that the same thing had happened every night since the lieutenant's arrival, and Ralph told himself roughly that he ought to be used to it, but this did not make him any. the happier. He sauntered into the summer-house and sat there for a long time, his eyes wandering listlessly over the trim lawn and flower-beds, the wall which enclosed the garden, the spire of St. Mary's Church, and, beyond, the tower of the cathedral. The weather was warm for the time of year, and all day a south-west wind had piled up the clouds for rain. Now all was still, as if the earth were waiting for the coming storm. It was not late, but the lack of sunlight gave a strange gloom and soft-ness to the outlines of the buildings, and made the cathedral tower seem greater and more dominating than usual. Ralph sat still wrapped in his thoughts. His brow was contracted with pain, his lips set tightly. It was his birthday, but no one knew it, or would care to know it. A Socinian's son! Was that the reason why he had been cast out of favour? Doubtless. Nay, more, they thought him to be a Socinian. This would account for many things, especially for a curious reserve with which Madam Cromwell had treated him of late. He had taken the hint given by Rachel, and on presenting himself before the old lady one August evening had been received most kindly. She had told him much of his father and grandfather, and had invited him to come and see her whenever he had leisure. But not long ago he noticed a sudden change in her manner, and once she was almost rude. This was a few weeks since, and he had not been to see her again. He had tried to find a possible reason for her rebuff, but had thought of none till to-night. It did not occur to him that he had rarely been in the old lady's room without meeting Rachel, and that he was a different person in that maiden's presence. But he remembered now that religious subjects were rigorously avoided, and once planted in his mind, the idea that he was an outcast grew rapidly. A score of incidents which at the time they occurred seemed of no importance became positive warnings now. There was the occasion on which Cromwell had nearly startled him out of his wits by requesting him to offer up daily prayers for the troop during his absence in London. Ralph's prompt refusal had been dictated more by ner-vousness than anything else, and Cromwell had quietly let the matter drop. But Capell had taken this duty upon his arrival as a matter of course, and had done it well. The manners of the troopers struck Ralph as more reserved than formerly; even the servants avoided him, or he thought so. Ralph sighed bitterly.

"A mere suspicion," he muttered, "born of my words to the old minister that first night. Psha! a slender rope upon which to hang a heretic. Yet, I'll swear they would hang me."

He sighed again; then his face became very thought-ful. What, after all, did he believe? He had read his father's book many times, and each time with interest and growing sympathy; and he had read his Bible — he knew most of the New Testament by heart. Yet, for all that, he had not thought deeply about his own religious belief. In the Low Countries he had been too busy learning the art of war; in England he had given the best of his mind, body, and brain to Cromwell; and in leisure hours he had — well, he had thought of Rachel Fuller-ton. It was a confession he did not like making; but he was in the mood for telling himself plain truths, and this weighed upon his mind. Then with another sigh, a very lingering one, he dismissed the thought. On the morrow this quiet life would be at an end; active service was coming at last. Oh, how he longed for it! Yet to-night he indulged in none of the dreams of glory which had lightened the burden of his loneliness on other occasions. He only thought of death, and shivered — not from fear, but from a sudden feeling of unprepared-ness. "Merciful God," he cried, "I am not fit to die!" He left the summer-house and feverishly paced the gar-den-walks. A religion — faith in a living God, in eter-nity, in Christ; these were what a man needed when his soul went forth at death. Were they his? They must be; and yet, like a dark, threatening cloud in a clear sky, he felt a doubt rising in his mind, a sickening uncer-tainty, and he was tortured by it. "This shall not be," he muttered, clenching his hands; "I will search my heart, and before I join the friends in evening prayer find out where it rests, and be prepared to avow my

faith before the world, even as my father did. Father!"
the word came from his lips like a cry, " how I need thee.
What would I not give to see thy face and hear thy
speech — so gentle, yet so steadfast! Almighty God,
breathe his spirit into mine! Thou who art my Father,
too, the Creator and Father of the world, Father of
Jesus Christ ——" He stopped, as if struck by some
sudden thought, and stood still.

"'Give up all, and follow Me,' saith the Lord. The
young man would not. I have naught to give. Yet
were I to declare myself as one who renounced my
father's faith I might gain much — perchance everything,
or near everything, that could make life worth the living.
And if I have doubts, why — but no," he drew a long,
sharp breath between his teeth, "I have no doubts. The
light hath come to me at last. I believe, I know. God,
my father, Christ, my brother!"

He doffed his hat, and a heavy drop of rain splashed
upon his forehead, while from the distance came the
rumbling of thunder.

"An omen!" he exclaimed. "I accept it, Lord, for
weal or woe. Come storm, come stress, the sorrow of
friends, the contempt of all, I fear it not, for I know
myself. Father, dearest, canst hear me, wherever thou
mayest be? I am thine now, of thy blood, of thy faith,
for ever and for ever. Amen, amen."

He replaced his hat, and with carriage erect and head
thrown proudly back, he returned to the house. As he
was about to touch the door it was opened, and Rachel
stood before him. He started as if he had seen a ghost,
while Rachel, her mind full of kindly thoughts, smiled
pleasantly upon him.

"This is well met," she said, "I was searching for you,
and feared you were in the town. Madam Cromwell
hath sent me. She requests you to come to her at once,
wishing much to speak to you."

Ralph bowed formally. "I will attend her bidding, madam."

Rachel looked surprised at the austerity of his manner. "'Tis to offer you her good wishes on your birthday, sir."

Ralph started, and the colour rushed into his face. "That is truly kind of her and of you, Mistress Rachel."

They were in the passage leading to the staircase, a narrow passage. Rachel was smiling again, and her eyes were brighter than usual, and very near to his.

"I was well pleased to do so," she said cordially. "We have not met much of late, and to-morrow you leave us. Now let us not delay."

She went on before him, and Ralph followed, watching as one in a dream her dainty, graceful movements, and feeling a sudden sense of happiness, rest, and peace. He did not, however, notice that the dress which Rachel wore, though a sober grey, was of silk, the broad, white collar above it edged with lace; nor, if he had seen it, would he have conceived it possible that they had been donned in his honour, and that Rachel had spent at least five minutes more than was at all necessary before her looking-glass. Madam Cromwell knew it — that is, about the dress — and Rachel knew that she knew it. The girl had no secrets from her dearest friend, and felt no shame in acknowledging to her the warmth of her regard and friendship for Master Dangerfield, the frankness of which was a proof to Madam Cromwell of the lack of anything more serious.

The old lady fully shared Rachel's feelings, and the girl knew that whatever reserve Madam Cromwell thought it prudent to show toward Ralph her heart melted at sight of him. To both he was the trusty family friend, and in Cromwell's absence the man to whom they looked for protection. They knew nothing of his former life at college or abroad, and they did not care to know; they watched, they saw, and judged him for themselves.

Thrice blessed is the man who has such confidence from pure and strong-souled women. Calumny may do its worst, yet through storm and shine and every change of fortune their regard will last unto the end. Such confidence as this had been given to Ralph by these two, and as he mounted the stair to Madam Cromwell's room and heard her cheery voice, and saw Rachel at the door with a smile of brightest, sweetest welcome on her face, he dimly realised it, and after one leap of joy his heart fell faint and chill.

"My God!" he thought, "she knoweth nothing, suspecteth nothing after all, and I must tell her to-night. It is hard, bitter hard; at the least I might have been her friend."

CHAPTER XVII

"WELCOME, and many happy returns of thy birthday," cried the old lady as Ralph entered. "Now sit ye. Rachel, bring forth the confections and cakes thou hast been so busy upon. We must have all in readiness against the coming of thy guardian and his lieutenant.

"This last evening, before you all set forth," she continued to Ralph, "I petitioned my son to spend an hour here before prayers. I wished also to see thee. That surprises ye!"

Madam Cromwell said the last words in her most abrupt tones.

Ralph could not help smiling. "Such a thought was indeed in my mind, madam."

"And why, then?"

He flushed a little, but met the keen glance she gave him. "I believed my visits were become too frequent."

"I did not tell ye that."

His lips tightened. "That was not needful. I saw it was so, and intruded not again."

Madam Cromwell laughed pleasantly. "Young sir, thou'rt thy grandfather to the life. How well I can remember —'twas not long before he went aboard the ship which carried him to his death — that he said those words in that very tone. It was his pride — all pride and vanity — yet it became him, and were I as young now as then perchance I'd say the same of thee. But I am an old, old woman, and should indeed know better than to chatter thus; the sea covers him, and the earth will soon cover me. Nay, thou canst never come too often, nor outstay thy welcome; yet I had reasons for not desiring thy visits. I will be so far plain with thee, boy. Let that be forgot. When thou goest away to the war — to thy death, or maybe to victory and honour — I would thou shouldst know I am greatly interested in thee. I am on the brink of the grave; thou a youth, and, I trust, of a pious mind, filled with true religion; yet my prayers may avail thee. They will be thine — aye, and the prayers of all this family; forget not that. We do not express our feelings freely in this house, but we have warm hearts. This is thy proper home. Believe me, my dear, we love thee very well."

It was very seldom that Madam Cromwell spoke with such emotion. Ralph was touched, and rose impulsively to kiss her hand. As he did so he met Rachel's eyes full of sympathy and feeling, and something in their expression quickened the resolve he had made when he saw her at the garden-door.

"I am grateful," he said in a low voice, squaring his shoulders and sighing as he spoke; "in truth far more than grateful. Your words, dear madam, make me resolve most earnestly to live even as the grandson of one honoured by your friendship, and as my father's son, should live; and with God's help I will do it. But I cannot ever make this house my home. Nay, for aught I know, after to-night its doors will be closed against me, or opened coldly to the cornet of the troop. I will give the reason. It is a simple one. I am a Socinian, so-called. My father's faith is mine. Though I can neither write nor preach, having no gift of words, what he held to be the truth I hold and ever will — I crave your pardon."

Madam Cromwell had interrupted him with a sharp question. She repeated it. "How long since thy conversion, if I be not too curious?" Her voice was cold and hard.

"My mind hath been exercised some years. I came

to full knowledge and conviction touching my belief to-night."

"Then I have hope," she rejoined more cheerfully, watching him from under her eyelids, "a day may soon come when thy present conceptions will wither and die, and thy nature recover health. Thou'rt young, Ralph, very young."

"I am a man," he answered quietly; "I have lived through much, and thought a deal. Madam, my faith will never alter."

"Then God help thee!" she cried. "None else can, here or hereafter. Thou hast arrayed the world against thee. Puritan and malignant alike will cry shame upon thine unbelief; all will cast out one who denies the Godhead of Christ. My son alone, for the sake of the love he bore thy father and thy usefulness as a soldier, will keep his hand in thine. I beseech thee, think and pause while there is yet time. I wish thee so well, that I would take any means to hold thee back; yet what are my words to thee? Rachel," turning in her agitation to the girl, "speak thou to him. I mean it. Thou hast more power than I — the power of youth and womanhood. He *must not* cast himself away."

Her voice rose almost to a shriek, and her face was white. Rachel bent over her and kissed her forehead.

"Dearest granny, what can I say or do? Sir, you hear her words. Must you so soon forsake your friends and — and their religion? Could you not seek counsel from some godly minister, who might dissipate your doubts? 'Twill be so sad, so terrible for you. Is there no hope?"

"Indeed, I trust not." He had drawn back a step, and now spoke with a proud dignity they had never seen before.

"Madam, you mistake the matter; I have found, not forsook, religion. I have no doubts. My faith is as sacred and dear to me as yours to you."

"Nay, I believe that," Rachel cried hastily, "I do, indeed. I meant not to insult your — what you believe; that would be my last thought. I only meant that — that there is but one religion in the world to me, and it was grievous to think a friend should depart from it."

"And if he hath done, if his mind and soul be set another way," Ralph cried with sudden energy, "doth he cease to be your friend? Cover not your real feelings, I pray you, with soft words. I would know naught but the truth, however bitter, from your lips to-night. We have worked together, you have called me friend. Is that friendship killed by this difference in our faiths? I know what others think," looking at Madam Cromwell, who was listening with strained attention, glancing from one face to the other with gleaming eyes; "but you — tell me your mind."

He stood with his back to the door, and, in his excitement, did not hear it open, and until he saw Rachel glance behind him was unconscious that Cromwell and Capell had entered while he was speaking. Even then he did not move or take his eyes from Rachel's face. Nor was she backward in her answer, and her eyes met his unwaveringly.

"I hold your friendship in too much honour, sir. God keep you always; I can only wish you well."

"Amen — amen to that," said Cromwell, now coming forward and taking her hand. "So do we all. Mother, we be come at last, late I know, but there was much to do. Now all is finished, and we are free to take our rest until break of day to-morrow. Now, Master Cornet, prithee put off thy black humours. Capell, this man is the most sensitive of fellows; see to it in your dealings with him. A look askance, a hasty word of doubtful meaning, and he will draw upon thee. These cakes thy handiwork, Rachel? Faith, girl, they do thee credit. I see my wife hath taught thee. And that reminds me, mother, she sent her duty, but being indifferent well was

fain to be excused to-night. Bridget and Betty are upon
their way. Here they come," as the door opened. " I
knew they'd not leave us long in peace. Now that we
are all assembled we might sing a psalm in parts.
Choose one for us, mother. Rachel and Master Ralph,
with that high voice of his, will lead us. Betsy, run for
the music-scrolls; they are in my library. Then join thy
sweet pipe to my untuneful one. Truth! we'll make
the old house ring with our psalmody."

He moved briskly about the room as he talked, gathering chairs into a semicircle opposite Madam Cromwell's,
and when Betty returned with some music-sheets he
handed them to one and another, and called upon Rachel
to begin with a verse alone. There were not enough
sheets to go round, and Ralph and Capell both made a
movement to share theirs with Rachel. Capell was nearest, but, thanking him, she took Ralph's. A very little
thing it was, yet never forgotten by the men. Then
Rachel sang, and her voice, pure and fresh as a bird's,
filled the room. The rest chimed in at the second verse,
Betty's shrill soprano and Cromwell's harsh bass making
a quaint discord; while Madam Cromwell, with her Bible
before her, watched Ralph's dark face and Rachel's fair
one bent over the same scroll, and sighed. They sang
the ninety-fourth psalm, a favourite of Cromwell's,
beginning with the words, " O God, to whom vengeance
belongeth, show Thyself. Lift up Thyself, Thou judge
of the earth; render a reward to the proud." The last
verse of all he made them sing twice, his voice rising
above the rest, Capell droning a grim accompaniment.
"And He shall bring upon them their own iniquity, and
shall cut them off in their own wickedness; yea, the
Lord our God shall cut them off."

When the singing was over refreshments were handed
round by the girls, and Cromwell, seating himself by
Ralph, told him in an undertone the latest news from
the army and the Parliament. He had often done this

before; but to-night there was more cordiality in his tone than usual. He made a timely reference to approval expressed in high quarters of a new system of cavalry drill which Ralph had introduced into the troop, and before their talk was over Ralph's gloomiest thoughts and forebodings had vanished. The struggle that was coming, and enthusiasm for the public weal and the practical problems before them, filled his mind and absorbed his thoughts, while behind it all, warming his heart and comforting him inexpressibly, were Rachel's words. Let the world do its worst; he had one friend.

After prayers Cromwell went again to his mother's room. He found her reading her Bible.

"Tell me, mother," he said, closing the door carefully, "what hath the youth said? Pish! he is for ever flaunting his heresy in some godly face. First, at Hepworth for speaking harshly of his father, now before this Capell. The first a fanatic, the second a — h'm! ——" Cromwell finished his sentence with a grimace. "No," as his mother looked up questioningly, "I say not what he may be, for I do not know. He is a soldier and a good one, that is certain. Moreover he gave up the commission of a captain to serve as my lieutenant. But what of Ralph?"

Madam Cromwell repeated his words from memory, adding with some emphasis, "But I do not despair. He is neither irreverent nor light-minded. One day the scales will fall from his eyes. He will stand aghast at his own blasphemy and repent."

Cromwell shook his head. "Tush! not he. I say he will not, dear mother. It is in his blood. I have foreseen this since he came first. You rate not high enough the strength of a young man's will. Dost forget what you said yourself about him were he to fall in love? His mind is very set. He will never come to me, and were I to attack him his answers would be sharp and heavy as a broadsword stroke. Nay, take him as he is. As the maiden said, God keep him always. We must leave the issue in His hands. Beshrew me, mother, but our little girl is of high courage. Not many would so address a youth in our presence. Yet she did it, and without the quiver of an eyelid. Pity she be not a man, she should be my lieutenant before them all."

"I pray nightly, son, that your Oliver may win her love."

At these words Cromwell, who had been falling into a thoughtful and dreamy mood, looked round, and a curious smile passed over his face.

"Your prayers, mother, will never go unanswered. And yet I have heard ye say that words spoken to the Almighty should come from the heart. Is it your dearest wish that Oliver should take Rachel to wife? He is your grandson, but you love one better than he."

"Sayst so, son," the old lady replied, looking back at him very keenly; "who could it be then?"

"Ralph, the heretic," Cromwell rejoined in his curtest tone, "who minds ye of your youth."

Madam Cromwell smiled a little. "Thy penetration, son, would pierce a shield of triple brass. But turn thine eyes toward thyself before thou blamest me. Lay thy hand upon thy Bible and then say ——"

But Cromwell stopped her by a gesture, and his face was stern. "Nay, that I will not. I have not blamed you — God is my witness! But was I not right to take my oath with Hepworth? God help our lad! He hath put himself to-night beyond a chance of happiness, even as by the same breath he hath awakened her regard. Truly, the heart of woman is unfathomable. Well, we march to-morrow. They shall never meet again as heretofore."

He stooped to kiss his mother's hand. She drew his face down and embraced him, and he felt that her cheeks were wet with tears.

"I cannot gainsay thee, Oliver," she said brokenly.

" God's will be done. Her soul, at all costs, must preserve its purity. They must not be united unless his
faith returns. But my heart is sore; and thine, I see full
well, be sorer still. Fear not that I shall vex thee by
a word. Thou'rt right as always. The Lord be with
thee, dearest son."

In another part of the house Lieutenant Capell was
writing a letter, covering sheet after sheet with a small
neat hand. It was addressed to Isaac Hepworth, and
began with a brief account of his recent movements,
present work and position. Then followed these words,
more interesting to his correspondent than all that had
gone before: —

" According to your wishes I have kept strict watch upon
both man and maid. Suspicions implanted at our first acquaintance have been daily growing upon me. To-night all have been
confirmed. Indeed I would suggest that when next you hear
our troop is quartered in this town it should suit your con-
venience to journey hither yourself. This evening he declared
before us all that he was a Socinian even as his father had been.
But there was more than this; he claimed her friendship, which
she gave unto him in a manner that might mean much more.
Further and lastly, her guardian with emphasis and meaning
said Amen to all she spake. Truly, when I say that none here
are to be trusted, and that as concerning true religion I feel as
a man among vipers, you will understand how grave be the
condition of affairs. The best news is that by dawn we shall be
on the march. The steel of a malignant may relieve your anxieties. If we all return, beware!

" I rest, your humblest servitor,
' GEOFFREY CAPELL."

CHAPTER XVIII

CROMWELL'S troop joined the Parliamentary army under Lord Essex at Stratford, on October 18th. The rumour ran that the king was on the march for Oxford or London, and that Lord Essex was to intercept him and give battle as soon as possible.

It was late in the afternoon when they arrived. The country round about was overrun with men and horses as with a plague of locusts. The farms and gentlemen's houses were full of officers; in the cottages, under hedge-rows and haystacks, in copses and woods were scattered the soldiers, taking such shelter as they could find. The march was over for the day. The infantry were cooking their supper; the cavalry, who had arrived first, were strolling about singly and in groups. None of the men wore uniform. Here were a regiment of pikemen with their weapons, sixteen feet long, of ash tipped with steel, stacked together like poles in a hop-field. These stalwart countrymen were dressed in brown leathern jerkins and hose, stout walking shoes, and grey worsted stockings, and were resting on the banks of a stream, examining tender toes and blistered heels after their march. Near them were two regiments of musketeers. Their dress was much the same as the pikemen, though many had a broad leathern lappet on the left shoulder to support their heavy muskets. A very weary set were these musketeers. Their matchlocks, heavy pieces of metal, had, before firing, to be placed upon the ground in iron rests, and were discharged by means of pieces of tarred rope, which were set alight before the men went into action and kept alight until the battle was over; and these rests, ropes, and matchlocks had to be carried wherever the soldier marched. On the right of the musketeers was a squadron of horse, the animals staked out on grass and furnished with a due allowance of corn. Their riders were clothed in long, loosely-fitting coats of leather or cloth reaching to the knee, with wide skirts ornamented by enormous buttons. Their legs were encased in baggy overalls of the same material, the dress completed by huge calfskin boots, and spurs in all stages of dirt and rust. Their clothes were rudely cut, stained and creased with the marks of their armour, which had been put off to ease their weary shoulders. Upon the arrival of the Ely troop these cavalrymen crowded up to examine its equipment. Their manner of doing this was various. Many did no more than stare curiously at the new comers; while other of facetious turn of mind made comments, trenchant and mostly coarse, concerning the carriage and dress of the East Anglians. Greatly to their surprise they received no reply to their banter. Reuben Sweetlove, aware of the ways of raw troops, and jealous of the dignity and discipline of his men, had induced Cromwell to give strict order that while on duty the troop was to be deaf to anyone save its officers. Therefore, upon the word being given to halt, while Cromwell went forward to report his arrival to Lord Essex, leaving his men under command of Capell, the troopers sat their horses unmoved by the gibes and questions of the crowd, stiff and stolid as though the speakers had been magpies. At this chilling reception the men one by one fell silent and were moving away, when a man — an officer, to judge by the orange scarf across his breast — dressed in full armour, but without his helmet, swaggered forward with gestures which drew all eyes upon him.

"'Sblood, boys, what have we here? Such mummi-fied loons I never beheld — on my life, I have not! What be they — sacks filled with sand, tacked together with staves and rusty iron? God a' mercy! lend me a pike, and let me see if they run water or wind — men they cannot be."

There was a roll in the speaker's gait, he was obviously tipsy. Yet a certain authority in his tone, and the idle humour of the men, gave him an advantage, and his words were greeted with appreciative laughter. This excited him. He drew his rapier with a flourish, and addressed the trooper nearest him, who happened to be Corporal Micklejohn."

"Speak, ye little pup! Tell me who and what thou art, or by Beelzebub, as the malignants have it, my sword-point shall prick thee into piping a shrill and proper tune."

It was a critical moment. Jem's gorge rose at the insult, and Ralph saw his hand stealthily seek the hilt of his heavy broadsword. In another instant blood would be spilt. Ralph glanced at Capell, but he looked on indifferently. The stranger, with a jeering laugh, made a mock pass at the corporal, whose eyes flashed fire. Ralph could endure no more, and, setting spurs to his horse, rode in between them.

"How now, sir! Keep your distance from my men, and put that blade away. Were you not an officer you should be well trounced for this. Draw off, and quickly! Corporal, be you quiet."

Ralph's action was so sudden, his tone so peremptory, that the man in spite of his bravado started backwards, and in his haste tripped over the scabbard of his sword, and fell sprawling on the ground. A peal of laughter greeted his discomfiture, hushed quickly however as he sprang to his feet. He was sobered by the fall, and his face was white with rage. He glared at Ralph with a haughty stare.

" Your name and rank in this troop? " he said.

" Ralph Dangerfield, Cornet. Yours, sir? "

"Pshaw!" was the contemptuous answer, "that you shall learn ere long. Thy captain's name?"

Ralph's blood boiled. "Nay, by my faith, I'll answer no more questions till I know thy name."

The stranger laughed unpleasantly, and Ralph noticed that he had a strong, clever face, heavy brows, and a pair of sinister, grey eyes which seemed familiar, though he could not remember where he had seen them before.

"By Gad, young 'un, thou'rt a froward slip of insolence. Why — Hillo! I spy a friend. Master Geoffrey Capell, what dost here, man? Serve you under him, then? 'Slife! fortune must have used you ill."

"I am lieutenant, Sir John," was the answer, spoken in a surly yet respectful tone. "'Tis to be regretted that the young man hath hasty blood, but, as you see, he knows you not."

The man showed his teeth with a mocking smile.

"Zounds, man! 'tis a riddle which of you is in authority. An' you be, prithee tell him my name and rank, and bid him beg my pardon."

Capell turned to Ralph with a slight shrug of the shoulders. "This gentleman, cornet, is Sir John Salingford, nephew to the Lord-General, and captain of a troop in his lordship's own regiment of horse. 'Twould be meet, perchance, if you explain that you spoke in ignorance of his station."

"I did, without a doubt," Ralph answered grimly. "Had I known whom I was addressing, truly my words had been more pointed. Your servant, Sir John."

A titter ran through the troop, and Micklejohn laughed aloud, but Salingford did not appear to hear it. He was looking hard at Ralph, muttering to himself: —

"Dangerfield — Dan-gerfield. Is that thy name? Faith, I recollect now where I have seen ye. Thou wert at Cambridge — a Sidney man — sworn boon companion of the rake-hell Charlton, now a captain of the Royal Guard." He gave a loud, ugly laugh. "Verily, but it

shall be my privilege to acquaint thy captain of the orna-
ment that his most godly troop of wooden churls hath
in thee. I must to my quarters. I bid ye good-bye, fair
lieutenant. If this cuckoldy braggart of thine be as rare
a hand with the dice and the women as he used to be
at college thou'lt have thy work cut out for thee. Is thy
captain of a piece?"

He laughed again, and swaggered away, with a contemptuous nod to Capell.

Ralph drew a long breath of disgust.

"Have you many such officers?" he said to the lieutenant. "Surely this one should be cashiered for a sot
and a wastrel."

"He hath sharp teeth and much influence," was the
curt reply. "Were I you I should avoid his company."

"Let him avoid mine," Ralph rejoined with curling
lip. "My sword is at his service day or night, though
'tis a pity to soil good steel."

"Brave words," sneered Capell, who was sore and
ill at ease, conscious that this incident had done him
no good with his men, angry with everyone concerned,
and particularly with Ralph. "Pity they were not
spoken in his presence. They have lost their flavour
now. Hist! here be the captain," he added in a low
tone, as Cromwell rode up, "he had better know naught
of this."

But Ralph was of a contrary opinion.

"If I have exceeded my duty," he said aloud, "let me
be punished. I will conceal nothing."

Cromwell, however, saved him the trouble of
confession.

"Hast been interfered with, lieutenant?" he said to
Capell. "I seemed to hear laughter and loud talking
hereabouts. I trust my order hath been remembered."

"There was but one offender," Capell replied with
unruffled countenance. "We dealt with him resolutely."

"One. That must have been the officer I saw without a pot, who raised his lip as I passed him. What said he?"

"The ruffle was not with me," Capell replied. "It seems that Sir John Salingford — that is his name, sir — knew your cornet formerly. The dispute arose between the two"; with which parting shaft he left Ralph to tell his own story. Cromwell listened with grave, unmoved face to a description of the encounter.

"You acted right," he said. "But mind me, friend, no duels. I know the man. An unworthy member of an ancient house. Hold thy tongue and thy temper fast. If he challenge at once acquaint me. Dost promise that?"

Ralph coloured high and bit his lip. It was a hard condition to make in those times, but with Cromwell's eye upon him he could not hesitate, and gave his word. Cromwell was pleased.

"That was worthily said," he rejoined. "We march now another half a mile. Quartermaster, preserve close discipline. There be more souls lost in camp at night than lives in day of battle."

The army marched for three days without hearing definitely of the king's forces, though it was known now that he was on his way to London. It was a slow and tiresome business. There was no organisation and no commissariat worthy of the name; and though the people of the surrounding country were favourably inclined, and brought in a fair supply of provisions, a certain amount of foraging was necessary, which added to the fatigues of the march, and rendered real discipline, even among the best regiments, very hard to maintain. Besides this, the uncertainty of the enemy's whereabouts, exaggerated reports of the equipment and strength of his forces, and a fatal hesitancy at their own headquarters, gave the Parliamentary officers much anxiety, and spread uneasiness like a disease throughout the rank and file.

The Earl of Essex was in many ways a worthy commander. A brave and conscientious man, he possessed valuable experience, was shrewd, careful, farseeing; he could be doggedly persevering also in pursuit of a purpose when he had once made up his mind, but it took him a long while to do so. The genius which at a critical moment could turn a defeat into a victory, the force and energy which could make that victory crushing and decisive, was not his. The officers knew this before a shot was fired. They knew, too, the rawness of their men, and especially the weakness of their cavalry — then the principal fighting arm — and it was with feelings of sore uncertainty and even forebodings of disaster that the thoughtful men in the army of the Parliament heard of the advance of Rupert's scouts from Banbury way, and quartered their men for the night in Kineton village.

The king was said to be but ten miles off, advancing steadily, and all knew that in the morning would be fought the first battle of the Civil War.

CHAPTER XIX

THE army of the Parliament in October, 1642, was not a model army. Discipline was lax, and *esprit de corps* scarcely existed. The troops had been hastily collected, the men were mostly without training, and their leaders had no fixed principle of action. They had, however, one feeling in common — all believed that the time had come when a determined protest must be made by force of arms against a system of government which had oppressed rich and poor alike, which defied the law of the land, narrowed religion down to slavish obedience to one arrogant sect, and rendered the lives of the majority of its subjects hardly worth the living; and so strong and widely-spread was this feeling among the average Englishman of the southern and eastern counties, that Lord Essex's army, in spite of all its faults, was a formidable body of men.

The day dawned fresh and cool on October 23rd, 1642. The air was sharp and frosty until the sun gained power; a keen wind blew over the Warwickshire vales, and breakfast was eaten with particular relish by all those who had not partaken too liberally the night before of the hospitality of the countryside. Cromwell's troopers, thanks to Sweetlove's vigilance and their own common sense, having remained sober to a man, were the first to answer the reveillée, and sunrise saw them vigourously cleaning armour, grooming horses, and putting the last polish upon spurs and bridle-chains.

It was Sunday, and the bells of Kineton Church were ringing for early service, answered in the distance by a peal from Radway, a village four miles southward, nest-

166

ling under the heights of Edge Hill. The army, however, was in no mood to attend religious services; and although their chaplains, of which every regiment, and in many cases every troop, had one, delivered discourses among them, these good men received little attention. The colonels were in council with the commander-in-chief, and every other man in the army was gazing southward and eastward across the valley below Kineton to the hills beyond, where the Royalist cavalry pickeerers had been seen the night before. The men of Cromwell's troop were soon at liberty to devote their full attention to this absorbing occupation and to speculate freely upon the probable position of the enemy. Cromwell was at headquarters, Capell was writing one of his interminable letters to London, and Ralph, as anxious as his men, attached himself to the group from whom he was likely to get the most information — Sanctify Jordan, Micklejohn, and the quartermaster. It was a sign of their confidence in him that his presence had not the least restraint upon their freedom of speech.

" Hearts, man! " Jem was saying to Sanctify; " don't give thyself the conceit that thou canst teach an old soldier his business. I see with thee some pike-points glistening in the sun on those heights to the right; but if the king's army lay there we'd see more than pikes. 'Tis a strong position; an' I say again, had my Lord Essex been advised by me he'd have advanced at dawn, swept away those straggling pickeerers, and commanded the heights himself. They will now be taken by the enemy sure, and o'erlooking us, they'll note our weakest places. Pah, what a mole the general be! Would I were in his boots a matter of some twelve hours."

" The Lord help the army then," said the quartermaster gruffly; " naught but a miracle would save it. A plague on thee, Jem, for the most feather-pated rogue that e'er wore spurs. Where's thy brain and sense run to, man? Advance to the heights, quota! Why the malignants ha' been there hours — pikes, musketeers, horsemen, and guns; snug in the dip behind the hedge, I'll wager. What they mean by letting their pikes twinkle in air for us to see the Lord knows; but there they be. Didst ever know infantry outstep cavalry? Are pikes mounted on horseback? Well, then, how could such be so close, and the rest far enough away to give us time to cross nigh two leagues of rough ground and scale the cliffs? Woof! get thee to bed again, thou muddlehead."

"Sooth, crack thy joke, then, comrade!" muttered the corporal, looking decidedly crestfallen. "I'll acknowledge I may have blundered. I'm but a trooper, and know naught of your lead-footed infantry-men. Give me a few squadrons of horse and I'd ——"

"Harry every hen-roost in four counties!" growled Sweetlove. "Out upon thee, scatter-brain! Now hold thy tongue and listen to me, who was soldiering over in Deutschland afore thou wert out of petticoats. When I've done make contradiction, an' you please. Younkers, mine eyes have been upon those heights and over every knoll and rise and fall o' the land since daybreak, and the plan of the battle that's to be is clear to me as sunlight at noon — not the outcome of it, mind. Nay, that is a different story. Many's the army put into the field wi'out a crease in its battalia-line, wi' every regiment in place, and every place the best, and yet when the scuffle comes 'tis beaten to dirt e'en by such gabble-tongues as our corporal. The general whom I'd lay my life upon must be one who sees straightest when his flank is turned, and, spying the enemy's weak place, fasteneth upon it, and strikes time and again. I doubt if we'll find that commander in our godly army yet. But he will come, and they over yonder may be no better furnished. Friends, pass your eyes along the ridge slowly, starting at the right — their left flank, can't ye see summat besides pikes? Chut! there's cavalry!

Look how the sun catches their breasts and plumes! Cuirassiers, i' faith! And there, further along, in and out 'tween those trees, come more helmets — footmen, musketeers, belike. Ah! and what is that o'er their heads?"

"A colonel's pennant," the corporal struck in confidently, glad of the chance of a word. "Truly, a gay bit of bunting, something larger than our own."

"Pennant — thou calf!" roared Sweetlove, with a loud guffaw. "Donner an' Blitzen, it is the Royal Standard! Colonel, sayest thou? The king himself is there. Then those men we see to the right and left must be the Royal Guard — Lindsey's red-coats, as the little spy we caught called them. 'Twill be the centre of the position, that's sure. Now, can ye see aught further to the left? My eyes are old. Ye cannot? There's more bush and timber than elsewhere. That may be the reason. But 'tis there somewhere that their right wing bides. Well, there they be. And now, 'tis we go up or they come down. God grant my lord yields not to any hot-bloods. On this plain we should make brave work of it."

The old man rubbed his hands and chuckled, and almost for the first time since Ralph had first known him his face relaxed into a genuine smile of pleasure and cheerful anticipation.

"There, hear ye that?" he cried, as the long blast of a trumpet came from the rear, and a number of horsemen were to be seen riding away from the house where Lord Essex and his staff were quartered. "The council's at an end. 'Tis all resolved upon, and we'll be in battalia 'fore the sun's at the meridian. The godly ministers will have to end their exhortations for a space. And here's our captain."

Cromwell was approaching at a leisurely trot, far too leisurely for his horse, which was excited by the bustle around him, and was exceedingly fresh. But his rider

was one who controlled on principle all inclination to
hasty movement until the moment had come for action.
In reality Cromwell was as nervous as the youngest man
in the army. It was his first battle. How would his
men behave? What words should he say to them beforehand? Such questions, and others born of the warnings
of comrades of experience, oppressed Cromwell's mind
sorely at this moment. But not a trace of this was upon
his face, and his faculties of observation were as alert as
usual. He noticed, and remembered, that while Sweetlove, in his excitement, had one hand upon Ralph's
shoulder while he indicated with the other the position
of the enemy, now clearly visible, and the Corporal and
Trooper Jordan stood by listening with all their ears,
Capell held himself gloomily aloof.

"To your posts, men," Cromwell said as he rode up.
" The army takes position two miles in advance of Kineton village, our regiment will be upon the right centre.
Quartermaster, put the troop in order with what speed
you may. Capell and Dangerfield, when you are
mounted advance a pace with me upon the plain."

They found him alone, moodily observing the slowly
increasing numbers on the heights.

" It will be a bitter, bloody business," he said, not
looking at them, and Ralph noticed that his face was
rigidly set. " Hundreds, nay thousands, will rush into
eternity to meet their God. May He deal mercifully
by us, miserable sinners as we are."

" Amen," muttered Capell fervently. Ralph said
nothing, and they saw him smile.

" How now? " Cromwell exclaimed in a tone of deep
anger. " Wouldst mock at death and hell? Is that thy
religion? "

" I mock at naught, sir."

" Why smile, then? "

" I was thinking that for me death would be a blessed
thing."

Cromwell frowned.

"Art so confident of God's mercy? Hast been sin-less? Nay, thy presumption is beyond all sense and reason." Ralph made a motion of dissent, but Crom-well would not listen to him. "Verily the curse of thy unbelief is manifest indeed. Pray to the Almighty with thy whole heart, that He may chasten thy wicked pride and impious imaginings before thou art brought to His judgment seat; or thy miserable soul, unwashed by the blood of Christ, naked and without grace, will be dragged down by devils to the pit, and endure for ever the tor-tures of hell-fire."

He paused, for his quick ear had caught the sound of horses' hoofs. "Sweetlove hath been prompt," he said in his natural voice, turning in his saddle as he spoke; "the men are in readiness. We shall be the first at the general's quarters. Come!"

He wheeled and put spurs to his horse. His eye was bright, his face calm again. The bitter mood had passed.

The army gathered fast upon the plain. All around Kineton, and down the gentle slope that sweeps unin-terruptedly to the foot of Edge Hill Heights, marched the regiments in column, deploying in line of battle two miles beyond the village, there to wait the advance of the king — if he chose to advance. The country was open, almost without cover, rough, waste, bottom land, somewhat sodgy with recent autumn rains, otherwise ideal ground for cavalry.

Lord Essex's regiment, to its great disgust, was placed in reserve, but standing on slightly higher ground than the rest, was able to obtain a complete view of the army as it swept into position, line by line, column by col-umn — fourteen thousand men.

Ralph and the quartermaster were again standing close together.

"A brave sight, Reuben. There will be few creases in our battalia line."

"Perchance not," the old man answered slowly, "if they rest where I have placed them in my eye. We have the downward slope to favour us — such as it be — and we are far enough from the heights yonder to see their plan of battle as they descend. Ha! look ye, look ye! My lord well knows his business after all. See, at our right flank there, those musketeers deploying behind that hedge! I have watched the place this hour, and wondered if 'twould be made any use of. Mark it well. It runs two hundred yards from Kineton way towards the heights, a stiff-set piece of cover — the only bit there is on all the plain. Then, see you, our horse are forming up at the Kineton end of it, three regiments or more — Meldrum's, Stapleton's, and Balfour's — and behind them the heavy guns. A strong position, sure! Should it be broken, Master Cornet, then may we of the centre say our prayers an' charge — mayhap for the last time. So, now, what is to stiffen this right wing of ours —infantry? Aye, here they come — purple coats, grey coats, and brown; Colonel Fielding's these, Lord Roberts's, and Sir William Courtenay's. Woof! you clumsy rogues. Why, the musketeers hold their guns like mopsticks, and the pikes are more like to prod their comrades than bear down malignants. Well for the churls they have time to blunder in and out of rank at their own time, and not to the music of squadrons spurring down upon 'em at the charge. They'll march more daintily a twelvemonth hence, I'll warrant, if," sarcastically, "there be any left."

He grunted with a veteran's contempt as the straggling files tramped awkwardly along, some treading upon the heels of those in front in their excitement, others moving heavily and mechanically with a lurch in their walk and a hunching of broad shoulders which sug-

gested more familiarity with a plough tail than a gun.
But, as Reuben said, there was plenty of time.

It was ten o'clock, the sun had risen high, and the air
was now pleasantly warm, and still no movement was
to be seen upon the heights. The royal army seemed
waiting, like a hawk poised in mid-air, uncertain
whether to pounce or to fly away. At length, on the
plain, the Parliamentary infantry rolled themselves into
position, the pikemen in the centre, flanked by the musketeers; the latter disposed in ten long ranks, so that the
front ranks after firing might retire and reload. To the
left of these was the centre of the Parliamentary army,
composed of Lord Essex's regiment of horse, another
under Colonel Ballard, a regiment of infantry commanded by Lord Brooke, and the train-bands of London.

"The weakest spot we show," Sweetlove muttered,
frowning, "be our left wing. All the way from that
knoll which hides the enemy's right there's naught to
stay him or break his charge — not so much as one tree
or bush as cover for our foot. And what men have we
to withstand his encounter? In numbers plenty, but
bad fighting stuff. Our centre and reserve be true and
tough; the London men are stiff-made rogues and will
stand some pushing, while these troopers of ours have
the best mounts in the army. But to the left they are a
dreaping lot, to my fancy, and if the attack be brisk 'twill
snaffle 'em all, horse and foot alike. Wharton's lads are
slow, Mandeville's ill-mounted, Cholmley's weak-hearted
— 'twas these swilled most liquor yestere'en. I'll wager
their pates under this sun feel as if strung with whip-
cord, and their tongues cleave to their mouths with
thirst. Never expect men in such a plight to stay. But
eh, Himmel! The enemy is coming on; the hills are
alive. They fight, then, on the plain. Give praise unto
the Lord!"

He spoke in full, sonorous tones. Half the regiment
heard him, and the troop smiled to a man.

"Hear that?" Micklejohn whispered to Sanctify. "'Slid! not a mite of doubt now touching the fighting. Old Reuben's never nigh praying till he smells blood."

Then he fell silent, watching eagerly with all the rest the advance of the army of the king.

From a brown-roofed hostelry on the brow of the ridge far to the right —" The Sun Rising "— and along the heights for three miles eastward, there came into view dark columns of men and horses, winding slowly down the hill. There were pikemen and musketeers in sober brown and grey; carabineers and dragoons in caps and breastplates of plain steel; and in places a flash of light and colour — a regiment of cuirassiers, the pick of the royal cavalry, gay with their plumed helmets and their plated armour. At first it seemed like the pouring forth of a confused mass — horse and foot intermingled without order or method; but presently, as the army began to deploy upon the plain below, its formation became easily distinguishable.

On the left wing, facing the Parliament right, were cavalry to the number of three thousand, supported by a small body of pikemen. From the centre came column after column of infantry, the extreme flank stretching some distance toward the thickly-wooded knoll mentioned by Sweetlove as the probable shelter of the right wing. Where was this right wing? Of what did it consist? These questions were in the minds of all the Parliamentary soldiers, but none could answer them. Now and then those with the keenest eyesight saw the flash of a helmet, or caught a glimpse of a few horsemen riding rapidly to and fro — enough to make them suspect that a considerable body of men, probably cavalry, was concealed behind the hill, but nothing more. And as the mysterious is always alarming, so greater anxiety was felt by many about this right wing than about all the rest of the Royalist army. By degrees, however, the attention of the soldiers became centred upon a small body of cavalry near Radway village, in the midst of which the great flag waved — the standard of the king. As Sweetlove had said, it was in the centre of the force, and before it, marching with a compactness and speed superior to all the rest, was a regiment of red-coated soldiers, the pick of the army, Lord Lindsey's Royal Guards. The chief interest of both forces clung to the standard. Wherever it might be there would come the hardest fighting. The Parliament men watched it descending the hill, and saw 'it planted on the plain near the foot of the heights, while the king and his staff rode forward hither and thither among the steadily advancing lines of men. About two hours after noon, when the army had completed its formation in line of battle, the standard was taken up and carried forward to the centre, just behind the Royal Guards, and exactly opposite Lord Essex's own regiment. A brave show they made, those red-coated men, and Ralph wondered sadly where Lord Charlton stood, and sighed at the hard fate which seemed bent upon casting them at one another's throats.

And now the hearts of men began to beat, the eyes of the fighters glistened, and the cheeks of the cowards blanched. At any moment the battle might begin. On either side officers rode up and down the ranks exhorting their men to do their duty. King Charles, dressed completely in armour, with a cloak of black velvet, his head covered by a plain steel cap, rode down his lines in person, and the cry, " God save the king!" which greeted him was heard for many miles. On the Parliament side the ministers prayed aloud to God, the men standing with bare heads, and answering with a long, fierce " Amen."

Cromwell addressed his troop himself. His face was all aglow, not a trace of anxiety or bitterness left upon it.

" Be firm, my lads, and list always to the word of command. Each think of his comrades, and fight not for himself. Our cause is God's. Be worthy of His blessing, and flinch not. Above all, hold ye together."

A cloud of smoke from the right and a dull roar. A gun had been fired from the Parliamentary centre, another and another, replied to by the Royalist artillery. The battle had begun. Now a movement on the enemy's left. The cuirassiers were advancing to the charge against Meldrum's and Fielding's horse and their musketeers behind the hedge. Both armies watched the encounter with bated breath. On they came, the gallant cavaliers, yet Meldrum and Fielding do not stir to meet them, though their horses paw the ground and the troopers draw their swords. Puff! the match-locks from behind the hedge belch fire and smoke, and right athwart the ranks of charging men strike the heavy bullets. The men fall in all directions, their horses stampede against their companions, troop after troop is thrown into confusion. And now into them pell-mell the Parliamentary troopers charge. The struggle is fierce and furious, and for a time doubtful. Behind the Royalist cuirassiers are pikemen, and on their right flank a regiment of musketeers, who return the fire of those behind the hedge. But the odds are against the king. The Parliament men gain ground. Their enemies give way — a few yards first, then many; and then the pikes and musketeers have as much as they can do to cover their retreat. Yet so manfully do they fight, that there is no rout, only a slowly-retreating, fiercely-struggling band re-forming behind a second line of infantry. The onslaught of the Parliamentarians is checked, and swinging round they retire to their former post, cheering and shouting in the first flush of victory. But their comrades in the centre hardly shared their complacency. The thoughts in their minds were expressed by Ralph to Sweetlove.

" Good heavens! what be we doing? Another charge well home, with a fresh regiment to add the weight, and that left wing of theirs would go. A shame, a burning shame, I say, to miss so fair an opportunity. Their colonels should be shot."

"What were my words?" Sweetlove growled. " 'Tis not in us yet. I tell ye, we tire of the swing of sword in half an hour. Stay, now, what have we here to our left? God Almighty! Here be their right wing at last. See them advancing from behind the knoll. Ha! a fine deployment and now for the charge. Eh, but they are rare gallants! Sure, they must be the bloods I've heard of under Rupert of Bohemia. Would to God they fronted us! Ramsay's horse will never stand such an encounter."

He paused with parted lips, and with every man in the Parliamentary centre held his breath.

Cuirassiers these. Mounted on the best of blooded horses, magnificently armed, expert swordsmen, and perfect riders — the proudest gentlemen of Europe and the bravest, confident even to contempt, laughing as they charged. Down they swept like a whirlwind upon the massed regiments of horse and foot. A few feeble shouts answered their fierce battle-cry, and then!

"We break — we run!" yelled Sweetlove. "Not a struggle made or stand attempted. God curse the cowardly curs! Our horse are flying right and left, the foot cut down like grass. A sight to make ye sick. What orders now for us?"

Steady, rigid, expectant stand the Parliamentary centre — two regiments of horse, two regiments of foot. Upon them depends the issue of the battle, and they know it well. On their right Meldrum's, Fielding's, and Balfour's horse are gathering into new battle line, flushed with victory, but a little weary. On the left the routed horse and terrified foot, crushed out of all shape, are flying into Kineton, two miles to the rear, crying that the battle is lost, Rupert's troopers hot upon their heels. In this juncture, by all military rules and precedents, the regiments which formed the Parliamentary centre, or at least the reserves, should have faced about to meet a flank attack from Rupert. At most they should have held close to their position and received there the attack now pending from Lindsey's Guards. But they did neither. Lord Essex, it may be, intended this; but the excitement of the troops, officers and men, forbade it. The long inaction, the sight of one wing failing to follow up an advantage, and the other rolled up without a blow, had acted like strong wine. "Forward upon them!" was the universal cry, followed by a shout of enthusiasm loud, deep, and earnest, as the leaders, after an instant's hesitation on the part of the commander-in-chief, galloped to the head of their regiments and gave the word "Advance!"

No more talking now; every man fell into his place and put his horse to a gentle trot. They rode in loose order; horses too unbroken, riders too clumsy to attempt the close formation of well-trained cavalry. In Cromwell's troop alone, thanks to Ralph's experience and Sweetlove's determination, the men rode in rank, eye to eye, shoulder to shoulder, and their captain, glancing back at them, felt a glow of pride. Forward for half a mile, steadily, steadily. Then the pace began to quicken, and the officers drew their swords. They could see the enemy clearly. On their left were infantry in six lines, under Sir Jacob Astley; on the right the beaten cuirassiers of Wilmot; in front the Royal Guards, and behind it the standard and the king himself.

"Forward, Lord Essex's own!" the cry rang out. "Make ready to charge!"

The moment was coming, and men settled in their saddles and tightened rein. The captains spoke their last words.

"Hold in to an hundred paces of them," Cromwell said, his face quiet and still, though dark as night; "then, as I raise my sword, in at the gallop and upon them heartily. God's with us!"

A few breathless minutes, then the captain waved his sword above his head, and his horse sprang to the gallop. " Charge! "

The spurs went home and the troop followed, guns flashing in their faces, comrades thundering in their rear. Stubbornly the redcoats met them with clubbed musket and raised pike, but they could not stay their course. Not in vain had Ralph and Sweetlove toiled to discipline the men and train their horses. These chargers were unwieldy brutes, far slower than Rupert's; but now, maddened by the spurring and the firing, they plunged forward furiously with distended eyeballs and bleeding flanks, and trod down the Royalist infantry as a hailstorm beats down corn. The guards met the shock valiantly, but the line of horsemen never wavered, trampling out of shape rank after rank — tireless, relentless, approaching nearer and ever nearer the standard in the rear.

Ralph had fought in many a battle already, and many more bloody than this was he to see in later times, but none made so deep an impression upon him as that under Edge Hill Heights. His interest was chiefly personal. His troop must be first on the foe and the last to leave, and Cromwell at all costs must be protected. So, though the captain led the charge, Ralph was at his side from the beginning, and they rode almost neck and neck. He thought they rode alone, but presently he found Capell at his elbow. The heavy face was clenched and inflexible in its passion, the sword-arm raised for the stroke. He was no laggard, then, this captain of train-bands! And now of a sudden the horse from the right wing, Balfour's and Fielding's, swept down again with a heavy flank attack upon the Royalist left, doing what they should have done two hours before. The Cavaliers gave way and fell back in confusion, and Balfour's horse, wheeling sharply, pressed hard upon the rear of the Royal Guards. This shook even their firmness, and then Essex's own, headed by Cromwell's troop, cut their lines in two. Cromwell rose in his stirrups and pointed with his sword to the left.

" At last, men; see the standard! Charge for it. Are ye ready? *Now!*"

He dug his spurs into his horse's flanks, and with Ralph and Capell on either side and the troop thundering after him, bore down upon the little knot of officers where the standard flew. The stag was at bay, and a gallant body of gentlemen had gathered round the flag. Cromwell's troop was a little ragged now, for many of the men were wounded and the horses were tiring, but their blood was up, and they were supported by the best mounted of the other regiments. Ralph found himself fighting between Capell and Sir John Salingford. He could fight, this man. He wielded his heavy sword like a feather, and once saved Ralph's life by cutting down a pikeman who had thrust at him. As for Capell, he seemed made of iron. His blows came slowly, but he never missed his mark, and when they closed in the death-struggle round the standard he ranged to the left of Cromwell, Ralph to his right, and together they kept watch upon their captain's safety.

The end was very near. For a few minutes the cavaliers held their assailants at bay by superior sword-play, but they were struck down one by one. Then a tall man in full armour sprang like a tiger at Cromwell, who was engaged with another; Ralph parried the blow, and struck him on the side of the head. He reeled; his helmet fell off, and Ralph saw that it was Charlton. The next instant Salingford thrust at his armpit, but Ralph threw his shoulder against him, and the attempt failed. Charlton saw this, and turned aside a blow he had aimed at Ralph. Then they looked into one another's eyes, and the fury of battle died away. There was a dash from the men behind, and they were crushed close together.

" Take quarter," Ralph cried, " for God's sake! "

"Nay," was the hoarse reply, "if we are beaten life is not worth the living, but I fight not with you."

He parried a blow from Capell, and then, as the crush lessened, turned about to defend Sir Edmund Verney, the standard-bearer, who was vainly struggling in the grip of Reuben Sweetlove. Ralph pressed after him. For the moment even Cromwell was forgotten. His design was perceived by Sir John Salingford.

"What," he snarled, "wouldst foil me and save him? By God then, I'll kill thee both!" and rising in his stirrups, he brought his heavy broadsword down upon Ralph's head. But as it descended a blade was thrust between, and Salingford's weapon splintered at the hilt. The next instant a hand gripped him by the neck.

"Verily, most honourable knight," a voice growled in his ear, the voice of Sanctify Jordan, "that was a fool's act, an' deserves my knife beneath thy ribs. Yet I'll spare thee. But get to the rear. At my back be men who'd take thy blood drop by drop didst thou but graze the cornet's skin."

While the words were spoken the grip tightened upon Salingford's neck and he was thrust aside with such force as nearly to dismount him. His brain was swimming, and he felt deathly sick. When he recovered he found himself far from the front, and a long, exulting cheer told him that the standard had been taken. The redcoats had been cut down almost to a man. From every side the Parliamentary troopers were spurring up, and in the centre of a wildly-excited group stood old Reuben, in his grasp the standard and his face streaming with blood, but quiet and composed, the only man among them all who kept his presence of mind. He was coolly scanning the enemy's lines to the southward.

"Captain," he said to Cromwell, "what's to do now, think ye? The battle be not over yet."

Cromwell shook his head.

"A horse for the quartermaster!" he cried sharply to

the men. "Nay, indeed it's not, old friend. We should deal with those pikes that are forming there with what speed we may. I have spoken to the colonel. I trust he will charge them."

It was the turning-point of the day. The Royalist left wing was completely broken, of the centre only five regiments of pikemen remained, while the Parliament horse was flushed with victory. They rapidly re-formed to the attack, and prepared to charge. Suddenly a trumpet sounded from the rear, and by the last gleam of the dying day, they saw Rupert's cuirassiers emerging from Kineton. They rode back to meet them. But the light vanished, the gloom of the autumn evening fell upon the plain, and Rupert, wheeling to the left, rejoined his army without striking a further blow.

CHAPTER XX

THE battle was over, and the last murmur of strife died away as the gloaming faded into darkness. Then the plain from Kineton to the heights became a mass of wandering lights as lanterns and torches were lit for the search for wounded comrades. Before midnight every cottage, farm and inn for miles round was full of wounded soldiers or hungry officers, and the inhabitants had to retire into garrets and barns to make room for their self-invited guests.

In a small farm-house, just outside Kineton, an officer sat before a roaring fire. He had taken off his boots, unbuttoned his doublet, and was smoking a long clay pipe, leaning back in a huge elbow-chair, with his feet tilted at a comfortable angle on a stool.

It was Sir John Salingford. At a table near him Capell was making swift play with knife and fork, dividing his attention between a plate of cold beef and a tankard of ale. He was booted and spurred; his hat and gloves were on the table, his cloak thrown back over his shoulder to give free play to his arms.

"A truly cursed business," Salingford remarked in a grumbling tone. "Would the rogue were one of my troop! I'd have him hanged and his pretty cornet court-martialled."

"That will be more than you can compass, Sir John, as the affair stands," Capell observed with his mouth full. "Better leave this Dangerfield alone."

"An' I do may I be d——d," was the answer. "Pish! d'ye think I can stomach his insolence? A psalm-singer like thou might, but not a gentleman. An' his captain had not spoken to my uncle Essex, who put me under strict promise to keep my sword quietly until this battle, I'd have trussed the cockerel ere now, be sure of that. Now I am free to strike, and it shall be at both of them."

Capell rose from the table and warmed his hands at the fire. "In duels, I've heard, it be not always the best man wins; he may pink thee."

"Leave that to my experience. Were it Charlton indeed! But there be another way to deal with that devil." He said the words spitefully, scowling at the wall. Capell watched him a moment, and then drew his cloak round his shoulder.

"Art going?" said Salingford, who seldom appreciated solitude.

"If my captain found me here when he supposed me to be seeing to my men's quarters it would be my last day in Cromwell's troop."

"'Slife, man, what odds? Cursed if I can tell what men see in that sour-faced country-man to look at him so! Were Essex himself to walk in at this moment he'd not move me."

"The lord-general," Capell rejoined drily, "is not my uncle. I must go."

Yet he warmed his hands again.

"There seems a great affection between this Danger-field and my Lord Charlton," he murmured.

Salingford swore loudly. "I have cause to know it. Not that I ever took much note of your cornet, he was a mere boy at college; but Charlton I knew, curse him, a tearing, gambling, fighting roysterer — and more; one who grudged others what he'd pluck by handfuls for himself. We'd a pretty quarrel. 'Slife, the man worsted me, I'll own as much to you, and now he'll rue it. Wounded, you said, and at Dangerfield's quarters, where-fore a prisoner. Good, very good! I'll so work upon mine uncle in the matter of my lord's black malignancy that he'll not release him at any ransom, but let me send him where I will; and once on his way to prison, guarded by my bully-boys ——"

He stopped to puff at his pipe, and finished his sentence with a malicious chuckle. Capell went on warming his hands.

"What was the cause of the attachment between them?"

"Satan, their best friend, only knoweth, I do not. They were never apart at college; dicing, racing, drinking, in company always. Dost love this cornet, that his name be on your lips so frequently?"

The question was asked with a sharp turn of the head. Capell raised his eyes, and the men looked at one another.

"I have known him no longer than a week. I have no cause either to love or hate. But "— he paused —" I'll be frank. One that hath been a friend to me distrusts him, and has set me to take note of his behaviour."

Salingford looked at him a moment keenly, then burst into a mocking laugh.

"Say no more, most godly brother; I'll leave that younker in thy hands. That is what thou desirest, is it not? I thought it from thy anxiety about the duel. Charlton is mine own; but the other you may deal with as you list. An' devil take me if I do not pity him! Give me for deadliest poison the hatred of a truly pious man."

"Psha!" Capell rejoined impatiently, opening the door; "an' I did hate him my way would be clear eno'; but I do not, so the way is dark, dark as night."

He strode out and walked quickly away toward the inn where Ralph Sweetlove, and the corporal had found quarters for the night, and in his ears, like an evil echo, rang Salingford's mocking laugh.

Capell was very weary, and the frosty air, for the night was very cold, cut him to the bone. A nervous reaction after the battle was upon him, and he felt deeply depressed. He had never been a cheerful person. His life had been a hard one. Even his childhood had been loveless and joyless. Like Ralph, Capell had lost his mother in babyhood, but, unlike Ralph, the father who brought him up was a hard and unsympathetic man. He meant to do his duty by the boy. He succeeded only in making him, in tender years, very miserable, latterly callous and bitter. Of Capell's later history we know the outline. Poverty had never been absent, and his friendships were but skin-deep. He was born and bred a Presbyterian, but his religion had been merely a ladder by which to climb into the favour of the elders of his father's church. He had succeeded, and when he came to London joined Isaac Hepworth's congregation from the same motive. Then came a change. In Hepworth, for the first time in his life, Capell found a man whom he could respect, and ultimately whom he grew to love, so far as it was in his nature to love any man. The minister's warmth and straightforwardness, his fiery earnestness and energy, and most of all his childlike faith in Capell's sincerity, pierced through the hard crust of the man's worldliness and reached his heart. The first result of this was that Capell's hitherto implacable distrust and hatred of ministers as a class died a natural death; next, his religious professions ceased to be a mere form and pretence; lastly, he began to have a real desire to live for something besides himself. This made him resolve to take active part in the struggle against the Crown. He was not naturally a soldier, but he had plenty of cool, steady courage, and a determined will. He trained himself thoroughly in military science, as he did in all things, and one day met Cromwell at Hepworth's house. Capell took a fancy to Cromwell, and not long afterwards asked for a lieutenancy in his troop. This again was indirectly due to Hepworth. The good man, who held no secrets from Capell, talked about his niece so much and so warmly that at length Capell was fired by a desire to see and know this maiden. He was thirty years old, an age

when life alone is doubly lonely. Why should he not
marry? he thought, and if he did marry — well, he would
like to see this girl, the dearest person on earth to Isaac
Hepworth. So, with characteristic disregard of all obsta-
cles when he had once resolved upon a thing, Capell
threw up his captaincy in the train-bands — an easy and
lucrative position — and prepared to journey down to
Ely. Before he went he had a long interview with Hepworth, who poured out his anxieties and suspicions about
Ralph, and begged Capell, as a proof of friendship, to let
nothing escape him concerning the youth's behaviour
to Rachel and her attitude towards him. The minister,
after receiving the news that Rachel had refused to be
betrothed to Oliver, had concluded at once that partiality
towards Ralph was at the bottom of it, and said so to
Capell.

As soon as the lieutenant came to know Rachel he
fell in love with her. Her quiet nature suited his own
precisely. A lively young person like Betty bewildered
and irritated him; Bridget's eager questionings and little
airs and graces bored him; but Rachel's quiet grace and
gentleness soothed his soul, and her cordiality, when she
found out his regard for her uncle, filled him with a hope
that if by some means she could be withdrawn from her
present environment he might have a chance of pressing
his suit with success. All this intensified the want of
sympathy between his nature and Ralph's, and fostered
an antagonism which deepened gradually into bitter
enmity.

Yet Capell was quite honest in his protest against Sir
John Salingford's accusation. He was persuaded that it
was a Christian duty to spare no pains to remove the
danger to Rachel's peace — nay, to her immortal soul —
which was so gravely threatened by the continued presence of this Socinian in Cromwell's troop. He would
use honest means first of all to remove him, but, come
what would, it should be done.

Among the many hundreds of wounded men on the field of battle that day, few had a narrower escape of death than Lord Charlton. He had been struck on the head, dangerously near the temple, and when Ralph, who never left him, was able to convey him from the press of dead and dying men, he found him insensible and bleeding profusely. Fortunately the first man he appealed to to help was Sweetlove, and the old quartermaster, who could refuse Ralph nothing, not only assisted him to place the Viscount in a rude litter, but found men to convey it, sending a trooper in ahead to Kineton, and by this forethought obtained decent lodgings there before the place was crowded to suffocation. Reuben, also, from his experience of wounds, was able to apply the right remedies without waiting for the overworked chirurgeon, and by the time Capell entered the inn, and was admitted to the sick room, the worst danger was past, and Charlton was asleep.

"Your friend will live, then?" Capell whispered to Ralph, eyeing with grim disapproval the signs of comfort and care which surrounded the wounded man.

"Aye," returned Ralph, glancing gratefully at the quartermaster, who was tearing up bandages for further use; "'tendance and quiet will do the rest, thanks to this skilful chirurgeon of mine."

"Tuts!" broke in Sweetlove roughly, "a mere trifle. I'd see no man bleed to death like a pig. The lieutenant, though, would say 'twere better if I had."

He stared at Capell with searching eyes, but the lieutenant shook his head.

"A life is a life," he said, "whether friend or foe. He is delivered into our hands, and should be dealt by honestly. Hast seen the captain yet, Dangerfield?"

"I am going to him now."

"Then let us walk together."

They left the house, and as soon as they were alone Capell said solemnly —

"You have done well by the cause to capture this malignant."

"I could wish he were free," Ralph answered, sighing. "Capell, this war is an accursed thing."

"Those be strange words, Sir Cornet," was the frigid rejoinder. "Accursed? How mean you?"

"This prisoner be my dearest friend. 'Deed, I would give my life for his. Yet through this war he may rot in prison, if he be not exchanged. And if that sot Salingford discover him, as I fear he must, he will die."

"He hath discovered him," Capell said shortly. "I saw him not half an hour ago."

Ralph groaned. "What did he say?"

Capell cleared his throat significantly. "He spat into the fire. Nay, you are right: my lord is doomed."

Ralph gave a short laugh. "Not so fast. He be my prisoner, not Sir John's."

"That will profit you naught. He has the ear of the Lord-General."

"So have I."

"How?"

"As an officer in his army."

"H'm! Well, if you think that will weigh against his blood relation, and a captain and a knight to boot, I have nothing more to say to you. Here are the captain's quarters."

They entered a small cottage, smoky and dark. Cromwell was sitting on a rude milking-stool munching a piece of dry bread. A jug of sour milk stood on the floor. He greeted the young men cordially, and then asked questions concerning the disposition and accommodation of the men.

"We fall back to Warwick," he said, when Capell had answered, "unless the king offer battle."

"But this will give the enemy a clear course to London," Ralph said indignantly.

"That was put forward for the Lord-General's consideration," Cromwell answered. "I could wish with you, our steps were forwards, not backwards. But we are subordinates, friend. We must abide by the judgment of our superiors, and murmur not."

He spoke with some emphasis, and nothing more was said. Shortly afterwards Ralph excused himself, and the captain and his lieutenant were left alone together.

Cromwell threw a log of wood upon the fire and pointed to another stool. "Draw nearer to the heat. An' thou canst keep awake I have a matter of some confidence to discuss with you. Is the door closed?"

Capell examined it, and then sat down to listen, the firelight playing about his burly figure and hard, quiet face.

"Know you this prisoner of our cornet's — the Viscount Charlton?"

Capell leisurely crossed his feet. "By reputation, sir, not otherwise."

"And that?"

"Bad, captain."

"Be precise, an't please you," Cromwell rejoined curtly, after waiting a minute for Capell to continue. "What is wrong with him besides his politics?"

"He is a gamester, a shameless libertine, a rake-hell Cavalier."

"Enough, I know the breed. Where did they who told you this obtain their knowledge?"

"At Cambridge, I understand. The Viscount was a student there."

"In what year?"

"I know not the date — more than twelve months since."

"Was Dangerfield his fellow-student?"

"I have learnt that they were boon companions, both by day and night."

Capell spoke in quiet, even tones, but with a peculiar distinctness that his listener noted. Cromwell bent forward slightly, and pushed the log with his foot. "I read reproach in thine eyes, friend," he said in a low musing tone. "You think I am rash to harbour such an one in my house. Believe me, I knew not this before."

Capell looked up in genuine surprise. "'Deed, sir, my mind ne'er nourished such a thought. And, mayhap, my informant was mistaken."

"You do not think so," Cromwell said. There was no answer. Cromwell sighed.

"You have a wide experience, Capell, and some wisdom of the world. I believe you are very sure upon this point. What advice have you to give me for the future? Nay, I mean my words. They are no mockery. See, then, I will bare my heart to you. This youth is beloved by my household. I have e'en a weak affection for him myself. But that, God is my witness, shall never overcome my sense of justice. I have forgiven to a point his backslidings in faith, because I believed him to live a sober and a proper life. Am I deceived? Tell me! These men have been as bosom friends this two years past. So much I knew. You have informed me of the Viscount's character. What is to be done?"

Cromwell paused, and there was a long silence. At last Capell answered brusquely, "I see but one course, sir."

At these words Cromwell, who had been gazing at the fire with listless, weary eyes, looked at him sharply. "Tell me what that should be."

"Enforce a test upon the young man and abide by its results. Refuse to aid him to exchange this Viscount. I know the man to be of lewd and vicious habits. Well, cast him into prison, and let him there remain until the war be done. If Dangerfield protest give him as the reason for your action his friend's character and disposition. Truly, if he be in earnest in his reformation, which God grant be so, then he will submit to your word. If not he deserveth not your countenance, for it will prove his sympathy with a man of bad, ungodly life."

Cromwell nodded and rose. "A wise scheme. I thank thee, man; thou hast pointed out a way from the difficulty I had not considered. Your words will bear fruit; a test there shall be. Get thee away now to thy quarters. Glance at the men as you pass; and — aye, I had forgotten — send me a man to bear a message."

"Hast any choice, sir?"

"No; yet stay. Send me the tallest of the troopers, Sanctify Jordan; he will serve my purpose best."

CHAPTER XXI

LORD CHARLTON had so far recovered the next morning as to eat a hearty breakfast, and express his obligations to Ralph and Reuben Sweetlove.

"Gad, dear boy, thou returnest good for evil to the hilt. After that dispute of ours at Sidney I'd made sure the next time we met I'd have thee by the throat, and my heart sank at the thought. And thou art a Roundhead and a rebel! Nay, then, grant me a hearing, though it be but five minutes. Your little doctor told me how you were cozened into rebellion. Faith, I'd forgive thee for it, and so would his Majesty — I'll swear he would — an' he knew the hard measure dealt in his name to your father. It was blood for blood with you. Well, blood you've had. 'Struth, I warrant you drew enough yesterday before you reached me to pay for a score of lives. Be content, Ralph, and return forthwith to thy allegiance. Your captain, say you, is a man to follow to the death. I won't dispute it, he hath a face of iron; but we've a score as good. When I get back again 'twill be to serve under the prince. Lord, how your heart would spring at sight of him. The royal blood in him! The force and fire and energy! He's a rider — I've only known one better, and that yourself — fearless as a lion, a leader in very truth, yet a brother to his men. Then he lives for his profession. He is no drinker, like Wilmot; no woman-hunter, like Goring; but a true man and a soldier. Did you set your eyes upon his face, Cromwell's would fade like a ghost. For the rest, pah! How canst breathe among these snuffling crop-ears? — men of such 'religion,' forsooth, that the cur Salingford, one of the

most infernal coistrils and rakes that I know, is captain
of a troop; and I'll swear that even your Cromwell stands
cap in hand before my Lord Essex's nephew. Nay, come
out of it all, for the Lord's sake. Get on thy nag this
night, let me hang to his tail, and before morning trot
into a camp of honest men and cast in your lot with the
king." He seized Ralph's hand, his face aglow with
earnest feeling. " Promise me," he said in a whisper,
" for there be steps outside. Swear."

Ralph pressed the strong fingers. " I swear," he said
with a smile, " by God Almighty, old friend, that the day
I break my faith to Cromwell you may take me to the
nearest tree and hang me. Open! "

It was Sanctify Jordan. He came stiffly to attention,
and saluted with a wooden, expressionless face, his helmet touching the ceiling.

" By order of the captain, sir, I be to enquire touching
the health of your prisoner. Commands have been laid
upon all with prisoners in a condition of body fit for
removal to convey them to headquarters by twelve of the
clock this day."

" My Lord Charlton is too sick to be moved," Ralph
answered quickly. " Bear that message to the captain."

The trooper saluted again and withdrew. He was
joined outside by Micklejohn.

" Is he going? " he said anxiously.

" Doubtless."

" Then the devil is looking after his own. Salingford
hath been prowling around headquarters all morning
I've been told by one of his men that he will do my lord
the worst mischief he can think upon once he gets him
there."

Sanctify said nothing, but when he caught the corporal's eye he winked.

" Hearts! " exclaimed the little man with a grin. " Be
there something afoot, then? 'Slid! but I feared you was
on his side, since you spent the night at Noll's quarters.

Do my lord lie here, then? Drat it, comrade, canst not trust me?"

"I obey orders, Sir Corporal," the other answered solemnly, "and those be strict. Nevertheless, I would beg of you, an your labours permit of it, to keep within hail of the house that lieth behind us. Touching thy question, *ask the cornet*. Fare thee well." And he strode away at a pace the corporal could not keep up with.

"I' fackins, old maypole," grumbled the little man, rubbing his nose, "thy captain's favour maketh thee stomach-proud, methinks. Have a care, then; I may find means to outwit you all. I care not for the malignant lord, but if by serving him I could chagrin Sir John! He called me 'pup'; he threatened me! Zounds, but to think of it makes my ears tingle! Give me but the opportunity, an' I'll make him wish he'd cut his ugly tongue out ere he mocked at me."

Meanwhile, within the house, Ralph and Charlton were in close consultation.

"It must be before the rise of moon, I tell you," Ralph was saying. "Art strong enough for the attempt?"

"If I choose to make it."

"Then will I find the man."

"Nay, 'tis madness. Let me be."

"To await Salingford's pleasure? Not I."

"You betray your captain. He will be held responsible."

"Pish! Trust me to prevent it."

"But that would be worst of all. This devil hates you, too."

"A fig for him!" Ralph rejoined. "Come, there be no other way but this. If you escape not, his malice will end you. My mind is made up. If any come to look at you to-day appear to be near dying; then, when it is dark, put on this cloak of mine, my armlet and hat. I know a man who will not betray us, and will guide you beyond the lines. Will your head stand it? That's the rub."

Charlton laughed.

"Pooh! where 'tis life or death you may depend upon my head, drunk or sober. I'll try it now. Hands off! I can walk alone!"

He swung himself out of bed, stood a moment until the first dizziness had passed, then quietly walked across the room. At the end he reeled, but still refusing aid, rested against the wall.

"A space for breathing, then back again," he said cheerily. "Gad, Ralph, put me on a horse, and I'd be good for a score of miles. Oh, a devil!"

There were steps outside the door, and Cromwell came in. Charlton fell on the floor with a groan.

"Vain boaster that thou art," Ralph exclaimed, his face many times redder than usual, "thou couldst not ride a furlong. Prithee, captain, lend me of your strength. My prisoner, wishful to disprove my message to you, hath overtasked himself and fainted."

Cromwell came forward promptly, and together they lifted Charlton into bed. Ralph was then about to administer stimulants with great show of anxiety, when, to his disgust, Charlton opened his eyes and stared at Cromwell with an intensity ill suited to a fainting man.

"I come direct from the Lord-General," Cromwell said, with a peculiar dryness of manner. "His desire to see my Lord Charlton is so strong that, hearing he could not move, the general hath decided to visit him. I expect him within a minute or so. While we converse with his lordship, Dangerfield, go you and find a trusty man to tend him. He must join the rest to-morrow, but he can remain in these quarters for four-and-twenty hours. I shall require your presence elsewhere."

Cromwell's tone was peremptory and precise, and Lord Charlton, serious as his position had now become, was secretly amused at the nonplussed expression which came over Ralph's face. It was gone in a moment.

"I will seek a man at once, sir."

"Whom will you take?" questioned his captain sharply.

"Corporal Micklejohn, an you can spare him."

Cromwell considered a moment.

"He will do. Lose no time. I hear the general below."

Lord Essex came slowly up the rickety stairs, for he was a man of weight and substance. He cast a sharp glance at Ralph, who stood aside to let him pass.

"Your cornet, captain?"

"Yes, my lord."

"A youth of gallant carriage. But I like not his dress. It lacketh seriousness and simplicity. He should take pattern by his lieutenant. Tell him so from me. Lord Charlton, your servant!"

He bowed courteously, and then, sitting down by the bed, began his examination. It lasted an hour, and by the time it was over Charlton's head was in a whirl. Yet he was sufficiently himself to keenly observe his new gaoler when he came in, and to feel that Ralph had done well. Jem had been a valet once, and the old deference to rank was not dead in him yet.

"Thou'rt a good fellow, by gad," Charlton exclaimed later in the day, "and shouldst become a Cavalier. Art not sick to death of living soberly and singing psalms?"

"Truth, my lord," the corporal answered, "it irks at times, I own. But then it pays. An I served the king, where'd the money come from, and the rations? I know ye have the braver words and the gallantest leaders. But we've the wages and the food. Then I've an old comrade in the troop, our quartermaster. And he says the Parliament has all the rights of the dispute, and never have I found him mistaken yet. While he lives

I'll bide here. Hist! there's a step, the cornet's. Why,
'tis dusk already."

"In two hours, Jem," Ralph said, signing to him to
retire, "not later."

The corporal saluted and disappeared. On the stairs
he stealthily drew a handful of gold pieces from his
pocket and counted them carefully.

"A rare youth this, my faith! No risk; that guzzling
gander of a knight discomfited, and ten pounds! There's
only one difficulty: how to spend it out of Reuben's way."

In the bedroom Charlton wrung Ralph's hand.

"Ralph," he said hoarsely, "ye make me feel hot all
over. Curse it, how shall I ever pay what I owe to
you?"

"Pooh!" Ralph answered, laughing; "my heart is
lighter than it hath been all day. What said the
general?"

Charlton gave an uneasy laugh.

"What did I betray? Gad, I think they got more
than I meant to tell. A murrain on them both! Essex
I could have fenced with all the day, but not your cursed
captain. No sooner did I set my Lord-General's nose
on a wrong scent, than whiz came a question from those
set lips like a cannon-ball against a troop of horse, and
put me to confusion. I hate that man. I pray to God
I shall meet him in battle where there be none between.
Essex may be a hypocrite — all you prating rebels are,
saving your presence — but he's a gentleman. When I
named the king he raised his hat, sir. I could have
shaken him by the hand for it. But your captain never
moved. What you see in such a man to love passeth
my comprehension. He is iron — body, soul, and heart
— iron, sheathed in steel; while in brain he is a very fox,
with a cunning that is fathomless. Talk not of him as
one to be compared to the prince, or I could find it in
my heart to strike thee. Zounds, it puts me in a fury."

"Then turn thy back upon it all," Ralph said, with

difficulty preventing himself from answering as warmly. "We have no time to quarrel. It's dark. Drink this cordial to give you strength, and let me dress you."

He had brought a cloak, which might have belonged to Capell, a high-crowned hat, and a scarf of orange silk. In these, with his hair tucked inside his hat, Lord Charlton looked such a comical caricature of a Parliament officer that they both laughed heartily, and the little storm blew over. The cognac had an immediate effect, and Charlton walked steadily to where Micklejohn held two horses. At the last Ralph had changed his plan of action, and he accompanied his friend himself beyond the lines. There was no mishap. The fresh night air revived Charlton, and the few soldiers who saw him took him for Capell. When the last sentry was passed the friends shook hands, and Ralph rode slowly back straight to Cromwell's quarters. Now that it was over, he began to feel limp and nervous. He regretted nothing, but the consequences were not pleasant to think of, and never in his life had he dreaded anything so much as the coming interview with Cromwell.

He looked through the window of the cottage as he rode up to it. Cromwell was alone, writing. At Ralph's entrance he held up a warning hand, and went on without stirring to the end of his letter. Ralph suffered tortures. When Cromwell at last rose from the table he looked at Ralph with severe reproachful eye.

"This is ill done," he said before Ralph could speak. "Nay, it is beyond excuse. I am most sorely disappointed in thee."

He paused, as if for a reply, but Ralph was speechless, all his faculties benumbed for the moment by sheer astonishment; for of one thing he had been confident: no one had had an inkling of his design.

"What cause had thou to treat me so?" Cromwell went on sternly. "Couldst not have trusted me to obtain the youth's honourable exchange, but thou must

tamper with my men and steal the malignant away from
his just bondage like a thief in the night? I know thy
thoughts," he continued, " that Salingford be ill disposed
towards thy friend. You feared a mischief from him.
Think you, then" raising his voice angrily, " that I would
let that deboshed tapster knight play foul with a prisoner
taken by my officer? Nay, that I cannot forgive. Get
you hence, sir. I will report to my Lord-General that
my cornet seeks another troop."

Then Ralph found his tongue.

"I plead nothing in my defence," he said huskily.
" You have stripped me both of weapons and armour,
and can stab where you list. But hear me. Had I
thought you would look upon my friend as aught but
a prisoner to be treated as the general might order, I
would have died rather than cozened, or tried to cozen
you; but I felt bound by my love for one who served
me in my sore need — when my father died — to place
his life before aught else. There lies my excuse; I have
no other."

Cromwell turned slowly round again and rested his
hand upon his chin.

" The man is dear to thee?"

" He was my nearest friend at Sidney. We are as
brothers."

Cromwell shrugged his shoulders significantly. Ralph
flushed to the temples.

"Ah! his enemies have spoken ill of him. I will not
hide the truth from you. At college I was fond of pleasure, most of all of horses. Charlton had the finest in
the town; thus we drew together — and — and we diced,
we drank, and once we fought."

" For why?" Cromwell interposed sharply.

" 'Twas about a girl," Ralph stammered. " He had —
I thought he had — insulted her, and I drew upon him.
He was the better swordsman, and disarmed me. I was
at his mercy, and when he saw that he threw his rapier

away, said he was i' the wrong, and begged my pardon. From that day there was never a cloud between us till the war began. At father's death he bearded the archbishop, e'en cursed him, I was told, for a bloodthirsty tyrant. Afterwards, by his sympathy to me, he saved my reason. We went together to Holland, and were two years in the same regiment; and there ——"

"You gambled still," Cromwell said drily, "and philandered 'tween campaigns with all the women of the town; is it not so? Nay," he added roughly, "speak the truth now, though thou'st kept it wondrous well hid these months."

Ralph's chest heaved.

"That is a lie," he exclaimed, "a black and damnable lie! An I knew the man who had said this to thee he would not live to utter many more."

Cromwell had touched the sorest point of all, and saw it. His face softened.

"Enough lad, enough," he said gently; "thou'lt rouse the troop. I but asked a question. No one has slandered you. Rest confident that I would bring anyone who did so to a speedy reckoning. I expressed but mine own suspicions. I have been young, and have known temptation. Hast not thou?"

He spoke very gravely, and Ralph's eyes fell.

"Of course thou hast," Cromwell continued; "but hast resisted it?"

Ralph looked up and smiled.

"Then God be praised! But thy friend, this lord, he did not resist. Nay, I judge him not. Let God do that. But how escaped thou contamination? Tell me this."

"There is no credit to me for it," Ralph answered with a sigh. "Father opened upon the matter before I went to college, with such gentleness, yet so clearly that I could not fail to take it well to heart, though I scarcely understood, for I was not sixteen. But when my manhood came, it seemed to me that for his sake I must keep pure though it cost me my life. And once resolved the rest was easy. I hated lewd talk; I would fight with anyone who uttered it in my presence. And when temptation strove with me I beat it back, taking a kind of pleasure in the strife because it was for his sake. This was at college. In Holland there was so much work for brain and body, and my mind was so burdened with the troubles over here, that I was seldom tempted. Now, since I came to know — your — family, the danger is over. The devil is dead."

Cromwell watched him for a moment.

"I have a letter from Ely," he said suddenly. "It arrived but this morning. Rachel writes and sends remembrances to thee from all. Shall I return thine?"

Ralph looked up with his heart in his eyes, and it was Cromwell's turn to sigh.

"I beg you will, sir. When shall we return?"

"A few days hence. Go to your quarters now. I must wait upon the general, and confess your breach of discipline."

Ralph's face lengthened, and a look of defiance crept into his eyes.

"Nay," Cromwell continued kindly; "be not anxious. Truth to say, I think his Excellency will be relieved. He wished no ill to the Viscount and feared the intentions of Sir John. Do you know the cause of ill blood between the men?"

"It is an evil business," Ralph answered, "but I am glad to tell it to you. There was a maid at Cambridge, daughter of one of my lord's tenants, whom Sir John would have ruined. That was his chief amusement in those days. But she would have none of him, and he was so angered that he spread a report that she was wanton. By good fortune Charlton heard of it, and next day in my presence, in the public street, he thrashed the slanderer like a dog. They fought in the fields, and the miscreant was in bed for a month. A pity he ever rose again. Charlton was too tender. I would have killed him!"

Cromwell raised a reproving finger.

" 'Vengeance is Mine, saith the Lord.' Yet it would have been well deserved. As for thee, thou'rt too hasty, Ralph! This impatience will lead to thine undoing if thou takest it not in time. Curb it, on thy life. Thou wouldst ever strike too soon. See to it that thou dost not wound thyself."

CHAPTER XXII

AT an early hour the next morning a messenger arrived at Capell's quarters from Sir John Salingford, requesting an immediate interview upon urgent business. The knight was pacing up and down in a very unpleasant mood.

"The bird hath flown," was his greeting. "What think you of it?"

"I am surprised ——"

"At what?" the knight snarled. "Thou lookest pleased. 'Sdeath! didst help in the flitting?"

"I am surprised," Capell repeated, without noticing the words, "and exceeding disappointed. I have been cozened also." He spoke with a bitterness which convinced even Salingford.

"'Tis a most cursed chance," the knight went on, slipping in an expletive at every other word; "I'd made sure I'd caught him. The meshes of my net were too wide. I wish I had not told thee."

"Psha!" exclaimed Capell impatiently. "Cast thy eyes a step above. I'd naught to do with it."

"Your captain?"

"Aye."

"Pish! what interest would he serve by setting a malignant free?"

"God knows!" Capell cried, with an irritation he very seldom showed. "But he it was; naught happens in the troop without his knowledge. Besides, he was forewarned. You knew this Dangerfield at college?"

"Aye, by sight."

"Didst ever hear that he was rich?"

"Nay, a poor rat. Doth Cromwell need money?"

"Not he. But I thought it might be he would favour a young man who possessed it."

Salingford stole a glance at his companion. His face was clouded, his lips compressed and drawn. "A young man," he repeated slowly. "The worthy captain perchance hath a daughter?"

"A ward——" Then he stopped, a little late.

Salingford laughed as only a sensual man can laugh.

"A fair lady! Lord! I have smitten thee, comrade. Nay, shake not thy solemn pate; I know thy secret now. Ha! ha! ha! A woman's in it? I might have guessed. Such rogues wi' the wenches are you pious men. Ye be jealous of the cornet, with his curly hair. This is rare. What is she like? Give me her charms."

Capell's lip curled, though his face was a dark, angry red. "You strike air, Sir John. I be no squire of dames."

"Thy denial weighs not a feather with me," retorted the other. "I have found thee out. I am like a hound red-hot upon the scent. Thou wilt not describe her? Gad! then I'll go to Ely shortly and see her for myself. Then look to thy fair. 'Struth, I love a pretty woman, and wil-she, nil-she, many a one's loved me."

He laughed louder than before and showed his teeth. Capell turned upon him suddenly, seized him by the collar of his doublet, and shook him till his teeth chattered.

"Thou d—d villain," he roared, "if thou darest to show thy face in Cromwell's house, and so much as casteth thine eye upon that maiden, I'll take thee by the neck and cut thy tongue in twain. I am no boy to be frightened by a rapier point. Beware, and keep thy distance from that town."

He loosed his hold, and Salingford staggered back into a chair. He tried to speak, but could not shape the words. The passion of a cold-mannered man is a terrible thing to see, and Salingford, though no coward, was so much astonished at Capell's outburst, his nerves so shaken, that for the moment he could only gurgle in the throat and gasp inarticulate oaths. Capell strode to the door.

"Forget not my warning," he said quietly, "for by the God above us, thou wilt get none a second time."

The instant he was gone Salingford leapt up in a fury, buckled on his sword, and called for his horse, intending to challenge the lieutenant before the troop, or before the army if need be. But on second thoughts, when his horse arrived, he bottled up his wrath and went about other business. Though he would not own it, he did not care to face that man just then. He would kill him, such words as those must be paid for with blood, but he would wait for a more favourable opportunity.

Capell also went about his work, and for the rest of the day did not speak a word, except to give necessary orders to the men. But no one noticed it; all were accustomed to his taciturnity. Perhaps no one cared to notice.

Ralph was in good spirits, and was almost ashamed of his light-heartedness, when, on the following day, order was given for the troop to return to Ely.

There were great rejoicings the night the men came home; mourning also, for only two thirds of the troop returned. As far as Ralph was concerned, he found that he had small cause to rejoice. Before he had been at Ely a week he discovered that his prophecy to Madam Cromwell was fulfilled to the letter. His confession of faith had made him an alien and an outlaw. Though admitted to the house as an officer in the troop, his company was shunned by the family there. No more invitations came from Madam Cromwell. When he met her by chance she would only acknowledge his bow stiffly and pass him by, her face set and forbidding. Mrs. Cromwell deliberately turned her head away; Ralph could have fancied she caught up her skirts for fear they might by chance brush against him. Bridget never spoke, and even Betty — and this was the bitterest of all — Betty, whose eyes used to light up and whose voice rang with merry greetings in old times, now cast down her eyes and greeted him in an awed half-frightened whisper, as if he were afflicted by some terrible disease. Only Rachel and Cromwell did not change. As, however, the strict proprieties of the time prevented Ralph from ever seeing the first alone, and his captain was far too busy ever to speak on any subject but the most urgent business, he did not thereby gain much companionship. Under these circumstances Ralph made a strenuous effort to win the confidence and liking of Capell. But here he met with the worst rebuff of all. From the day of Edge Hill fight the lieutenant had encased himself in an armour of reserve. He did not avoid Ralph, but met all his advances like a stone wall. He did not seem to hear or see them, and more than this. Day by day his manner as senior officer in the troop became more curt and arbitrary. In Cromwell's presence he said nothing, but when the captain was absent, as he frequently was in London and elsewhere, then did Capell show a quiet, tenacious masterfulness, which galled Ralph's proud spirit intensely, and caused him more suffering than all the rest of his troubles. It was not that the man was overbearing, or, at least, dictatorial at first, but simply that he asserted to the full all the authority which his position of second in command allowed him; and let it be known that there was only one way in which the work must be done — .Geoffrey Capell's. In short, he was for ever finding fault.

The position of junior officer in a troop was a very difficult one in those days. He had no clearly defined responsibility, no authority, except what his lieutenant chose to give him. In most cases he was a stripling, often the captain's son placed there to learn the use of arms, laughed at by the men, and snubbed by the quarter-master. Ralph, of course, had never suffered in this way, but as soon as Capell began to impress his personality upon the troop Ralph's place became a very thorny one, and grew steadily worse as the months went by.

The district round Ely was honeycombed with Royalist plots. Warnings, anonymous and otherwise, reached Cromwell daily of houses stored with arms; of squires, clergymen, and farmers who were boiling down plate, their own and other people's, for the use of the king. Edge Hill fight had fanned the flames of loyalty on many hearthstones, even in the eastern counties. To deal with such matters was now the principal occupation of both officers and men of the Ely troop. Ralph found it very heartless, miserable work. Little resistance was made to the troopers' raids. It was a question of acute cross-examination, brisk searchings of households from cellar to garret, and frequently the intimidation of women and old men. A deaf ear had to be turned to all excuses and pleadings. Whenever suspicion rested on a person or family their homestead had to be turned literally inside out. Ralph detested the duty, and more than once was found by Capell to have allowed some important clue to slip past him through lending a too willing ear to the prayers of distressed ladies to respect their household gods. Such mistakes were never allowed to pass unreproved, and by degrees Ralph perceived, what Capell was at no pains to conceal, that his lieutenant took small notice of his reports, and that where a search of real importance had to be made, if unable to take command himself, he sent Sweetlove, or even Micklejohn, rather than their officer.

Life spent in this way soon became a grinding misery and torture to Ralph, only to be endured because to resign would mean separation from Rachel, and because of the loyalty and friendship of the troopers, which never failed him. Then he felt, it could not last for ever. As soon as the spring came the war would be renewed, and this would mean freedom and the work he loved.

In such manner Ralph reflected when in his quieter moods, and took comfort; but there were other times when he became so furious and savage with his sufferings and the cause of them that he would resolve point-blank to go to Cromwell, empty the vials of his wrath, and depart. He never doubted that he would have to go, for every complaint Capell made had some foundation in fact, and neither by word nor look did the lieutenant betray the least personal feeling or dislike. Had Ralph known the spasms of jealousy that tortured Capell when Rachel greeted him with her cordial, pleasant smile, he would have been astonished. Still more would he have wondered had he known that the tone of Cromwell's voice as he greeted him after an absence of a few days — his " Good-even, lad," with just a touch of softness in it very few would notice — seared Capell like a red-hot iron. No, he knew none of these things, only that the man seemed possessed by a demon of fault-finding, and a capacity for discovering every weakness in his armour which was more or less than human. Nor was he aware that though Christmas was now at hand, and for three months the lieutenant had exhausted every art he pos-sessed to ingratiate himself with Madam Cromwell, he was exactly in the same position — that of a stranger, respected but disliked — as on the first day of his acquaintance. As for Betty, she treated Capell as a pugnacious kitten would a strange dog, refusing to answer when he spoke to her, running away when she met him alone, and mimicking him behind his back until Rachel, to prevent serious trouble with Mrs. Cromwell, had to threaten Betty that she would complain to her father.

The three girls, Betty, Bridget, and Rachel, slept in the same room, and night after night the sisters engaged in a battle royal over the two officers, for Bridget rather affected an admiration for Capell, though he never treated her with more than very formal politeness. At the end of each dispute they would refer their respective arguments to Rachel. Neither, however, received any satisfaction.

"You talk nonsense, both," she would say; "I will not listen to such rubbish. It would be better far if you went to sleep." And then she would turn over, close her eyes, and refuse to say another word. Yet she listened, and long after the dispute had ceased and the sisters were dreaming, Rachel would lie awake, thinking and brooding.

It is ever the silent looker-on who sees most of the game, especially when the witness is a woman with an interest in the players. And Rachel had exceptionally good opportunities. As the captain's secretary, she was present at the daily meetings of the young men during Cromwell's absence, and though Capell's manner and speech were guarded in her presence, her perceptions, coupled with her knowledge of Ralph, were too quick to be deceived; and as time went on both men became less careful and circumspect, and Rachel saw with dismay that a crisis of some sort was inevitable. At first she was merely sorry. Ralph was her friend; Capell had her guardian's confidence and was a religious man. For no one, much less Rachel, could doubt the sincerity of the prayers he said for the family every morning and evening in his captain's absence. But gradually, almost insensibly, her feelings altered. Ralph's face was always like an open book, and Rachel had learned to read faces. He grew thin and pale, and the grim droop of his lips she had spoken of to Madam Cromwell long ago became much more marked. He had the look of a man who was worn down by a life of petty miseries. His evident suffering began to prey upon her mind. How long would he bear it? and when he ceased to be patient, what would he do? More especially, what would her guardian do?

Such thoughts as these were bad companions for a girl who seldom shared her thoughts with another. Rachel herself began to look worn and anxious, and to suffer from want of sleep, and one day Madam Cromwell took her soundly to task and asked what ailed her. Rachel made an excuse, and after reading a chapter of the New Testament aloud to the old lady retired quietly to her room, and locked herself in to think it out. It was a bitterly cold day in December, and there was no fire in the room, but Rachel needed none just then. She was hot all over, feverishly restless, her mind full of a desire that she frowned at — but which would not go — to do or say something herself to end this suspense and clear the air.

"Why doth he not speak to my guardian?" she thought; "he is being unjustly treated. The lieutenant hates him, though for why I cannot think. But he does, and that is not right. Captain Cromwell should know it. Were Oliver here, I'd make him tell his father. As he is away, there is — there is only me." She flushed slightly, and her eyes became very bright. Then she sighed. "Life is so hard now for Ralph. He stands alone. They hold aloof because of his religion. It is cruel — cruel; and the lieutenant is cruellest of all. He hath some purpose in it, I believe. 'Tis to rid himself of Ralph, perhaps. He wants his captain's favour to himself, yet sees, as I see, that he loves Ralph the best. Ah, now I know it; and so —— But I will not endure such meanness. My guardian shall hear it; it will soon be too late. Naught but cowardice keeps me silent. I ' will speak, and that to-morrow, when he returns from London."

She rose from her bed, on which she had been sitting, and shivered. "How cold it is — bitter cold! I must to my work."

She hastened away, and was soon busy with her customary household tasks. No one who saw her quiet face that evening as she sewed before the fire would have guessed the thoughts that were chasing one another through her mind. It was a severe struggle to Rachel to resolve upon aggressive action. To be patient and constant was her nature, but not to step forward and act. Yet when once she had formed a resolution that something must be done, the fates themselves would not turn her from her path.

CHAPTER XXIII

THE news that Cromwell, who had been in London two weeks sitting in his place in Parliament, was returning on the morrow had been brought by special messenger to his wife. There was also a letter, a bulky one, for Capell from Isaac Hepworth.

"An opportunity," it ran, "hath been vouchsafed to me to leave my post for a few days, and these (D. V.) I spend at Ely, travelling thither with thy captain; expect me, therefore, the day after this reacheth thy hands. I have read with an eagerness and pleasure not to be expressed thine accounts of the Socinian's manifold discomfitures. May the Lord be praised! Indeed, thou hast deserved well of godly men, and I discern with sincerest joy that even Cromwell begins to appreciate thy true worth. He cannot, he says, praise thy diligence too highly. My dear friend, let me beseech thee to crown thy good works by exposing upon our arrival, in some direct and powerful manner, the backslidings, the impious scoffings, and the sinful pride of this youth, so that Cromwell be deprived of further power or justification for keeping him in the troop. It would appear to me an opportunity we should not allow to pass; for though against thee alone, as once against myself, Cromwell's obstinate tenderness for the youth's father might lead him to overlook much misconduct, yet he cannot withstand us both, and especially if proof be forthcoming that the youth fails by his own standard in the carnal duties of an officer. I am already acquainted with young men who would take the youth's place should Cromwell declare, as he did once to me, that there be none to be had. Thus, given evidence of some gross neglect of duty — and I am sure thou canst produce such evidence — the object for which I have prayed for so many months may be attained at last. I pray you consider this in your prayers. May God bless you! My affectionate remembrances unto my niece. The Almighty hath, I am confident, raised a champion for her defence in thy person, to whom neither she, nor anyone who hath her eternal welfare truly at heart, can be too grateful.
"I rest.
"Your affectionate friend,
"ISAAC HEPWORTH."

Capell lay awake for many hours the night he received this letter, not to decide whether he should follow the minister's advice — the course recommended he had resolved upon before the letter came — but to think out in all its bearings a plan he had been maturing for some days, and to decide whether the time was ripe for putting it into execution. After careful consideration he thought that it was.

Directly after breakfast next morning the officers met as usual in Cromwell's library to arrange the business of the day. Rachel was present — Capell took particular care of that — and all letters which had arrived since the evening before were opened and read. One of these seemed to cause the lieutenant peculiar concern. It was a scrawl in an almost illegible hand written on a dirty piece of paper. He read it several times before he passed it to Ralph.

"A very vilely worded thing, upon my life," he said in a tone so quiet and unusually courteous that Rachel raised her eyes and looked at him over her pen. "But we must attend to it without delay. I shall put the execution of the business in thy hands, cornet."

Ralph read the letter and uttered an exclamation.

"Surely, lieutenant, this be a piece of spite." Then, turning to Rachel, " I would have your judgment in the matter. Here's some knave who declares that in the dwelling of Mistress Deborah Brampton, The Grange, Milton, there are secreted a thousand pounds of silver, ten hogshead of salted beef, one hundred muskets, fifty swords, and a store of armour, placed there by malignants for the behoof of the Royal army."

Rachel's eyes opened wide.

" Mistress Brampton! That is indeed strange. I have heard my guardian say her husband was always a most well-affected man."

"There," Ralph exclaimed, "you hear that, lieutenant. Why, the matter is absurd."

"I am not of that opinion," was the answer, very quietly spoken, in a slightly sarcastic tone. "The man is dead. The woman ——"

"A most gracious lady," Ralph said shortly, "whom I've met in Madam Cromwell's presence, and have heard is a distant kinswoman of hers."

"The woman, I say," rejoined Capell, "is a Papist."

He paused as if there was no more to be said. Ralph's lip curled.

"That is unfortunate, indeed. For then in your eyes must she be guilty of crime. But methinks we have known that long. What else know you concerning her?"

"Naught I shall tell you," Capell replied coldly. "The task must be set about at once. Take the quartermaster and ten troopers. See that you search more thoroughly than on the last occasion. Mistress Rachel, I will ask you to write from my dictation replies to these questions from the commissioners in Cambridge. I do not wish to leave more labour for the captain than is necessary. He will be much fatigued belike, for it is rough travelling weather. Address the chairman — Sir Francis Bacon."

He had turned his back upon Ralph, taking no more notice of his presence than if he had been a trooper. For an instant Rachel thought there would be an outburst, for Ralph's eyes were ablaze. But, controlling himself, he bowed to her, and stalked out without a word. He saw Capell smile as he left the room.

"When I return," he muttered, as he strode to the men's quarters, "I will tell Cromwell he must find another cornet. My patience is at an end. I shall do that man a mischief. He maddens me."

The men were nearly as much disgusted as Ralph when they found they had to turn out on a bitterly cold day, and ride ten weary miles on such an errand as Capell had given them.

The Bramptons were much respected, and though the

lady of the house was of a Catholic family, it was known that her relatives had cast her off upon her marriage with the Puritan squire, and she was so good to the poor, so simple and unpretending in her life and habits, that her name stood as high in the fens as that of her husband, who had been in his lifetime a strenuous Parliament man.

Ralph was in so bad a temper that he made no secret of his disbelief in the anonymous letter. But orders were orders, and until he was relieved from his present post he must needs obey Capell. So, in spite of the grumblings of the troop and his own anger, he got his men smartly into the saddle, and they set off briskly along the Cambridge road. As his custom was, Ralph made Sweetlove ride with him, and after a time could not resist unburdening his soul.

"A pretty business, Reuben. What think you we'll find at Brampton Grange?"

Reuben pursed his lips and made no answer. Ralph went on hotly —

"An we come upon an ounce of silver or one hogshead of beef not properly belonging to the family, I'll forego my commission and leave the troop."

Sweetlove grunted. "What doth the lieutenant know besides the letter?"

"Nothing, I believe, except that the captain returns shortly, and he wishes to see him in my absence."

"Nay, you wrong him, sir; I'm sure of that. 'Sides, what can he say that will not bear the light?"

Ralph laughed.

"You take me in the flank there. Truly I hate the man, wherefore I am prejudiced, and should hold my peace. But, tell me, what shall we find at the Grange?"

Sweetlove wagged his head sagely.

"That is as it may turn out, Master Cornet. I am truly sorry for the circumstance. I knew Squire Brampton's father and his father's father; but where you've women and Papists besides. God knows what a coil there may be. One thing be certain, quite. Th' lieutenant hath more in his mind touching this business than he has dropped to you. We must beware lest we be caught napping."

Brampton Grange was a plain, square house of stone. In summer its hard outlines were softened by creepers and climbing roses; but at this time of year it stood in the midst of a grove of elms and poplars without a redeeming feature; staring, uncompromising, as if the architect, called upon to construct a mansion on this flat, fenny land, bare of a single picturesque feature, had given way to a kind of despair, and erected one in keeping with the landscape. It was a large house, however, with ample barns and comfortable accommodation for the throng of farm-servants, who crowded in from field and byre to stare at the troopers.

"Be it a holiday, or what?" muttered Sweetlove. "They are doing no work to-day."

Ralph ordered his men to dismount and search the outbuildings while he went himself with Sweetlove to the front door. There was something more than usually mournful in the aspect of the great gaunt house; the blinds were down at all the windows, and the knocker was muffled in black cloth.

"Good lack!" Ralph exclaimed irritably, "'tis a death. That accounts for the crowd. The whole place be in mourning. He knew it; I'll wager he did. I've two minds to do naught but make inquiry among the servants."

Nevertheless, he raised the knocker of the door, and beat a subdued tattoo on the great oak panels. Experience had taught him that in these cases to question household domestics was the most hopeless waste of time. He knocked thrice before anyone answered. At last the grey head of the house-steward was thrust out. Ralph noticed that his eyes were red.

"What would ye, then, sir?"

There was a pathetic appeal in his voice that went to Ralph's heart.

"We would speak a moment to your mistress, friend," he answered. "Tell her that it is a matter of great urgency, or we'd not trouble her. Have you a death here?"

The man rubbed his sleeve across his eyes with a groan.

"'Deed, yes, sir. Master Jack — he was the only child — was took yesterday; a wasting fever it was. Mistress had the best of doctors. One from London is in the house this minute, but no good came of it. As to seeing her, I hardly know how to do your bidding, sir — captain, I mean. She's crazed with grief; the joy of her life be gone. We are all nigh dazed with the shock of it."

"I will first see someone in authority then, good steward. Admit us, at least; it is cold upon this step. Send me whom you will."

The man opened the door at these words with a hasty apology, and leaving his visitors in the hall, hurried away.

In the hall was a roaring fire of logs. Reuben, who was very cold, stood as near the blaze as possible, and placidly rubbing his hands, carefully scrutinized everything, counted the doors, noted a crack in the panelling which might mean a secret spring, and calculated the number of rooms that a house of this size would be likely to contain; while Ralph, who scarcely felt the weather in his irritation of mind, walked up and down biting his lips, and trying to think how he could express in the least offensive terms the demand he would be obliged to make. The steward was away some time, and they were about to go and look for him when they heard a step above, and Ralph gave an exclamation of astonishment, as Doctor Taunton came leisurely down the stairs. He bowed to them both with great politeness, not recognising Ralph in his helmet and armour.

"I greet you, gentlemen, on behalf of our poor madam here, stricken in grief. She desires —— Good God! Ralph!"

He started as if he had seen a ghost, and for the first time Ralph saw the coolness of the little man desert him. He looked thoroughly disconcerted and abashed; then he smiled, a faint reflection of his old smile, and shook hands.

Ralph was overcome for the moment by the joy of seeing a friendly face. "An amazing piece of good fortune this!" he cried. "So you be the London doctor the steward spoke of. Certes, I did not expect to see *mine!* Are you well? You seem weary and jaded. What ails you, sir?"

He took the doctor affectionately by both hands. They were icy cold.

"'Tis like enough," the little man said in his quiet tone; "this, boy, be a house of death. But now tell me your purpose here. You ride not in these things," touching his breastplate, "for pleasure."

He held Ralph's hand while he spoke, but did not look at him. His quick eyes were busy with the quartermaster.

Ralph became grave again at once and sighed.

"We hear there are stores of provisions, arms, and money here which have been collecting for some time past for the malignants — I mean the Royal army. We must find them, doctor; mind, we will do it with small inconvenience to anyone," he added as Taunton looked very grave. "My men are discreet, and the quartermaster is my friend. You need have no fear of rudeness from us."

"Tut! I have none," the anxiety upon his face vanishing more quickly than it came. "I am but a guest here, sent for to see the child who was sick; but I will answer for the lady. She has nothing to hide, and I have but to mention your name — she knew your father — and all will be left at your disposal. Search you then, and welcome. While you go call your men to aid you I will find that steward fellow. The family is Puritan, after your hearts, not mine." He made a comical grimace that set even Sweetlove grinning. "The husband, lately dead, was, I understand, John Hampden's nearest friend. There is but one thing to say — I speak as man to man — forget not that a mother crushed with the sorest blow that ever fell on woman, the loss of her only son, lieth overhead. Bear this in mind, and may God speed you. You are but doing your duty. Now to work! My time is short, yours also."

He nodded pleasantly, and went briskly down the hall.

"What think you now?" said Ralph, as they went to call the men.

"A gentleman of ready speech and gentle manners. Know you what he is?"

"An old friend of my father's; indeed, my guardian, a gentleman and a man of honour. I will stake my life upon it."

Reuben nodded gravely.

"You should know your friends. A little too honeyed in his choice of words. Be he a confirmed malignant?"

"Yes."

"Is he a chirurgeon?"

"One of the best in London."

"H'm!"

Reuben could not be persuaded to say more, but on the whole he seemed well satisfied."

The door was open, as if by invitation, when they returned. The barns had been thoroughly searched without result, and no servant or other person could be persuaded to talk about anything but the boy who had died the day before.

"Now friends," cried the doctor cheerfully, "lead on where ye will. If any door be locked the steward must find the key. I have seen the mistress, and she makes the house your own to search through."

They began with the cellars; then the ground floor, kitchen, sculleries, pantry, and buttery; next the reception rooms, the library, and the hall; then upstairs. By this time Sweetlove and the doctor were on very friendly terms, Taunton's dry humour, the promptness with which he caused every door to be opened, often obviously against the steward's wishes, and his total absence of resentment at the extremely thorough manner in which Sweetlove and his men did their work, began to impress the quartermaster in his favour, and though he did not relax in the least the vigilance of his search, the business proceeded more rapidly than usual. At length they reached the upper stories. The first room they entered was a touching sight. It had been apparently a nursery. Two women were gently laying away in drawers a heap of playthings, weeping as they worked. Doctor Taunton signed to them to withdraw, but Ralph stopped short.

"Hold, men; this is a sanctuary. Don't move, my good women. Reuben, do your work alone, and quickly."

The quartermaster stepped inside and made a swift examination of cupboards and walls.

"Naught there, cornet."

When they were in the passage again, Doctor Taunton said quietly to the steward: —

"Go thou ahead and warn thy mistress that she will be presently disturbed."

But the man drew back and wrung his hands.

"God preserve me, doctor, I cannot. Let them go an they must, but I'll be no witness to it, nor carry such message to my lady. She's abed, gentlemen," he cried, turning with a desperate appeal to Ralph, "a-laying white and still and speechless, scarce breathing in her misery. She cannot even weep. I cannot go; I will not."

"Thou fool," the doctor cried angrily, "then must I

go myself. I have sworn to this officer that no room shall be shut against him. Thinkest thou I shall break my word?"

"It will kill her," muttered the man rebelliously; "ye said so yourself."

"And if I did," was the sharp answer, "I know enough — I have heard enough — of Cromwell's troop, to be sure that even a woman's life will not hold them from their duty!" He said the words bitterly, and Ralph saw that his face was very white. "What if the information they act upon turn out to be a lie? What even if they know this in their hearts? It is naught to them. They are not men, but soldiers, bound by the iron discipline of their godly captain. They *dare* not disobey. Stand aside, then. I will go before; do thou let them pass."

He pushed the man roughly out of his way, and walked down the passage.

"Stay, doctor." Ralph spoke in a tone sharp and decided, the tone of a man who has taken counsel with himself and made up his mind. "We leave that chamber unentered. Open not the door."

Taunton gave an impatient grunt.

"Nonsense! Now thy feeling overcomes thy sense. Canst, in the face of all these men of thine, withhold thy hand? What will thy captain say? Why, he will call thee chicken-hearted, or court-martial thee for insubordination. Thou must obey — obey as a servant those who respect not the widow nor the weak."

Ralph's face grew stern. .

"Peace, sir! I obey my conscience first. Neither I nor any of these men who are under my command enter that room. Whither doth this passage lead?"

They walked along it past the chamber door, and the steward muttered a fervent blessing on Ralph's head. No one else spoke. Not by word or gesture did Taunton show either gratitude or pleasure. In two hours more the house had been searched from top to bottom.

Nothing had been found. Refreshments were now offered, of which the visitors partook, and then the order was given to mount.

As the men obeyed, Sweetlove, who had been standing apart frowning to himself, drew Ralph aside.

"Master Cornet, I must speak. Bethink thee, I pray. We should search that room."

"At risk of the lady's life? No, Reuben."

"Suppose it be a trick?"

"Then I will suffer for it. Come, the men are ready." The old man sighed.

"As you will. You always will do as you will, and I might have spared my breath. Yet if I commanded ——"

"Pish!" Ralph cried, "a truce to it all! I have no doubts, and, thank God, I have not the lieutenant to reckon with to-day. The captain is at home by now, and I report to him."

CHAPTER XXIV

CROMWELL'S library, where Ralph upon his return from Brampton Grange found the captain, was a room with an amazing number of nooks and corners, a plainly furnished, severely practical, uncompromisingly unornamental room, much like its master, as rooms tenanted solely by one person are so often wont to be. There was one square window to the south, and two doors, one opening to the outside, by which the farmers entered from the courtyard to pay their tithes, the other communicating with the rest of the house. The fireplace faced the inner door, and was large for a room scarcely twelve feet square. The furniture consisted of a worn table of black oak, solid as marble, and marked with generations of chippings of knives in youthful fingers; half a dozen high-backed, hard-seated wooden chairs, and book-shelves on three sides of the room. The books were moth-eaten and dusty. The floor was covered with coarse matting, worn into holes from Cromwell's habit of pacing up and down the room. It was a room for business, thought, and meditation, not the chamber of learned leisure. Here countless letters were read and answered, but no books, except the big Bible, which was in constant use and stood in dangerous proximity to the inkstand, were read; no study, except that of human nature, ever thought of.

The afternoon was waning when Ralph, booted and spurred and splashed with mud, came in to report his search of Brampton Grange. He had been told by the servants that Cromwell was alone, and was much put out to find not only Capell with him, but Isaac Hepworth. They were sitting round the fire, and Ralph was certain by the look the minister gave him at his entrance that he had been the subject of their conversation.

All rose, and Cromwell extended his hand.

"The storm hath caught thee, Ralph. We were more fortunate. What is thy news?"

His tone and manner were as cordial as usual, and Ralph's temperature, which had been falling with the weather, rose again.

"My report, sir, will be a surprise to your lieutenant, and perchance a disappointment." He turned to Capell. "In execution of orders received, I journeyed to Milton, and there searched the house, barns, stables, and all dwellings pertaining to Brampton Grange and found naught — not one ounce of silver, not a pound of meat, neither arms nor armour. The letter was a fabrication of the enemy or some false friend, I know not which; but of one thing I am sure; it was a lie."

He spoke with slow bitter emphasis, glaring at Capell. The lieutenant's face, however, showed not the least emotion, unless a slight, a very slight, smile of satisfaction, which passed quickly over it and left it graver than before, could be called so. His answer was to glance at Cromwell. But the minister could not contain himself, and had cleared his throat for an outburst of vehement speech, when Cromwell silenced him with a motion of the hand, and addressed Ralph in harsh, questioning tones, looking from him to Capell and back again.

"Cornet, what mean you? You speak at the lieutenant with looks that seem to say you would gladly draw upon him. What means it, I say?"

"But this, sir," was the hot reply: "I believe him to be mine enemy, and mayhap yours."

"A lie," Capell answered in a cold, contemptuous tone, "a double lie!"

"My meaning, sir," Ralph went on, taking no notice of the interruption, "is this. For months past I have not known a quiet mind, nor taken satisfaction in my work. At first I searched for shortcomings of mine own, but found none to account for what I suffered. Day in, day out, it hath ever been the same. With quiet malice, persistent, yet ever underhand, he hath pursued me with blame and bitter carpings. In your presence they are well hid; in your absence they come forth and goad me till I am nigh distraught. I have never spoken to you, for never until to-day had I sufficient cause; but I will now. I have been sent with ten men to Milton. What to do? Why, harry a poor household, a household known to be well affected, and its lady a kinswoman of your own, who lieth in her chamber mourning for her only son. I say naught of the fruitless journey and mis-spent time. Doubtless some inquiry had to be made into the letter we received. But if it be as I suspect, if your lieutenant knew well what I should find at my journey's end, and hugged himself to think I'd have to do what he knows I most detest — deal hardly with defenceless folk — then I tell him in your presence 'twas an action mean and spiteful, a coward's thought, a trick unworthy of a man."

His words came fast and hotly, and when at the end Capell broke into a low sneering laugh he clenched his hands, and, but for the presence they were in, would have struck him on the mouth. Cromwell stepped between them.

"Peace!" he said. "Ralph, thou hast been cozened. Lieutenant, keep thy mirth for a fitter season. Tell him the truth."

"I tested you to-day," Capell said very slowly. "I, like yourself, awaited the captain's coming before I told him what for these months I have known touching the nature of your principles. Now answer this before the captain. It is he shall judge, not me. Was any chamber in the house left unsearched?"

"That where Madam Brampton lay."

"Where it was *said* she lay. Then, indeed, you could

not but return empty-handed, friend. There, and there only, was the treasure. There be two chambers with a secret door between. A chest of silver, not a woman, lieth in the bed; beneath it arms and armour, in the next apartment the provisions. You have indeed been fooled. Yet that is but part. The captain, perchance, will wish to know why."

He paused, leaning on the table and drumming his fingers upon it, looking grimly at Cromwell. For an instant no one spoke. Ralph's teeth were set; the colour had left his face.

"How know you this?" he gasped.

"The house steward told me. Did you see him?"

"He admitted us."

"No doubt, a clever rogue, who hath played a many parts. At the present it suits him to profess to be a Papist. He writ that letter; I know his hand. If you think I lie," he continued in a tone of quiet contempt, "wait until to-morrow. To safeguard the treasure I gave orders for a score of men to start for Milton if you returned empty-handed. They will be there in an hour."

Ralph groaned. He saw it all now, and how easily he had stepped into the trap, and brought about his own undoing. An overwhelming sense of shame drove from his mind even his hatred for Capell. He was too much crushed even to resent the deception which had sent him without a clue on a doubtful errand. All he saw was that he had been deceived, and by the man he would have trusted as a father — Doctor Taunton.

"I have naught to answer, sir," he said miserably to Cromwell. "The house appeared in mourning. We searched, but left that room untouched because I trusted their good faith, and thought the mother of a child which had been dead but a few hours was there. I have been cozened, and to rights."

He stood like a guilty man, with bowed head, and Hepworth, even Capell, felt a sudden pity for him. The latter was about to speak, when Cromwell, whose face was very stern, broke in.

"Wait; I have not done yet. Sweetlove was with thee. What was he about?"

Ralph winced, but raised his head in quick reply.

"Blame not him, sir. He would have searched the room, he pressed me afterwards, but I laid strict orders upon him not to enter. The fault was mine, mine only."

Cromwell nodded in stony acquiescence.

"What possessed thee?" he said after a pause. "What spell was thrown upon thee? Didst meet a friend of thy younger days? Ye have so many friends."

The shot went home, and again Capell smiled his quiet, malicious smile. Ralph blushed scarlet.

"Who was it, then?" Cromwell continued. "Another of Rupert's roysterers?"

"A man who was once as a father to me," Ralph answered, "one Doctor Taunton, of London."

"Taunton the chirurgeon?" cried Isaac Hepworth, breaking in. "A Papist of Papists, Cromwell, a familiar to the queen Jezebel herself. God preserve us, this is a blacker business than ever we suspected."

Cromwell frowned, and turned once more to Ralph. "What did you think this man could be about in a well-affected house?"

"He said he had been dealing with the sickness of the boy."

"You believed him?"

"Yes."

"Go on, then; tell me all."

"He was in authority, and kept us company, opening all doors freely. Indeed," Ralph went on doggedly, "he would have led us into Madam Brampton's chamber had I not refused to enter. So understand that even he, malignant and Papist though he be, is not to blame."

"Were you aware of his malignancy?"

"Yes."

" Still you believed his word? "

" In that particular."

" What would he not believe," muttered Capell, as if to himself, " if a malignant told the tale? "

Cromwell was silent a moment; then he said with sharp decision, " Leave us, Dangerfield. I will see thee in thy chamber later."

Ralph obeyed, and without looking to right or left walked down the dark, narrow passage which led from the library to the hall. His tread was heavy and uncertain. He felt as if he had been severely beaten. He was crushed and sore in body as well as mind, and nearly mad with self-reproach and shame. At the moment he had only one wish — to reach his room without meeting anyone, and there make plans for a speedy departure, unless, indeed, Cromwell wished to place him under arrest as a delinquent, a Royalist sympathiser, a lax, unworthy officer. To be alone, alone — it was that he craved, and when, turning the corner, he came suddenly upon Rachel, standing before the great hall fire, he started violently, and tried to pass her by. But at his step she raised her head and came towards him.

" You have returned? But what is this? Are you wounded or sick? You are deathly pale."

Ralph tried to smile.

" Only wet and cold, dear madam. 'Tis stormy weather without. Hearken to the wind. I am going to my chamber to change my clothing."

But Rachel did not listen to the wind.

" You are in trouble, sir," was all she said. " May I know it? "

Ralph stood before her astonished. This face, flushed, but determined, was not the gentle one he knew; even her tone was different. The reserved girl, with her sweet voice and retiring ways, had become suddenly transformed into a strong and earnest woman. Her tone was almost a command, and, as if in response, his own mood changed and he craved for her sympathy. He looked round. The household were busy elsewhere. They were alone. He stretched out his hand, and clasping hers as if she were a sister, told her everything. He did not try to screen himself; he made no accusation against Capell. He simply described what had passed, taking for granted that this was what she wished to know. Rachel listened with quickening pulse and angry eyes. It was natural she should see it from a woman's point of view, and not a soldier's, and that the tenderness and sincerity of him who blamed himself should be uppermost in her mind rather than his rashness and lack of self-control. At the end, when he said sadly, " What think you of me now? " she could not trust herself to speak, but turned away and pushed and poked the burning logs. When she rose from the fire her face was bright and animated.

" I would rather say what I think of the lieutenant," she answered. " My guardian at present hath only heard one side. But this Master Capell hath wronged you sorely. I can find no excuse for him. He knew your kind heart and your chivalry. He played upon these things for a foul purpose. I would I might never see his face again. His purpose is clear indeed. He would push you out from this house, from the troop, and above all from your captain's favour. But he will not prevail, for you will endure him and stand your ground."

She gazed at him with parted lips and eyes aglow, and Ralph's heart beat so fast that he could scarcely answer her. Yet he was not so much in love but that he felt she asked too much.

" Indeed, I cannot think so, fair friend. How can I stay? Nay, even if I could bear the jeers of all my men and the continued rule of one who hath so shrewdly rolled me in the mire, would the captain trust me? It is not possible. I have been tried and found wanting, and with Cromwell, if I judge him aright, that is the end. He will dismiss me."

Rachel smiled a quaint smile of confidence.

"I do not think so. But will you promise me — for I can hear we shall be interrupted—that naught but such dismissal shall make you leave the troop? Will you give your word upon it?"

She held out her hand, and Ralph bent and kissed it before he answered:—

"I promise."

An instant later Capell came into the hall. All he saw was Rachel gazing at the fire; but he heard a step on the stairway, and knew whose step it was.

CHAPTER XXV

RALPH had made a promise, and he was one who prided himself upon keeping his word. Moreover, he had made that promise to Rachel. Yet alone in his chamber, with time and opportunity to think, the difficulty of carrying out what he had promised seemed almost insuperable. What a fool he had been all these months! In the light of Capell's explanation, he had been inconceivably weak and credulous. And how his want of toughness and strength threw into relief Capell's shrewdness and success. It had been a struggle from the first which of them should win Cromwell's confidence. The struggle was over, and he was beaten. What would it matter to Cromwell, Ralph reflected bitterly, that Capell had laid traps and dug pit-falls? Capell could fight; he could command men though he was not loved by them. If he did not take the same interest in the art of drilling and manœuvring of the troop as himself, that was only because for the present the man's thoughts were otherwise engaged. Ralph Dangerfield once dismissed and a suitable cornet appointed in his place, Capell would turn his attention to his military duties, and under Cromwell's eye, make the troopers efficient soldiers, as easily as he had made them efficient sleuth-hounds. How, then, could he, Ralph, after all that had passed, expect to retain his present position? Capell would insist, and reasonably, upon his dismissal.

So Ralph the soldier reasoned, while Ralph the man raged at the injustice he had suffered. It was as clear to him now as to Rachel that Capell had been for a long time determined to oust him from the troop, and that this blow was but one of many, the heaviest and the last.

"I told them 'twas cowardly to send me to the Grange," he muttered, pacing the room faster than ever; "but, my faith, he deserves a worse word now. Could we but meet with the sword? Yet that would be as unfair the other way. I'd pink him blindfold before he had time to raise his heavy eyes, and I'd love to do it. As it is, I shall have to go and leave him master. If Cromwell will give me one more opportunity! But that he will not do. His face was hard as stone. Once deceived in men, he neither forgets nor forgives."

A knock came at the door. "Master Dangerfield," cried Betty's voice, "prithee, come to supper. Father has sent me and charged me to wait for you. I know not why, unless he thought you'd be asleep," and a smothered giggle followed. Ralph listened in surprise. Not only had such a summons been the last he expected to receive, but the child's tone was the old merry one. She spoke like the Betty of former times. Hastily changing his doublet and hose, he joined her in the passage. Betty was in the highest spirits, and danced on tiptoe all the way downstairs.

"We have heard from Oliver to-day. Did you know it? Such news! He's a lieutenant; think of that! Oh, we're so proud! Father pretends to be sorry, saying he will but spend more money on his dress and be no better soldier; but he is really as pleased as any one of us, for I caught a glance of his eye to my grandmother just as I left the table."

"Is Madam Cromwell present at supper this evening?" Ralph asked in so abrupt a tone that Betty looked up startled.

"She be indeed. It is father's first meal since his home-coming."

"Ah! I had forgotten," he muttered, and Betty heard him sigh. The next moment a hand was slipped into his, and she whispered:—

"What ails you, Ralph? I should not call you so, because mother told me not; but I will this once. You look so thin and white, and your eyes are as fierce as when I saw you first. Hath anyone been speaking ill to you? The lieutenant, perchance. If he hath I will tell father, and he will punish him."

Ralph pressed the little hand.

"Punish me, Betty, rather; I am in fault."

"I'll not believe it," quoth the child stoutly, "not unless father says so; and that he never will, for he loves you. He does," as Ralph involuntarily shook his head, "I know it," she added with a little stamp of her foot, "and what I know I *know*."

They entered the supper room, and Ralph, seeing that everyone was present, felt like a prisoner sitting down to break bread with the court-martial that has just condemned him. But his pride came to his aid, and he slipped quietly in the place which had been left vacant for him, between Madam Cromwell and Rachel.

"It is the last time," he thought; "that is why they do it."

There was not much conversation during the meal. Ralph glanced once at Cromwell and met a look so stern that every mouthful he tried to eat afterwards almost choked him. Yet he was obliged to talk, for Madam Cromwell asked him many questions. She was so gracious and so kindly that but for the cloud upon her son's face Ralph might even have taken heart of grace and tried to be cheerful too. When they rose from the table Cromwell beckoned silently to him, and leaving the others, they went into the study.

"Now," said Cromwell, standing where he stood when he told Hepworth that Ralph was to be cornet in the troop, "what have ye to say? Tell me briefly."

Ralph looked perplexed.

"I mean," Cromwell added in deepening tones, "touching your lieutenant. What hath he said or done that is amiss? I have heard his side of it; I have seen you together. I wish now to hear your tale."

Ralph considered a moment before he answered. He might now tell in detail all that he had suffered at Capell's hands. Cromwell would listen, weigh, and judge fairly. It would be one way of keeping his word to Rachel, probably the only way. And yet it was telling tales of his superior officer behind his back, blackening the character of a man to serve his own purpose. No, he could not do it.

"I have naught to tell," he blurted out at last. "If you question me I must answer; else I'll be silent."

"I wish your judgment of the man."

"'Twould be of little worth."

"I want it, I say."

"I will not give it."

"Why then?"

"He is my enemy."

"That is enough. Tell me why and wherefore."

"I know not why, but it is so. Since Edge Hill in all ways he hath found me blameworthy."

"That is his zeal for the cause, or thy soul's welfare. Well?"

"My religion is such an abomination in his eyes that he can see nothing well-favoured in me."

"It is so in mine, yet have I trusted thee. What more?"

"My presence in the troop is hateful to him. Above all, he'd thrust me from you."

"Why?"

"I do not know. But that it is so I am confident."

"Tut, tut!" Cromwell ejaculated impatiently. "So were you of the tale told by the malignant doctor, and a dozen other cozening lies which have brought this trouble upon ye. But no more. Would you make him out a treacherous knave, then, scheming only for thy undoing to serve some selfish end? Answer me that."

Ralph flushed and shut his teeth.

"I do not know," he said.

Cromwell watched him with cold and unsympathetic eyes, his heavy under-lip thrust forward, a dour, relentless face.

"I will tell thee," he said slowly, "something which thou hadst better hold within thy mind when thou thinkest of Capell. I know, as well as thou dost, that he be not tender of the feelings or the pride of other men. None have considered him. He knoweth not what it means. He is a Puritan and a Presbyterian of the strictest school. These things, with thine infirmity of temper, lack of patience, and hot, unreasoning impulse, are enough to account for all that he hath done. And now, mark me well, he hath been justified for every word he spake over this affair at Milton. A messenger hath come in bringing word from Reuben, who returned thither with fresh men, that the treasure, arms and provisions as described, are in their hands. There hath, however, been one miscarriage. Your friend, the Papist, hath escaped — a mercy for him," Cromwell added drily, "unless, indeed, they catch him yet. Our quartermaster is a hard man to deal with when he hath been outwitted, a little cruel, I have heard. He learnt it oversea."

"What would he do?" Ralph exclaimed.

"Nay, you know best. I have been told that in Holland it is the custom to draw a knotted bow-string above the eyes when there is contumacy, and twist it twice or thrice. At times they gouge an eye, or both."

"What! Such an outrage upon one who hath not borne arms, and is an old man? By the Lord, I'd crack the skull of any man, quartermaster or lieutenant, who even made threat of such a thing. But you are playing with me, sir."

"That is not my way. I know men in our army who would do it to their own brother an' he were caught playing such a trick as your doctor. You have much to

learn, Master Cornet, if you think all godly people are
as soft-hearted as yourself. But this brings me to a
point," pausing an instant, and changing his tone to one
of grave reproach and sadness. "Thyself, what is to be
said, what is to be done, touching thyself?"

They were face to face, and Ralph's eyes fell before
his captain's glance. The heat in his blood died away.

"I have blundered," he muttered; "I have been sorely
fooled. And to-day — to-day — it hath been worst of all.
Yet, sir," raising his head, "I do not call this war. I
learnt nothing of this — this harrying of homesteads in
my two years abroad. Did you find me in the rear at
Edge Hill fight? Oh, were I in the field I'd make them
tell a different tale!"

"Which is but to say," Cromwell rejoined stonily,
"that, having teeth, you'd keep them sharp on flesh. A
dog could say as much. Enough; I ask for no excuses.
I am sorry for it; God knows that. When I first saw
you I read strength of will and purpose in your face. Thy
father's death" — he spoke now with peculiar distinctness — "his cruel persecution and bitter sufferings, had,
I thought, bred in thee a maturity of mind, a steadiness
of purpose, that would be proof against the weakness and
hasty impulses to which thy nature is so prone. Brave I
knew thou wert, and with some military knowledge. I
was not mistaken there. But, for the rest, I find thee
thin-skinned, proud when thou shouldst be humble, soft-
fingered when thy grip should be of iron, flinching at
pin-pricks to thy dignity when thy mind should be fixed
upon thy country's wrongs. Truly, Ralph, thou art not
worthy of thy forbears. Thy father, with his infinite
patience — where be thine? Thy grandfather, the grim
old Ralph — was it thus he dealt with the Spaniards on
the main? Think not it is through the business of to-day
that I lay all this upon thy shoulders. I have watched
thee. Thou art weak just where I'd have thee strong. I
blame thee not for thy soft heart. But only women i'

these times may listen to their hearts. We must be steel until our country's free, steel that may bend, but never break. Thou'rt not that yet. And proof of this hath come at a time when I need thee most. Yesterday I was made a colonel, and commissioned to raise a regiment of horse. Money hath been placed in my hands and more promised. In three months we should take the field, and there are six hundred men to be enrolled, armed, horsed, drilled. I have work here for a score such as you and your lieutenant. But though I needed ten score, I'd not take one on whom I could not depend. Capell must now have his troop. And you? Believe me, boy" — his voice had changed again; it was earnest, almost tremulous — "I would be just, aye more than just, to thee. But what can I do but tell thee to be gone? An' I loved thee as my first-begotten son that is in heaven, what could I do, when, in striving for the godly cause, thou hast but half a heart, the rest being given to thy malignant friends?"

He was walking up and down the room in short, quick jerks. Suddenly he stopped and looked into Ralph's face with a question in voice and attitude that wrung his heart. A moment before Ralph had been white and speechless with anger and outraged feeling. Now he only said hoarsely:—

"That be not true — and yet it is. For though I fight and would die if need were on the Parliament side, it is because you are there. You misjudge me, and cruelly. But I complain not. I bow to it all, for it cometh from your lips. Had another man said it, I swear to God I had struck him down, but you — there, I cannot speak. Do as you will; put me to any work. I am yours, only put me to the proof once more."

Cromwell's face set into its grimmest lines.

"Any work?" he said slowly. "Hunting for arms under Capell?"

"As you judge best. I'll do it."

"Nay," was the rejoinder in a kinder tone, "I could not, lad. Thou and I must part. Serve my cousin, John Hampden. He will suit thee better; I am too rough. To-morrow I will give thee a letter ——"

"I shall tear it up."

"I repeat," he said sternly, "I will give thee a line from my hand which thou canst read thyself ——"

"And I repeat to you," Ralph answered, "I will tear it up."

"Wouldst defy me? Nay, this passes patience."

"Defy you? Aye," Ralph cried, " so far as this — I will serve no other man. Dismiss me if you're tired of my poor service. But I will not go to Hampden. I have a little money, enough to take me where I choose to be. That may be far or near — I say not where. But if not in your service I'll be in no other. Keep me at your side, and if it be but to groom horses or clean armour I will do your bidding. Now, tell me your decision; I have nothing more to say."

They were close together now. Cromwell raised his hand, paused an instant, then let it fall upon Ralph's shoulder.

" Boy, boy," he said huskily, " I should drive thee from my presence. I should, but I cannot. God is my witness — I cannot. Stay, then; the troop will not be sorry, and I — well — I loved thy father dear, and, with all thy faults, thou art thy father's son."

CHAPTER XXVI

CROMWELL had promised to tell his mother before she slept that night the result of his talk with Ralph. He had warned her that the friction between his subalterns was too acute for compromise, and that Ralph had been in the wrong from the beginning; but he had spared her particulars and said little or nothing of Capell, for he knew that Madam Cromwell was not one of the lieutenant's admirers. He had now to tell her that Ralph was not to leave them. His plans were already made to prevent further disagreements: Capell should have a troop, Ralph retain his cornetcy, and if he were zealous and sensible be promoted before they took the field. Cromwell made up his mind upon these points just as he reached his mother's door, and had opened it, after one sharp knock, before he heard from within the sound of heavy sobs. At Madam Cromwell's feet knelt Rachel, her face buried in her hands, crying as though her heart would break. Cromwell drew back and looked inquiringly at his mother, but she nodded, and he came in.

"God be praised!" she cried fervently. "Surely, son, He hath sent thee in answer to our prayers. We need thee sore. Hush, childie," to Rachel, "calm thyself, and tell thy guardian — thy true guardian — all thou hast told me."

The sobs ceased, and Rachel rose to her feet; but she shook her head at the proposal with a shrinking negative.

The old lady added quickly, "Thou dost not wish it? Well, let me speak first. Run to thy chamber for a few minutes; but see thou returnest in a short space. This matter shall not rest here."

She drew the girl towards her and kissed her on the forehead. Rachel fled.

" 'Tis the minister," Madam Cromwell exclaimed. " Truly, son, thou wilt have to take him between thy fingers once again and make him feel thy strength. This evening, after you took Ralph away, the man pounced upon Rachel like cat upon a bird, led her to his chamber, and there burst forth with abuse and railing which would disgrace thy corporal. He called her ' hussy,' ' Jezebel,' and the Lord knows what — she would not tell me all — frothing at the mouth like a wild beast. He impugned her modesty, and all but called her virtue into question. And for why, think you? Because he heard in some manner that she conversed alone with Ralph this afternoon. This news, it seems, had angered him to such degree that he had only waited until they were alone to condemn the lad in furious terms and forbid Rachel to speak to him again. Was ever such a fool? He thought in his blind ignorance that she would cower at his revilings like some dumb animal. But she did not. She endured it, she tells me, for a little space; then she withstood him boldly, called his evidence in question, even asked plainly where and from whom he had learnt such things. Thereupon, as I have said, he drove his teeth into her tender flesh and left poison in the wound. It maketh my blood hot to think what she hath suffered. An that man cometh within my reach he shall hear what he hath never heard from a woman's lips before."

The old lady said the last words slowly between her teeth.

Cromwell looked at her anxiously, for she had risen to her feet and was trembling all over.

" Sit you down again, mother," he said tenderly. " Nay, disturb not yourself for this nor anything. Leave all to me. Be sure Rachel shall receive just treatment in the end. But we must be discreet, nor must we hurry lest we trip. There is more behind this than we know as yet. What speech did Rachel and Ralph have with one another? Know you when it was?"

"After his return from Milton. A few words touching that incident and its consequences."

"A few words only?"

"For certain but a few, for Rachel told me all, words any friend might say to another with the whole world to listen."

"Give me their sense."

"He passed her in the hall. She asked the reason of his woeful countenance, and he told her that he had been betrayed; he did not try to screen himself. Then she counselled patience, and urged him to await your after-judgment. He promised this — promised he would not go unless you gave him his dismissal."

Cromwell coughed.

"He promised that? Then it explains — but tell me all."

"There is no more. He was in too much sorrow to be gallant had it been his nature. Aye, an' if he had attempted it," her voice rising again in its indignation, "does anyone who knoweth our Rachel think she'd permit familiarities? That minister is mad!"

"A bag of nerves," Cromwell said with quiet scorn. "He hath good intentions, an eloquence of preaching, and much earnestness for the godly cause, but his is an acrid temper and a narrow mind. We have too many such. Yet, Parliament thinks there be no minister to compare with Hepworth. He hath more friends there than I. If he again demand the custody of Rachel I shall have little power to prevent it. He is her blood relation. Her spiritual welfare, all will say, must be in danger now Ralph hath declared his heresy. Should the minister on such plea make application to Parliament for authority to control her movements, I know not what answer I could make. We must be wary, mother, and keep our anger within bounds. First, tell me this: What will be the posture of the girl after his words?"

"'Deed, you put me a hard question, son," the old lady rejoined, hurt at his coolness. "Were Rachel such a wench as I was at her age, she'd be over head and ears in love with Ralph, aye, though he were as graceless a heretic as her uncle calls him. Oh, a fool, I say! Is it not the surest way to breed love in a woman's heart to abuse, behind his back, a man already in sorer straits than he deserves? But how it will turn with Rachel I know not. There is your Oliver. Saw you how bright she looked when his promotion was read out? The advantage lies with him still, for when a woman knoweth that a man looketh longingly toward her, burning with true love, she is for ever brooding on it, thinking. ' Shall I — dare I — take it?' Other men stand on a different level to her mind. Yet this minister's foolish tongue may have gone far to carry Ralph forward. Ideas have been planted in her pure soul which can never leave it, though the fruit that cometh from them may be picked by Oliver, not Ralph. We cannot know, we never shall, until it be too late. I know this: the child will suffer sadly, and it will be a bitter pain for her even to see Ralph's face after her uncle's words."

" Then she shall not see it," Cromwell said with emphasis. " He shall leave us."

His mother smiled and raised a warning finger.

" Nay, Nay! Good lack, fair son, wouldst thou, too, run thy head into the very snare thou shouldst most carefully avoid? Not see him! Why, then she would think of him both day and night. Nay, that would be fatal. Better that she speak with him every day until thy regiment be ready to depart. But thou hast not told me what was the upshot of thy talk. Be the lad to go?"

" I had decided not, so absolutely did he seem to desire to serve me. This, I will own, touched me not a little. Now "— he gave a short laugh —" I spy another motive."

"Nay, have a care, my dear," Madam Cromwell interposed, "lest you misjudge. The lad's love for you is deep and pure. As for Rachel, until this afternoon she hath not met him, except in thy lieutenant's presence, since ye all returned from Edge Hill fight. Of that I am confident. This foolish minister hath been crazed by some evil tongue."

A suspicion darted through Cromwell's mind, and he knit his brows.

"That may be so," he said slowly. "Yet if the minister should make good his reason for insisting that Ralph depart, what am I to answer?"

"That you will make due inquiry before giving judgment. 'Tis unlawful to condemn anyone unheard."

Cromwell considered a moment.

"The principle be just," he said, musing, "and applieth in this case without a doubt. Yet the boy must go sooner or later. These meetings must not continue. Touching Hepworth's words to Rachel — ah! here she comes, just in right time. Leave me to talk with her, mother."

He kissed the girl with a kindly, fatherly caress, and leading her to a chair, asked her to describe what had passed, assuring her by a kindly word or two of his sympathy and confidence. But for once Cromwell was baffled. No tears were in Rachel's eyes. Her manner was as quiet as usual, though she was rather white. She thanked him for his kindness and consideration, but refused absolutely to repeat what her uncle had said, or discuss his action in any way. That he had startled her she admitted. He had made accusations which were totally unfounded, but they were for her ears alone. She would neither repeat his words, nor question his right to say them if he chose. In fact, Rachel made it clear that though she had told Madam Cromwell a great deal in the first shock of her grief and pain, she had not told her everything, and would on no account say more, or appeal to one guardian against the other.

Cromwell was half pleased, half annoyed, at this sudden reserve. But he could not try to force her confidence, and stopped his mother promptly when she would have upbraided Rachel for her reticence.

"I must away," he said; "farewell, my child. Nay, mother, reprove her not. You and I have slept while the maid hath grown into a woman. That's the trouble. I like her none the worse in that she can keep her counsel."

He saluted his mother and had turned to go, when Rachel ran to him and took his hands in both her own.

"Be sure, dear sir, that my heart is full of gratitude, though I cannot utter it. I pray to God to preserve and guard you, kindest, noblest of my friends. I will do nothing, either now or at any time, without your sanction. And — and I would ask your blessing. I need it sorely."

Cromwell's eyes softened. He took her in his arms and laid her weary head upon his shoulder.

"Child, art thou not my very dear daughter, dear as my own flesh and blood? Thou must know that. Then a truce to thy foolish fears! I cannot say more. Thou owest a duty to thine uncle — a pious and godly man. But mind me, Rachel, thou hast been hardly used," with a deepening of tone that made Madam Cromwell smile, "and in my house that is not to be permitted. You ask not for my protection. You are one of those who can suffer in silence and murmur not. So be it, then. But let them that despitefully use my daughter have a care! There is no man — understand *no man* — that shall stand between us if you appeal to me. Sleep sound, good daughter; happy dreams!"

He strode away after kissing her again with a look upon his face that made his mother mutter under her breath: —

"An the minister meet him now, there will be tribulation for that godly man. I trust, I pray, as I be a living woman, that he do." Then aloud: " Rachel, I pray you read me a chapter from the Book of Job. My mind is something feverish to-night."

In the library, as Cromwell turned into the passage, he saw a light burning, and a tall, slight figure standing by the table. The minister was waiting for him. The expression of Cromwell's face changed immediately. The cloud upon it gave way to a mask of cold passivity. He had donned his armour and drawn his visor down. Isaac Hepworth was reading from a pocket Testament. At Cromwell's entrance he closed it with a vicious snap, as a man might cock a pistol, and thrust it on a pocket of his gown.

A dignified and imposing presence was the minister's, changed somewhat since we saw him in the summer. His grey hair was now a snowy white, his face thin and colourless as parchment, and seamed with lines of thought and care, but his eyes were as bright as ever, and his bearing haughtier and more dignified than of old. He was a man who led others and knew it, one accustomed to be listened to with respect by the leaders of his party, and to speak with authority to all. Well might Cromwell tell his mother that matters had altered since his last debate with the minister concerning Rachel.

It was the end of December, 1642, and throughout England men were strenuously arming for or against the King. The result of Edge Hill had quenched all hopes, indulged in by so many, that one pitched battle would end the war. King Charles was in Oxford, surrounded by a brilliant court, unyielding and confident. The Earl of Essex had fallen back upon London, where Parliament still met and held the reins of government.

Hepworth was not a member of the House, but he was so well known for his force of character, intense earnestness, and boundless energy and enthusiasm that he had great influence there. All that belonged to him — his money, time, and strength — he gave without stint to the cause. He had written and printed at his own expense an immense number of pamphlets, which were distributed broadcast all over the country, impeaching the divine right of kings; he had published a refutation of Popery, and a bitter, not to say ferocious, attack upon Arminianism, Erastianism, and all other heresies, all of which speedily placed him in the front rank of militant Presbyterian divines. From the pulpit he preached simplicity of life for rich and poor alike, passionately denouncing the worst sins of the age — profligacy and drunkenness, and calling upon all men to obey any demand from Parliament for funds or service, and to resist to the death the prelates and the King. And so pithy and vigorous were his pen and his speech, that what he wrote was eagerly read, and his preaching drew immense crowds.

All this, as we have seen, Cromwell knew. He knew also that the stricter Presbyterians, of whom Hepworth was a leader and prophet, were gaining power by leaps and bounds. It was a time when people craved strong food for the mind and the emotions; so the men who lived without pleasure or ease, who called all religions other than their own damnable heresies, and held men of other parties to be the enemies of God, were coming to the front. The time was soon to come when these Presbyterians were to become the dominant caste. On the other hand, the "godly party" was not as yet sure enough of its strength even for its most powerful members to push their authority too far.

"We are well met, reverend friend," said Cromwell courteously, drawing two chairs up to the fire and settling himself into one. "Hast waited long? I trust not. I see by thy face that thou hast something on thy mind of weighty consideration; so, indeed, have I. But speak thou first. What can it be?"

The minister coughed. He had meant to lead Cromwell first to commit himself about Ralph's delinquencies before clinching the argument with his talk with Rachel. This sharp challenge put him out.

" 'Tis a matter we have touched upon before," he said " which I trusted would never again appear."

Cromwell faced round with an air of surprise.

" What can that be? "

" Rachel, my ward."

" *Our* ward," said Cromwell quietly. " Well, what of her? I trust you have no tidings of Oliver that should cause you to repent of your consent to his addresses? "

" Nay, nay," Hepworth began with some impatience.

" The Lord be thanked," Cromwell interposed solemnly. " That would have been a serious blow. What ails the girl? "

" Vanity, strange presumption, a spirit over-proud, and a deceitful heart," thundered the minister, breaking forth at last. " Thou hast been cozened, Cromwell, and I have been undone. Didst not swear before thy Maker that if any sign of love became manifest between her and this Socinian cornet of thine, thou wouldst part them as with a sword? Those were thine own words. I trusted thee, dolt that I was, and left the child within thy house. How hath my faith been requited? Daily, nay hourly, all these months this youth hath had access to her. Until Capell arrived she acted, forsooth, as thy secretary, and at that time, in thy absence, the Socinian even opened letters with her, to which she wrote replies at his dictation. Since, she hath declared a friendship for him under thine own eyes. What is the result? Why, this — that when I, standing in the relation of a parent to her, and by law entitled to respect and obedience, telled her the truth concerning this youth—his leaning towards malignancy, his laxities and insubordinations — she contradicted me unto my face, questioned every word I uttered and with a warmth of language I never heard her use before, justified him. 'She believed me not,' her very words! She 'knew another side'; he was 'too brave to oppress women,' 'too generous to let his friend the malignant lord be a victim to an enemy,' and so forth. Truly my mind almost refused to grasp what mine ears had heard. I could not believe that Rachel stood before me, for she was transformed from the maiden I knew into a woman that defends her lover. Oh, she loves this viper that thou wouldst press unto thy bosom spite all of my prayers. Thou wilt part with him now, doubtless," he went on with bitter scorn. "Thou thoughtst he would be a useful tool; but now that he hath turned in thy hands and wounded thee, thou wilt drop him. But let me tell thee it is too late. Harm hath been adoing; seed hath been sown that will be reaped with tears of shame. For this youth is no mere youngster to be frighted or brow-beaten. He hath courage and determination, and he knows his power with her. And for all this thou, and thou alone, art to blame. 'Tis written, 'Put not thy trust in princes.' Before God, Cromwell, I declare this: 'Put not thy trust in friends.'"

He paused, breathless.

"Hast finished, then?" said Cromwell, in his quietest, driest tones.

"For the moment, aye; but there be much more upon my mind."

"Then I pity you. But I would crave your attention for a little while before ye conclude your sermon. What is your purpose? I have seen one in your eyes from the beginning."

"I shall convey Rachel to London to reside with me. I have a house of moderate comfort, and have engaged a discreet gentlewoman, a lady of ripe years and strictest principles, to be a companion to her."

"All this provided? There hath been forethought here. Methinks the present sad condition of affairs hath been foreshadowed in thy mind for some considerable time. Be this so?"

Cromwell's tone was still quiet and courteous, his face, slightly shaded by his hand, calm and reposeful, while Hepworth's twitched with nervous intensity and excitement.

"Assuredly," was the reply, in a tone of dignified complacency. "Didst imagine I would trust my niece with anyone, even with thee, without a means of knowing something of her doings and behaviour from a trusty source? Thou must surely deem me very simple."

He laughed as only a man to whom diplomacy was a sealed book could have laughed. "Nay, friend," he continued, "I know much, aye, more than I have told thee. But I have said enough, I trust, to open thine eyes to the mischief that hath been abrewing."

"Not yet, reverend sir." And now, though Cromwell still held his voice in check, it was like low thunder. "I would know a deal which as yet thou hast but hinted. First, who has supplied thee with such minute and particular information? It must be a member of my household, or my troop. Give me his name."

There was a pause. Hepworth saw that he had gone too far.

"Nay," he said stiffly; "that would be to betray confidence."

"Then I will tell *thee*." Cromwell left his chair and stood at the table, a glitter in his eyes like the flash of steel in firelight.

"In the month of September last, thou, a Christian minister, sent into the house of thy friend a spy. There is but one man who could have told thee what thou thinkest thou knowest, and that man is Geoffrey Capell. Deny it if thou canst."

He paused for an answer, but Hepworth, cautious now, only remarked: —

"I commit myself to nothing."

"Thou dost not deny it?" Cromwell exclaimed. "Then 'tis true. Capell, the pious soldier, my trusted officer, I now know to be a spy, and worse. Pretending zeal for the cause and true religion, he hath plotted the undoing of a comrade, hath watched his movements and speech, and followed him about as a tiger tracks its prey. Silence," as the minister would have protested angrily, "silence! and hearken to me. I have listened patiently to thee. As thou'rt an honourable man, answer this question: Hath not Capell, since his sojourn here, writ to thee twice or thrice a week? I know he hath. Has there been one letter in which he hath not told thee of Dangerfield's misdoings? Has there been? Answer."

The minister looked, as he felt, uncomfortable; but he said with dignity, "The lieutenant is my friend. Whate'er he has said to me hath been in strictest confidence."

"Dost mean thou hast kept the contents private?"

"Aye, indeed."

Cromwell shrugged his shoulders.

"Thy memory is faulty, or my Lord Essex lies. Two weeks ago he told me he had seen such a letter, handed him by you."

Hepworth changed colour, then became more dignified than ever.

"Maybe thou art right. I deemed it wise my lord should see that letter. We had been speaking of Capell."

"You deemed it wise?" Cromwell said fiercely. "'Pon my life, sir, that would be a poor excuse were you to be brought before a court for defaming an honest man. I have seen men hanged for less. But to return to Capell the spy. You've told me much, you said. Indeed, I know more than ever you intended. Who was it reported Dangerfield to be lax, malignant, insubordinate? Capell. Who told you of his misdemeanours and said he was to be thrown aside? Who but Capell? Twelve hours have not passed since you crossed my threshold. You have not exchanged a word with Dan-

gerfield or asked me for my opinion of his conduct.
Nay; solely upon this information garnered from your
spy, and through the itch and fever in your blood, you
must needs rend this child, your niece, as if she had been
guilty of illicit dealings with the lad. Perhaps this, also,
your spy hath led you to believe. She defended him, you
say? Aye, her soul hath so strong a sense of justice that
not even dread of your cruel suspicions could subdue it
to silence. 'Another side'? 'Fore God, there be
another side, indeed. You do not know that maiden.
As for you and your plans, I refuse now, or ever, to part
with her. Your suspicions are without foundation.
Said I the word, she'd be betrothed to Oliver this night.
And were it not so, naught should drive me to relin-
quish her unto your hands. By your foul attacks you
have proved yourself unworthy to have the charge of
such a maiden. What?"— as Hepworth, whose anger
had been growing moment by moment and now flamed
out in a volume of threats —"you'll appeal to Parliament? to Essex? Get ye to your bed. Were you not
a minister, and I well aware of your good faith, and how
you have been nose-ringed by this spy of yours, I'd deal
by ye far more rudely than with a few rough words.
You'll see the maiden? Only in my presence, not alone.
Never again shall your tongue so wound her tender
heart. As to my cornet, I still hold him culpable to a
degree. But he hath been falsely charged. There will
be a reckoning there for someone. My worthy lieutenant shall explain some things to me before he sleep."

CHAPTER XXVII

IT was now ten o'clock at night. Cromwell had ridden thirty miles that day over heavy roads, and since his arrival at Ely had not been at rest for a moment. He was very tired. Nevertheless, with scarcely an effort, he put aside his weariness and went straight to Capell's room. The lieutenant was kneeling in prayer, and Cromwell stood at the door with bent head until he rose from his knees.

"You, sir? Be there fresh news from Milton?"

He took up his doublet.

"Stay, man," Cromwell said, seating himself on the bed. "Put your clothes aside. I have no work for ye." His face was grey, his eyes weary; there was no anger in them now.

"We have had much talk to-day," he went on, "concerning my cornet. Yet, after all, I have not put direct the question that concerns me most."

He paused, and Capell wondered what was coming.

"You told me he had been careless in his duties; indulgent to the disaffected; blasphemous on occasion in his language; a bad example to those under him, and a thriftless and unwilling servant to the cause. This was much, but I would know more. Hath it ever crossed thy mind that he was given to gallantry?"

A gleam came into Capell's eyes. He turned them away and sat still thinking. Was this an answer to his prayer, or was it a snare of Satan? He was not easy in his mind this evening. He had played his cards well, and Dangerfield had been trapped even more completely than he had expected, but would he be dismissed?

Capell had not forgotten Cromwell's change of front after Edge Hill, and was apprehensive that even yet he might retain Ralph in the troop. The evidence against Dangerfield was strong enough for most men, but Capell was far too astute to fall into Hepworth's error and underrate Cromwell's affection for the delinquent. It was a desperate business. Capell had the strongest reasons for feeling that Ralph must go; but though he was confident that he, himself, had gained Cromwell's good will by his work since September, yet — he was not on safe ground. He tried to read his captain's face, but it told him nothing. Then, slowly but decisively, he made the plunge.

"You ask of me that which I am loath to tell you," he said. "This cornet of yours be not, like myself, a stranger here. Again, it may be reasoned that I have no concern with aught that does not touch his conduct as an officer, or the performance of his duty. All this would persuade me to silence, and if I speak it is only because you question me." He paused to glance swiftly and suddenly at Cromwell. There was no change in his attitude, no hint of foreknowledge in the grave, tired face.

"But, as you bid me speak," he went on more rapidly, "I must, though in strict privacy. That youth is amorous to a degree, that is, he is in love, as the term goes. And in my poor judgment the backslidings in conduct that you wot of are to be traced more to that cause than any other. I have never been in love myself," he added, in cold, decided tones; "I am not well-favoured, and have not the gift of speech with women: but I can tell the signs in another. If your cornet, sir, be not in love with your ward, Mistress Rachel Fullerton, if he dotes not upon the very ground she treads on, then call me a lying knave, take my commission from me, turn me from thy doors."

He spoke with an emphasis and an earnestness very

seldom seen in him. Cromwell raised his eyebrows and coughed with dry and irritating incredulity.

"This is strange news, indeed. Where be your proof?"

Capell smiled with peculiar grimness.

"That is not wanting. Since I came first to Ely scarce a day hath passed without fresh tokens. An I even spoke to his fair mistress the cornet would fret and fume. When it became meet that I should examine letters with her in your absence — and let me say the maid hath rare business judgment and good sense — he chafed, cursed beneath his breath, cast glances at me, and got into such a taking over it — faith, I thought he'd challenge me. Poor wretch, I'd have found it in my heart to pity him but for the danger to the maiden's peace. That made it grave, and because of that I bring the news to you."

"A consideration worthy of your reputation," Cromwell replied, "yet why, good sir, came you not before? You have been here two months. Hadst weighty reason for your silence?"

Capell was silent a moment. He had not expected the question. He thought that Cromwell would continue to pooh-pooh the whole affair.

"There was a reason," he replied.

Cromwell nodded. "Aye?"

"I feared it would do him a mischief, and judged it right to wait until I perceived a leaning on the other side."

"When saw you that?"

"To-day, since your return. 'Twill be best, perchance, to give you particulars in detail. It was after your dismissal of the cornet in the library, after I left you and the Reverend Master Hepworth in conversation there. When I was in the passage leading from your room, I heard voices from the hall, his voice and hers. Before I reached the place Dangerfield had retreated up the stairs, but Mistress Rachel stood her ground and for an instant met my eye unblushingly. Yet when I looked at her in passing a deep colour came into her cheeks, and she turned around with a kind of anger and defiance. Of a truth "— Capell smiled sardonically —" the maiden might have been the queen and I a traitor to his majesty. Then I spoke some word touching the weather. But instead of answering she moved away with a haughty bending of the neck, and so passed into her chamber. I was amazed, for until then we had not fallen out in any way. I had a mind to ask in what manner I had offended, but I did not. I saw her cheeks were wet with tears; even her hands were trembling. That, sir, be my evidence and the proof."

Cromwell nodded.

" 'Tis well I spake ye on the point to-night. The matter is of importance. Doth any other person know this but thyself?"

"I know of no one."

"None? Hast told any other person what you saw?"

"Aye; the reverend minister, being her relation, was informed of the circumstance."

"It was your words, then," Cromwell muttered half to himself, "that brought such a tempest on her head from him."

"I fear so," Capell said hastily. "The good man — I say it with all respect — is of a hasty temper. I think he was over-harsh in what he said."

"She does not say so," Cromwell replied. "How much have you told him — all?"

"Only enough to set him on his guard."

"Guard? 'Gainst what? My cornet?"

The storm was rising, and Capell held his peace.

" 'Gainst Ralph Dangerfield — thy comrade in arms," Cromwell said, quietly still, but so bitterly that it set Capell's teeth on edge, "the man whom you disliked. Now, was this well? I ask you, was it well done?"

Capell frowned. He was in no mood to allow his action to be questioned.

"I obeyed my conscience. An it hath displeased you ——"

"Me? What am I? Was it pleasing unto God? Wait before you answer. You said that Hepworth knew of the maiden's danger two hours since. Also you told me you'd held back all knowledge from my ears, though I be his captain and her guardian, because until this day there was no proof that she was touched with a feeling for the youth. Hast ever let your suspicions escape you to others? I would know that."

Capell set his teeth. His back was against the wall, but he would not flinch.

"I have done naught dishonourable toward Dangerfield, neither by word nor deed."

"Thou hast kept thine counsel, then, breathing no word that might injure him and profit thee? Answer me."

"I — kept my counsel."

"Thou liar!"

Capell sprang to his feet, his teeth bared like a dog's. Cromwell rose also slowly and glared at him with a glance so withering and contemptuous that the lieutenant, though a man of strong nerve, positively shivered, and could not speak.

"I say liar, and again *liar*," Cromwell thundered. "Thou hast corresponded with Isaac Hepworth behind my back for months about this matter. The boy was right when he said thou wert his enemy and mine. Liar, hypocrite, slanderer of a man's good name — such an one art thou, Geoffrey Capell, and thou knowest thou art. Were these times of peace, I would arrest thee and have thee tried as a common criminal; but the press that is upon us forbids that. Thy sword is wanted, and thou shalt be free to use it, but not in my service. Thou leavest my house to-morrow never to enter its doors again, and quittest the troop until God in His good time shall have punished thee and brought thee to repentance. Now say thy say if thou wilt; I will hear thee."

Capell did not speak for a moment. His face was colourless, his mouth hard, and there were drops of sweat upon his forehead; but he did not quail.

" Perchance," he said hoarsely, " I have been to blame; but I am not what you say. One day you will confess as much. Dangerfield hath cozened you. Your love for him robs you of your understanding. He cannot help himself. Passion is his god; he is without religion."

" I have heard that said before," Cromwell replied; he had regained his composure. There was such misery and bitter sense of failure in the proud face that he could have pitied the man had he been less angry with him. "Aye, the youth hath some lack of faith, I grant ye that; but he hath honour, and he tells the truth. If thou wert more like him thou hadst never sunk so low as this. Yet thou art a believer. If God dealeth with thee, according to thy deserts, Geoffrey Capell, woe betide thee! "

CHAPTER XXVIII

WHEN Ralph woke the next morning he remembered with disgust that it was his turn to give the men their daily drill. It was the custom in the troop — a custom instituted by Cromwell in early days at Ralph's suggestion — that all the men not on special duty should turn out for an hour at sunrise and perform such evolutions as the officer on duty might direct. Capell and Ralph took this duty between them day and day about, and in this way discipline and smartness in action, both of men and horses, was kept up to the mark. It was the happiest time in Ralph's day. He was doing the work he understood and loved, and he did it well. Even Cromwell, when at times he turned out and watched the manœuvres, rarely criticised his method of handling men. But on this particular morning Ralph wished that the drill had never been thought of. It would be hard to face his men in any case, and it was more than likely that Capell would make an excuse of being present also, and in a dozen ways make his cornet feel the humiliation of his position after the fiasco of Brampton Grange. However, the thing had to be done, Capell or no Capell. Cromwell had *not* dismissed his cornet, and therefore that cornet must do his duty. So, with the grimmest of faces to hide his internal qualms, Ralph dressed himself with scrupulous neatness and arrived at quarters punctual to the minute. One glance showed him that Capell was absent, and, mounted on a fresh, spirited horse in the crisp, fresh air of a winter's morning, his spirits rose, and he faced his men with a composure that he flattered himself would have done credit to Cromwell.

By the time the drill was over Ralph was himself again. As he rode back to town with Micklejohn, who had taken Reuben's place, he saw that the little man had something on his mind, and looking down at the round face and turned-up nose, nipped by the frost to a bright carnation, he said cheerily:

"Speak up, Jem, and be not so bashful. Though I am your officer, you are twice my age, and should be twice as wise. We are beyond hearing of the men. Now tell me thy mind, and plainly; rid it of the spleen that my blunder hath given ye all."

Jeremiah looked up sideways with a mischievous twinkle in his eyes.

"Marry, sir, if my conscience rode me as hard as thine does thee I'd throw and trample on the cursed thing. Pardon my speech. My tongue wags as it lists into thine ears. My thoughts were but these: I wondered thou shouldst look so gloomy when thy cause hath triumphed, and we troopers, aye, everyone of us, could sing a *Te Deum* for joy at thinking thine enemy is gone."

Ralph looked at him in amazement.

"What mean you, man?"

"Hast not heard? God's sake, I dare not tell thee. Yet I must in very truth. I cannot hold it. But betray me not. At earliest dawn, an hour before drill, who should come upon us, but the captain — I should say the colonel! I'd my clothes on, for which the Lord be thanked, and Sanctify, who never sleeps, was rubbing down his mare. Otherways we'd have been caught napping, for the lads slept too long to-day. 'Saddle the lieutenant's horse,' saith the colonel in that sharp tone of his that means he be exceedingly short of temper. Not a man of us but hastens when he hears that tone. 'And another,' he adds, briefer still, 'a quiet nag; see it be quiet. Let both be at my door within ten minutes. But rouse not the men.' 'Twas done in the time, though I was so nervous, Sanctify declares I'd nigh put the saddle on pommel hindmost; and there on the steps we saw the old minister and Capell. I call him not lieutenant," Jem added, with elevated nose; " he be none now. They were departing, and Noll — I ask thy pardon; it is our pet name, I mean the colonel — speeded them. There were few words passed, and those civil ones; but the stiff carriage and angry eyes of the presbyter, Capell's lowered brows and face yellow as a drum-head, the colonel's cold address, all told a right plain tale. And, alack for me, I've lost a heavy wager I made with Reuben before he went again to Milton. Yet I lose my crown with a light heart to think that man hath gone."

He laughed and slapped his thigh, then suddenly stiffened his features, reined in his horse, and dropped behind. They had reached the town, and turning a corner of the street, had been met by Cromwell.

In the course of the day Reuben returned in triumph with a trail of waggons loaded with the intercepted treasure and provisions, and surrounded with cheering townspeople. The news of the seizure flew far and wide, and greatly facilitated the recruiting of the regiment.

Into this work Ralph threw himself heart and soul. Capell away, he was Cromwell's right hand once again. No colonel ever had a more industrious one. Ralph never knew the exact reason for Capell's departure. Cromwell on the first morning told him that until other arrangements were made he was to take command of the troop, and aid him as occasion arose in other ways. He admitted curtly that circumstances had arisen which justified Ralph's view of Capell's sentiments, but he said no more. It was natural that Ralph should credit Rachel with the chief share in all this, and the thought made him happier than was at all desirable or wise. Soon afterwards, however, Oliver paid a flying visit to Ely, and Ralph's hopes fell to zero. He saw nothing of Rachel. Oliver was with her most of the day, and confided to Ralph, from whom he had no secrets, that he believed his betrothal could not long be delayed.

Yet, in spite of the pain and sinking of the heart which this news gave him, Ralph enjoyed Oliver's visit. There was a heartiness in the grasp of hand and in his burly voice; an infectious cheerfulness in his ringing laugh, which cheered Ralph as it cheered the rest of the family. Besides, Oliver put his father's attitude in a new and pleasant light.

" I' faith, friend," he exclaimed one day, " why harpest thou upon this string of ' retrieving reputation '? What is there to retrieve? My father be not angered. Eh? You think so because since then he hath been short of manner and close of speech? That is nothing but the pressure of the times. Man, he was never really angered, but he had a part to play before those worsted stockings, Hepworth and Capell. Bah! think you he loves raking homesteads, scaring women, squeezing malignant purses, and spying upon his neighbours any more than thee? He knew you were too good for it — depend upon that — and only kept you at it to give Capell rope enough to hang himself, which, at length, the dreaper did. A curse upon such rogues! Well may those rascally Cavaliers call us crop-ears and hypocrites while we kennel hounds of such a breed! Father hates them, though, as much as we do, and if he lets them strut on stilts a while, he strikes them down before they choke him or his friends. My fakins! Ralph, but there has been, and is, a rattle over you. Father angry forsooth! He is your toughest friend. The Speaker of the Commons writ him a private letter. I know not its contents, but he told me it concerned grave charges made by Master Hepworth, and which he feared might come before the House. Essex hath written too, demanding your dismissal. Now you know father! Thinkst him to be a man who'd allow such a storm to gather round his head if he did not know you were worth it? And you be worth it, comrade.

Thy religion is the only weak part about ye, and what matters that in a soldier? I am your friend, and father be too, till death and after. Let the world wag as it may."

Drilling, drilling, drilling — this was Ralph's work. Recruits poured in, for Cromwell's reputation of being the poor man's friend, and paying his troopers regularly, stood higher than ever. His enemies used it against him then and afterwards, declaring that it was made by truckling to the mob. The accusations would have had little real foundation in fact, for among all the gentry in the south of England no one had greater command over the purses of wealthy friends and neighbours than Cromwell. It is certain that his democratic sympathies and gift of winning the hearts of common men served him best of all. It followed, therefore, that while most of those who raised a regiment at this time had to be content to enrol any who chose to volunteer, Cromwell was able to select his men. Quickly the ranks filled up, and by February the regiment was recruited to its full strength of twelve troops, six hundred and eighty men. The appointment of officers was a slower business, though not so hard as it had been before Edge Hill. Ralph watched this process with peculiar interest. He had been duly appointed lieutenant of the first troop, and the captaincy was a matter of the first importance to him.

But January passed, and February, and though one after another of the troops were duly officered, the first troop remained captainless. Ralph, moreover, though nominally lieutenant, was filling half a dozen other posts. He personally tested, inspected, and bought the horses; gave riding lessons to awkward squads; superintended the arming and clothing of the men; planned with Cromwell, and passed on in his name to the other officers, the regulations which were to be observed concerning the punishment of breach of discipline among the men. He

organised a commissariat department on a small scale,
and while Cromwell was absent was paymaster to the
regiment. It was excellent training for a young soldier,
but the responsibility was very heavy, and the labour
intense. He was never idle, indeed, for a moment except
at night, and his nights were short. There were no
visits to Madam Cromwell's room now, no more consultations on business with Rachel. The only time he ever
saw her was on Sunday, and then it was but a glimpse
of her face at table, for the pressure of work was too
great even for a strict observance of the Sabbath. Yet
Ralph was happy. Every morning early he reported to
Cromwell, received his orders, and discussed briefly the
business of the day. Sometimes, as Cromwell's aid-de-
camp, he attended meetings of the committees of the
associated counties — bodies of shrewd merchants,
squires, farmers, and tradesmen, who like some commit-
teemen of the present day, readily voted supplies of
money subscribed by other people, and sent forth eloquent appeals to friends and neighbours to go forth to
war; but stayed at home themselves. There were, however, strong and earnest men among them, and wherever
Cromwell sat, work, not words, was the order of the day.
Ralph, a silent spectator of it all, was never tired of
watching the colonel work his will in everything he
touched; appealed to by all, guiding all, and in return
quietly taking upon himself burdens and responsibilities
few men would choose to bear. Yet all the time he
seemed to be constantly deferring to the will of others,
and few realised the power which lay in his hands.

In such a rush and whirl did Ralph live now that he
had hardly time even to think of Oliver, who was again
with the army in the north under Fairfax. But from
what he heard Betty drop one day he gathered there was
no formal betrothal yet. The question of the captaincy
of the first troop now became acute. Ralph's anxieties
in the matter were not so much for his own sake as for

the men. There were good soldiers in other troops, and even a sprinkling of veterans, but none to compare for a moment with "Cromwell's Own." Ralph knew them all, and what each man could do, and they knew him. During Capell's time there had been murmurings at his want of religion, but the majority, headed by Sweetlove, Micklejohn, and Sanctify Jordan, had staunchly supported him from the beginning, and whatever might be Ralph's infirmities of temper and speech, he inherited enough of his father's sensitive respect for the feelings of others, and reverence for all true piety never to say or do anything which might offend the most Puritanical trooper, nor rouse the antagonism of the most democratic. Then he was mindful of their comfort, spared them in illness, procured them leave of absence to see their families and friends, and though he could be severe enough on occasion, he never punished wantonly, and, as a consequence, the men of the first troop were the most contented and orderly in the regiment; worked early and late without a grumble, and suffered very little deduction of their pay in fines. That such men should have a worthy commander Ralph felt was absolutely necessary; and when the winter weather fairly broke up, late in February, and Cromwell went to London for the last time; when the equipment of the regiment was all but complete, and still there was no hint or sign of any appointment there, he could hardly bear the suspense. It was in those days that he felt the keenest regret for his want of self-control with Capell. Oliver might say what he pleased and the men be loyalty itself, as indeed they were; but Ralph knew well that Cromwell had blamed him, and blamed him still. He was as kind and considerate now, as he had ever been, but there was a reserve, a certain curtness of manner, a lack of the old cordiality, which Ralph felt bitterly at times, and which prevented the least hope that the captaincy could ever be his. The most that he could hope for was that a man would be chosen who would treat him as a comrade.

One morning, the 27th of February, Ralph rose an hour earlier than usual to make an excursion of thirty miles through muddy lanes to a village where he had heard certain horses of peculiar merit were for sale at a very low price. It was a hard ride, and to Ralph's extreme annoyance he found upon his arrival that the beasts had been picked up by someone else. By the time he reached home he was tired out, and when Betty met him at the door and announced in a great state of jubila-tion that her father had arrived, a depressing presenti-ment overcame him that bad news was coming.

"Anyone with him, Betsykin?"

"Marry, no, Ralph; who should there be?"

"The new captain of the troop, belike."

"Oh dear!" the girl cried petulantly. "Expect you another man? Not Master Capell, surely? I thought he had quite gone from us."

The name made Ralph start. Could it be possible that Capell would be appointed? It might be. The abruptness of his departure could not have been wholly through Cromwell's displeasure. Not a word had ever been said against his work or capacity, and to conciliate the Presbyterians such an appointment would be an excellent stroke of policy. A cold shiver ran down Ralph's back as these possibilities occurred to him, and when, late in the evening, he met his colonel alone, his spirits were at the lowest ebb.

"You are aweary," Cromwell began, lighting a long pipe and taking a sip of spiced ale — the only luxury he was ever known to indulge in. "What rode ye so far for after half a dozen horses? It was waste of time."

He spoke impatiently, as if seeking an opportunity to find fault. An unpropitious beginning.

"I have seen all there are about here," Ralph answered, "but they do not satisfy me. They be too light in bone or else very coarsely bred. It is not easy, believe me, to find just what we need."

" 'Tis you who are so hard to content. We spend much on horseflesh, too much."

"You will find it well worth, sir," Ralph cried, forgetting weariness, suspense, and all else in his favourite hobby. " Remember you — it was you who remarked it — the difference between the charge of Rupert's horse and ours at Edge Hill? I believe if Ramsay's had been our best, 'stead of our worst, they must have broke before that charge; and it was speed that did it. Their beasts were each worth three of ours. But take your regiment, or, at least, the first troop. I'll swear they'd make Rupert's bloods look to it now! Regarding the other troops, until they have more training, and their officers more experience, and I have weeded out a score or two of their nags, they'll never be more than second-rate. I have done my best, but truly "— and he sighed wearily —" so much is there to do, and so little time, that I feel small contentment in my work."

"That is a pity," Cromwell said in a musing tone, puffing huge clouds of smoke and gazing into the fire. "The officers complain that had you your way, you would keep their men and them at exercise until they were like to drop from weariness."

Ralph gave an impatient snort.

"Your officers, sir, may mean well. They be zealous in preaching and most pious, but never did I know men more ignorant of their profession. Truth, I believe they think victory will come far more by long prayers than by hard work. 'Fore Heaven, I would not scoff at any man's religion, but it is hard to be patient when you see precious time wasted in long-winded sermons."

Cromwell made no answer to this outburst. He smoked in silence until his pipe was empty, then laid it down and slowly paced the room.

"The first troop," he said suddenly, "is the best, you think?"

Ralph smiled proudly.

"Need I answer? That troop was of your making."

Cromwell shook his head.

"Ah, but it was," Ralph persisted; "you chose every man. They learnt the use of sword and carabine under your eye. You carved it with your own hands. And, sir, it be worthy of you, though, perchance I should not say so."

"To a point you may be right," Cromwell said thoughtfully. "But only to a point. Others have done more, Capell for instance."

Ralph gave a start, a perceptible start, and Cromwell turned and looked him in the face.

"Do you deny it?" he said gently. "Be quite frank, I pray you."

"Nay," Ralph said, biting his lip; "that would be unjust. Capell did his part; he was in some ways a good officer."

"How compareth he with your comrades here?"

Ralph went very white indeed. The notion of Capell's return became something like a certainty now. But he forced himself to answer.

"I should judge him superior in knowledge and in industry. But as a man, sir, God help the regiment if he come back again!"

"And wherefore? Because he is your enemy?"

Cromwell's face had hardened, but Ralph did not flinch.

"If that be your reading of my motive ——" he said bitterly, when Cromwell cut him short.

"I say not that. I will be plain with thee. Thy power and character is what perplexeth me now, not Capell's. I know that man. Do I know thee? I have been pondering many days upon thee. I have had occasion." He sighed. "Thy name has been dinned into

my ear in London by many tongues, some poisonous, all
harsh — but one. Capell, whom I have seen, said little,
and that in thy favour. But none other had a good word
for thee. Mark that. Thy life at college was laid
before me in blackest colours, thine intimacy with that
malignant lord, and lastly, and worst, thy dependency
in money, until very late, upon that black-minded Papist,
Taunton. Some were not backward in declaring that
thou knewest as much concerning that treasure at the
Grange as anyone. Peace now!" as Ralph, unable to
contain himself any longer, swore aloud; " prithee, peace
till I have done. I heard, I say, such things as these:
Thou art a Papist in disguise thyself; a malignant spy,
a rake, a debauchee — oh, there is no end to thy delin-
quency. Well, to all of it I made one reply: ' I will
tell him this,' I said, ' on my return, hear his reply, and
then in writing send unto my Lord of Essex my decision
upon it all.' Now, what dost reply, Ralph? "

He paused and smiled, a smile Ralph thought sardonic
and hard.

" My answer, sir," he cried hoarsely, " be this: If you
believe one of these foul, damnable lies, aye, even the
smallest of them, by my father's soul I leave this roof
never to enter its doors again."

He was roused at last, roused as Cromwell had never
seen him yet.

" I have served you," he went on more quietly, " to the
full measure of my strength. I have done it gladly.
But if in your mind there rests one grain of disbelief in
me I serve you no more. I would trust you with my
life; I ask such trust, and no less, from ye."

Cromwell watched him a moment with drooping eye
lids before he spoke again, then slipped a hand beneath
his arm.

" Come to my mother, good Ralph. I will answer
thee in her presence. She is acquaint with all that has
been said. Come."

He turned and led the way upstairs, Ralph following in wonder and perplexity. A griping pain was at his heart that this would be the last time he should see the old lady's calm, strong face.

Madam Cromwell was sitting in her accustomed place, and, as usual, Rachel was with her. The girl rose at their entrance, and would have left the room, but Cromwell gravely signed to her to stay.

"Mother, I have brought him to thee according to my promise. I have questioned him, and my mind is well made up concerning all that I have heard. Thou hast greeted this man as lieutenant for the last time. He is the captain of my first troop."

CHAPTER XXIX

THE week that followed Ralph's promotion was a time to be remembered all his life. Before he slept that night he learned that a public announcement of his appointment was to be made to the regiment next day.

"It is absolutely necessary," Cromwell said when he gave the order. "There be many to cavil and say you have crept up my sleeve. I intend to stop that once and for all."

The men were in full uniform, a goodly sight on that bright spring morning, twelve troops of horse in buff and steel. They were disposed in a crescent on their usual drilling ground outside the town, their movements watched by a crowd of people, for it had got wind that some ceremony was to be performed.

"Men," Cromwell said, in the conversational tone he always used when addressing his soldiers, yet so distinct that no one ever missed a word, "men and officers of my regiment, I have assembled thee this day because I think it fitting thou shouldst hear from my lips that I have appointed Master Ralph Dangerfield to be captain of my first troop. It is a position of trust and responsibility. The men of that troop fought well on Edge Hill field. The quartermaster of that troop it was"— Cromwell spoke with particular distinctness now —" who took the King's standard on that day. The commander of such men as these must be one with courage above the average, zeal beyond question, integrity, and filled with the fear of God. Captain Dangerfield hath all these qualities. I speak not from my own knowledge only, though since the war began he hath been an inmate of my house, but from the fidelity and the brotherly love manifested toward him by his men. Soldiers of the first troop "— Cromwell raised his voice now until it rang over the field —" I speak in thy name. Tell your comrades whether this man hath not been your faithful friend, through good report and evil report, whether you will not follow him as your commander whithersoever he may lead, though it be to certain death. The regiment awaits your answer."

A pause while one might count five, and then from the sixty throats of " Cromwell's Own " there came a gruff and mighty cheer, which set the horses of half the officers curvetting, and made Ralph blush like a girl. Then from their ranks a horseman advanced half a dozen paces, drawing up before Cromwell with a salute — old Reuben.

" Faith! Colonel, I will answer for them." He wheeled round and faced the regiment. " Comrades, list to an old man who'd drawn blood o'ersea when the most of ye were in your mother's arms. The colonel hath chosen well. I've known none braver than Captain Dangerfield. At Edge Hill, when we disputed with the King's guards, but for him the colonel would have been a dead man a score of times. As we followed him then, so we'll follow him now. And more "— he drew his sword and shook it in their faces — " there were some who planned his destruction, and mayhap they will do it again. Let them mark this, then. His enemies are our enemies; those who would slay or misuse him will have to reckon with the troop to its last man. God ha' mercy on them; we'll have none."

His words were greeted by the troop with a shout louder than the first, and then, Ralph having tried to make a speech in reply, and signally failed, the regiment marched back to its quarters, the officers to formally congratulate Ralph, the men to stare at him furtively for the rest of the day.

As time passed the work grew harder and harder, but, with Cromwell to direct, and Ralph to carry out his orders, it went merrily on, and the afternoon before they were to depart Ralph found himself with nothing more to do. An intense longing to see Rachel came upon him, and searching stealthily through the house, he found her to his great joy alone in the library.

"We march to-morrow," he said, with an unusual abruptness of tone; "I would bid thee farewell now, an I may, having so fair an opportunity."

She frankly extended her hand.

"Must it be good-bye, then? Yet I know you are longing to be gone. God keep you."

They were quiet, friendly words, spoken without tremor of the lips or voice. Ralph's face, which had been very hot, grew cool again.

"I thank you," he said, though not quite in the same tone. "Thou hast indeed kept thy promise, and proved thyself my friend by deeds as well as words — the best friend I have."

There was so much meaning in his tone, that Rachel looked startled a moment and very faintly blushed.

"Truly, I know not why you should say that."

"Does that mean I have presumed too much?" Then before she could answer he went on: "I must speak my mind, for we may never meet again. Thy guardian, my dear colonel, hath been the kindest commander and the truest master I could need. But the day I spake you in the hall he was sorely tried, and but for the strength you gave me I could not have withstood him, but would have resigned and so lost all chance of the position I hold to-day. How much I owe to you I know not. But through all you have been the anchor that hath kept me here. Oh that I might do you a like service! Were I a hundred miles distant, if you were in trouble I'd find a way of coming to thee. Good-bye, and God bless thee friend — sweetest friend and best."

His voice broke at the last, and taking the hand she had extended, he kissed it passionately. And Rachel — she was not the child who had listened half fearfully, half wonderingly, to honest Oliver's declaration. These few months had taught her much. She was a woman much perplexed and sad at heart; thinking long thoughts in leisure hours, burdened with a vague sense of coming trouble and a yearning which she could not understand. Ralph's words found their way straight to her heart and made a home there. Months after he had gone, and the house was quiet, and dull, and lonely for the women left behind, Rachel would recall them, whisper them to herself guiltily, and brood over them. At the moment she could answer nothing, only stand helpless, letting him keep her hand and do with it what he chose. They were both silent — a silence that for Ralph was golden — then he took her other hand and kissed them both.

"My sweetest friend," he murmured, the passion of his love rising higher and higher, "and one day to be my dearest ——"

"No." She tore her hands away, and put them behind her. Her face was white to the lips. "No," she panted, "you must not say it, nor think it. You must not."

"Why?" The words came in a whisper, too, but were hissed from between his teeth. "Have I again presumed too much?"

"I said not that," she cried, biting her lips hard to control a fatal inclination to burst into tears; "I meant it not — you know I meant it not," with an accent of reproach that made his heart leap up again. "'Tis — 'tis something very different, sir — it is our religion. We can be friends; we shall be, but never more than friends. It would be wicked, impious. Think you not so, too?" she added, an appeal in her voice which made Ralph's heart ache.

"Nay, I do not," he said firmly; "I swear to God I do

not. If that be your only reason it is not enough. 'Tis nothing — Rachel."

He drew nearer, but she shook her head, and he could see that now her eyes were steady and her face like marble.

" It is everything to me."

His hands dropped to his side. Once he tried to speak, but no words would come. They were in his heart, words of burning love and supplication, but as he looked on the white face, so sorrowful, yet so steadfast, they died upon his lips.

" Good-bye," he muttered, turning to the door.

" Good-bye," she answered softly, so softly and, oh, so tenderly, " good-bye, dear friend."

He reached the door, and fumbled at the lock. For the moment he was stunned, only feeling that he must go, because she wished it. But as he looked back once more into her face, so sad and pitiful for all its firmness, his eyes flashed into hers defiantly.

" I do your bidding now. But some day I shall return and claim your love, and will not be denied. I swear it by the God in whom we both believe."

The door closed behind him with a slam, and Rachel heard his footsteps echo down the passage. They did not meet again before the regiment departed.

The men were to have left quarters at sunrise, but there were so many things that the younger officers had forgotten, and were obliged to look to at the last moment, that the morning was well advanced before the long columns of steel-clad horsemen streamed through the streets of Ely, and, leaving the cathedral and the deanery on their left, marched on towards the plain brown house where the colonel's family was assembled to see them pass.

They made no brilliant spectacle. They were plain yeomen mostly, with a sprinkling of farmers' sons, officered by squires and merchants — men of the middle class. There were no waving plumes or gilded armour. Yet, to those who knew the faces under the plain steel caps, no bravery or gay trappings were needed, still less to us, who as we see in imagination the grave, stern men advance in their polished armour and plain buff coats, on their stout horses, shining with the grooming overnight, must feel, if we be Englishmen, a glow of honest pride. The "Ironsides" these, fated, as we know, though they do not, to withstand and conquer all their foes, and later to fill the finest troops in Europe with wonder and admiration; yet plain British men, sirs, nothing more, their leader only a stout, broad-shouldered country gentleman, with harsh features, massive chin, and a rugged, melancholy face. The face lights up now, and the heavy lips are parted with a tender smile. He is passing his own door, and his officers, sitting erect and gallantly, are saluting with their swords the ladies gathered there.

On sweeps the regiment, four abreast, a space between each troop; and last of all comes "Cromwell's Own."

"Oh, look ye, mother; Rachel, look. How differently they ride from all the rest," cried Betty, pointing at them, and forgetting in her excitement that her shrill voice carried far. "There — there's Ralph. Aye, I'd know him in a thousand were it but for the way he sits his horse. He minds me of a picture of the king," then to Rachel in a lower voice, oblivious of an outcry from her mother at such a shocking simile, "Be he not the finest officer you ever saw save father? I know he be. Oh, there's the quartermaster. I must wave my hand to him, and the little corporal man on his great horse by big Sanctify—sure 'tis like a David and Goliath—and, oh, now, mark the rest! How their horses step together, Their very stirrups clash in unison. Hark to the trumpets and the peal of bells in their honour, and the people cheering there in the roadway. I shall cheer too — nay, mother, I *must, I will.* Hurrah, hurrah, hurrah!"

And then Betty the irrepressible ran beyond the doorstep and waved her handkerchief and shrieked at the top of her voice until the troop passed by.

The men heard her, and many a stern face broke into a smile; while, as for Ralph, he nodded gaily, half turned his horse, and gave her a magnificent salute. Then they broke into a trot, and in a few minutes were but a cloud of dust upon the Cambridge road. Many, many months were to pass before they were seen on that road again — months of such suspense and anxiety that men grew grey, and women aged more than in a score of years in times of peace.

War was over the land, desolating it, ruining lives and breaking hearts — war, with its carnage and waste, its furious hate and despair; war, cleansing by fire and the sword the foulness that had been growing in the country a century past; tearing up by the roots and casting aside institutions which custom had made men believe were divine; the war of a nation against itself, a nation destined to stand and flourish and put forth greater strength than ever it had done yet; the war of a people for freedom, won when all the fighters were dead, and mostly forgotten; the war won by Oliver Cromwell, and Oliver Cromwell alone.

CHAPTER XXX

WHEN the chronicler of a true romance of war sends forth a regiment with blare of trumpets, equipped for fight and thirsting for it, it is considered his bounden duty to provide immediately an account of a fiercely contested battle, or series of battles, in which the reader's favourite characters will do great deeds of glory and renown. Unfortunately, hard historical fact is too definite to be set aside, and as we have set ourselves, so far as the limits of our story will allow, to follow faithfully the fortunes of the Ironsides — we must tell the truth!

The regiment marched to Cambridge, but no further. The town and all the neighbourhood was in a panic, for rumour said that 20,000 bloodthirsty Cavaliers were spurring from the west to sack the county and hang the commissioners for the Eastern Counties Association, who had been the persons chiefly instrumental in providing the means for equipping Cromwell's regiment and others, from the gates of the colleges. The welcome given to the grim Ely men may be imagined, for they were the first soldiers to arrive. Next day, and for many days, men came pouring in until 12,000 had assembled, fairly armed and moderately disciplined, and all agog with anxiety to meet and slay Cavaliers. But no Cavaliers appeared. It was not the habit of the marauding portion of the royal army to raid where disciplined troops had assembled for their reception. No sooner did the good citizens of Cambridge discover this than they became as anxious for the departure of their protectors as they had been for their presence, and in three weeks only two regiments remained — Cromwell's and another.

But if there was no fighting there was hard work in abundance. Ralph, to his great joy, was requested by the commissioners, at Cromwell's instance, to inspect the fortifications of the town with his colonel, and, thanks to his studies in fortification in the Low Countries, was able to point out their deficiencies, which were manifold, and was thereafter appointed a member of a committee, with Cromwell as its chairman, to set about putting Cambridge into a state of defence. This work was completed in two months; the committee received the thanks of the town and dissolved; the troops were formally turned into a garrison for the time being, and their chief occupation became the daily drill and exercise to perfect their knowledge of the use of arms and horses.

A wearing time it was, severely trying to the temper and patience of everyone. To realise the difficulties of the officers of the regiments and the irritation of the men, it must be remembered that they were drawn from the land or from small businesses, which were in very many instances going to rack and ruin through their owners' sacrifice for the opportunity of coming to blows with the absence, also that, while all were willing to make any enemy and wresting their country and themselves from the rule of the prelates and the king's favourites, they had not bargained for months of monotonous life under military rule, out of sight of their loved ones, living on very insufficient food, and frequently exposed to the grumbling and complaints of the citizens out of whose pockets their subsistence came.

These feelings were not rendered less acute by the reports that Sir William Waller was doing great things against the Earl of Stamford in the west of England, and that in the north Lord Fairfax and the Marquis of Newcastle were circling round one another like two bulldogs awaiting but an opportunity to get to death grips and perhaps, it was said, decide the war.

Nor were the good folk of Cambridge and the eastern counties generally at all more content at the state of things than the soldiers. To men in other parts of the country, exposed to Rupert's depredations and the plunderings of the " Newarkers," these eastern counties — Norfolk, Suffolk, Essex, Hertfordshire, and Cambridgeshire — were havens of security. But the East Anglians did not appreciate their blessings. Trade was not as good as it had been, and men were getting poorer, and yet they were expected to contribute from their failing means towards the support of these armed men and their fat horses, which did nothing but eat and sleep and exercise at their expense. In one thing the soldiers and citizens heartily agreed, if we except the majority of Cromwell's regiment: they were unanimous in laying the responsibility for all their troubles upon the shoulders of their leaders, and in especial upon Colonel Cromwell.

Was it not Cromwell who, sitting on every committee throughout the association, pressed hard and ever harder for more money, more food, more arms and ammunition for the soldiers, and even had the hardihood to declare in a manner no one cared to contradict, that were the things he advised *not* done he might as well disband his men, and invite the malignants to do their will on Cambridge and devastate the country? A most pestilent, unconvinceable, obstinate, and overbearing man, thought the citizens then; as for the soldiers — always excepting those who knew him and saw him daily in drill and camp — was it not Cromwell who drew up a code of regulations against the plundering and drunkenness, blasphemy and disobedience, so stringent, that if a man swore he was fined a shilling, and if the least complaint was made by a citizen of rude behaviour there was flogging for the first offence, and stripping of arms before the troop and ignominious dismissal for the second, and even, if the crime were wounding an unarmed man, or lewdly threatening a woman, hanging?

Aye, it was Cromwell, and Cromwell alone. But the things that he directed to be done were done. The men were fed somehow and decently housed; their arms were sufficient for their use, and their horses sound and in good condition; while, on the other hand, depredations or lawlessness on the part of the troopers were almost unknown. For of Cromwell it might be written that all his life he never made a rule, or caused one to be made, but he enforced it to the bitter end, and exacted full penalty for its disobedience, whether the culprit were a common trooper or His Majesty the King of France.

In this work Ralph played a subordinate but very active part. His own troop being above suspicion both as to discipline and conduct, and their drill requiring little supervision, Cromwell made use of him as an aide-de-camp when instructions or suggestions had to be delivered to the commander of other regiments, and at times as his proxy on the committees of defence. The intercourse between them was strictly confined to business, but the fascination of Cromwell's strength and patience to Ralph's eager, sympathetic temperament grew steadily as the weeks passed, until it became a byword among the regiments, both officers and men, that the least wish or suggestion from the colonel was to his captain more sacred and binding than any laws made by God or man.

In such work as this, with now and then a dash at a town or village where Royalism showed signs of ferment, quenched at a blow by Cromwell's dragoons, did the spring pass, and the early summer, and then at last, when the discontent of the soldiers, in spite of Cromwell, rose almost to semi-mutiny, and the committees contributing were sinking week by week, the news flew through the country-side that the Parliament had ordered the army of the eastern counties to move northwards to the succor of Lincolnshire, now swarming with malignants daily growing in power and confidence, and that pending the arrival of Lord Willoughby of Parham, now in Gainsborough and besieged there, Colonel Cromwell was to be in command. Among many of the officers there were serious apprehensions that the men would refuse to march; perhaps some of these officers, smarting under the pressure of hard and disagreeable work Cromwell had laid upon them, would have been not altogether sorry, but be that as it may, they were entirely mistaken.

The men were Englishmen, and, grumble as they might at drill and discipline, the moment they knew that the time for action was at hand, and that they were to try their strength against Newarkers, Camdeners, and possibly even the Marquis of Newcastle's famous army, now pressing Lord Fairfax hard, they forgot their grievances and troubles, received their scanty rations with great cheerfulness, and gave thanks to God.

On Thursday, July 24th, on the dawn of a hot summer's day, the regiments marched quietly northwards. No one knew except their commanders precisely where they were going or what they were going to do. But they were to fight; that was enough. They marched until noon, when a halt was called, scouts sent out, and orders given for men and horses to take their fill of food and rest for two hours.

" Ye will all need it, lads, mark me," Cromwell said, walking among them as they settled down. His face was pleasant and cheerful, his manner kindly as a father's. Cromwell in garrison and Cromwell campaigning were two different men. " I say you will want all the strength and skill that the Lord hath given you," he added. " See it be forthcoming presently. But rest ye now; eat and drink and take your ease. In two hours or less our task beginneth. And it will be a heavy one, though not too heavy for such men as ye."

Then he retired to his own quarters, and swallowed a

hasty meal, mounted a fresh horse, and with his major, Whalley, a bluff, plain-mannered, straight-forward soldier, and Ralph, he rode out some distance from camp.

The day was hot and hazy, and it was not easy to see far, but when they reached the top of a hill Cromwell pointed to the north, and his officers saw what he saw and needed no words to tell them what it meant. A volume of smoke was resting like a long, low cloud over a grove of trees, another creeping like a snake over a bit of sunny valley.

"Plunder of the helpless, rapine, murder! O, God, hold not Thy peace. For lo, they that hate Thee have lifted up the hand; they are confederated against Thee. O my God, make them like a wheel; as the stubble before the wind, as the fire burneth a wood, and as the flame setteth the mountains on fire, so persecute them. Let them be confounded, and troubled for ever; yea, let them be put to shame and perish. Whalley, bid the men to saddle; haste ye down to them. They have had rest eno' and must set to their arms in the name of the Lord, and stay this devil's work."

A few minutes of bustle and running to and fro, a few brisk words of command, and the men were in saddle, ready for anything. Cromwell led them in person. He knew the country and had reliable information of the movements of the enemy. The Royalists also received timely notice of the Puritans' advance, but they did not know yet with whom they had to deal. The Cavaliers were drawn up on an open heath, and as the East Anglians formed in line of battle charged them in loose order, gaily and confidently. The Ironsides withstood them as a rock withstands a tidal wave, and, like that wave, the Cavaliers were dashed asunder by the shock of their own assault, scattering to right and left of the solid mass of men whose ranks they could not pierce. Then from Cromwell's lips came the word to charge,

and with one deep-resounding shout of " God with us,"
the Parliament men leapt upon their foes and crushed
them. In half an hour the Royalists were flying headlong across the heath, many cut down as they ran, the
rest to take refuge in a great stronghold of the neighbourhood, Burleigh House. By the time the sun had
set this stronghold was surrounded and blockaded, and
while the men had some refreshments Cromwell called
a council of war to decide its fate.

The officers were of opinion that they had not force
enough at present and should send for more artillery.
Cromwell listened to all they had to say, then quietly
unfolded his own plan of campaign. At the first streak
of dawn, at that time of year about 3 a. m., the siege was
to begin. Before night the house must be taken and
the men allowed a few hours' rest. They would then
march to Grantham, forty-two miles, receive reinforce-
ments there, and press on without delay to Gainsborough,
thirteen miles further on, to relieve Lord Willoughby.

The officers, with the exception of Whalley and Ralph,
looked at one another aghast.

" 'Tis beyond all reason," an old veteran exclaimed.
" Colonel, dost not know that thy troopers be only flesh
and blood? "

" Sir," Cromwell answered gently, " I be commander
here, and what I desire will be carried out. If less than
this be done the cause hereabouts will perish. This
cause is God's; if He be in earnest in this business He
will give us the strength needful. If not, His will be
done. Captain Dangerfield, to you I give the task of
placing the ordnance for the breach; Major Whalley,
you will lead the charge when the guns have done their
work. Gentlemen, the council is at end. When the
trumpet sounds let each do his part, and God be with
ye all."

CHAPTER XXXI

BURLEIGH HOUSE fell before the sun went down. It was a bitter struggle, for the terms Cromwell offered were refused, and no quarter was given to any found with arms in their hands. The Parliament men had seen the burning homesteads as they rode; the sufferings of the country people had goaded them to fury; and there was no mercy in their hearts that day.

When it was over they slept with their arms beside them, too tired even to eat; but at dawn they roused, ate heartily, and set forth on horses fresh after a good rest, and so marched briskly northwards towards Grantham, covering the distance, with short rests for food, in twenty-four hours. At Grantham they stayed an hour, breakfasted, and picked up 300 men from Nottingham and a train of waggons laden with food and ammunition for Gainsborough. This town was still thirteen miles away, the weather was hot, and the roads dusty. Presently the pace began to flag, and from officers and men alike an unspoken prayer went forth that the Royalists around Gainsborough might have raised the siege. On they marched, however, steadily, until within two miles of the town; then a halt was called, and it was whispered that a score of pickeerers Cromwell had thrown out ahead had returned to report that the enemy was awaiting them in force.

Then Cromwell himself rode down the lines. "Men," he said, "you have done marvellous well. In so far as I am aware, not one hath faltered through the fatigue of this long march. Now we are within sight of our goal. Praise be to God!" He doffed his hat, and his words were greeted with a heartfelt "Amen." "We be, indeed, but one mile and a few furlongs from Gainsborough town, wherein a garrison of godly men faint for lack of the provisions we have brought with us from Grantham. Yet the Lord hath not yet released us from our travail. Between us and the town lieth the enemy, proud and scornful as he ever is, assured that thou, being aweary with marching, wilt shrink from the issue and turn and fly before him. Even now "—he raised his sword and pointed to the brow of a sandy knoll of heather and gorse a few hundred yards away — " see, they come upon us with their pots glistening in the sunshine. Men, we must charge them home, drive them before us as the rabbits yonder flee into their holes. Art ready?"

His voice rang out over the field, harsh, sonorous, and soul-stirring, and, as if by magic, the faces of the weary men brightened, a hoarse shout of approval came from the parched throats, and backs straightened under the heavy armour — the men were ready!

Cromwell beckoned to Ralph.

"Order fifty dragooners to advance unto the foot of the hill and open fire. Bid them not dismount, but advance slowly, firing; for their support send one Lincoln-shire troop and four of ours; Brandreth's and Sugden's, Crook's and Farrington's. Tell them to charge briskly and yield not a foot. The rest will follow as reserve. Let them act swiftly; the malignants descend the hill."

Ralph followed his colonel's eye, then rode for his life, for the ridge was black with armed men. A few minutes later the dragooners,* in loose order, were toiling up a steep incline of yielding sandy soil, covered with rabbit burrows, firing as they went. It was a hard task, for with a flash of swords and a yell the advance guard of the Royalists above dashed down upon them at speed, and several saddles were emptied on either side, but the

---

* Mounted infantry carrying short guns.

dragooners held their ground stubbornly; and now in
solid order, advancing at a steady trot up the hill,
came 400 Lincoln men. Back went the Royalists'
"forlorn hope" before them, but only to turn and
charge again, reinforced by 200 men. It was a stiff
struggle, but the Lincolners inch by inch forced
their enemies back to the hilltop. And then, for
a moment, their hearts failed them, for ahead, not
more than a hundred yards off, was another large body
of horse, and still further to the rear a regiment of
cuirassiers. But as they drew rein and paused to breathe
their horses for the onslaught that was coming they
heard the steady tramp of the Ely regiment behind them,
Cromwell himself leading the right wing.

"Upon them," he cried, as the long line overtopped
the hill and the pace quickened to a gallop, "steadily,
steadily! Lose not your order, but hold together — all
together — *charge!*"

Like an avalanche they swept down the gentle slope,
with a crash broadsword fell upon breastplate and helmet, and the real battle of the day began. These Cavaliers were no drunken plunderers expecting an easy
victory. They were veteran men-at-arms, well mounted
and well led. For some minutes, despite the impetus
the charge of the Ironsides had received from the fall
of the ground, the result was doubtful, but at last one
Royalist troop gave way, another, and another, and then
of a sudden all wheeled and fled, and a yell of exultation
and joy went up from the men of the Parliament. Their
blood was foaming in their veins; to cut, and hack, and
slay for the glory of the Lord their one desire. The
enemy must be destroyed, crushed out of existence. So
felt the men, and their horses, as excited as their riders,
responded gallantly to the spur. Few noticed that
though the squadrons whom they had conquered were
flying for their lives, yet to their left rear, standing
firm and vigilant, with tightly drawn rein and sword
points flashing in the sun, a regiment of cuirassiers, a

compact and perfectly appointed array of horsemen, was awaiting its opportunity. How they smiled, those court gallants, as they saw their hated enemies ride recklessly past and give themselves into their hands. How eagerly, though all in silence, they obeyed their leader, General Cavendish, as he raised himself in his stirrups and drew his sword. " Now, gentlemen, we have the Roundhead dogs. Charge, and God save the king! "

They charged with closed ranks, and with deadly swiftness and precision, fell on the flank of the Lincolners, who had just been recalled by Cromwell from the chase. Yet the Lincolners were sturdy fellows, and at sight of their new enemy, with a hoarse cry of defiance, they turned about and met them bravely. But they went down before the cuirassiers as grass before the scythe; they were thrown into confusion, beaten to pieces. And now — but what is this? Another battle-cry, as confident as that of Cavendish, and of a grimmer tone; a rush of galloping hoofs, regular and rhythmic, and then a terrible crash of steel on the flank and rear of the cuirassiers. The biter was bit. In the excitement of watching his own men fly and the regiments chasing them, General Cavendish had not perceived that Cromwell had halted three troops the instant the fight on the hill was over, and awaited his action while the Lincolners dashed on. These troops were the first and two others. They were only one hundred and eighty men all told, and the Cavaliers numbered six hundred, but they were the pick of Cromwell's force, and with the Lincolners in front and these in rear, the regiment of cuirassiers was as helpless as a buffalo with a leopard on its back. Silently the Ironsides fought. They gave no respite and no chance. In vain the Royalists tried to form a new front. In vain their officers, spurring into the midst of the Ironsides and fighting with desperate energy, sought to gain time for their men to rally and for their reserves to stiffen the yielding line. No individual efforts could stay the fierce vigour of Cromwell's chosen troopers. The cuirassiers gave way before the weight of their serried line, sweeping onward with the swing and force of an Atlantic roller. In an hour not a Cavalier remained upon the field; General Cavendish was dead, and the road to Gainsborough was open.

It was not, however, until nearly noon that the gates of the beleaguered town, with loud rejoicing from its citizens, opened wide to receive the weary, mud-stained victors and their train of powder and provisions. Free quarters were immediately offered to the men, and Lord Willoughby, the commandant of the town and titular chief of the army of the eastern counties, received the officers in his own house, and ordered a collation to be spread for them.

Lord Willoughby of Parham was a slight, handsome man, with bright eyes and a gallant bearing, which Ralph liked, but with a cynical manner of speech. He was dressed in correct Puritan fashion, but there was an elegance in the cut of his doublet of finest black cloth, a neatness and spotlessness about his attire generally, which denoted that the fine gentleman in him was only sleeping. Ralph, glancing at Cromwell, could hardly help smiling at the difference between the two men. They sat together at the head of the table, their officers at the side, Whalley at my lord's right hand, Ralph on Cromwell's left, and it was easy for Ralph, who knew the meaning of every expression and turn of his colonel's face, to see that no love was lost between them. Nothing, however, could exceed my lord's courtesy, or the neatness and aptness of his compliments to "his most worthy and gallant friend" when he drank his health. Ralph was curious to hear how Cromwell would respond, but he never had the opportunity, for as the colonel rose to his feet, glass in hand, the door of the room was hurriedly opened, and a trooper, covered with dust and foam and sweat, stumbled in, and clumsily saluting, cried that troops in large numbers were approaching from the north.

The commanders looked at one another, Cromwell quaffing his wine in silence and waiting for Lord Willoughby to speak. His lordship smiled.

"A false alarm, I think. These poor rogues of mine be so dazed with awaiting succour, which at last hath come, that they see Cavaliers under every bush, and if sheep wander down a hill they report a troop of Newarkers at the gates. Cholmley," to one of his officers, "take this man, swill his throat with small ale, and listen to his tale while we refresh. 'Fore Heaven, it is hard indeed for a man not to be able to enjoy his wine."

"With your leave, my lord," Cromwell said, "I will question the messenger. It seemeth to me an urgent matter." Then, without waiting for an answer, he turned to the soldier.

"How far be they off?"

"A mile by this, sir, I swear not more."

"Didst see their strength?"

"I counted six troops of horse, and nigh a regiment of foot."

"No more?"

"No, colonel."

Cromwell rose.

"It would appear, my lord," he said with dry politeness, "that these are not sheep. Hark! There be some more awake than we — our men!"

There was a rattle of hoofs and clink of steel bridles. The troops were hastily forming outside the house.

Willoughby was on his feet now, calling for his helmet.

"Nay, there is no need," Cromwell said at the door. "Finish thy dinner, sir. Lend me five hundred foot, and I will see to this force."

Willoughby laughed.

"Thou'rt truly modest, colonel, as indeed I have always heard. I have but four hundred, and can ill spare those."

"Four hundred, then," Cromwell said impatiently; "but do not delay."

He hurried away; the foot — pike and musketeers — were hastily assembled and marched cheerfully out of the north gate, with the horse of Cromwell's regiment on either flank. They found the enemy approaching at a steady pace, but not apparently disposed to fight. One charge of the cavalry drove back their advanced guard, and they retreated rapidly to the crest of a high hill, too quickly for any effective pursuit from the weary horse of the victors. This hill was steeper and loftier than the battle-ground of the morning, and nothing could be seen beyond it. Cromwell, giving orders that the enemy were to be followed for a few miles, but warily, returned to Gainsborough to consult with Willoughby as to the future destination of his force. He had barely reached the town when a message came that on the other side of the hill were a large force both of horse and foot, among which had been detected the red-coats of the Marquis of Newcastle's own regiment, proving that Cromwell's tired horse and the Gainsborough regiment of foot were opposed by the greater part of the royal army. A hurried consultation followed, and Cromwell rode back at headlong pace to recall the foot. But it was too late. The Royalists had advanced briskly, and the Gainsborough men were retreating in a disorder which grew worse each minute. Nothing could save them unless Newcastle's advance was checked, and to do this there were but twelve weary troops of horse. But Cromwell was at the front, and his orders flew right and left.

"Major Whalley, charge with two troops. When thou hast broken their first line, retire; and thou, Dangerfield, and, Brandreth, do the same with thine. Thus by removes we may yet get in with safety to the town. Seek no more than to baffle their advance. God be with ye; march."

As the orders were given, so were they carried out, though each trooper felt that he was going to his death. Twelve troops of exhausted men and worn-out horses against an army fresh and vigorous, led by a great soldier; and in the rear of the Parliament horse the disordered foot, whose confusion acted like fresh blood to whet the Royalist appetites. It was a manœuvre so strange and unexpected that many of the Cavaliers thought the enemy had taken leave of their senses. Then Whalley's troops charged, and their onset, though but at the trot, was so well and compactly made that they broke the first line fairly, and before they could be overwhelmed by the solid mass behind, at sharp word of command, they wheeled and swept aside. And when the Royalists, with triumphant cheer, re-formed their first line and spurred on to the pursuit, they were met by a fresh handful of troopers, and they were once more beaten back. So the struggle went on, the Ironsides, dogged and silent, retreating inch by inch; the advancing Royalists, loud in their defiance, chafing furiously at the delay, but unable to crush their stubborn, well-handled foes. At last the signal came that the foot were safe within the walls of Gainsborough; and with one last charge the Ironsides turned and followed, leaving Newcastle's army growling like a hungry lion for the prey which had escaped its jaws.

Yet there was no rest for either man or horse. In a few hours Gainsborough would be surrounded, and Cromwell and his regiments retreated southwards. They left the town disheartened and miserable. It seemed as if all their exertions had been in vain and their blood spilt for naught. But they were mistaken. With the fall of Cavendish, his army had dispersed, and Gainsborough, though once more beleaguered, was now well victualled and provided with good store of ammunition; and in the days that followed, wherever the Marquis of Newcastle made inquiry, whether from the relics of Cavendish's force or from his own troops, he heard the same account. A regiment of Parliament horse, as well mounted and armed as the best accoutred cuirassiers, with a discipline and a method of fighting never heard of hitherto among the Roundhead cavalry, led by a man with a heavy face and rasping voice, one Colonel Cromwell, of Ely, carried all before it.

"Such an ill-favoured rascal," one of the captains said within hearing of the Marquis, "that I could have struck him down once in the push, but, by my faith, I was feared my sword would be turned by the wart on his nose."

"Sir," said his commander in a tone that quenched the ready laughter of the staff, "should it ever be my fortune to take prisoner the man you honour with your raillery, I trust he will give me the privilege of sitting at my own table. An' we be not careful the day is drawing nigh when we shall know this Cromwell as the first general of horse in England."

CHAPTER XXXII

THE regiment marched to Huntingdon, and remained there to recruit and rest. They reached the town late in the evening. Thanks to the forethought of their commander, shelter and food were ready for them, and no labour awaited the worn-out men. Cromwell, Whalley, and Ralph were quartered in the same house, and ate their supper in tired silence. Before it was over Ralph noticed Cromwell eyeing him askance, and knew that there was work for him to do. He rose and stood at attention with a wan smile, for he was terribly weary.

"Your orders, colonel?"

Cromwell motioned him aside.

"Nay, get thee to a couch. Thy face is white as this napery here," lifting the tablecloth. "Pish, get thee to rest, I say."

Ralph did not move.

"You have a message or letter to deliver that is urgent, sir. I am ready."

"Whalley," cried Cromwell with mock anger, "this man be a spy upon my thoughts. What say you? Ought he not to be arrested?"

"He is in the right, sir," was the blunt rejoinder. "But an he be too weary give me thy message."

"Worse and worse," Cromwell said, a pleased smile lurking round the corners of his mouth, "major and captain of a piece. Beshrew me, Ralph, but it cuts me to the heart to bid thee, sir, yet it is imperative. Lay thee down, man, for half an hour. Whalley, seek you a fresh horse for him. He must to Cambridge with letters to the commissioners."

He drew out writing materials, and while Ralph,

wrapped in his cloak, did as he was bidden, and the major went to find a horse, Cromwell wrote with set lips and frowning brow. The half-hour passed; the horse was ready, and Cromwell's letter sealed and directed.

"This is to Sir Francis Bacon, Chairman of the Association. Place it in his hands, and see to it that he calleth a meeting of the rest this night, and leave him not until you have assurance that the help I demand is forthcoming. Drive into their minds the extreme urgency of our position and the true condition of affairs. Though these men fear God, and have honest minds, they are timid and tight-handed through narrowness of view. Rouse them. I might have sent Whalley, but he hath not thy power of tongue. Thrust upon them the facts with all the eloquence that is in you. Remind them that Fairfax is beaten into Hull, Waller crushed at Lansdown Heath, Bristol taken by Rupert. Tell them that no place in England owns allegiance to Parliament now but the eastern counties and London. This, put forth as you will express it, should strike some fire into their souls. But mind you, lad," grasping Ralph by the arm, and speaking with as much warmth as if he were addressing the commissioners, "waste not your breath with accounts of the urgency of our own danger; that will not move them. They hold it is but a soldier's business to be killed. But show them that if they give us not the means to stay Newcastle's advance their homes will be ablaze and their towns laid waste."

The night was clear and cold, and Ralph, with a fresh horse under him, covered the distance in two hours. He had a racking headache, but Cromwell's words had roused him to so keen a sense of the danger of the country that for the time his weariness disappeared.

Sir Francis Bacon had been in bed some time when Ralph arrived; but a message from a scared servant that an officer had business with him of life and death brought that worthy gentleman into the hall in a few minutes, and after a hurried word or two with Ralph

a messenger was despatched to the houses of the other
commissioners, summoning them to an immediate conference. Ralph was regaled with bread and wine, and
had begun to answer some eager questions from Sir
Francis, when the door opened, and who should enter
but Isaac Hepworth. Sir Francis smiled an embarr-
assed smile. He was an amiable and peace-loving man,
forced into his present position by a high sense of duty.
Hepworth was his intimate friend, so was Cromwell. He
knew all about the feud between them, and had done
his very best to pour oil upon the troubled waters. It
was an evil fate which decreed that the bone of conten-
tion, the Socinian himself, should be the messenger
chosen by Cromwell in this crisis, and that Hepworth
should be staying in the house. Sir Francis was thoroughly loyal to Cromwell, but foresaw the extreme difficulty of persuading his colleagues to agree with his
views, with Hepworth present to dispute them. Yet
there was nothing to be done. The minister was far too
influential a person to be banished from the conference.
Events must take their course.

Ralph, at sight of the minister's entrance, rose and
bowed very stiffly. Hepworth formally acknowledged
the salute, and addressed Sir Francis.

"I hear there be news from the army."

The Chairman of Commissioners handed him Cromwell's letter.

"Assuredly, yes, reverend friend. This gallant officer must have much to tell us. But he may, perchance,
prefer to wait until the commissioners arrive. Read
this."

Hepworth, without again looking at Ralph, or showing by the least sign that he was conscious of his presence, read the letter slowly. By the time he had finished
— and it seemed to take him a long while — the commissioners made their appearance.

Puritans of the Puritans were these gentlemen, grave
and elderly, dressed in black coats and doublets of the

strictest, plainest cut, and white falling collars of snowy unstarched linen. Their faces were clean-shaven, their hair closely cropped. They sat motionless and wooden as carved images round Sir Francis Bacon; and Ralph, standing in their midst, his armour soiled and stained with blood and dirt, his long hair lying disordered and lank with perspiration on his shoulders, his left hand grasping his belt, his right resting upon his sword as if in the last resort he would use it to strengthen his arguments, seemed an altogether different species of being.

The business of the conference was opened by the Chairman, who, after introducing Ralph, read Cromwell's letter aloud. It was a short pithy account of the engagements around Gainsborough. The last paragraph and the postscript the Chairman read very slowly and emphatically, and Ralph, watching the faces of the commissioners, felt a sinking of the heart as he saw them change from quiet attention and approval to uneasiness and dissent. The words were these:—

" Thus you have the true relation as short as I could. What you are to do upon it is next to be considered. If I could speak words to pierce your hearts with the sense of our and your condition I would! If you will raise 2000 foot at present to encounter this army of Newcastle's, to raise the siege " (of Gainsborough)," and to enable us to fight him, we doubt not, by the grace of God, but that we shall be able to relieve the town, and beat the enemy on the other side of Trent; whereas, if somewhat be not done in this, you will see Newcastle's army march up into your bowels, being now, as it is, on this side Trent. I know it will be difficult to raise this many in so short a time, but let me assure you it's necessary, and therefore to be done. At least, do what you may, with all possible expedition! I would I had the happiness to speak with one of you. Truly I cannot come over but must attend my charge; the enemy is vigilant. The Lord direct you what to do.
" Gentlemen, I am your faithful servant,
" OLIVER CROMWELL.

" P. S.—Give this gentleman credence; he is worthy to be trusted; he knows the urgency of our affairs better than myself.

If he give intelligence, in point of time, of haste to be made, believe him; he will advise for your good."

A silence followed the reading of the letter. The Chairman coughed deprecatingly.

"This, gentlemen, be what the colonel saith. God hath granted him some notable successes, and it would seem strange that after these the resources of this poor Association should be taxed again. Yet these words, being the words of Colonel Cromwell, need no verifying. What answer will it be your pleasure to return, or are there questions you would wish to ask this gallant officer commended to us by the colonel?"

"Questions, Sir Francis! What questions?" said one of the commissioners sharply. The speaker was a small, thin man, with an aggressive snub nose and restless eyes. "Of a surety, it would appear to me that enough hath been said out of the colonel's own mouth or writ by his pen to end the matter. He asks what is impossible. And, were it within our power, I should decline to advance him a man until I had received a full account in detail of lives lost, the present strength of the army, and in what manner he would propose to use the foot he asketh for; yet, as we have not these, I shall not waste my breath."

The Chairman sighed.

"There be truth in your words, Master Barrow. None can deny our poverty, but the colonel hath been truly painstaking and forward in his doings. Would you indeed" — appealing to the rest — "send him nothing? I thought that if four companies, mayhap a regiment ——"

"And I say none," quoth the little man, wrinkling his snub nose obstinately; "neither man nor musket, pike nor pistol would I send to this soldier till he present himself before us in person at the least."

The Chairman looked round at the other commissioners and saw indecision written on the faces of all.

"Captain Dangerfield," he said, with a grave bow to Ralph, "if thou hast aught to say, we'll be pleased to hear thee."

Ralph bowed and stepped forward. The contemptuous tone of little Master Barrow, a Cambridge attorney, who rarely ventured to open his lips in Cromwell's presence, irritated him extremely. He wondered whether Hepworth's presence had made this difference, for he felt assured that nothing but the bitterest and most rancorous hostility was to be expected from him. The position was desperate, and desperate measures must be taken. At Sir Francis Bacon's call he drew his sword, and at the scrape of steel on scabbard and the sweep of Ralph's arm the commissioners started violently, and Master Barrow's face went a sickly yellow.

Ralph held the weapon out for their inspection.

"I have much to say, sir," he cried; "too much for my tongue ever to express. But an this gentleman requireth evidence let him observe this blade. 'Tis still wet with blood, the blood of Newcastle's redcoats; and blood drieth quickly on a sword. Thus you may measure in your minds how short a time it is since we were disputing, foot by foot, inch by inch, with the king's great army of the north. Then it was at the gates of Gainsborough; in a week, nay, in a few hours, it may be at Cambridge. See my doublet here, and there upon my hose — blood, sirs, again. 'Tis the enemies', thank God, but how soon may it be mine own or thine? Can two regiments of horse withstand an army very long? They did it to-day at the sword's point, as you have heard, and all for your sakes, and your wives' and children's sakes, and all the helpless ones that will now, it seems, soon be at the mercy of malignant plunderers. For we are but men, though Cromwell lead us. And we can do no more. Bethink you, since Thursday —

and it be now Monday night — we have had no respite
from our labours.   In that time, your colonel — whom
this honourable gentleman, in his absence, dares to
speak of in terms that are scarce civil — laid siege as
he hath writ you, and took by assault Burleigh House;
marched fifty-five miles to Gainsborough without rest
day or night, defeated there a superior force of very gallant Cavaliers, relieved the town, and attacked and held
at bay the finest army the king commands, and all this
with no more than a thousand men.   And now, through
these men being exhausted and only horse-soldiers,
while Newcastle hath a many regiments of foot as well
as cavalry, Cromwell asketh you for a matter of two
thousand foot, and offereth then to meet the enemy and
drive them home again.   Think you he cannot keep his
word?   Did he ever fail?   But no "— Ralph was in a
passion now, recking nothing of his language and little
for his manners, while the commissioners sat and eyed
him apprehensively —" no, the failure hath been on the
other side.   'Tis you who would grudge, and even now
question, his success.   You, sitting securely in your
homes like dogs in kennel, order him, to whom you owe
your lives, to come to you and bow the knee to your
Majesties!   It is an absurdity, and to me, who hath
known what he hath done, 'tis monstrous.   But I waste
your time.   If you have naught to give or promise me,
then I have nothing more to say but this.   Our blood
hath been spilt in vain.   In vain Cromwell hath plucked
the beard of the Marquis.   In a few days at most you
will find the Royalist troopers at your gates.   Perchance
then blows will have more influence than prayers.   Not
a general throughout England, fighting for the Parliament, hath been victorious but Cromwell, and he hath
never yet been beaten. If he faileth now, and the malignants clutch your throats, upon your heads be it.   I bid
you farewell."

He would have walked out in his heat and disgust,

and ridden, weary as he was, straight back to Huntingdon. But the Chairman plucked him by the sleeve and
said persuasively: —

"Nay, nay, gallant captain, be not so hasty. Thy
appeal hath moved us, me at least. Gentlemen, I pray
you, let not this officer return with such a message to his
colonel; it would be a grievous thing."

He looked appealingly round again, and Ralph
paused.

"What can we do?" Master Barrow said in acrid
tones. "The officer is pleased to call us dogs. Then
I reply we have no bones to spare for wolves. We are
nigh penniless, and could but appeal in any case to Parliament. That will take time. Let the worthy colonel
send direct to London. I propose that this message be
returned to him, with our good wishes and regrets."

A murmur of assent came from the others, with here
and there an ejaculation, "What men we have had better guard the town!" "Enough hath been done by us;
'tis the turn of Parliament."

Ralph muttered an oath, not so low but that it was
heard and remembered. Then he turned to Sir Francis,
who was trying to warm the coldness of his colleagues
into some message more grateful to the ear, and, inter-
rupting the good man, he respectfully proffered his hand.

"'Tis vain, sir. Besides, what matter empty phrases?
If I bring not men, or tidings of their coming, to my
colonel, think you he will value words? Nay, I must
be gone. I am grateful for your countenance; indeed,
I will not forget to report how you inclined toward us.
To these gentlemen "— Ralph bowed low with sarcastic
politeness —"on my faith I have nothing more to say."

He strode to the door slowly, hoping against hope
that someone would take the Chairman's part, but not
a word was spoken. He reached and opened it, when a
hand was laid upon his shoulder, and turning, he found
himself face to face with Hepworth. The minister's

eyes were aflame, his lips trembling with indignation; and with a thrill of excitement and joy Ralph felt that he had misjudged this man, and that in the fiery old presbyter he had found a friend in need.

"Stay, sir," Hepworth said in a low, rapid tone. "I beg you will delay a moment even now. Let me have speech with them first."

Then, as Ralph stood where he was against the door, the minister turned to the startled commissioners.

"Listen, sirs, unto me. I would fain have held my peace. Ill doth it become a Christian minister to venture his judgment and opinion in a carnal matter such as this. But I must speak — I will. Would I had the tongue and the power of the prophet Moses, to smite your sloth and backwardness. Oh, ye craven hearts! Are ye not ashamed? Where be your manhood and your patriotism? Is it for such as ye our soldiers give their lives? Hearken ere it be too late. Hearken, I say, though at the eleventh hour. This young man hath spoken the truth. He is a worthy representative of a brave officer. Most of ye know that I have had a mortal feud with Cromwell. Aye, and I have denounced this youth as accursed and ungodly. Sirs, I call you to witness that I withdraw my words now and henceforth. He hath fought and suffered as a Christian soldier in a sacred cause. And as he hath fought, so have his comrades, upholding against most fearful odds the standard of the godly. And now in this crisis, faint and battleworn, he cometh to us, to thee and me and all those who do not fight, but who watch and pray and should give freely of their substance. He asketh in his colonel's name for your support. Shall it be withheld? Answer me, men of Cambridge, so-called commissioners of the public weal of the city; *dare* ye, as followers of Christ, withhold it? Prate not to me of keeping men to guard your town. That is but arrant cowardice. Gird up your loins, and guard your town yourselves. If ye have men, though they be your brothers and sons, send them forth. If ye have but a penny-piece i' the world give it to arm and equip them. Ye talk of Parliament. Hast not one grain left of self-respect? Art so ignorant and so short-sighted that ye cannot see that Parliament will only help after ye have done your part? Sir Francis Bacon, speak from thy heart unto these commissioners, or I will shake the dust of Cambridge from my feet, and before the bar of Parliament bear witness against thee and every one here present as traitors to their country, their soldiers, and their cause."

He paused and glared round for a reply. Then Sir Francis rose with flushed face and a dignity that well became him.

"Reverend friend, I thank thee from my heart. Thy reproof hath been bitter, but 'tis timely and rings true. Friends, we have been backward, I, perchance, the most of all. I must pay the forfeit. I be not rich, but I do herewith promise the sum of one hundred pounds within two days toward the equipment of a regiment of foot for the use of Colonel Cromwell. Who will second this with a like amount?"

Two of those present did so, and then the Chairman, thanking them, went on:

"That maketh three hundred pounds. Now, there be men at our disposal. I propose that 500 be sent forth to-morrow under Captain Dangerfield's command, more to follow as there be opportunity. Hath this your approval? If not, let those who would oppose it bear in mind that I resign my chairmanship this night and accompany my reverend friend to bear witness in the House."

He waited for an answer, but none came. The commissioners were conquered, the good fight was won. In the relief and excitement of the moment by a mutual impulse Hepworth and Ralph grasped hands.

"We owe it all to you," Ralph whispered.

"Nay, friend," the minister replied, "to thyself — thyself, and thy worthy colonel, for the deeds thou both hast done."

CHAPTER XXXIII

R ALPH slept that night the sleep of the weary. When he awoke at last the sun was pouring into his chamber, and he found it was nearly noon. Sir Francis Bacon was out, but in the room where the conference had been held he found Isaac Hepworth busily writing.

The minister greeted Ralph cordially.

"Art well rested? See, here is breakfast ready to thy hand; eat while I finish this letter. I have then something of import upon which I desire your counsel and opinion."

Ralph did as he was bidden wonderingly. He was more astonished, if it were possible, at these kindly words, than at Hepworth's championship the night before. What could have happened to take away the violent prejudice and dislike which the man had nourished against him so long? The matter was not to remain long in doubt. Something in Ralph's face expressed his thoughts, and no sooner had Hepworth finished his letter than he abruptly struck the nail upon the head.

"Thou'rt surprised, young sir, that, after all I've done and said against thee, I should now seek thy friendship. Of a surety had any person by way of prophecy declared a few months since that I should do so, I would have scoffed at him. But the ways of God and His manifold providences are beyond the ken of the wisest, and so I, who have denounced thee and thy colonel, and exalted other men, even such as this Master Barrow, who would have given thee stones instead of bread, now find that my thoughts were vain and foolish, my speech the babble of the ignorant. That I do thee justice at last, Ralph Dangerfield, thou hast to thank the times and thine high courage and thine earnestness."

He paused as if to give Ralph an opportunity to speak, but receiving no answer, went on again, striding up and down the chamber.

"Truly, I believe, these days of stress and mortal danger to our cause are but a mercy and judgment vouchsafed by Almighty God to purge from us our pride and bitterness of heart. It be in such times that a man knoweth his brethren and discerneth them that have been but wolves in disguise, or at least poor, white-livered knaves, without courage or virtue. Not that I disguise from myself or would have thee doubt the shame and iniquity of thy most damnable heresy. Nor do I justify thy colonel's harsh and arbitrary treatment of that brave and godly soldier Geoffrey Capell. But these things are naught beside the welfare of our country, and the duty that I feel lieth in my path to do. I would even take my place beside you, even to wielding the carnal weapon in the day of battle, otherwise offering my poor services as chaplain to the regiment. Stay; I know what thou wouldst say," as Ralph raised his head quickly to speak. "The regiment is full of sectaries and heretics, presumptuous men who would expound the Holy Scriptures out of their own mouths. And they, you would tell me, need no chaplain. Nay, I know this; but if I came it should not be to argue or dispute, except with the malignant at the sword's point, but to speak comfortable words to the wounded and the dying, and, if I preached, to utter words of encouragement and love. Truly, good captain, I am most earnest in this thing. I am weary of the talkers in London and the Parliament, who prate, but never act. I have not long to live; my body is feeble for my age, wherefore I must live usefully and suffer in the foremost ranks. Tell me, dost think

Cromwell would take me? Wilt thou give me thy support with him?"

He spoke earnestly, pleadingly, this elderly man, weak of arm and body, but so strong of heart, and Ralph was deeply touched.

"Why, sir, you will be more than welcome," he exclaimed; "I will answer for the colonel. Yet I fear how your strength can endure our life. 'Tis rough and hard."

"Tush!" Hepworth interposed with his old impatience of tone. "Fear not that I shall faint by the way. The Lord hath given me some will and spirit; I shall not fail ye there. Then it is settled. Now let us find Sir Francis Bacon. He should have returned by this. I trust it will be to report that a goodly regiment shall accompany us to cheer thy colonel's heart; this he promised me last night."

They found that the knight had been as good as his word. Four hundred men were to march for Huntingdon that afternoon, and as many more as they could recruit six days hence. Hearty was the welcome they received from those in camp, and Hepworth had nothing to complain of in Cromwell's greeting.

"You have done well to bring him," Cromwell said afterwards to Ralph. "He is greatly changed, and I doubt not will much encourage the men by his exhortations; but we must contrive to keep him out of danger."

The cause of the people was at a low ebb this summer. Well might even Hepworth feel that all private disputes must sink before the common danger. In the south and west the king was everywhere victorious, Gloucester alone holding out for the Parliament. In the north the Marquis of Newcastle, having shut Fairfax up in Hull, made a determined movement upon Lincolnshire, took Gainsborough, stormed and captured Lincoln. and lowered on the horizon of the eastern counties like a thunder-cloud. The condition of affairs became more and more critical. In spite of promises from Cambridge and elsewhere, Cromwell could get neither food nor clothing in sufficient quantities for his soldiers; while the few men sent to him were the sorriest, raggedest of recruits. The only chance of success lay in a stronger administration of the association which held the power and the purse-strings, and in a thorough overhauling, and severe drilling of all new men. With this end in view, Cromwell gave up for the time the attempt to regain Lincolnshire, accepted the governorship of the Isle of Ely, and devoted himself to reorganising the machinery for raising and maintaining an army, and to supporting from his place in Parliament measures for strenuously continuing the war. His regiment he left under command of Major Whalley, and to Ralph he gave command of all recruits, sending him to Boston with his own troop, and with instructions to take all the men who were sent to him, teach them the use of arms, and fit them at the earliest possible moment to take the field. The means by which he was to do it were left to his discretion. He was responsible to Cromwell for his acts, and to Cromwell alone.

Such a position should have been after Ralph's own heart. He called no one master but his absent chief; his skill and faculty for organising men were brought into fullest play; and as helpers he had his loved and trusted soldiers, the men of " Cromwell's Own," on whose devotion and fidelity he could absolutely rely. Yet Ralph was not elated by his responsibilities, nor even content. This was not because of the difficulties he had to face, though many a man of tougher fibre and greater experience might well have despaired of the rough, half-starved, discontented rabble, out of which it was his business to create soldiers for the Commonwealth. Nor did he complain of the meagre food, and the dreariness of being far away from friends and without companions of his own rank. The source of his discontent lay deeper. He was separated utterly and hopelessly from Rachel, and he more than suspected that the work allotted to him was part of a deliberate plan. How or when this feeling first came to him, Ralph could not have told. He had hoped against hope after his appointment was made that before he was thus banished he would have a glimpse of Rachel at Ely, and get an inkling of the state of her mind; and whether, as he could not help hoping, these months of separation had not led her to regard their religious differences with a more lenient eye. Ralph was confident that she loved him. Some girls might say as much as she had done, and mean very little — but not Rachel. She was too reserved by nature, too refined, too sensitive. She would cloak her feelings until the last moment. That she had drawn the veil aside, even for an instant, was a pregnant sign of what lay deep — deep in her true heart. Oh, she loved him. Poor Oliver, poor old lad! He would sigh in vain. It was only the question of creed which kept them asunder. And some day, if there were a God above them, a way to reconcile their differences would be found.

Thus thought Ralph in his cheerful moods; but he was not always cheerful. And as time went on, and September passed, and the fens became drearier and duller, and his men, though smarter in their drill and appearance, were discontented to the verge of mutiny at his strict discipline, these thoughts came very seldom, like glimpses of light in a sky gathering for a storm, until at last they disappeared altogether. Another idea, a very troublesome one, began to trouble him. If Cromwell had some suspicion that the "Socinian" was something more than Rachel's friend, and for that reason had banished him from her presence, was he likely to stop there? Cromwell was one who never stayed or rested until all that he had at heart was carried out beyond all possibility of miscarriage. As long as Rachel was free he — Ralph — was dangerous. But once she were betrothed to someone else, Oliver, for instance, he would be but as a viper without fangs. At present, it was true, Oliver was beleaguered in Hull with Lord Fairfax; but might they not find a way to spirit him out? Did Cromwell ever fail to find a way? And once at Rachel's side, how Oliver would pray and press his suit. Why, he had nearly won her before. Now, with both guardians at his back, he could not fail to win. "Cromwell, if determined, will stay at naught," Ralph said to himself. "He loves her so dear that did he believe it to be for her welfare he would kill me. Nay, if I do not take some action, try one more appeal, I shall have lost her, and she her happiness. For Rachel is one who, loving once, loves always; and losing her love, never loves again. By God, it shall not be, though I've to beard them all and leave this regiment to grill!"

It was late in the evening when the thought began to burn in his brain, and until long past midnight he tramped up and down his room, making plans and rejecting them, only to begin afresh, at last throwing himself upon his bed tired out. But when he slept the gruesome fear crept into his dreams and took form and shape. He was in St. Mary's Church at Ely, the place was full of people, and up the aisle came Cromwell, leading Rachel dressed as a bride, while at the altar stood Hepworth, Bible in hand, and Oliver in gay attire. The ceremony was performed, and though he would have given his soul to interfere, he could not move nor utter a sound. But at last, when the minister reached the words "Those whom God hath joined let no man put asunder," of a sudden he seemed to find his voice, and leapt up before them all crying, "Not God — not God, but the devil," and woke to find the dawn breaking. It was time to begin another weary day.

After breakfast Ralph laughed at this dream, and threw to the winds the notion of Cromwell trying to coerce Rachel's inclinations — Cromwell, with his tenderness and high sense of honour. Yet the idea that something of the kind might happen, nay, must happen ultimately, would not leave him, and a visit to Ely, an interview with Rachel alone, presently became his settled determination.

The difficulties in the way were very great. Though his recruits, whom he had now handled for two months, were vastly improved, it would not be safe to leave them even for twenty-four hours in other hands. It would be direct, inexcusable desertion of his post. Yet, to ask Cromwell's permission by a false pretence, that seemed worse still. No, he would go, leaving old Reuben, who was acting as his lieutenant, to take command. He would see Rachel, ascertain his fate, and then tell Cromwell. Let them do as they pleased with him. Either he would be too happy or too desperate to care. He had served Cromwell and the Parliament faithfully without reward; they must now let him serve himself. The hot and rebellious blood of the Dangerfields was at fever heat. It must have its way, though the skies fell, and the stars went out!

So Reuben was summoned to his captain's quarters one dark evening in October, and told that he must take command, as a matter of great urgency required Ralph's presence in Ely. Then a letter was written to Rachel, just to say that she must receive a visitor at nine o'clock of the day in the large sitting-room alone. Ralph knew from experience that this room was empty and unused at that hour. This letter was to be delivered by a messenger early in the morning, Ralph himself riding all night and going to an inn on the outskirts of the town until the appointed time. What was to happen after the interview would depend upon circumstances.

The time passed very slowly after he had made his preparations. As he swallowed a hasty supper he heard the tramp of his horse outside. His servant had brought it round before the time. Ralph emptied a glass of cognac, drew his pistols, and examined their primings, buckled his word belt, and strode out. The moon had risen, but only shone faintly through a thick autumn mist. Ralph took the reins from the trooper, and the horse, his favourite charger, smuggled his nose into his hand, seeking the caress he never failed to get before Ralph mounted. Then he started with a nervous snort as the figure of a man loomed through the mist.

"Good-even, captain," said a voice at Ralph's elbow. "Whither away so late?"

It was Cromwell. He had left his horse with a trooper, and had come up unperceived across the sandy waste. Ralph's heart flew to his throat. For an instant he thought of riding away without reply; but the blood rushed back, his nerves regained their tone, and he said coolly:—

"You, colonel? I was bound for Ely. Now, perchance, I'll be spared the journey. Jonas, take Viscount to stable; I do not ride to-night."

He went into the house without another word — Cromwell following — relit the candles, closed the door, and faced his colonel with clenched teeth and steady eyes.

"You're surprised to see me thus, sir. Well, you shall know all, and at once. But wait," his voice changing, for he saw that Cromwell was tired. "Eat and drink first; here are victuals. Pray, sit ye. I will get some ale."

Cromwell made an impatient movement of dissent.

"Pish, man! your news first. The rest will wait. What of your men?"

"I have a good account to give," Ralph answered. "They be nearly ready for the field, so that you provide good officers. They know their business fairly, and, though wild rogues, have courage and a great wish to fight. Two I have shot, as I writ you, for attempting my life, and a dozen I flogged soundly. The rest, seeing what befell their leaders and coming to some knowledge that I would do my best for their welfare, have become quite docile. Naught is amiss there. It was of myself I wished to speak."

"Art thou sick?"

Cromwell said the words with such sharp solicitude of tone that Ralph winced, but he replied without change of manner: —

"Nay, not the least in body; in mind, yes. I would I might take a brief holiday in Ely."

He saw Cromwell's lips tighten.

"Thou deservest a holiday, truly, friend. But why at Ely? London would be a better change."

"Not for me, sir. My friends are at Ely."

"And they would welcome thee," Cromwell rejoined, then, after a slight pause, "If this were all, thou mightest have written. Is it a holiday only that you seek?"

His lips were pressed together more tightly still as if from some painful thought, and he watched Ralph keenly.

"I wish to see my friends."

"Friends, or one friend?"

"One friend," Ralph answered in a tone which he had never before used to Cromwell — hard, resolute, defiant. "I would go to Ely to get speech with Rachel Fullerton."

The murder was out, and Ralph braced himself to meet that stern inflexibility he had seen so often of late in Cromwell's face. But it did not come.

"And what wouldst thou say to Rachel?" The words came sadly and slowly, and filled Ralph's mind with a presentiment of evil.

"You know what I would say."

"You love the maiden?"

"As my life, more than my life."

"But — thou hast no hope?"

"Indeed, yes. She loveth me, I am sure. As sure of

it," he continued doggedly, as Cromwell gave an emphatic shake of his head, "as that there is a God in heaven. I know that — there is a difficulty."

But Cromwell would hear no more.

"Hold thy peace, man," he cried. "Thou art a fool demented by a vain imagination. Nay, look not at me as if thy sword were at my throat. I'll have none of such bravado. See here: Yesterday, at noon, my son Oliver escaped from Hull by water, and came among us safe and sound. Last night he asked my leave to renew his suit. I gave it, and early this morning they were betrothed, and in God's good time Rachel will be his wedded wife. How now?"

There was no answer. For an instant Ralph stood and glared at his colonel like some wild creature brought to bay. Then his eyes fell; he shivered, and mumbling an excuse, left the room. In a minute or two he returned with a haggard face, but his voice and manner much as usual.

"The night has grown very chill, sir," he said. "Will you not taste my cognac at least — unless, after all, you will eat as well?"

"Thou are right there, lad," was the answer in a brisk tone. "I am hungry. Let us set to. Thou must eat with me."

Ralph sat down and obeyed mechanically, and they talked business for an hour. Cromwell had come to inspect the recruits, as a determined effort was to be made to drive the Royalists out of Lincolnshire before winter set in. Ralph would be relieved of his present command and serve under Cromwell once more at the head of his troop. At the first pause in the conversation Cromwell proposed that they should retire to rest, and Ralph, eagerly assenting, was alone at last. He threw open his casement, for his brain seemed on fire. The night was dark and dreary; the faint moon had sunk; a bitter wind was blowing across the fens.

So his dream had come true in a way. Yet he felt no bitterness either toward Cromwell or Oliver. There had been no coercion, no time for it. Besides, he knew, being now in his senses, that such a thing was impossible. She had done it herself, and by herself. Oh Rachel! Rachel! Well, it was her right. She had promised him nothing — said nothing. He closed the window, threw himself on his bed and after a time slept. Yet even in sleep his face was drawn and pitiful — the face of one suffering from a mortal wound dealt by the hand he loved.

CHAPTER XXXIV

CROMWELL found the recruits satisfactory, and at once gave necessary instructions for drafting them into the army. By midday he started home again, reaching Ely late in the evening. He was met at the door by Oliver and Betty arm in arm.

"What cheer, son?"

"The best, sir. I' faith, father, I be so lighthearted, that were the war over, I should dance a jig with Betty here, and scandalise my dearest friends. Truly, I am as happy as man can be. How's our dear captain?"

"Well," Cromwell said. "That is as well as one who's done the work of three these many months can be."

"I'd a hope he might be with you," Oliver said wistfully. "It is a long time since we met. I could not love a brother more than this Ralph. I'd have liked for him to share my happiness. Did he send any message?"

"Best wishes"— Cromwell was unbuckling his sword as he spoke, and it took him longer than usual —"and a long life to both. Where be Rachel, then?"

"With grandmother," Oliver said, wrinkling his brow with a comical look of jealousy. "Even now, though she be mine, I can only have her company in little bits. This comes of loving one who is precious to so many. Come, Betskin, and help me mend my clothes, and leave father to his letters."

A little later, Cromwell, whose wont it was on coming home to retire at once to the library to work, heard a soft knock at his door.

"Come in, daughter Rachel; come in and let me look at thee," he cried. He held her at arm's length when he had kissed her. "So, missy, thou art going to be my daughter in very truth?"

"If God will, dear sir."

"I should thank Him from my heart; I do thank Him. Thou hast made two men happy, my child."

"Then I am happy," she said smiling.

He smiled back at her, but Rachel detected a latent watchfulness in his eyes.

"Sit here on the arm of this chair of mine, it be strong enough for two; then lean thy head against my shoulder. There, now my spirit is at rest, as it seldom is these times. Sure, thou wert formed by thy Creator, child, to bring peace into men's lives, peace and goodwill. Now tell me, daughter"— he put his right arm round her, and with the other hand stroked the soft hair from the white forehead, their faces close together —"art thou at rest in thy betrothal with this lad of mine, thy mind at peace for ever and for ever?"

She smiled again, smiled into the deep, sad eyes, and thought what tenderness lay in them, and how ignorant and foolish were those who said this man was hard. Yet, with a characteristic particularity, she noticed that one eye was larger than the other, and that the wart which lay between them was more prominent than it used to be.

"Need I make answer? An I was not so I should be wicked, most ungrateful too. It is not many women who possess so faithful a lover as mine, none who will have such a father." She whispered the word softly, and then kissed the offending wart as though she would charm it away. Cromwell patted her cheek with one finger.

"How know I whether thou art not wicked and ungrateful, mistress? Women, the best of them even, are so full of wiles. By my faith, our father Adam is to be more excused, I think, than some allow. Yet thou art right about Oliver. He is faithful, and will be unto death. I mind me thou saidst if he would submit to a probation from thee and returned as full of love as when he went away thou wouldst not say him nay. Was it not so?"

He paused, and still behind the tender smile there lay that watchfulness. Rachel's only answer was a pressure of the hand. Then a long silence followed, till Cromwell, turning slightly away, said with a sigh: —

" 'Tis well that some are happy these dark days. I feel as if there were two worlds: the one a heaven, this sweet home of mine; the other purgatory, if not worse. Which minds me, I have forgot to deliver a message Ralph Dangerfield bade me carry to thee."

He was not looking at her now, but her hand was still in his, and he felt her pulse slacken and her fingers twitch.

"What said he, sir?"

The words were quietly spoken, no tremor, no hardness, but just as one should speak about a friend.

"He begged that you would receive his best wishes, and that he would pray to God, in whom you both believed — he seemed particular about these words, wherefore I repeat them — that your choice would bring you happiness. 'Twas a right friendly and proper greeting," Cromwell went on, raising his voice slightly. "Thou hast made a friendship there, my daughter, that will last your life and his."

He turned his face towards hers; and now no smile was in his eyes, only the watchfulness. But he gained little by his scrutiny. Rachel's smile had vanished, it is true, and he could fancy that she had turned paler, but her eyes met his with the same steadfastness, and she answered in her usual quiet tone: —

"I do believe it. He is a noble gentleman. Even my uncle acknowledgeth that now."

"Hast any message thou wouldst wish me to take back to him?"

" My thanks, my best thanks, and "— she paused, and
he thought he detected a slight catch of the breath, but
he could not be sure —" and say that I have prayed for
him, with others, daily, since he went away."

Cromwell nodded, and again they were both silent.
A minute afterwards Rachel slid from her perch.

" I must go about my duties, dear sir. Indeed, I have
interrupted you too long. But it seemed a weary while
since I had you to myself."

Cromwell rose also, and laid his hand upon her head.
" God bless thee, child, and give unto thee in full
measure the comfort and solace thou givest unto others.
I will not forget thy message to the lad."

" And yet," he muttered when he was alone, " it will be
small comfort to him. She prayeth for him daily. That
means he is ever in her thoughts. Yet it is Oliver who
has won her. What was it the boy said? ' She loves me,
but there be a difficulty.' That meant his religion.
Tush! why, now 'tis all explained. Some fancy there
must have been. Truly, he's a gallant youth, and when
he strove to take advantage — the dog, I never smelt it!
—she put him off, and, like the true Christian that she be,
thrust away all thought of him for the sake of her
religion. Ah, 'tis a rare maid, with a wondrous strength
of principle and soul. Mother was wrong. Obstinacy
Rachel hath in truth, but 'tis in the clinging to her faith,
not passion. And now all's well."

He cleared his throat and sat down to his work, and
with a grunt repeated the words twice, aloud. But when,
later, he went to Madam Cromwell's room, for some reason he said nothing of his talk with Rachel, nor his own
communings upon it. The old lady was not well, and
the news from the Parliament and the country was too
grave for Cromwell to say very much. In the midst of it
she exclaimed:—

" I thank you, son. God has the cause in His hands,
and He will shield His own, and make ye victorious in

His own good time. Truly, my mind is full of private matters. So they are betrothed? What think you of it?"

The question came sharply, almost bitterly. There was not a pretense of pleasure in the speaker's face.

"I think it be the best that is possible," Cromwell replied in a firm, but very gentle tone. "There could be no safeguard greater than this to the child remaining here. Now, though Hepworth turn and rend me, which he may at any time, he'll never so much as talk of taking her away. Of Oliver I need not speak, and our lad be greatly altered for the better. The war hath been a good school of manners. Where would you find one more manly, or more honest, or more loving?"

"Where!" the old lady exclaimed petulantly. "Nay, ask me not, lest I make confessions that will sorely wound thy father's pride. I complain not of Oliver. He hath held well to the chase, and run fairly throughout. But I be not content with her. That's where it bites. I care not to conceal it now from thee. There was a time I could have sworn Rachel saw the full difference in those two men, even as I should have done at her age. I watched her close after thy departure to Cambridge. The last sign of the child in her departed too that day. A woman she was in very truth, and a woman with a sore heart and grieving spirit. Yet but eight months later on, we see — this! I am disappointed, though she knoweth it not. Oliver thy son, is dear to me; and dearer still is the religion which Ralph hath thrown away; but now that it is all over, now that she has passed her word to give her hand, I will confess my heart was set upon Ralph's grandson, and not mine, winning this fair jewel. Ralph — young Ralph — was thy true son; a strong man, with brains as well as courage, commanding others; able to uphold and follow worthily wheres'ever thou didst lead. He's but a captain, but I know, though thou hast kept thy tongue so close, that all this while he has been doing a colonel's work, and shortly, if God spares his life, will win the rank, and go on and on until he'll have a place and name of which we'll all be proud. And what perplexeth me is how this girl of ours hath failed to see this. When I was young, naught would have blinded me to the love that was in his every look and motion. Had I seen such love from him, not the powers of all the world, parents, guardians, ministers, be they who they might, would have turned my face aside. But women nowadays have not the strength or constancy of purpose we were taught. Their love cometh lightly, and goeth more lightly still. God forgive the child, and see to it that she be not punished by an aching heart in later days. Good-night, son; I would be alone. I must to my Scriptures, and learn patience and submission to God's will. But it is hard. She be our ewe lamb, and he ——"

"Be a Socinian," Cromwell said sternly. "Surely, mother thou forgettest what the word implies, what thou thyself hast said."

"I forget naught," the old lady said tartly, with a look that showed she was not in the mood to be reasoned with even by her son. "A good-night to ye."

Thus dismissed, Cromwell kissed her and departed, but before he closed the door he heard her mutter aloud: —"Socinian, bah! how we all harped upon this. Were we right? Mayhap. Yet a lad of that spirit, and his grandson; of a truth they'd have had my blessing."

Cromwell went back to his library, expecting to find Rachel there to write for him. But he was disappointed. Oliver, who had come in to try and tempt his father from work, in order to talk of future plans, said she had gone to her chamber with a headache.

This was true enough. It was one of those blinding, crushing headaches when the sufferer must creep away to some dark corner, and, after hours of pain, hope to lose herself in sleep. Rachel lay on her bed waiting for the healing slumber that was so terribly long in coming. She was in the room which had once been Ralph's, and had been set apart for her use as soon as he went away. Alone, yes, she was very much alone these days, wrapped round with a reserve within reserve which even Cromwell's piercing eye had failed to penetrate, and which no one else realised at all. Loved and trusted by everyone, even by Bridget, without an enemy in the world, she was understood by none. There are many people in such a position, both men and women, but few, perhaps, who have as many friends as had Rachel, friends anxious to understand her, and who craved as earnestly as she did to be understood. It is from such cases as hers that some of life's saddest tragedies are drawn.

Under favourable circumstances, once emancipated from her uncle's rigid rule and lack of sympathy, Rachel would have as fair a chance of happiness as most women. Ralph's nature, outspoken, masterful, strong, yet sympathetic and sensitive to gentle influence, was ideally fitted to match with her sweetness and steadfastness, her warm affections and well-balanced mind. But then circumstances were anything but favourable, and the further matters went between them the more impassable became the barrier which the difference of religion raised against their love. To love a man who denied the divinity of Christ Rachel believed to be a sin. Marriage was out of the question. This was her standpoint from the moment she discovered what was growing in her heart — and Ralph's. This, had it been in her power, she would have said to Ralph the day he declared his love. Indeed, afterwards, thinking over the incident in the light of her own intense convictions, she persuaded herself that Ralph, when he cooled down, would feel this as strongly as herself; that absence would do the rest, and their lives be separated for evermore. That her own heart ached sadly enough; that every scrap of news of him was treasured up as sacred; that a casual

word against him from Bridget made her hot with anger,
and Betty's quick defence drew tears of gratitude,
Rachel thought of little moment. It was so much a
matter of course, and besides — were they not friends?

Thus the months, weary, weary months, passed by,
and he never came even on the shortest visit. Finally,
when the news was brought by Cromwell that he was
in Boston, perhaps for the whole winter, at least for a
long time, Rachel finally made up her mind that her
past conviction had been a true one, and she finally
dismissed the whole matter. Then came the fateful day
when Oliver returned, ragged and thin almost beyond
recognition, but the same eager lover as of old. Yet
he was graver, more tender — a man now, all the blustering boyishness ground out of him. He was neither
bumptious nor obtrusive, but told her in simple, fervent
words how his love for her had been the greatest blessing of his life, and would remain with him till death.
Then he asked her if she could not give him any hope.
It all came suddenly, like a river swollen by spring rain
dashing itself against a dam that has been worn by time.
She yielded, and though when he took her in his arms
she shivered, and the lips that met his were cold and
white, yet afterwards, touched by his honest gratitude,
comforted by the joyous and heartfelt congratulations
of the rest, and the knowledge that nothing could now
part her from the household which she loved so well,
Rachel felt she had done right, and humbly thanked
God for having guided her safely to this goal after all
that had gone before. So Rachel thought and felt until
this evening, until Cromwell, in words that beat upon
her brain and heart like red-hot hammers on a tender
nerve, gave her Ralph's message. Oh, how his words
had hurt her! She could have cried out with the pain.
"The God in whom we both believe"! Back into her
memory came that white, defiant face, full of misery
and love, and smote her like a crushing blow. It was

marvellous that she had not betrayed herself to Cromwell; that afterwards she had forced herself to do her usual work until such time as she could escape and hide her face. Yet she had done it, and no one knew, not even Cromwell, what that message meant to her. But now, alone, she could give way, and let the horror run its course, and do its will upon her. How Ralph would despise her — Ralph, who, though she had loved him, had always seemed from his heresy a little at her feet. Now it was she who had proved wanting. Why — why had she ever doubted that he had won her heart wholly, utterly? She loved him as only once in all her life she could love. She knew and acknowledged it now when it was too late. They could never have been united it was true — even in this supreme moment of her distress that resolution failed her not — but to wed another; to go into the temple of God and vow to " love, honour, and obey " one who was *not* her dearest, it was enough to bring a curse upon the house. It was treason to Ralph, to Oliver himself, and yet what was to be done? She was betrothed to Oliver; she had bound herself by a pledge almost as sacred as the marriage tie to love this man, this good and honourable man, who loved her with a true and honest love. "Oh, if she could but die!" she thought. "Such a creature is not fit to cumber the earth — a woman who, in the crisis of her life, hath told a lie."

So Rachel said to herself, and believed every word, and far into the night lay sobbing in her shame and misery, until exhausted nature could endure no more, and she slept soundly, dreamlessly, like a tired child.

When she awoke next day, she was so weak and ill, that after dragging herself downstairs to do her work as usual, the family pounced upon her and drove her back to bed, and nursed her with a care and solicitude that made her sufferings still more bitter. But the rest did her good; her mind soon regained its balance, and by the following day she was herself again. No one except Madam Cromwell saw much change in her. For Rachel, like many another woman in the same position, when she came to think the matter out, felt that what was done could not be undone, and that if she could not give Oliver the love she wished, she could give him that which would content him well enough. Ralph — well, he could not love her now. He could only feel a loathing, or at best a pitying contempt. In any case, that must be set aside, ruled out of her mind, kept utterly at a distance out of sight. To make Oliver happy, care for all the rest, think nothing of herself — that was her duty now, and she must do it unto the end.

She did it, and only Madam Cromwell's eyes spied anything amiss; but the old lady said nothing, though she pondered much, and people said she aged a great deal that autumn. She was so silent, and so much less brisk in temper than she used to be.

CHAPTER XXXV

IT was a cold, blustering afternoon in the fens. A
north-west wind swept across a dull grey sky, driving
heavy clouds before it like a flock of sheep. It did not
rain, but there was every sign that as soon as the wind
fell there would be a deluge; and it behoved all travellers to make haste to shelter. One horseman, however,
riding towards Ely, urged his horse past cottage, and
inn, and hamlet, indifferent to all warnings, though he
knew the weather in these regions well. It was Ralph,
his face white and drawn with weariness and pain, his
left arm bound closely to his side, and a bandage dis-
coloured with blood about his head. When the first
cold drops of rain struck upon his forehead, he gave a
low, bitter laugh, and patted his horse's neck.

"It cometh then, Viscount; let it come! Five miles
still to go, lad; then a warm stable for thee, and a well-
earned rest. And for me a fever like enough. I neither
know nor care. Hasten on, good beast."

The rain came down, a cold, heavy, drenching shower,
and by the time Ralph's horse's hoofs struck the familiar
stones of Ely streets he was wet through.

With extreme difficulty — for every joint was stiff,
and he was weak with former loss of blood — he dismounted and knocked at the door.

It was opened by Betty, who gave a little cry of dismay at sight of his face.

"Why, Ralph, you be deadly sick. Oh, what hath
happened? Where is father?"

"He is well," Ralph answered, trying to speak cheerfully and distinctly, though his teeth chattered with cold,

and he shivered all over. "There hath been a fight, a glorious one, at Winceby. We beat them off the field."

"Oh, I am glad," she cried, clapping her hands; "but won't Oliver be in a fury at being a-bed and helpless! Truly his temper will be worse than ever now."

"Oliver a-bed!" Ralph cried stupidly, drawing a chair before the hall fire, and falling heavily into it. "Be he wounded?"

"Didst not hear from father? Why, it was just a week ago, three days after his betrothal. He rode a horse that had thrown two men — a wicked beast, but such a beauty. It was offered him at a low price, and now has cost him very dear, for it fell upon him and broke his leg, and he be a-bed for many weeks. Rachel is a-nursing him. But, Ralph, I will not speak another word to ye; you're ill yourself. Your arm be broke, or worse. Nay, I am off, and will send Rachel to ye. You must be doctored too."

And away she ran upstairs, and Ralph sat and waited. He heard a step, a light, quick step, that but a week ago would have brought a hot colour to his face. Now pale, and stern, he rose painfully and bowed. He had pictured this meeting to himself a score of times on his long ride. He would be courteous, distant, and she, no doubt, dignified and cold. And now — well, he bowed as he had planned, and mechanically said the words that he had learnt by heart.

"Your servant, madam. I have a message from the colonel."

But there he stopped. For when Rachel saw his stooping figure, the ghastly paleness of his face, and the bloody handkerchief, she interrupted him, and her voice, though quiet, was full of nervous tension.

"What hath happened to you? Nay, take your seat again. You have ridden far on little food, and have lost much blood. I know the signs full well. Then you are wet "— touching his doublet —" soaked through and through. Stay still; nay, I command you," as Ralph would have protested. "Stir not a finger until I have brought some cognac. Betty! Oh, you're here. Quick, to the kitchen! See that a fire be lit in the guest-chamber, and the bed there heated with all the speed that may be. Sir, I will bring the cordial instantly."

She sped away without another word, and while Ralph, who was now feeling exceedingly faint and giddy, fell back into his chair again and closed his eyes, the household set to work on his behalf. In a moment, as it seemed, Rachel was back again with the brandy. It was hot and very comforting, and he felt better at once, when he thanked her his tone was no longer formal. But her own face, grave, watchful, solicitous as a nurse's or doctor's should be, did not relax or change.

"You will now to bed, sir, as soon as the chamber is warmed. Pray do not heat yourself by conversation. Oliver would see you, but I told him to wait until to-morrow."

Ralph, however, would not wait. He was feverish and could not sit still, and demanded permission to go to his friend at once.

"Faith, comrade Ralph," Oliver exclaimed in the old cheery tones when he caught sight of him, "this be indeed good fortune, though truly it is unbecoming to express contentment at the misfortune of another because one has a knock from fate oneself. News, news — give me the news first. Betty only says a 'battle,' not knowing if it be of three thousand men or thirty. Tell me."

"A very pretty fight," Ralph said, falling into the other's humour, and grasping the warm hand with a feeling of relief and pleasure that surprised himself. "Three thousand of us under Manchester, thy father in command of the horse, disputed the advance of a part of Newcastle's army at Winceby, and, after standing to our weapons some three hours, we forced them back, and our lads following briskly, killed nigh a third and drove the rest some miles."

"Victory then, indeed! The Lord be praised. And thou, I'll warrant, wast at the head of thy famous troop and turned the day."

"Nay," Ralph said with a peculiar smile, "I saw little of it and did less. I was unhorsed at the beginning; that's to say, my horse was shot, and I was cut down. I lay unconscious until they found me, and then, being of no use, your father sent me here a while."

"What was thy wound? I'll warrant it severe."

"Not much," was the indifferent rejoinder, "a shoulder out of place and a broken crown. I'll soon be well. Now tell me of thyself."

"That will I not," said Oliver, raising himself upon his elbow and now observing his friend closely. "Thou'rt fainting, man. Betty, fetch Rachel. There, I knew it; he has swooned."

While Ralph was speaking his face had gone ashen pale, and slipping from his chair, he fell prone upon the floor.

In a little while they had carried him to a well-warmed room and put him to bed. But, in spite of all their efforts, he did not return to consciousness, and the doctor who had set Oliver's leg, and was reputed a skilful chirurgeon, was hurriedly sent for.

This doctor was an imposing personage. He was highly esteemed by the well-affected in the neighbourhood for his piety, and reported to be extremely learned; a handsome man, who knew it, and with a face which, though more remarkable for solemnity than intelligence, was honest, with wide-awake eyes.

When he had examined Ralph he shook his head.

"He hath, first, a dislocation of the shoulder." he said to Rachel, who in Mrs. Cromwell's absence from home, and with Madam Cromwell in bed with rheumatism, was the acting mistress of the house, "a bad one, but that is the least part. The blow and fall that caused it hath been so severe that I judge it hath shaken his system, nerves, and, in a measure, his mind. These, with a sword stroke he received across the hinder portion of the skull and the exertions of a long ride following, causeth his case, young madam, to be serious enough to be fatal. We should reduce the fever that is now upon him, yet the loss of blood may remove the means of recuperation. I would I had further advice. I possess some poor skill of chirurgery, but this needs a physician and one acquainted with the humours and distempers of the brain."

He felt his patient's pulse, while Rachel's face became almost as pallid as the unconscious one upon the bed.

"I see but one thing to be done," she replied, "we will send to Cambridge for any gentleman you may advise."

The doctor bridled at once.

"Indeed, madam! I should then withdraw. I hold myself as competent as any in this county. In London alone, where reside the greatest men in the profession — but London is too far. He'll be dead, an the fever run its course, before the fastest messenger could bring a doctor back. I will take a little blood and watch the symptoms. Nature hath secret reservoirs of strength we know not of. Pray let me have a basin and some bandages."

Rachel retired to get them; but first she went to Oliver. He was much shocked.

"Nay, but it looks hopeless indeed. Copestake is as good a leech as any. What a pity Ralph came here! All the best chirurgeons are in the field."

"What would you do?" Rachel said in a strangely quiet tone, and with an expression Oliver privately thought rather hard.

"Why, what can I do? But for the doctor's words I'd have sent to Cambridge ——"

"Whom will you send? There must be no delay."

Oliver looked up surprised; but there was no change in her face. It was white and rigid.

"You think so; then let's do it. Send Ned Worthyface; he's our best rider and a trusty lad."

"And if there be none in Cambridge he is to ride to London."

Again Oliver stared. It was not like Rachel to put words into other people's mouths.

"Why, yes, sweet, yes; do as you will. You've the best judgment of us all, I do believe. Yet to whom are we to send? I know no doctor in Cambridge or London."

"Write to the most considerable man your father knows and ask him to find one out. Give the groom orders even to go into the colleges. There be many learned doctors of medicine there; I was told so once."

"A shrewd notion," Oliver exclaimed. "Bring me pen and paper, and then to the kitchen! By my faith, dearest, we must save this man — thy friend and mine. It shall be!"

In the shortest space of time the letter was written, and the messenger on his way. Rachel, after rendering Doctor Copestake such assistance as he needed, returned to Oliver. She found him very restless and cross. He had just snapped Betty up so sharply that the girl was in tears.

"Tut! never mind then, baggage," he said with a growl as Rachel entered; "I am but a saker rammed with powder, but unshotted. I make a noise like a petard, but I hurt no one. Go now and talk to granny. I tell thee again Ralph's but asleep. He'll waken presently, and tell thee battle stories without end. Rachel, comfort the chit; then shut the door and let us talk."

But Betty would not be comforted.

"You are but fooling me," she sobbed, "and that is wicked and so silly. I saw him swoon, and I know as well as you that he lieth there unconscious, if indeed he be not dead."

"Dead! what stuff!" Oliver exclaimed. "Get thee away. He is as quick as me, and like to have care, tendance, and prayers, mayhap, that would cure a man at the last gasp of breath. Dead! not he."

"I hear you say it," Betty said viciously, slowly retreating; "I believe what I choose. But this I know, I am glad, yes, *glad*, that Ralph hath been wounded — if only he recover — for now you will find Rachel hath ofttimes something better to employ her time than you, though she be your bond-maiden." And then away the wrathful kitten bounced, slamming the door.

"How is he?" Oliver said hastily.

"Just the same. I trust the physician will come quickly. I cannot think it wise to bleed him so. His swoon seems to me from weakness and exhaustion, rather than from blood upon the brain. But of course I know not. One can only wait."

Oliver bit his finger-nails.

"Thou'lt grieve sore, Rachel, if aught happen untoward to thy friend."

He spoke hoarsely, and Rachel started, and for an instant her cheek flushed. Then she looked him in the face, and his eyes fell before hers.

"I shall grieve, so must all who love thy father. For he will lose the best officer he hath. He told me that had he not seen the men at Boston when they enlisted, he'd never have believed such sound soldiers as he took into the field the other day had only two months since been rude churls, and common wayfarers. He would feel the captain's death most woefully."

"And thou, I say," Oliver retorted with the petulance of sickness — for he was far from well — "an my father miss the officer, wilt thou not miss the man?"

"In a manner, yes," Rachel answered without the quiver of an eyelid, though her heart throbbed until she thought she must run from the room. "But, you will remember, it is long since we have met. And now"— she paused a moment to be quite sure her voice was under control—"I can have little thought for friends. My life hath changed since—the day that you came home."

He caught her hand and kissed it passionately.

"Darling, forgive me for a rough and peevish boor! I was but playing with thee. Nay, look not away. Tears! Why, Rachel, sweet, have I really hurt thee? Then I shall not sleep to-night for very shame and anger with myself."

He spoke in real distress, and she had to let him take her other hand, and then with a kiss bid him talk of brighter things. And all this time her heart was aching —aching for the man who lay upstairs.

The hours passed. The household one by one went off to bed, until only Rachel and Oliver, who would not sleep, and Doctor Copestake, remained awake. But the lamp burnt in the hall, the fire glowed on the hearth, and they waited, listening for every sound outside. At last, soon after midnight, a knock, gentle, but thrice repeated, came at the front door, and Rachel flew down the stairs.

"This Colonel Cromwell's?" said a strange voice, clear and rather acrid, with a refined city accent. "I am a physician, madam," the voice continued, and a man wrapped up to the eyes stepped over the threshold and made her a low bow. "You will guess my errand. I understand Captain Dangerfield lieth seriously ill."

"You are welcome in God's name," she answered tremulously. "Ned Worthyface, is that you?"

"Aye, Mistress Rachel, all that the rain hath left."

"Where are the horses?"

"In the stable, please you. This worshipful gentle-

'man would see his beast stalled 'fore he's come in."
There was a suggestion of grumble in his tone.

"Indeed, he was right," Rachel replied. "Go you
into the kitchen and find your supper and dry clothes.
Sir," turning to the doctor, "I cannot express how
grateful all in this house will be for your arrival. .You
must be drenched to the very skin."

"Nay, nay, was the answer, accompanied with a
strange chuckle, as if he found some secret amusement
in her solicitude; "I am well equipped in a defence of
my own contrivance. See, I'm dry as a bone."

While he spoke he wriggled himself free of an
immense cloak, pulling it finally over his head and dis-
closing the features of a very short man, with a head of
shaggy white hair and a long grey beard. His dress
of plainest black cloth was that of a professional chirurgeon of the Puritan persuasion.

"And now, madam, waste no time, an't please you,
on courtesies or aught else. My patient — take me to
him. He be alive still?"

"Thank God, sir, yes, but I fear in sad case."

"Who saith so?" was the sharp rejoinder.

"Our chirurgeon, who is attending him this moment."
The doctor gave a slight but perceptible start.

"His name, Mistress?"

"Copestake."

"Graduated he at Cambridge, taking his degree in
London?"

"I believe so," she said wondering why the man had
started, and beginning to feel decidedly uncomfortable.
"Do you, then, know him?"

"Without doubt. Go we up these stairs? I address
Mistress Rachel Fullerton?"

"That is my name."

"Good. I will tell thee mine in good time, but not
now."

He chuckled again, and so uncannily that Rachel was

thankful to see Doctor Copestake's tall figure at the stair-head. The little doctor saw him too, and bustling up to him, said in a gruff, deeper tone that he had used yet:—

"Your servant, sir. I have come by request of this honourable family to examine a wounded man. I am a physician. You, I understand, are Doctor Nathaniel Copestake. Let us proceed to business. Where is the patient? where is he, sir?"

He extended his hand to his majestic colleague, touched his fingers, dropped them, and strode into the room beyond, which was lighted up, and where Ralph lay still unconscious.

Rachel and Doctor Copestake exchanged glances.

"Do you know him?" she whispered.

"His appearance be quite strange to me, but I seem to have heard the voice. We must demand his name."

He strode in and motioned to Rachel to shut the door after them.

"Now, sir"— he coughed with a grave solemnity that was somewhat spoilt by the anxious inquiry in his eyes —"before we touch upon the matter of your visit, I must beg you to favour us ——"

He paused, and then his eyes dilated, his jaw dropped.

"God Almighty!" he exclaimed; "whom have we here?"

The stranger answered with a chuckle that was grimmer and more unearthly than the last, and, turning from the bed, calmly pulled off his beard with one hand and the white hair with the other, and stood before them a wizened, bald-headed, shrivelled old man.

"Aye, Copestake, thou art right. Madam," turning to Rachel, "I told ye that I'd tell my name. I only waited till I saw my patient's condition. It is desperate, and though ye hold my life now between your finger-tips, I hold his 'tween mine. My name is Taunton — Sidney Taunton. I am chirurgeon-general to His Majesty the King."

CHAPTER XXXVI

D OCTOR TAUNTON made his announcement with a relish which not even his anxiety about Ralph nor the imminent danger in which he stood himself could spoil. The horror on Copestake's solemn face tickled his fancy hugely; and he faced round, expecting to hear Rachel scream. But she disappointed him. After giving a slight start she remarked quietly, rather, he thought, in a tone of relief: —

"Whosoever you be, sir, if you can aid us, you are truly welcome, and ——" but she got no further, for Doctor Copestake drew his sword.

"Madam, you know not to whom you speak. But I do, thank the lord. This man, once a great physician, be not only dyed with deepest malignancy, but is a Papish and a notorious spy. Through a miracle, surely, a direct act of the Almighty, he hath now thrust his head between the lion's jaws. Stir not, you sir, or I run you through. Call the servants, madam; we will bind him fast."

He flourished his sword at Taunton as if he would have pinked him then and there. But Rachel stepped between.

"Hold, sir," she said in a tone so peremptory and commanding that Copestake, who had known her for two years, stared in amazement. "You forget yourself. This is Colonel Cromwell's house, not yours. If this gentleman can prove that he hath come on this errand of mercy, he shall be protected, though I send to the town for a company of musketeers. Put away your weapon on the instant. There shall be no violence here."

A woman thoroughly roused is a difficult person for a man to deal with, and if she is usually a quiet and gentle person the effect of her anger is doubled. So Doctor Copestake found, and though he muttered words which were neither complimentary nor polite, he sheathed his sword and retired glowering to the door.

Rachel addressed Taunton.

"Are you acquainted with Captain Dangerfield? I — I have heard him mention such a name."

"I am his guardian, young mistress, or was until he took his life away from me. His father, when a-dying, commended him to my care; thus I came, hearing of his sickness, and, if need be, I will give my life to save him. That is the truth."

There was a dignity in the way these words were spoken that won Rachel's confidence at once.

"You shall be protected, sir; I say it in the name of Colonel Cromwell and his son, who is in this house to give me full authority. Sir," to Copestake, "I pray you mark my words, and I would know what you intend to do."

"His intentions!" exclaimed Taunton, resuming his abrupt caustic manner and speech. "Bah, madam, trouble not thyself there a whit; I know him of old, and he knoweth me. Before this curse of Puritanism seized upon the land he was not too proud to be my pupil in the gentle art of chirurgery. He'll help me now. Come hither, Nat," bustling to the bedside and holding a candle so that the light fell upon Ralph's face, "hither, I say, and listen while I tell thee what's amiss. Politics be d——d! Our fair mistress will excuse me the word; I be half a soldier. We are doctors, you and I; before we fall to blows we have to save this man. Here now, and help me. 'Tis lucky I have your steady hand and head; I mind me you were to be relied upon of old."

The moment was critical, and Rachel felt that Ralph's life hung upon a hair, otherwise, she would have been amused at the sudden change which the little stranger's brief, decided words had upon his big colleague. Copestake's truculence vanished in an instant, and obediently going to the bed, he took the candle from the doctor and with a respectful, not to say reverential, air, watched him as he gazed keenly at the white face on the pillow and felt the sick man's pulse.

"Pish! what's this, man? Blood-letting here! Hadst not more sense? There, excuse not thyself to me; I know thy theory. A rush of blood to the brain, and fever; wherefore draw blood. Aye, aye, always the same tale. Mistress," jerking his head at Rachel, but otherwise keeping perfectly still and timing the pulse-beat with his watch, "cognac, at thy best speed, and a spoon; delay not.

"'Tis nerve exhaustion," Taunton continued to Copestake; "the lad's worn to a bone. A few ounces more, and you would have drained him, friend. What, the fever? That be but chill and excitement; his wound is healing. Nay, we must nourish and strengthen first. Here be our young mistress. A deft maid truly," he muttered to himself, "and as resolved to save my boy as if — See now, the spirit already taketh effect. Madam, hast some beef in the house? Cut it up, then, and boil the essence from it; he must have some broth; give it to him every half-hour in little sips; alternate with spirits in water. I will prepare a drug to soothe him, lest he be excited, and that bring the fever to a head before he hath stamina to stand against it. Copestake, thou wilt find the materials; I have none by me."

Ralph was conscious now, very feebly conscious, and inclined to murmur and babble foolishly to himself; but even this was better than the dead motionless coma, and Rachel, on her way to the kitchen, hastened to report progress to Oliver. He looked very much taken aback when he heard Taunton's name.

"It is a by-word for black Papistry, and even worse.

They say he is a master of the black art, and can raise the devil, if indeed he be not Satan himself in human form aiding the queen as her familiar. What will be said when it is known that we have harboured him? But there, there," he added hastily, " think not I blame you. An he saves Ralph's life he may be the devil for aught I care; and I warrant father says the same."

Rachel did not go to bed that night. She brewed the broth, and at the same time cooked a hot supper for the doctors, and sat by Ralph afterwards while they enjoyed it. He was sleeping now, but uneasily, and once she heard him call her tenderly by name. This made her weep. But after a minute she had dried her eyes and was frowning at herself, and the doctors saw no trace of tears when they returned. Towards morning Cope-stake took his leave. He pressed Rachel's hand paternally, and after looking round to see that there were no listeners whispered: —

" You were right, dear mistress, and may depend upon my silence. The captain's life resteth in his physician's hands, and I think be safe. There be no one in this land, nay, in Europe, with Doctor Taunton's skill in medicine; but no one must know he be in this house. The Parliament would give a thousand pounds to take him. Fare you well, and silence!" He put his finger solemnly to his lips and bowed himself out. Rachel returned to the sick-room, but Doctor Taunton met her in the passage.

"He is fully awake now," he said, "but must not see a face or speak to anyone. The brain hath been sorely taxed by some trouble of mind, while the body hath been strained and received a severe shock from the fall which put his shoulder out of joint. What happened? Do you know? "

Rachel was willing enough to tell the story which Cromwell had described tersely in a letter to his mother.

" Indeed, sir, he saved the colonel's life. I understand

339

that the regiment was charging full upon the enemy —
I crave your pardon, the Royalists — when one of their
dragoons in firing struck the horse of Colonel Cromwell, who was riding in the van, and he was rolled
upon the ground, whereupon Captain Dangerfield dismounted, intending to give the colonel his horse, when
another shot killed that poor beast also, and so they
were both afoot, the troop gone onwards. Just then a
troop of the enemy, making a circle to attack our army
from behind, bore down upon them, and the captain
placed himself in front, and receiving the full onslaught
of the enemy, was thrown backwards and sore bruised
and hurt. Both must have been killed but that the first
troop, having seen the straits of their officers, now came
back at the charge and broke the Royalists to pieces.
Captain Dangerfield recovering partially, returned here
last evening; the colonel's injuries were slight."

Doctor Taunton thanked her abruptly; went back into
the sick-room and shut the door.

"Saved his life, the life of the bloody rebel colonel!"
he muttered to himself. "By rights I should e'en kill
thee, Ralph, for such a deed." He shrugged his shoulders and smiled. "The humour of it is, though, that
mine own life dependeth upon the will of this very
Cromwell. So for that reason, if for no other, I must
cure my boy."

Taunton did not leave his patient's side for forty-eight
hours. Then he sent for Copestake suddenly, and
before night it was known that Ralph was in high fever,
and lay at the point of death.

Bad news travels fast, but the news that one wishes
most carefully to conceal travels faster still. Doctor
Copestake was loyal to his trust, so were the Cromwell
household servants. Yet within a few days of Taunton's arrival at Ely an agent from Parliament, duly
armed with a warrant for his arrest, was following him
there. Afterwards it turned out that Ned Worthyface,

who had met the doctor in his hunt among the colleges
for a physician, Taunton being in hiding there, had a
sweetheart in Cambridge whose mother was cursed with
a gossiping tongue. Taunton's notoriety as a spy and
a Papist did the rest.

Sir Francis Bacon was writing in his library when a
servant announced an officer from the Parliament, and
in walked a burly, hard-faced man, with cold blue eyes
— Major Geoffrey Capell.

Capell had aged in these months. His hair had
grown grey at the edges, and there were deep lines
about his face which would be wrinkles before he was
forty. Sir Francis, who had not met him before, thought
that a more forbidding representative of the godly army
would be difficult to find. But he greeted his visitor
with great politeness, for Capell had won no little
renown by his services with Sir William Waller in the
west, and was known to be a zealous and determined
officer.

" Be there any service I can render you? " Sir Francis
said, after they had exchanged greetings. Capell's
reply was to hand him a letter from the Clerk to the
Parliament.

" A score of troopers will suffice," he said carelessly,
as the commissioner read it. Sir Francis looked aghast,
and, gentle as he was, his spirit rose.

" A score, sir! Nay, then, expect you the household
of our worthy colonel to take up arms in defence of a
malignant spy? You are surely not acquaint with him.
Besides it hath been reported to me that this doctor,
Papist though he be, is trying to save the life of one
Captain Dangerfield, a most gallant, well-affected
youth."

" His dear friend." Capell rejoined briefly, cutting
him short without ceremony. " Anyone who knows
Dangerfield as I do understands that when he calleth
any man friend, though he be the blackest enemy of

this cause of ours, yet would Dangerfield hold him harmless even at the point of the sword. But I have not time to bandy words, worthy sir. Give me ten, and I'll be content, if I may procure them quickly. This Papist is a very fox, and must be run to earth at once, or he'll escape."

With a sigh Sir Francis signed the required order to the officer in charge of the garrison.

"Be wary, sir," he pleaded gently, "and be not too forward in your zeal. At least the doctor should have gentle treatment. I remember that they despaired of the young captain. The man is on a Christian errand." Capell bowed without reply, and departed to collect his men. He found, however, that no one was very anxious to go. A Papist might be bad and a spy worse; but to search Cromwell's house — that was another matter.

Once on the march for Ely, Capell forced the troopers to a swinging pace, and reached his destination at dusk. As he approached the familiar house a sudden hesitation came upon him. It had been originally his intention to make as much stir as possible, and publish far and wide the fact that a malignant had been found under Cromwell's protection; but now another thought came into his mind, and dismissing his men to an inn, he went to the house alone. The servant admitted him with evident unwillingness, and left him standing in the hall while she went to call Rachel. He stood by the fire and kicked the logs about. He was bitter and angry and unaccountably nervous. He laughed at himself scornfully. There was no reason for it whatever. Though still a step below Cromwell in rank, he was in high favour with the chiefs of Parliament and of the army. Moreover, in the present instance, he was master of a situation which he could and would make very unpleasant for Cromwell.

It was the end of October, 1643. A sudden change had come over the face of public affairs. The covenant was being signed, and this meant aid from the Scottish army for the Parliament, and, what is more important to us, the triumph of Presbyterianism over other sects and all "unbelievers." Capell knew this; he also knew that Cromwell's tolerance of "sectaries" was bringing him into strong disfavour with many influential men. It was from Capell's point of view a most auspicious time in which to let it be publicly known that an accursed Papist was domiciled in Cromwell's house, and in constant attendance upon one of Cromwell's most trusted officers.

Why then this nervousness? The answer to the question lay in the start he gave and his change of attitude when he heard Rachel's step in the passage. There are some things in a man which die hard, and the more unreasonable they are the more vitality they seem to possess. If Capell, when he had left London for Ely, had been asked on oath — and he was one who under such circumstances would never lie — whether the attraction he felt toward Rachel a year ago held the smallest place in his heart to-day, he would have stoutly denied it. He knew of her betrothal to Oliver, he knew of the reconciliation between Hepworth and Ralph, and he was, before all things, a practical, hard-headed man of the world. And yet — and yet — it was for Rachel's sake that he had left his men at an inn; and no step but hers would have made him give that start. He tried to harden his heart. Cromwell's bitter words rose in his memory. What was Rachel, what could she be, to him? He said the words to himself as she approached him and then forgot them, for Rachel came with a cordial greeting on her lips.

"This is a surprise, sir. Truly, when the maid said a soldier was below on some grave business from the Parliament, I feared to see a stranger who would require a very laboured explanation of our position and even then might not be content. But now I can have no fears."

Rachel spoke so naturally, with a face of such quiet composure, that it would have deceived a cleverer man than Capell.

"I trust I shall merit thy confidence, madam," he answered, smiling uneasily. "I would serve you, an it were in my power, be assured of that. I hope Master Hepworth is in good health. He is still with the regiment, I hear."

"I am writing to him soon," said Rachel with a chill at her heart as she looked at the hard determined face. "Have you any message that you would send?"

"My humble service, and tell him that all his friends in London desire his presence among them very urgently. And now, madam, there be a duty I must do which hath brought me here."

His tone changed; his face grew stern. Rachel felt desperate. Then an idea struck her.

"I wish to tell you, sir," she said in gentle tones, "that if a rumour I have heard be true, and you have come to Ely to search for one Doctor Taunton, he is in this house."

Capell's eyes became cold as steel. Rachel's heart sank again.

"I thank you, madam. It was this that caused my intrusion. I must see the man and——"

"Pray come now," Rachel said quickly; "your time is of great value. I would not unduly waste it."

She led the way upstairs, Capell following closely. And now Rachel, glancing up at him, thought that his face wore a pleasanter expression, and began to hope. What a merciful chance it was, she thought, that Ned Worthyface happened to be in Cambridge when the major arrived, and getting wind of his errand, tore back to Ely in time to warn them before he could arrive there! The matter was terribly critical. Doctor Taunton had refused to fly. The fever had been reduced, but Ralph was so weak that nothing but unremitting attention and great skill would save his life. "Let them take me," was all the doctor said; "only see that they budge me not until my boy is round the corner. Be not Cromwell strong enough to hold them back, or his son?"

Rachel promised to do her best, but did not answer the question. Cromwell was too far away, Oliver a cripple, and even if he had been able-bodied, Capell, she knew, would be too strong for him. Already, though this she did not tell the doctor, Oliver was fretting himself into a fever over the danger of the doctor's presence in the house, and the stain on the family honour of harbouring a Papist. Thus the burden of the day fell upon her shoulders; it was a heavy one to bear.

They mounted the stairs and reached the landing at the door of the sick-room. There Rachel paused, her hand upon the lock; Capell was at her side now; she touched him on his arm.

"Sir, I believe you to be a just man as you are a strong one, wherefore I will tell you two things before you enter. First, 'twas I who sent for the doctor; none knew him but me. If, therefore, there hath been wrong done, I alone must be punished. Secondly, if you move him now, you kill his patient. Once, long ago"— here Rachel's eyes grew bright and large, her voice firm — "you did Captain Dangerfield a wrong. I will not say you had no aggravation, but you wronged him. Now it lieth with you to save his life; come in."

The room was nearly dark; a single candle was the only light, and this was shaded. In the corner of the chamber furthest from the door Capell saw a bed, and crouched by it the doctor — the spy and Papist — his finger on his patient's pulse.

"A visitor," Rachel said in a low voice, but very

clearly, looking hard as she spoke at Taunton, "one who could not be denied — Major Capell."

She lifted the shade from the candle and motioned Capell toward the bed. He went there slowly, and then stood still, with a curious, quite new, feeling clutching at his heart. He had seen death and wounds in plenty, but never a man, whom he had last known in vigorous health, lying a thin, wasted shadow, with hollow eyes and sunken cheeks, helpless and weak as an infant. Ralph's eyes brightened.

"Capell," he said faintly, so faintly that Capell could barely recognise his voice, "this be a good meeting. Thou hast been in my mind of late, and I am right pleased to see thee. Dost know my doctor? Yes, of course; faith! 'tis strange that we three should be together."

He paused, faint with the exertion of having said so much; but he was quite himself, and his eyes went from face to face with a wistful look.

"How are ye?" Capell said to break the pause. He began to feel the air of the sick-room oppressive. "On the mend?"

Ralph shook his head. "I think not, but ask my doctor; it lies in God's hands and his. Thou art a major now?"

"Aye, of foot."

"It was a just promotion."

Another pause; then Ralph stretched out a hand, and Capell put his into it.

"We may not meet again," Ralph said; "I would ask your forgiveness for any wrong I did thee. Wilt give it and be friends?" His voice was low and tremulous; Capell's face twitched.

"The forgiveness will have to be double-edged," he answered. "I wronged thee sore."

The words came jerkily, as if against the speaker's

will, but the strong hand closed over Ralph's and held it; Ralph smiled.

"I gave thee much provocation. I know it now, comrade."

Tears came into his eyes, the tears of weakness, and then Capell's other hand joined the first.

"Think no more of it, Dangerfield," he said hoarsely. "The matter's at an end, and God bless thee."

He rose from the bedside and looked round at the others. His mind was a queer medley of emotions. He was touched, and really meant his words, yet above all his heart was joyful with the conviction that this man could not live. And so thinking, he met Rachel's appealing glance.

"Madam," he said, watching her, "I came to make an arrest; I hold the warrant from Parliament. Naught could stop the course of it but mine own will, but you have turned my purpose. I return as I came — without my prisoner."

He bowed and was leaving the room, expecting Rachel to follow him, when she ran to the bed, and he saw that Ralph's eyes were closed and that he lay insensible. A fierce excitement seized him.

"He is dead!" he exclaimed.

"Nay, friend," said Taunton drily, speaking for the first time, "not dead, nor near it; 'tis a faint. He'll live, if my experience hath taught me anything, to be as strong and lusty as thyself."

CHAPTER XXXVII

CAPELL remained that night in Cromwell's house, an honoured guest, and went away the next day well pleased with himself. He spent the evening with Oliver, who laid himself out to be agreeable, and found Capell in his present mood good company.

"I like the man," Oliver said with emphasis after the major had gone. "He hath been maligned. Indeed," he added with a queer laugh, "it surpriseth me that father should have given preference to Ralph as a soldier. This Capell, mark me, is a stronger man. I'd have called him one after the dad's heart. He'll be a good commander some day."

Rachel, who was at work in the corner of the room, did not reply for a few minutes. When Oliver saw her face it was rather flushed.

"None can doubt that he hath strength and a shrewd brain," she said. "But a man if he would win your father's heart must give evidence of honour and high principle. Yet I say not," she added hastily, "that he is without these qualities. We owe much to his forbearance. And yet I am truly thankful he hath gone. I fear him now more than I did. I think it is because there is a depth in him, a kind of reticence, that maketh it impossible to read his thoughts."

Oliver laughed.

"He might be thine own brother for that, mistress. Eh," as Rachel looked up surprised and hurt, "dost not know that thou, too, art deep, deep as a well? 'Deed, but thou art, and that is why I like Capell, which surely is a very pretty compliment," he added teasingly.

Rachel smiled and turned the conversation to other things.

Meanwhile Capell journeyed to London, dropping his men at Cambridge without any explanation to Sir Francis Bacon. He reported to his superiors that the Papist, being in attendance as physician on a dear friend of Cromwell's and under his protection, could not have been removed without a desperate quarrel with the colonel, an explanation believed readily by those who knew Cromwell, and as the moment was not at all opportune for a serious difference with him, Capell was complimented upon his discretion. Soon after this he received the offer of a commission in a regiment of horse in the army of the eastern counties, which was now commanded by Lord Willoughby, with the Earl of Manchester as lieutenant-general. Capell readily accepted, but in the midst of preparations to go north he heard from Hepworth that Ralph was out of danger, and that Doctor Taunton had left Ely. This news changed his plans, for he had intended to call at Ely on his way to the army. He had no wish to do so now, and it was in a very bitter mood that he took up his duties in Lincolnshire. In defiance of all reason and common sense, he had nourished hopes and built castles in the air, which now began to crumble slowly away. He bore no ill-will to Ralph, of that he was confident, nor did he regret having spared Taunton, though he failed to follow up this thought and acknowledge that had he not done so he would have estranged Rachel. But he felt it hard, nay, positively unjust, that God should have spared his rival's life. Capell lived in an age when even grave, acute men of the world thought it no shame to solicit direct intervention from the Almighty in their daily affairs. Their belief that their supplications would be answered by miracles was the result of a very literal interpretation of the Scriptures, and a confidence that, as they had obeyed God's will,

He would carry out their wishes to the letter. Capell hitherto had been far from sharing this extraordinary creed, but his secret broodings, the loneliness of his life, and the strength of his passions brought him by degrees to this conviction: that, as he had served God all his days, living soberly and piously, enduring a very hard and joyless life, he had now a right to his reward. And there was only one reward he cared for — Rachel Fullerton. That Rachel had no feeling for him but a distant friendship, tempered by distrust, and perhaps fear, was a minor matter in a time when women too often did not what they desired, but what they must, and when war had inflamed men's passions and made all things possible to the successful and the strong. Her betrothal to Oliver was an awkward fact. But with a lover's quick instinct, Capell saw that her heart was not in it, and he was confident of his power over Hepworth, and of his ability, when the right time came, to foment so violent a quarrel between Cromwell and the minister, that, backed by the influence of Cromwell's superiors in the army and in Parliament, he could draw Rachel once more under her uncle's care, and remove her to London. After that all would be easy. There remained, however, Ralph Dangerfield. In this man Capell saw the greatest obstacle to all his hopes. This gloomy presentiment did not come from any exaggerated notion of Ralph's strength; Capell still looked upon him with a certain contempt as a sentimentalist, but he respected his courage and determination, and, above all, he feared his capacity for making friends. It was that which kept Cromwell and every man in the first troop upon his side, and that which now caused even Hepworth to speak of him in a way which was gall and wormwood to Capell.

"Why, if the man should turn, or pretend to turn, from his unbelief," he thought, "Hepworth would embrace him as the sinner that repenteth, and I'd be left in the cold."

He made ready to journey north, however, none the less quickly for his despondency, and before he had completed half the distance to Lincolnshire had forgiven his Creator for sparing Ralph's life, and become possessed of a stubborn belief that all would yet be well—a train of thought which, translated into plain English, meant that if his reward were not to fall into his lap he would go forth and take it for himself, using any means that were necessary to gain his end.

At Ely the invalids mended day by day, and the mental irritation at being useless and inactive from which both suffered was mitigated by the knowledge that until winter was over there could be no fighting. The armies of the king and Parliament were waiting, making ready as best they might for the campaign of next year, which both felt must decide the war.

It was a quiet winter in the house at Ely. Ralph only gained strength at a very slow rate, and Doctor Copestake found him a most trying patient. At one time he was furiously restless and inclined to attempt any mad thing to prove that he was stronger than he seemed and might return to his duties; at another he was dull and spiritless, avoiding company — grimly hopeless. These moods were only known to his doctor and Oliver. Before the rest of the family Ralph was grave, polite, and quiet. But with Oliver, with whom he naturally spent a good deal of his time, he attempted no concealment; and Oliver, who was very fond of Ralph when he did not think Rachel did too much for him, was distressed on his account, and spoke to his father about it. Cromwell, however, pooh-poohed the matter, and said these were humours which active service would soon get rid of; it was but bodily weakness. But Cromwell was anxious, and watched Ralph closely. He watched Rachel also, and satisfied himself that all was well with her. She looked pale and tired, and had lost much of her former briskness of movement; but that was natural after all her anxiety and hard work.

Ralph steadily grew stronger, and by January, when, owing to a mild, dry winter, the army was to begin active operations, Doctor Copestake pronounced him fit to return to work. He went in a hurry at the last. One afternoon, when all were out but Madam Cromwell, a trooper arrived in hot haste, bearing a letter from Cromwell, who was now with the army, saying that the first troop had been chosen to share in a "brisk piece of work," and asking Ralph whether he would come and take command. Ralph did not hesitate a moment. He despatched the man to the kitchen for refreshments, and went to Madam Cromwell's room.

"Must thou then leave us so suddenly?" she said with a sigh. "Yet why do I say that? 'Tis far better so. I'll give thy farewells, Ralph, to all — all," looking at him keenly. "Thou'rt to be envied, friend. Indeed, thou art! Thy life has been spared by a miracle, and not for naught. Thou hast the world to conquer, and I believe thou'lt do it, for thou hast overcome thy worst enemy — thyself! Farewell, and may God protect thee!"

Ralph was very weary and faint by the time he reached the end of his long journey, but the reception from his troop put fresh life and vigour into him. As he rode among them the men made blunt comments on his worn looks; while Reuben, Micklejohn, and Sanctify grasped him by the hand and thanked God he was with them again.

When Ralph reported himself to Cromwell, he found his colonel engaged with the commander-in-chief, so he went back to his own quarters for supper. He had not been there long before, to his great surprise, in came Capell. Ralph greeted him with the cordiality of an old friend, but received a chilling response. The major was as cold as in former days; his manner, though polite, had no heartiness in it: it was that of the old Capell.

"Hast not seen Cromwell?" he inquired. "Then you know not what is forward. A stronghold of malignancy, a very nest of them — one Stainsby House, ten miles to the north of us — is to be reduced on the morrow, and Lord Willoughby hath given the business unto me. He alloweth two troops and some ordnance, the men to be picked for the work. I chose a goodly company from mine own regiment and then bethought me of thy troop, for I knew the men of old as trusty, and I knew thee." Capell smiled here, adding in a more cordial tone than he had used yet, "We have had some differences, Dangerfield, but none that I remember on the field of battle. Yet, now that I see thee, art strong enough?"

Ralph reassured him with emphasis.

"Well, then, let it be so. Now we will consult. I have obtained a plan of the place."

A discussion followed as to the best mode of attack, and Capell's manner grew distinctly more natural and friendly; but at the end, when they were about to separate, he stiffened again.

"I have not asked the mettle of the garrison," said Ralph. "Dost know it, and who commands?"

"The men be mostly Papists drawn from Newcastle's army, the governor a man of some mark, one of Rupert's colonels, the Viscount Charlton."

Ralph started and looked hard into Capell's face. It was composed, even stolid in expression, but paler than usual, the lips a little pinched — a mask.

"Foul play!" Ralph muttered as he turned back into his quarters. "I was sure of it. I felt it when he said he 'knew' me. So this is why he chose us out of all the troops who'd so gladly serve with him. Oh, thou cunning hypocrite! But this time I see through him;

and now I have Cromwell at my back. Beware, Capell, beware."

Ralph awakened at a very early hour next day, and made a very careful inspection of his men. This was just over, and they were waiting for the order to march, when Reuben drew him aside, his weather-beaten face purple with excitement.

"I've waited sin' ye came up, captain," he whispered. "Now tell me, have ye worked out the plan of attack?"

"Aye."

"Himmel! 'Tis too late, then. Where's the troop to lay? East or west of the main door — to front or rear?"

"Eastward, in the rear."

"God be praised," and he mopped his brow. "I' faith, His finger is in it, I swear. 'Slife, sir, but now we have 'em without doubt. The Lord be thanked, the Lord be thanked."

It was now Ralph's turn to ask questions, but Reuben was not communicative.

"Nay, nay, I can tell ye nothing now. In a space, when the time comes, you shall know all. Only mark me, case I forget. The credit belongs to my little comrade, Jeremiah. 'Twas a rare, keen bit of work. Oh, how they'll bite their tongues when it comes through. There'll be some strange prayers to-night from the high-snifting ones. Ho, ho!"

"Mean you the malignants?" Ralph exclaimed in bewilderment.

"Malignants!" cried the old quartermaster, chuckling. "Nay, sir, not the malignants."

He turned on his heel with a salute, and became preternaturally solemn, for Capell rode up. It was time to march.

They arrived at Stainsby House at noon — one hundred and twenty men, and two pieces of artillery. All was in order; the ground had been well surveyed beforehand, and in an hour Capell had sent a subaltern with a trumpeter to demand surrender. His terms were the lives of the garrison, nothing more. Ralph awaited the answer with the worst forebodings, for, according to the usage of the time, if the terms were refused, and the house carried by storm, no quarter would be given. The subaltern was not long on his errand. He returned with a sheet of paper, on which were these words: —

"If Major Capell desireth this poor house, let him take it. Charlton."

The major handed the note to Ralph without comment, and then addressed the troops: —

"These Papists send us insolent defiance, wherefore we shall make the assault forthwith. You have full knowledge of your duties; see ye fulfil them. Captain Dangerfield's troop will remember that they commence not to attack until they hear a drake fired. Then let them plant their ladders with all speed. Now to your posts! Let none forget"— he raised his voice —"that our terms have been refused. I charge ye, therefore, to spare not any, be they whom they may."

Stainsby House lay in the midst of a great park. It was an old, rambling manor-house; and though difficult to approach in front, where Capell was placing his guns, in rear, once the high outer walls were scaled, it would offer no serious difficulties to a determined assault, unless defended by a very numerous garrison. It was probable, however, that these walls would be well watched, and Ralph was to place his men under cover of the thick timber in the park until Capell gave the signal for attack. This he was about to do when Reuben plucked him by the sleeve.

"Hold a moment, sir; keep the troop back. Jem, ye cockerel, come hither and tell thy tale. Quickly now! There be no time to waste."

The little corporal came forward with a complacent grin.

" 'Slid, sir, I have little to tell. Being sent to spy about the place, I thought it my duty "— he coughed — " to make acquaintance with a maid I met hereabouts, who served the household, she telled me, by coming to and fro from the village. She knew not my persuasion, my dress being of a smarter cut than this, and — and we presently came to confidences, and then I found she entered the place by a postern in the wall, hid by ivy and the like. She would not tell me where it lay, though I pressed her hard, but I followed her by stealth one night, and by good fortune I found it. When I told the quartermaster, he——"

" Came to you, sir," Sweetlove chimed in, " but not until 'twas sure those dreaping Lincolners of ours had gone another way. Forgive me, captain, but I feared you'd tell the major, and our game be spoiled. Now we await your orders."

He drew himself up and saluted. His face was per- fectly wooden once more.

Ralph tried to frown.

" 'Twas not right, quartermaster. He would have changed the plan of attack."

" I' faith he would," was the reply, " wherefore — but 'tis done, sir, and what now? "

Ralph smiled.

" I see thou'rt incorrigible. Certainly there is but one thing to do. Lead on, corporal. Men, extend your lines and be wary as we advance. They may have got wind of this and make a sally. Steady now — march! "

A proud man was Jeremiah as he strutted along at the head of the troop, his helmet tilted a little on one side, his step the swagger and swing characteristic all the world over of an old cavalryman. But though a coxcomb, he knew his business well. He had marked the place in the wall, and now drawing his sword, knocked gently three times at a little iron-studded door about four feet high. It opened in answer to the sum-

mons, but only a few inches, and would have been
quickly closed had not Jem's sword prevented it. In a
moment the postern was forced back, the sentinel, a
half-sodden, drowsy pikeman, secured and gagged, and
the Ironsides were in a long, dark passage. Now came
the boom of a gun; the attack in front had begun. The
troop, with Ralph leading, strode quickly down the
passage to a stairway, up a flight of steps, into the main
hall. They met no one on the way. In the hall they
found a score of musketeers on guard.

"Make ready to fire," Ralph cried; then, catching
sight of Charlton himself, "My lord, surrender. You
are outnumbered. Your sword!"

Charlton's reply was an oath and an order to his men
to fire, but it was not obeyed. Already half the Ironsides were in the hall, their carabines at the shoulder.
The Royalists held back.

"Cowards! fools!" Charlton cried, not recognising
Ralph for the moment; "wouldst be cut down, then,
like sheep in shambles? Knowst not that these dogs
give no quarter? Upon them with the sword!"

He turned to lead the charge, then paused suddenly.

"God! 'tis Ralph! Pish, man! I saw thee not. All's
well, then. Men, lay down your arms. I know this
gentleman."

He lowered the point of his sword, and was about to
hand it to Ralph, when a man from the Ironside ranks
rushed at him crying: —

"Quarter! nay, accursed antichrist! 'Tis to be hip
and thigh. Our major laid upon us the command.
Comrades, what this captain says is of no worth. Come
you on."

The speaker was a lay-preacher and bitter fanatic, and
had only lately joined the troop. He rushed past Ralph
and thrust savagely at Charlton, but his lordship was
too quick for him, stepping lightly to one side, and
before his assailant could recover Ralph had dealt him

a buffet under the ear that threw him heavily to the ground.

"Mutiny, wouldst thou? Lie there, or I'll kill thee like a dog. Men "— he faced his troop, and saw uncertain glances and uneasy movement —" men of Cromwell's Own, will you dishonour me, or wilt stand by me? There be the issue. I have called on the governor of this place to surrender, and he hath offered me his sword. His men have not fired on ye. No blood is spilt. Will ye butcher helpless men?"

He looked down the lines of faces, but he gained little assurance of support from them. Then a man left the ranks and stood squarely by his side. It was Sanctify Jordan.

"Verily, sir," he said in his deep sepulchral tones, "I think, saving your presence, 'tis madness to stand 'tween lions and their prey; yet, since you've chosen to so stand, I must e'en stand by ye. And, to my sorrow, I warn all in hearing that the first, aye, and the second and the third who shall gainsay ye, will taste my broadsword's edge. Prithee, friends, art men or devils. *That* be the true issue. As concerning command, who be this major that one hath prated of? Did not Noll cast him from us; and did we not approve? Then see to it that you keep your sense. Strike ye enemies who can strike back, or those who'd hound ye on to murder unarmed men, but dispute not with thy best friend, the captain. Have I not spoken aright?"

"Aye, by God, thou hast," yelled little Mickeljohn, who, but for Sweetlove, would have pistolled out of hand the man whom Ralph knocked down. "I'd not ha' thought 'twas in thee, sop-stick. Reuben, raise thy voice."

"Not I," the old quartermaster said coolly, "there be no need. We be all united, and will stand by the captain to a man."

He walked slowly up to Ralph and, to Charlton's amazement, laid a paternal hand upon his shoulder.

"Take it as past," he said in a low tone, "and give your orders; the men are thine."

Ralph sheathed his sword and whispered back, "Thanks, old friend! Sanctify, command me," then aloud, "Quartermaster, see these prisoners be disarmed. My Lord Charlton, prithee hoist a flag of truce and open the gates. I solemnly assure you that this household shall receive protection."

CHAPTER XXXVIII

THE firing slackened at the gates when the white flag was raised, and ceased as the doors of Stainsby House opened to admit the Lincolners. Capell's company was in a very sulky mood; they now foresaw that Cromwell's troop would claim all the credit of the victory, and they asked each other, with many muttered imprecations, how the Ironsides could have made such easy work of it. They were in no mood to be merciful to the garrison. Capell was as furious as his men, though he showed it the least.

"Steady!" he said sternly, "no crowding, no disorder; there may be treachery in this. Mind the words I spake —'*No quarter!*' March."

Stainsby House had been built in the fourteenth century, but in the days of Elizabeth its owner had added a new front, with a magnificent entrance hall, paved with white marble. The walls were hung with tapestry, old swords and lances, armour of a bygone day, and trophies of the chase. A broad carved staircase, facing the door, led to the upper part of the house.

The Lincolners advanced briskly to the door, then, halting with one accord, waited for orders with an exclamation of disgust. In the centre of the hall, the Ironsides stood in rank at attention. Their lines as carefully accurately dressed as if upon parade. They filled the body of the hall, only leaving clear a narrow space down which three men could march abreast, forming a lane from the door to the staircase. On these stairs, unarmed, but without bonds, and showing no signs of ill-usage, were a crowd of prisoners — men, women, and children, to the number of eighty; and above them, standing in a gallery which led from the stairway to the upper chambers, were a guard of ten more troopers.

At the foot of the stairs stood Ralph and Lord Charlton. The Viscount was a brave and gallant figure, dressed in scarlet doublet, edged with gold braid, his fair hair falling over his shoulders in long curls; his head was erect, and his bearing courteous, yet dignified. Had he worn his sword, one would have judged him the victor of the day. Yet he was a very different man from the Charlton of olden times. Responsibilities, care, and hardship had worn away all the coarseness in his strong face; there were no traces left of the man of pleasure. And more than that, these hard years had not been without sweet fruit; love had found its way into his life. Beside him now, her hand within his arm, stood his wife. They had been married a month, and this was the last day of their honeymoon. A tall and winsome lady, with soft dark eyes, which have a nameless terror in them, for she distrusts these grim soldiers in the hall, and those fierce, flushed faces crowding through the doorway fill her heart with a sickening dread.

Capell, after a swift glance round him and one instant's hesitation, walked swiftly up to Ralph.

"The place is ours, then?"

"Aye, major. A secret postern was discovered in the rear, so we took them by surprise. No lives were lost. This be the governor and his lady, yonder the garrison; their arms are in our hands. Lord Charlton will sign such terms of capitulation as we desire."

"What say you?"

There was an ugly gleam in Capell's eyes. It seemed to him that Ralph spoke in a tone deliberately calculated to lower his authority, and make him an object of ridicule to his men and the prisoners. There was also an easy confidence and suggestion of superior rank in the bearing of Lord Charlton which galled him terribly. Under other circumstances he would have acquiesced in the necessity of sparing the lives of men who had yielded so easily. He was not naturally cruel, but now his bitter temper was aroused, and Lady Charlton, anxiously scanning his face, shuddered and shrank closer to her husband.

"I make no terms," he said, with a cold distinctness far more terrifying than any outburst of wrath, "neither is it your place to suggest them after my orders touching the assault. But you ever counted Papists and malignants dearer than your comrades or their cause. I'll have none of it. His lordship can expect no mercy at my hands. He chose his path; let him tread it to the bitter end. My orders are from the commander-in-chief; I'll obey them to the letter. See that thou hearken sir. Retire with me without the gates, and leave these wretches, male and female, to the fate to which their past usage of the godly justly condemns them. The Viscount and his wife shall be prisoners in our hands; the rest I give unto the men to work their will upon. Quartermaster," he beckoned — and a man left the ranks of Lincolners, and came slowly, very slowly, towards him —" secure this man and woman, and safeguard them to the camp. Captain, follow me."

He turned on his heel and moved away, and a cry of terror and dismay rose from the women on the stairs. Ralph gasped for breath. His rage was so intense and overpowering that for an instant he could not speak, but before he recovered a gruff, deep voice rang through the hall, and between the advancing quartermaster of the Lincolners and Capell the gaunt form of old Reuben Sweetlove barred the way.

"Thou speakest thy mind, major," he said, "as thou hast a right to do. But, by God's life, sir, I am a free soldier of the Parliament, and not thy servant, and therefore I'll speak mine. Halt, thou cur!" addressing the Lincolner in a tone that rumbled and echoed through the hall; "an thou advance within the swing of my arm thy life shall pay for it. Captain Dangerfield, orders have been given to the men without. What hast thou for thine?"

He paused, and the answer followed swiftly:—

"Withstand by force of arms all who interfere between ye and your prisoners. Men, close your ranks."

The clang of spurred heels on the marble hall, and, with the precision of the drill-ground, the Ironsides ranged themselves in four lines across the hall, and stood between the panting Lincolners and their prey — a wall of threatening steel.

Capell's eyes flashed fire.

"Insubordination! mutiny! Thy wits are a-wandering, Dangerfield. A little more, and thou wilt be a prisoner thyself. Down arms, ye fools! Lincolners, advance to the attack! If any resist ye it will be at their peril. March!"

He drew his sword, and to give the men the encouragement they obviously needed dashed away the carabine of the trooper nearest to him. The next moment Ralph, whose blood was at boiling point, struck his sword from his hand.

"Nay, that thou shalt not do," he cried, then to his men, "Give not an inch, lads. Make ye ready to fire."

An uncertain forward movement of the Lincolners, a click and the carabines of the Ironsides were at the shoulder. Then the Lincolners shrank back. Seeing this, Capell picked up his sword and dropped it into the scabbard. His face was livid with passion, but by a great effort of self-control he preserved his coolness of manner.

"Halt, men of my troop. Captain Dangerfield, thou hast filled thy cup until it runneth over. There be nothing now but for me to leave thee to deal with thy merry companions here according to their desires. Give orders to thy troopers to let me pass." Ralph bowed politely.

"Fall back, men, as you were. Major, I will meet thee shortly at headquarters. I take full responsibility for all that hath happened here."

He bowed again, and Capell rejoined his troop, which withdrew in sullen silence.

As they went Charlton struck Ralph on the shoulder with one of his old laughs.

"My faith, but thou'rt the same Ralph — the very same! Truly, dear boy, an there be many like thee and these brave lads among thy Puritans, thou'lt put us Royalists to shame. Sure, I'll tell Rupert the whole tale. But I would to God," he cried earnestly, "that I might help thee once. Fate is cruel indeed. Each time we meet I am thy debtor, and all the reward thou gettest is the cursing of thy friends. 'Tis hard measure, lad, for thee."

Ralph forced a smile, though he was in no smiling humour.

"A truce to that nonsense! Fear not! Your turn will come. To-day it is my quartermaster, not me, who has been thy friend. Reuben, my lord would speak with you. You remember him, Charlton, first in the master's room at Sidney, after at Edge Hill?"

"That indeed I do. Give me thy hand, good friend, if thou'rt not too proud, like the major yonder, to have speech with a poor gentleman. Truth, there is little hardship in defeat when the conquerors be such as thou, quartermaster, and these true men of thine. In God's name and my wife's," he continued, addressing the troop, "I do most sincerely give you my best thanks, and I hereby grant ye this house and all that's in it as a free gift, providing that ye share not a cask with the snuffling rascals ye withstood so gallantly. Furthermore, mind this: fortune may turn again. Should any of you fall a prisoner in our hands and suffer ill-treatment, let him send for me, and the devil's in it but I'll see he gets full satisfaction and a quick release."

A short cheer greeted his words, and while the articles of capitulation were written out and signed the steward brought out a store of wine and food, and in a few minutes victors and vanquished were mingling together round goblets and pasties, the best of friends and comrades for the time being.

The terms Ralph granted were safe conduct for all who desired it to the royal lines, with their personal apparel and belongings. Their arms and the contents of the house were surrendered to the Parliament. The arrangements occupied two hours, and then the garrison marched away northward; while Ralph, leaving the house in charge of a picked body of men, turned his steps to camp to keep his tryst with Capell.

CHAPTER XXXIX

THE Ironsides had not covered more than two-thirds
of the distance to their quarters before they were
met by a man who rode at furious speed. It was Major
Whalley.

"What, in God's name, hath happened?" he cried,
drawing Ralph aside and lowering his voice. "The army
is in a ferment, and our regiment like to come to blows
with all the rest, because it hath got abroad that you,
with your troop at your back, hast taken side with the
malignants, nigh killed Capell, and threatened to shoot
down his men. I'd ask your pardon," the honest fellow
said, "for repeating what must be a lie had I not met
Capell himself just after he had been to my Lord Willoughby. But my lord ——"

"What said Capell?" Ralph rejoined grimly.

"Little enough. Truth to tell, the man looked as
though he had been ghost-ridden. I have never seen him
so concerned. He begged I'd bear a message to you.
'Twas this: 'Tell Dangerfield to bethink him
of the best defence he may. His life will rest upon it.'
Thus Capell, and beshrew me, Ralph, I judge the man to
be in earnest, and wishing ye well out of the coil. He
looked like a boy that, hurling a stone at a companion in
a pet, hath struck him in a vital part. I'll swear he means
you no ill now."

Ralph laughed savagely.

Thinkst so? He's a devil, Whalley, a hypocrite of
hypocrites! But what odds? Let him do his worst, I'm
in the right. Here, then, is the story of it, and a plain
and true one."

366

He described all that had had happened, to which
Whalley listened with strained attention. At the end he
swore in a way no Puritan officer had any business to
swear. Ralph felt hurt and angry.

"'Sdeath! would ye rather, then, that I should have
allowed those coistrils to set teeth into the helpless
churls, even as wolves turned loose in a fold? Should
I break my word and see murder done, and worse,
because the butcher who ordered it was one step above
me in rank? I'll swear Cromwell will uphold me."

"Oh, curse ye for a hot-brained fool!" cried Whalley.
"I blame ye? Man, I was swearing because I was not
there. As for Cromwell, were he with us who would
care? But he is away in London."

Ralph's face fell, and he began to feel anxious.

"That is a blow indeed. His departure be very
sudden."

Whalley laughed significantly.

"'Tis a call from Parliament. It is whispered that my
Lord Willoughby's doings with the women of Lincoln
and elsewhere have got wind, and that Cromwell is to
make a statement in the house upon it. Woe unto my
lord if this be so, but the worse for thee now. Indeed,
I gather from Capell's looks that an example will be
made of ye if it can be done. What defence have you?"

"That, whereas the garrison disarmed without a blow,
to slaughter them in cold blood would have been the act
of a beast."

Whalley grunted doubtfully.

"I see, I see. But were the majority not Papists?"

"What matters that?"

The major laughed.

"Ask the Presbyterians; ask Crawford, the Scotch
general of whom they say Willoughby is afeared; ask
our chaplain. Ralph, 'tis a bad business. Harkee! Do
thy best to get the clock put back, and judgment sus-
pended until Cromwell is here to plead thy cause.

367

Believe me, thou'lt have no other friend. Nay, comrade, I will tell thee the truth. I fear the worst, the very worst. But here be the provost-marshal. Now, will he arrest thee only, or has he a warrant for the troop?"

He arrested Ralph alone. The men were held blameless, as Capell was not their regimental officer.

The trial was held on the afternoon of the next day, January 22nd. It was conducted with due dignity and decorum, and Major-General Crawford, the president of the court-martial, was courtesy itself. Yet from the first Ralph felt that the day was going against him, and he marvelled at the self control of Capell, whose evidence was treated with marked respect by the judges, and who seemed to lose spirit rather than gain it as the trial proceeded.

The ceremony lasted an hour, and for half an hour longer the court discussed the matter within closed doors. Then Ralph was recalled, and General Crawford rose. He was a little man, but powerfully made, with red hair, harsh features, and prominent blue eyes.

"Captain Dangerfield, thy case hath received full and weighty consideration, and the judgment of the court upon it be unanimous. They recognise that thou hast done good service to the cause in the past, but find that thou art guilty of the offences laid to thy charge, and these offences be so grave when committed by an officer in thy position, that there be but one punishment which can justly meet them — death."

He paused an instant, as if expecting a protest or exclamation, but the prisoner's mouth only curled slightly, and he held his head a trifle higher than before, and looked hard at Capell.

"Death," the General repeated with solemn emphasis. "Thou disobeyed the orders of thy commanding officer, urged thy men to resist him by force, and when he would have reasoned with them thou assaulted him with thy weapon. It hath been under consideration of this court whether signal punishment be not given to thy troop as well. But the court is inclined to mercy, and only maketh the order that thy sentence shall be executed by a file of these men, and witnessed by the rest. Hast anything to say?"

He smiled now for the first time, the smooth dog smile that Ralph remembered of old.

"Naught, General," he replied, struggling hard with a desire to break out into bitter reproach and defiance, "naught but this. Is it your intention to kill me before Colonel Cromwell returneth to the army? If so, I would pray that the execution be deferred, so that I might see him once again. He is my friend, gentlemen," appealing to the rest; "I had almost said my father; I have none other."

An uneasy expression crossed Crawford's face for a moment. Then looking straight before him, speaking rapidly and decidedly, he answered:—

"Nay, Captain Dangerfield, that may not be. Colonel Cromwell hath chosen to leave his post in the face of the enemy to attend some private matter in London. He may be gone some days. Meantime justice awaiteth her dues. I regret his absence, as he be, you say, your friend. But be assured of this: had the man all the will to serve you which, some say, he hath to serve himself, his presence would not avail you anything. Thou'rt guilty, captain, and at rise of sun to-morrow must pay the penalty. Provost-marshal, remove the prisoner."

Ralph was then led away out of the close atmosphere of the court-house into the crisp, frosty air of a winter afternoon. He felt like a man in a dream, a nightmare he might awaken from at any moment. He could not realise that he was doomed, as surely as any common felon with a halter round his neck, but only that something had happened which had set his brain a-buzzing, and snapped a spring in it that was vibrating helplessly.

As he walked from the court-house, he was conscious that there were a group of soldiers looking and pointing at him, talking loudly and laughing, and that further away was a body of men with familiar faces, men who muttered to one another in low and bitter tones. Then he was in the guard-house alone, the door behind him closing with a clang.

Sentenced to death! He realised it now. To be shot in cold blood — why? Because again he had been trapped, and this time most successfully. Capell had chosen him to share in this enterprise because Charlton was governor; had refused quarter because he foresaw that such orders would be disregarded; and, finally, had struck down the trooper's weapon to bring upon himself the assault which he knew well would provide the court-martial with full and adequate grounds for sentence of death.

"Why, why did I not kill him long since?" Ralph muttered feverishly. "Why had I not the wit to see that he should be treated as one treats other vermin? If Cromwell — but there is the crowning piece of devil's cunning. He knew, no doubt, that Cromwell was like to be called away. Oh, he has made sure of his prey this time."

A step outside the door, and the grating of the bolts, and Capell himself came in. Ralph drew a deep breath, and his eyes gleamed.

"This is truly kind," he said, breathless with the passion that was within him. "What service can I do thee now?"

Capell looked sharply into his face, then unbuckled his sword and laid it upon the table.

"I have come," he said in a monotonous tone, "because mine own company was burdensome, and I felt it would be an easement to my spirits were I to talk awhile with thee. Dangerfield "— he had thrown himself into a chair, and now, leaning one elbow on the table, stared hard and fixedly at Ralph —"thou thinkest I have plotted for thy death, as a sleuth-hound followeth a blood-trail. Nay, speak not; I read it in thy face. Thou thinkest this damned tribunal hath condemned thee unto death by my desire. Well, thou art a fool."

Ralph's lips were white now with the force he put upon himself to put his passion down. But he trampled on it still, as a tired swimmer keeps his head, by desperate efforts, above the waves.

"Capell," he said hoarsely, "dost think that I would believe the words of so damned a villain as thyself? Thou art the fool to tempt me."

He laid his hand upon the sword, swiftly drew it, and felt its edge and point. Capell smiled sardonically, without stirring an inch.

"Lieth the wind that way? I might have known it. Nay, man," with a contemptuous motion of his hand, "wait then, and watch events; it will not profit ye yet to shed my blood. Wait, I say, wait."

He spoke with more impatience than anger, but his eyes grew watchful, and his hand tightened upon the hilt of a dagger as Ralph, without answering, turned back the sleeve of his right arm.

"Tell me," he said at last, "why hast played the hypocrite? That first."

"Hypocrite! When was I a hypocrite to thee?"

"At my bedside in Ely, when you took my hand. Pah! the slime upon thy fingers clings to me yet."

Capell sighed.

"I was no hypocrite. I loved — nay, not loved — liked ye."

"Why?"

"Because I thought that thou wouldst die," was the cool reply, "and thought, being then a fool, that thy thin face and feeble body would never stand in my way again, so I wished you well, and asked your forgiveness. 'Twas honestly meant; indeed it was."

Ralph dropped the point of his sword to the ground and leant upon it.

"Stand in thy way! What mean you by that?"

"You do not know?" Capell smiled, more bitterly than before. "Then my face hath kept its secret well, it seems, since I betrayed myself to Salingford. I loved the maiden, friend, whom you love; I love her yet. You were in my path, and now I sometimes ask God wonderingly why I let ye live; but it was so. I withheld my hand from grasping that old Papist doctor and left him to cure ye. It was for her sake, for she had supplicated me. Truly, the love of woman driveth the wits out of a man. Aye, I let you live."

"Only to kill me now, even as a cat playeth with a mouse."

"So it seemeth to you," Capell rejoined in the same cold tone in which he began, "and, indeed, when I heard of your recovery, Satan entered into my soul and gained such power with me, that of a surety I had not spared ye. But when this opportunity was given to me, though I refused to let it go, I had no intention of pushing it further than to humble your pride and gain an advantage over Cromwell. I did not think that even your hot blood would drive you to such resistance, and afterwards I knew not till I delivered my report to Willoughby that Cromwell was away, nor was I prepared for such a bitterness and hostility as the court showed toward you. God knoweth this, and before the night is gone you will know it too."

Ralph stood and looked at him in deep perplexity. After all, was the man a hypocrite? Or if he were, what did he expect to gain by it? What did he mean? The time was now late; it was just upon midnight. A lamp, which Ralph's gaoler had placed upon the table, was burning low; the fire was a mass of red embers, dwindling fast.

"How shall I know it? Tell me that."

Capell answered with a shake of the head.

"I will not waste my breath. How can a hypocrite tell the truth? Nay, I will not, but, if I be not mistaken — hark! was not that a challenge from the guard? I must see to this."

There was a murmur of voices outside the door, and Capell, rushing past Ralph, taking no kind of notice of his bared sword, went out. A minute after he returned and threw the door open with a salute.

"Colonel," he said to someone following him, "you are an hour and more before the time I had expected ye, but you're not too soon, methinks."

Then he stepped back and shut the door behind him, and Ralph sprang forward with a cry.

It was Cromwell.

CHAPTER XL

GOD ALMIGHTY, sir! how came you here?" Ralph cried, astonishment overpowering every other feeling for the moment. Then, noticing that Cromwell was plastered with mud from head to foot, and his face haggard and his limbs trembling with weariness, he added impulsively, "You are tired out. Prithee lie on my bed, and let me send for refreshment."

But Cromwell only gave an impatient grunt.

"Tush! a trifle. I had a fall i' the slush, my horse not being up to my weight. They are bringing food. I heard Capell give orders. Now thyself, Ralph. This is a desperate affair truly; how ran you into it? Tell me from the beginning."

He threw aside his cloak, sword, and hat, and as Ralph began his narrative leisurely drew off his boots and warmed his feet at the fire. He made no comments, only asking sharp questions now and then. When the story was told he said: —

"Thou misjudgest this man. I have done likewise. He aimed not at your life; you've others to thank for that. When Capell saw their intention he sent a message to me; that I am here at all we owe to him. See that you acknowledge this; the times are too critical for honest men to be at variance."

The door opened now, and a trooper came in bearing a huge pasty and a stone bottle of spiced ale, Capell following.

"By my faith, thou art a good provider, major," Cromwell exclaimed, smiling. "I will now attend diligently to the business. Ralph, see to thine."

374

He settled himself down to the pasty with a sigh of satisfaction, and Ralph held out his hand to Capell.

" I ask thy forgiveness," he began, when the other stopped him.

" A truce to all such words. They be out of place. I have, I trust, foiled those who'd undo thee in cold blood to serve their selfish ends. But I love thee not, nor thou me."

Soon after this he left the room.

Cromwell then asked more questions, but said no word of praise or blame. Yet Ralph knew that all was right between them. The tired eyes flashed when the colonel heard how his troop behaved, and a smile crossed his face at old Reuben's words. But when Ralph gave an account of the court-martial Cromwell's face became unreadable. He made no remark, except to desire Ralph to repeat his statement over again.

Then for a long time he sat before the fire deep in thought, only rousing at last to say he should sleep there, and asking Ralph to lend him a blanket. Ralph made him lie upon his bed, and, tired out himself, slept soundly. He awoke at dawn, and found that he was alone. Food was brought him, and then he ate and tramped up and down the room waiting for news. The sun rose, and he heard the sound of marching feet outside, the clink of bridles and trampling of horses' hoofs, but no one disturbed him, and he was still a prisoner.

Meanwhile Cromwell soon after dawn held a short conference with Lord Willoughby, and a meeting of the court-martial was convened for nine o'clock. The members of the court came with surprise written in their faces in a very angry mood.

The tribunal was held in Lord Willoughby's quarters in a large disused room, formerly a banqueting hall, a gloomy apartment, panelled with black oak, with heavy, cumbrous oak furniture, the walls covered with old tapestry, now moth-eaten and rotting away. The offi-

cers sat at a long table, the president at the head. When
they had all assembled, the commander-in-chief entered,
Cromwell with him. The doors were then closed, and
Lord Willoughby rose to speak. He was very pale, it
was remarked, and his eyes, shifty at the best of times,
were more restless than usual, like those of a fox which
has heard the hounds thrown off; but he bore himself
with a determined and dignified air.

"I have called you into conference, gentlemen, to
prove unto the Colonel Cromwell, who hath so suddenly disposed of his business in London and come
among us in the night, that the decision of yesterday
touching the captain of his first troop was not, as he
seems persuaded, an ill-considered and vindictive action
of mine own, but a true rendering of your united judgment, after hearing of evidence, a decision absolutely
in consonance with the usage among all military tri-
bunals, both here and abroad, for the proper maintenance of discipline and order. Gentlemen, if I have
by a word misrepresented you, I beg ye to signify it
to Colonel Cromwell."

He resumed his seat, and there was a long silence.
Then he rose again, a slight smile lurking about his lips.
"There be your answer, colonel. Do you wish to
address the court?"

Cromwell bowed, but he seemed in no hurry to speak,
and before he did so General Crawford, the President,
who had been impatiently drumming his fingers on the
table and fidgetting in his chair, sprang up with a sharp
cough, like an engine letting off steam, his eyes gleaming like an angry wolf's.

"My lord, I speak in deference," he cried in a high-
pitched acrid voice, " but I would know why it is that
our authority is set at naught, and ourselves become the
contempt of the whole army. Yesterday we passed
sentence upon an evil-doer, a friend of malignants and
Papists, a scoffer at all true religion, a mutineer, who

hath taken up arms against the godly, indeed a most
damnable sectary, one whom the devil hath made his
own long since. This man, I say, we condemned, and
when the sun rose to-day I expected to hear his death-
knell. In place of this he lives, and we are met here, at
the will of this Colonel Cromwell, to consider whether
we have acted aright. It is monstrous, my lord, beyond
all reason and excuse. Colonel Cromwell is to address
the court; let him have a care what he says. The nation
I represent giveth its support unto you Parliament that
England may repent her sins, and become godly. Were
so scandalous an incident as this to become public in
Scotland, I'd tremble for the consequences. I warn
Colonel Cromwell to beware of his loose sympathies,
lest he also fall into the pit."

He fell back into his chair with another snort, and
now Cromwell rose in good earnest.

"My lords and gentlemen," he said in a tone low,
quiet, and controlled, in startling contrast to Crawford's.

"I have much diffidence in addressing you, so strong
be my humble sense of the respect due unto this honourable court, that were it not a matter of deepest and most
vital moment to myself, yourselves, and the army, I
had not dared to thrust myself between your judgments.
Nay, I had upheld them, though they cut off my nearest and my dearest. That I do adventure a protest against
the sentence passed upon my captain must go for an
evidence to the worthy general and to others who have
known me longer than he that I consider this matter
to be of an importance which transcendeth all bounds
of military usage. I do think this, indeed I do, and,
with all the strength that is in me, I must tell ye so.
What are ye doing?" his tone suddenly changing and
filling the hall with its harsh vibration. "What are you
doing? I know your answer, putting one to death for
open mutiny. Well, mutiny be a crime, but when ye
say mutiny, I would ask against what? — just authority

or petty tyranny? God or the devil? For the one a
man should die; for the other he deserveth the encouragement of all good men. The man Charles Stuart
calls ye mutineers, and worse. Be he right? As to
the matter of my captain, I have closely questioned
Major Capell, and he telleth me that he informed this
honourable court, in clearest terms, that he held his
subordinate guilty of no crime, but only of assuming
in a manner which he thought deserved your censure,
authority that by right belonged not to him. Is Capell
a perjurer, or a false witness? Dare even General
Crawford make that accusation? The issue, an I be
not much mistaken, rests there. If you doubt me, call
the major now before your honourable presence and
question him yourselves."

Lord Willoughby smiled sardonically.

"You hear the colonel, sirs. In what manner will
you answer him?"

"Why, thus, my lord," cried Crawford, "that we took
evidence yesterday; we came to a judgment on it, and
we reverse not our opinions at the bidding of any man.
Let this Socinian be executed forthwith as he deserves."

Willoughby smiled again, but Cromwell interposed.

"A vote by hands, an't you please the president."

Crawford protested angrily, but, in response to a
request from Lord Willoughby, consented to allow it.
All voted for the prisoner's execution. It only remained
for the commander-in-chief to confirm the sentence.

Lord Willoughby bowed sweetly to Cromwell.

"I cannot hesitate. By heaven, no; the sentence is
confirmed. This man must die."

There was a crash of a falling chair, and Cromwell,
springing to his feet, struck the table a blow with his
fist that made it shake again. His face was a deep red
from neck to brow, his eyes aflame with passion.

"No; I say, no," he exclaimed, turning upon Willoughby with the glare of a lion at bay. "Thou hast

no authority to sentence this man, nor any other, were
he the meanest soldier in the army. That be the privilege of the commander-in-chief, and thou, Lord Willoughby of Parham, art *not*, and never wilt be more,
commander of this army, for which many thanks be
given unto God, and the Parliament that yesterday
ordered thy dismissal."

A chorus of exclamations greeted this astonishing
statement. The officers leapt to their feet. Crawford
drew his sword.

"Thou liar!" he yelled; "'tis naught but a vile conspiracy of sectaries, and thou the head of it. My lord,
order his arrest."

But in the midst of the clamour Willoughby himself
stood still and quiet. He was white with fury, but,
with a dignity that did honour to his name and rank,
he waved them all aside and raised his hand for silence.

"Peace, friends, peace! I thank thee, Crawford, but
thou must sheathe thy blade. So now let me speak.
Colonel Cromwell, for this insult thou shalt answer to
me as a man. For the present I take no notice of thy
words. But understand this: were thy news as true as
I believe it to be false, it would make no difference to
this business. If Parliament, through lending a willing
ear to my enemies, chooseth to appoint another to command the army, I am still commander-in-chief until that
successor arrive bearing his authority in writing. And
as such I have full power to confirm the finding of this
honourable court. I swear by the God who made me
that the sentence shall be carried out; aye, and within
the hour."

He left his chair, and with a slow and steady step
strode down the room, and would have passed out
haughtily when Cromwell laid a hand upon his arm and
pointed through the window.

"Wait, my lord," he said grimly. "He that giveth
such a sentence had better execute it. Look and see

the task which lieth before those, be they Scotch or English, who would take my captain's life."

Lord Willoughby glanced up carelessly, started, and stood still. His officers seeing this, crowded round him.

A hundred yards away stood the guard-house, which, when the members of the court-martial had passed it an hour ago, had been guarded by two musketeers. Now the pale winter sun, shining through a frosty haze, glanced upon helmets and breastplates, glittered on the blades of swords. A regiment was there, a perfectly appointed regiment of twelve full troops, seven hundred strong. Stirrup to stirrup, shoulder to shoulder, they stood, motionless, as if cast in bronze, yet every face alive with sternest resolution, every eye turned toward the court-house with grim inquiry, waiting, waiting.

" Who and what be those? " someone exclaimed.

" 'Tis a body of horse," Cromwell said in a quiet tone. " They be violent and froward fellows. Every man, I have been told, will sell his life full dear for the comrade that lieth within. My lord, I know the men. Take my word for it, they will spare none if they be roused. At present they wait, as I do, to know the ruling of this honourable court."

A deep silence followed these words. Even Crawford did not speak. All looked at Willoughby. For some moments he stood still as marble gazing at the lines of men as if he were counting them; then he shivered.

" I countermand the sentence," he said hoarsely; " the affair be not worth bloodshed. Captain Dangerfield goes free."

CHAPTER XLI

THERE was mourning in the house at Ely. Isaac Hepworth, setting out upon a visit to Rachel the day the court-martial sentenced Ralph, told the Cromwell household in all good faith that their friend was dead, for Hepworth arrived at Ely two hours after the execution was to have taken place. The minister performed his task with a tact and judgment few who knew him would have expected. Madam Cromwell and Oliver were the only two to whom he told everything. The rest knew no more than that the unfortunate young man had met his death through an act of mistaken clemency to malignants, with which military law dealt severely. Hepworth, however, might have spared himself the trouble. Ralph, to those who loved him, could do no wrong. Little Betty sobbed bitterly, and could not be comforted all day. Madam Cromwell, after making so sharp an attack on every officer in the army who might have had a hand in the matter that Hepworth was glad to escape from her presence, gave way to a grief she had not felt since her husband's death. While Rachel —

She listened to all that her uncle had to say with a face as cold and white as the snow which was beating softly against the window-pane. She assented mechanically to his kindly meant expressions of regret at the loss of a brave life, and, then escaping, went straight to her room, and was not seen again that day.

Oliver was out when the minister arrived; he was taking riding exercise daily to get back the strength of the broken limb, which took long to heal. Mightily astonished and dismayed was he at the news, and in his

381

excitement expressed himself without restraint concerning the "cursed bigots who would ruin the cause by taking harsh measures with their gallantest officers." In old days Hepworth would have exploded with wrath at such language; now he patiently held his peace. Oliver's next anxiety was about Rachel. When he heard that she had received the tidings with a calmness which had much impressed her uncle, he was greatly relieved.

"I'd feared it would have greatly put the child about. Poor sweetheart, how she slaved to save his life. Sure, sir, I was jealous; in very truth I was. Now I will comfort her in every way I can, and she will, I trust, soon have brighter things to think about."

It grew late, and when no Rachel could be found, and Oliver heard that she was in her room with a bad headache and that he would not see her till the morrow, he began to get anxious, and passed a very bad night.

The next morning at breakfast her chair was still vacant.

"She be abed," his mother said shortly, "and refuseth food, complaining of her head, but declareth that she'll be stirring presently. I know no more."

After breakfast Oliver went to his grandmother's room, but Rachel was not there, and the old lady was in so irritable a mood that he soon retreated. In despair he went to his father's library to write a letter, and there, in her usual place, quietly reading the correspondence which the messengers had brought from London, he found Rachel at last.

"My dearest, art better?" Oliver exclaimed, striding up to her with both hands out.

At the sound of his voice Rachel dropped the letters and came to meet him, but when he would have kissed her she took his hands and very gently kept him at arm's length.

"I am much better, thank you, dear, and very glad

we have met. I have a deal I wish to tell you. Would
you close that door, that none may overhear us?"

He stood a moment as if he had not heard her, seized
the door handle, and slammed it with such force that
the room shook, then returning, caught her hands again,
and held them in a grip which made them numb and
powerless.

"Rachel, why holdest thou me off this way? Thou'rt
in sorrow. Thy cheeks are pale, thine eyes heavy with
weeping. Why may I not comfort thee? God's life,
what hath happened? Thou lookest the picture of
death. Tell me what it means."

He was in a fever of excitement, and clasped her
hands more and more tightly, till she could have cried
out with the pain. But she did not mind; it was almost
a relief to suffer physically after the mental torture she
had undergone all night long. There seemed, too, a
vague justice that he should give her pain.

"I will tell, I must tell," she said, her voice strangely
altered, an intensity and passion in it which struck him
with a kind of chill. "Yet how — how shall I tell
thee?" with a catch in her breath. "Oliver, our
betrothal hath been a lie. Not with you, but me. I
promised to be your wife and should have been, and
yet all the time, though I loved you — I did indeed — I
loved another more, him who is dead. I wronged you
and Ralph, and now he is dead and will never know —
never, never!" She caught her breath again, but still
controlled herself. "I have been wicked, yet I tried to
do right. I did not know how much I loved him. But
now I know. Curse me, kill me, an you will — I deserve
it — but this is the truth, and we can be betrothed no
longer."

He laughed at her, a ghastly caricature of the laugh
of other days.

"Nonsense! I say thou'rt talking nonsense, child,"
he cried hoarsely. "Be silent. It is that your brain is

crazed with grief. The undoing of thy friend, and mine, hath turned thy head. God Almighty! must it come to this? But I say, 'tis nonsense, nay, worse. What! think ye I will let thee break thy troth now, thou, who art *mine*, and for a dead man? Nay, were he an archangel he should not now rob me of mine own. Why, bethink thee, darling," lowering his voice to one of tender entreaty, "how I love thee. Since we have been together these months I swear thou hast become a part of me, 'bone of my bone, flesh of my flesh,' as the book hath it. In a sense thou'rt my wife already. Without thee as my loadstar I shall go to wrack. Dost fear my jealousy, that I'd be hurt to think that once thou cared more for Ralph than me? Oh, thrust that from thy mind. He was a better man — I've always said it — be his religion what it might. Had he lived, indeed — But now to let you go away alone, where there be no arms to enfold thee, no happiness, no answering love, naught but a grave and saddening memories — nay, I cannot, will not, give thee up to that. Thou hast promised me. 'Slife, sweet, thou shalt keep thy word."

The old Oliver came out in the last words, and he stood before her now with his old masterful smile, his voice full of the old determined ring. But he had not to deal with the Rachel of old days, a shy young girl, startled, uncertain of herself; she was now a woman, with infinite sadness in her face, and a determination in the steady eyes and closed lips greater than his own. When she spoke the words came slowly, firmly, and the chill which had fallen on his heart when he first entered came back again.

"Oliver, thou dost not understand. Alas! how should you? How trust any words of mine, since I so deceived thee? But thou must, dearest friend and brother, more than brother. I will lay all bare unto thee. Thou canst claim that, surely. I have loved him long. Once he told me of his love, and I then refused his suit because

I'd never marry one who believed not in true religion.
This was a-many months ago. I thought I had forgot.
It seemed a duty to our Lord Jesus Christ. Then you
came home from Hull, and caring for you very much,
I gave consent to your entreaties. Afterwards, when
he lay wounded, sore doubts came upon me, but when
I prayed for guidance, an answer seemed vouchsafed
that as I had sown, so I must reap. It was not hard,
dear," with a sudden break in her voice, "for I loved
you, too. Then came yesterday, and all last night I
spent upon my knees. In early morning peace came
unto me. A voice seemed to whisper, 'Thy life belongeth to the man thou lovest, and to none else. He be in
sorest need of thee. As on earth he was for ever fighting men, so now he is beset by devils, and his soul
wrestleth desperately for salvation. Give thyself to him;
let no thoughts turn thy mind from his welfare. Pray
continually to God to show him mercy, and thou shalt
then at last bring him to peace and eternal rest.' Thus
said the voice, and then just as I was, kneeling by my
bed, I fell asleep, nor wakened till they came aknocking
at my door. After this I could not longer bear me
towards you as I used. And now thou knowest all."

She looked at him with eyes which were full of a mute
pleading, as of a culprit who has confessed a sin, and
awaits punishment with confidence in the justice of the
judge. Oliver tried to speak, but his throat was so
parched that he choked until tears came into his eyes.

"My darling, thou hast conquered. By my faith, I
have not a word to say. Blame not thyself. 'Struth,
no! It is I who am to blame; I was blind and froward,
thinking of myself, not thee. I stole thee from Ralph,
thee, to whom I had no right. Forgive me, sweet; I
did not know; and now 'tis over!" His chest heaved,
and he shivered. Then he drew himself up, and his
mouth became like his father's in the firmness of the
lips. "'Tis over. I trouble thee no more, not an

instant. 'Deed, I have troubled thee too long. I am rough and rude, and never was worthy of thee. But at least I be a man, and not a brute. I give thee up, and may God grant thee peace, the peace that my love could not give."

His voice grew husky, and was scarcely audible at the end. He turned abruptly, as if to leave the room, then drew his hands across his eyes and wheeled again.

"Nay, I will not run away, but this will be good-bye. I join the army to-night, and 'tis better we should not meet again. Bless thee and fare thee well!"

Again he turned to go, but Rachel called him back.

"Let me have thy hand once more, or I shall think that thou never can forgive."

He ran to her with a cry, and after one glance at her tear-stained face clasped her in his arms.

"May I then once more, for the last time? My darling, my darling. Forgive, sayest thou?" He dropped upon his knee and reverently kissed her hand. "Rachel, thou little knowest a man. I loved thee for thy worth's sake, not because I was beloved. Thou loved another, yet gave me months of purest happiness. Shall I forgive thee for that? Now 'tis over; but as thy heart was never mine, how shall I complain? Forgive! Thou'rt pure as crystal, and ever while my life lasts I will love thee in the far distance, as if thou wert a saint in heaven."

He kissed her hand once more, and then the door closed behind him, and she heard him whistle merrily down the passage and call to Betty.

"Hey, kitten, where art thou? Lessons? Quit them, then. I mean it i' faith. News hath come that sendeth me to the north to-night. So thou, Betsy mine, wilt have to work thy fingers to the bone to get my clothes in readiness. No resistance now or pouting! I say thou'lt come with me, and what I say everyone in this house doth do."

"Not Rachel," was the shrill reply. "She is your mistress, and her wishes be your laws."

His reply was inaudible, but Rachel, sitting in Cromwell's chair, buried her face in her hands and wept bitter, scalding tears.

It was perhaps the most miserable day in Rachel's life. Oliver's face haunted her, and she was tortured with doubts. He was so unselfish, and so honourable, and his love was of purest gold. Had she a right to reject it now? No one would think she had; all the world would be against her when the news was known. But this thought brought about a reaction. Had not everyone been against Ralph? He had stood alone, and braved them all; was she not strong enough to do likewise? Nevertheless, all the rest of the day Rachel spoke little to the other members of the family, and steadily avoided any visit to Madam Cromwell. The next morning her nerves had regained their tone, and she went in at her usual time; then her heart reproached her. The old lady's face wore an expression of grief and yearning and such sad wonder at their little one's neglect that Rachel broke down, and kneeling at her feet, her head buried in her lap, told her all. Madam Cromwell embraced her and solemnly blessed her, and then eased her own heart by confessing all the love she bore to Ralph. It was noon before Rachel left her chamber.

Madam Cromwell's apartments were upon a tiny landing, half-way up the staircase. As Rachel opened the door she heard a tread in the hall below, accompanied by the clink and ring of an iron-heeled boot. The sound surprised her, but before she could look over the banisters Madam Cromwell asked some question which obliged her to turn back. Having answered it, she closed the door, and took a step downstairs, one step, but no more. A man was at the foot of the stairs, looking at her with eager eyes and parted lips — Ralph!

Rachel gave a stifled scream. Was it a spirit? Then

the stairs creaked and swung with his weight; the eyes she thought were closed in death gazed into hers; strong and tender hands supported her as she stood dizzy and faint, clinging to the banisters.

"Mistress Rachel, have I startled thee so much?" He paused breathless. A swift flush of colour swept into her face, and her eyes brightened in so wonderful a way that his heart was thrilled with a sudden desperate hope. He had only come to say farewell. The night before he had been to Cromwell, and said that he must see her again for the last time. He had no thought of claiming a word or a look for himself, but see her he must, and Cromwell, after hesitation, had granted his wish. He had ridden all night, and stolen in quietly, mud-stained and weary.

Now his breath came quickly, yet a terror was upon him — the fear that after all he might be mistaken.

"Rachel," he panted hoarsely, "have a care. I love thee so that I would not — oh, God, I would not — wrong our friendship by a word; but if thou smilest so when thou art close to me, I'll forget all that hath passed since the day when thou wert mine, not Oliver's."

He paused again, and bent over her, for now she was trying to speak "I am not his," she whispered, and then, as Ralph caught her in his arms, "I told him it was past. He hath gone away."

By something very like a direct intervention of Providence, the Cromwell family on this particular morning were so much engaged in other parts of the house that, though Rachel and Ralph stood together on the landing for a full half-hour, no one disturbed them, or indeed knew of Ralph's existence, for he had opened the front door himself. At the end of that time Rachel bethought her of Madam Cromwell, and taking her lover by the hand, led him to her room.

"A visitor, grannie," Rachel said, opening the door

a very little way, "who hath brought surprising news. May I admit him?"

She peeped in, keeping Ralph out of sight, but at the first glimpse of her happy face Madam Cromwell sprang up.

"What hidest thou? Nay, only one thing could turn thy mourning into such joy. Is it Ralph arisen from the dead? Hath he escaped?"

"Reprieved, dear madam. Indeed, I am no runaway."

He knelt to receive her blessing, and the old lady wept.

"May the Lord God Almighty bless thee, dearest son. Aye, and may He bring about in His good time thy happiness and hers. I do pray for it," with a return of her brisk, curt tones; "but methinks, young sir, thou hast stolen a march upon them all by thy avowal. Ah, I thought 'twas so. Then mark me well. Though thou hast won a maiden's heart, the world, and my son in the front of it, will be against thee. And none knoweth better than thou what ill-hap cometh to those who have to oppose him. Thou wilt have to fight hard, Ralph, if thou wouldst win."

CHAPTER XLII

RALPH had very few hours to spend at Ely. He had promised Cromwell that he would be at his post the next morning, and was obliged to start early in the afternoon and spend a second night in the saddle. No one in the family, except Madam Cromwell, knew of what had happened. After an anxious conference in the old lady's room, it was agreed between the lovers that, until Cromwell gave his consent, they should not meet, and that they would not marry without his sanction, Ralph being confident that it would be given sooner or later. Madam Cromwell, however, who was an interested listener to the discussion, though she approved of the decision, sighed and shook her head.

"He cannot. Think him not stony-hearted, Ralph, though I need not say it — thou knowest him too well — but 'tis impossible. I can't tell thee why. The only chance will be to wait with patience and with constancy, and ask God to find a way."

Twenty-four hours later Ralph was in Cromwell's quarters. Cromwell listened to the confession without the least surprise.

"I have seen Oliver," was all he said. "No, thou canst not; he is away with Fairfax, and thy place be here. So, after all, her heart is thine? A pity, a pity! Thou canst never marry. NEVER! She is a Christian, thou one who denieth the God-head of Christ. Thou must not even see her; I have thy word? Good. I trust thee both. Do thy duty, lad. Pray for guidance, pray earnestly by day and by night, and may God's will be done."

Then he turned to military matters, and Ralph felt that, for the present, all was over; he must wait and pray.

Events were marching swiftly in the north of England. The day Ralph was sentenced by the court-martial, the Earl of Manchester was given the chief command of the eastern counties, and Cromwell appointed a lieutenant-general, with command of the horse. At once the campaign, which, in Lord Willoughby's hands had begun in a sluggish and uncertain manner, became brisk and effective, and one after another of the strongholds and towns in Lincolnshire taken the preceding autumn by the Marquis of Newcastle were recovered. Meantime the Scottish army under Leslie, Lord Leven, was steadily advancing from the north, and Fairfax broke out of Hull and joined them. The Ironsides were hard at work, and Ralph soon had an opportunity to recover his reputation even among the strictest of the Presbyterians, and in February received promotion, becoming major of the regiment, with Whalley as colonel.

In May, Cromwell, who had been campaigning in the south, returned to Lincolnshire, which was now in the hands of the Parliament. Leslie reached York, to which city Newcastle had now retired, and the attention of all England turned northward, the Parliamentarians with hope, and the Royalists with keenest anxiety. By June the three armies, under Leslie, Manchester, and Fairfax, joined hands before York, and the king sent an urgent message to Prince Rupert to succour Newcastle at all hazards.

Rupert was in Lancashire, carrying all before him. He marched eastward at once, with 20,000 men, and coming before the Parliament generals were prepared to meet him, slipped past their armies, and on the 30th of June relieved the city. Again the fortunes of the Royalists were in the ascendant. Newcastle and Rupert were the strongest men in the king's army; their troops were veterans; together they outnumbered the Parliament, and the fiery Prince declared the time had come to take the Roundheads by the throat and crush them by one decisive battle.

This was expected by Manchester and Cromwell, and, after some dispute among the generals, the Parliament army fell back a few miles, and spent the night of July 1st on the ridge of Marston Moor.

It was the evening of that day. Ralph had been busy with Whalley putting the regiment into the best trim possible, for the rumour had spread that Rupert's Life Guards, and the famous "king's old horse," under Goring, were in York. These were the men who had broken the Parliament left wing at Edge Hill, and had never been beaten since. Every man among the Ironsides prayed fervently upon his knees that God would give his regiment the opportunity of meeting these men next day. Sweetlove was captain of the first troop now; Sanctify, lieutenant; Micklejohn, quartermaster. In Cromwell's regiment promotion went by merit, and merit only.

Ralph was tired and hungry, and devoured with relish a plain supper of black bread and water, and looked forward to an undisturbed sleep to fit him for the fatigues of the morrow. He was in sound health now, and hard fighting condition. Life was anxious, and the future dark, but there were no more doubts or fears. He was beloved, and Rachel would wait, wait a lifetime, if need be. He had only one wish now: to see Oliver. His heart smote him at the thought of what the old lad must be suffering. Ralph would have given much, very much, to have had him at his side in the fight that was coming. Bitterness between them was out of the question, yet they never met. And now, perhaps, they would never meet. Ralph thought of this as he ate his supper, and was thinking of it when he heard the ring of hoofs, a sentry's challenge, and then a man came in and greeted him: Capell.

Capell was panting and exhausted, his face streaked with blood, blood on his armour and doublet, blood and dust on his boots.

"I've been sent for thee. I will tell my errand as we ride. Come quickly."

Ralph was on his feet in an instant. He asked no questions, but ordered a horse for himself and a fresh one for Capell, made him drink a stiff glass of cognac, and mounted.

"Where go we?"

"Northward for ten miles, to a village they call Knaresborough. A man lieth there at the point of death: Oliver Cromwell, the General's son."

"Wounded? How?"

"In a very bloody skirmish, thrust through the lung. He was able to ask to see thee; then he fell speechless. If we find him alive it will be a miracle. But I swore to bring thee."

"Doth his father know?"

"A trooper went for him. He will be there before us."

There was another question on Ralph's lips, but he did not ask it. Capell read it in his face.

"You'd know how I came to be the messenger? I was sent by Manchester to seek Fairfax, who hath been riding broadcast all the day, taking observation of the enemy's position. I lost my way upon the moors, and by evil chance I came upon a picket of malignant dragooners, and should have lost my life — for their horses were swifter than mine own — when I fell in with young Captain Cromwell and his troop. All would have been well had he not chased the enemy into an ambuscade, where two troops set upon him. By the grace of God, our troopers beat them off handsomely in the end, but our loss was heavy, and the captain was first to fall."

He hastened the speed of his horse, and Ralph asked no more questions. Yet he wondered why had Capell ridden so furiously, nearly killed his horse, and wearied out himself for a man he scarcely knew?

Knaresborough was reached as it was growing dark and chill, and Capell pointed to a labourer's hut, before which stood a sentry. Another trooper was holding a horse, which Ralph recognised as Cromwell's.

"Go thou in," Capell said, dismounting. "Wait not for me. I may come again to thy quarter to hear, to know, if his mind was eased before he died."

Ralph clutched him impulsively by the shoulder.

"Capell, tell me, why didst thou come to me thyself when a trooper might have served?"

But the major drew away frowning.

"Ask him; I will never tell."

Ralph went in, and Capell, remounting, rode slowly back to the army. He was deadly weary and allowed his horse to go at its own pace. What a failure his life had been of late! The only hope of Rachel's freedom, since Ralph had recovered from his wounds, had been his death in action; now this hope was gone. Oliver had told Capell why Rachel had broken their engagement, and frankly stated that his motive for doing so was to prove that, whether Ralph were alive or dead, no one else could win her. Capell had been touched by the words of the dying man, and so became the bearer of his message to Ralph, and no trooper would have ridden at such speed.

Now, it was over, and Oliver dead. Dangerfield need fear no rivalry from anyone.

"Why should I desire a woman that hath been ever cold towards me?" Capell said bitterly to himself. "It hath been a most cursed weakness; I will never think of her again, or him. 'Twas a sort of fever in my blood. It hath passed and left no effects behind. I am free, free!"

He filled his lungs with a deep breath of the fresh moorland air and rode on. Suddenly his horse neighed, and in the failing light he saw a horseman approaching him. He was still two miles from the army; not a human creature was within hail. The stranger and he were alone.

"Who goeth there?" Capell said, drawing his pistol. There was no answer, and he raised it; then a harsh laugh grated on his ear and made him start.

"Put away, put away, psalm-singer. Zounds, have I indeed found thee at last, and in fair and open field? Nay, then, but my luck hath not forsaken me. If my friends desert, mine enemy cometh to meet me. Stand, damned hound! Rememberest me not, the gentleman whom thou dared to lay thy hands upon after Edge Hill fight? Hast won that girl to wife? If so, then let her say her prayers and marry someone else; she'll see thee no more. Stand!"

It was Sir John Salingford; yet Capell could not have recognised him but for the voice. His armour was rusty, his boots in holes, his doublet in tatters. He was a mere wreck of the man who led his troop against Lindsay's Royal Guards. Debauchery and drink had ruined him. His relations had disowned him; he had been drummed out of his regiment, and now had become that loathsome species of human brute, bred by civil war, which plunders helpless villagers by night and hides all day from the men-at-arms.

The men dismounted, secured their horses, and threw off their armour and heavy boots. A moment at the guard, and then they closed upon one another, fighting desperately, savagely — a duel to the death. Blood soon flowed freely from both, but neither gained much advantage, for they were a good match. Then Capell's strength began to tell, and, of a sudden, Salingford tripped backwards and fell, and the major's sword was at his throat, his foot upon his neck.

"Repent!" the victor gasped. "Call on Christ, thy Saviour, for mercy; I will give thee time for that."

"I have no breath," was the answer. "Thou chokest me."

He had dropped his sword, and his hands were held stiffly at his sides. Capell removed his foot.

"I give thee three minutes."

"Nay, one will do. Devil, I have outwitted thee."

He leapt from the ground, and, too late, Capell saw that he had secreted a dagger up his sleeve. Again they closed and fell together upon the ground, and twice a thin thread of blue steel gleamed in the air, and twice it was buried to the hilt. But now Capell knelt upon the villain's chest, and he struggled and struck in vain. A gurgling cry, a fearful straining and contortion of the limbs, and he lay still. Capell rose slowly, feebly, and pressed his hand against his side; then he tried to reach his horse, but dropped upon his knees before he could get half-way, and among the moorland grass a stream of life-blood trickled slowly. He raised his hands in prayer.

"Be merciful, Lord, to a sinner. Bless her; give him faith. Give — give happiness to both."

He began to rock to and fro, a shudder passed through him, and he fell forward on his face. A cold wind blew over the moors, and the horses shivered and shrank close to one another and neighed pitifully. A pale moon rose and shed its light abroad, and shone upon the sleeping army and on these two men lying dead.

In Knaresborough the sentinel stood before the door, the trooper held the horses, and Cromwell and Ralph sat in silence by a rude bed of straw. They held Oliver's hands, Cromwell the right, Ralph his left, Oliver, who was conscious, though speechless, having signified this to be his wish by a turn of his head and faint movement of his fingers. Thus they waited — waited for the end. At intervals the dying man would make desperate efforts

to speak, but his lips seemed too stiff to shape the words.
At last, gazing into the wistful eyes, Ralph read a meaning in them, and laying his other hand in Cromwell's,
whispered: —

"Father!"

A smile, happy and content, lit up the face on the bed,
and became almost joyous when Cromwell grasped
Ralph's hand, and in a deep whisper answered: —

"Son!"

Then they sat in silence again, and now moment by
moment the dying face grew whiter, the feeble hands
cold and flaccid, the eyes dull and heavy. Of a sudden
he roused, and with a strength amazing in his condition, brought both Cromwell's hands and Ralph's
together within his own, grasped them strongly, and
whispered: —

"Father, love him! Naught"—he choked and fought
for breath —"*naught* must stand between them. I
know — I know"— his face worked convulsively, great
beads of perspiration stood upon his brow, but his will
conquered his weakness —"I know now that it be God's
will."

He stopped, coughing violently and spitting blood,
then lay quiet again and smiled upon them. All at
once he turned his head on the pillow, like a child falling
asleep, and murmuring, "Rachel — dearest — my dearest!" closed his eyes, and his breath stopped.

Silently then Ralph and Cromwell rose and kissed him
on the forehead, bathing it with their hot tears. Then
Cromwell said in broken tones: —

"'The Lord giveth, and the Lord taketh away;
blessed be the name of the Lord.' Ralph, there'll be
battle on the morrow; God knows the outcome. After
it is over, if we be alive, come ye to me, and we will
open our minds and hearts to one another. God's blessing rest on thee, my son."

CHAPTER XLIII

THE sun was near its setting after a day of hail and rain, with bursts of hot sunshine in between. The wind had dropped, the thunder only growled sleepily at long intervals in the distance, and though the clouds were still heaped up in dark masses to the eastward, they rested on the horizon like tired warriors, spent with the warfare of the day. On the plain six miles from York, fronting the ridge of moorland above the village of Long Marston, lay the Royalist army. It had been gathering there since early morning, approaching the army of the Parliament which lined the ridge, and since four in the afternoon the forces had only been separated by three hundred yards of bushy, marshy ground; the men on either side could recognise by uniform and standard those with whom they were to wrestle when the signal came to charge.

It seemed to the Parliament cavalry that this would never come. All day the Ironsides, under Cromwell, on the left wing, and Lord Fairfax and his Yorkshiremen on the right, stood facing the plain that stretched towards York, watching the columns of the enemy draw nearer and nearer, while their own infantry, which had been ordered southwards some miles early in the day, under a belief that Rupert would not risk a battle after all, were hurriedly marched back again and took up their position in the centre. Yet both armies stood in line of battle for two hours, and no advance was made on either side. The Parliamentarians were on higher ground; but in front of the Royalist lines was a deep broad ditch lined with their musketeers — a nasty break-water for charging cavalry.

It was nearly seven o'clock; the rays of the sun, gleaming horizontally athwart the plain between clouds of inky blackness, flashed upon the breast-plates of Rupert's squadrons on the right and Goring's on the left, and lit up the facings of Newcastle's famous " white-coats" in the centre, leaving the Parliament men dark and threatening on the ridge above. And now, like the first flash of lightning and growl of thunder which heralds the storm, from this ridge there came the report of cannon, and the Parliament line swung forward and advanced at a foot pace down the hill. They marched two hundred yards, then halted, and then the armies were within a hundred and fifty feet of one another. A pause like that curious stillness that precedes the heavy patter of thunder rain, and then sharp and clear and shrill rang out a trumpet call.

"Praise ye God; praise ye the Lord," cried a deep voice in the van of the Parliament left — Captain Reuben Sweetlove's. "Men, we lead the attack against Rupert's Life Guards, and Noll himself rides with us."

That was Reuben's address to his men, and had he been able to pour out words of burning eloquence, they would not have served his purpose half so well. Though the Ironsides were veterans worn with two years' constant fighting, and with a discipline more hardening than warfare, when Cromwell — the man had made them what they were, the friend of each, the idol of them all — rode quietly up to lead the fighting line, a cry went forth of deep joy and exultation. As Cromwell heard it, he wheeled round, and Ralph, who was nearest to him, saw him flush deeply and his lips tremble.

"Men, old comrades and tried friends, upon ye more than others will rest the issue of the day. I thank you for your welcome, but I've naught to say. I've proved your courage and your strength. May God prosper the right. Fall in."

Fifty yards of spongy ground, covered with whin-bushes, the ditch, by good fortune, dry, with sloping banks, and then the enemy. Behind the Ironsides were four other regiments of horse, and in their rear the reserve, three regiments of Scottish bordermen under one David Leslie. And as the cavalry of the left wing swept down upon Rupert, the musketeers and pikemen of the centre, under Manchester and Leven, advanced at the double; and Fairfax on the right charged gallantly upon the king's old horse, under Goring.

Down the hill, across the ditch, not a horse stumbling, rode the Ironsides, and, with swords high in air and a mighty swing and crash, charged the front ranks of the Royalist right wing, " Byron's horse." The Cavaliers met the charge bravely and well, but the onset of Cromwell's men was irresistible, and their perfect discipline carried all before it. Vainly the royal troopers dashed themselves against the iron wall; on it went resistlessly, and Byron's horse, Rupert's advance guard, gave way. But now behind them there was a sound as of the rising of the sea. A thousand horses at a gallop, a thousand helmets with their tossing plumes, a thousand broadswords flashing in the setting sun, and Rupert's guards charged in.

The Ironsides were ready. Above the tumult and the rush of troopers, above the war-cry of the Cavaliers, the regiment heard Cromwell's order: —

" Close, men, close. God with us!"

Stirrup to stirrup, shoulder to shoulder, they met that onslaught which none had ever stayed before, and then was fighting such as had never been throughout the war.

The minutes pass. Swords crash home through breastplate, bone, and flesh; horses reel, lifted by rein and spur, rear, and spring forward for the counterstroke. Their riders hack and hew, and often clutch and grapple hand to hand and tear one another to the ground, and struggling still, die beneath the plunging hoofs.

The minutes pass, and there is no advantage yet for either side. The Ironsides hold together, but Rupert's guards are better horsed and more expert with the sword and force them backwards. The fiery Prince is fighting in the van, and once Ralph and he cross swords. But before they have time to deal any fatal blow they are separated by the press about them, and Ralph grinds his teeth and curses aloud. The thought of his old vow to Taunton is in his brain. He would dearly love to slay the nephew of the king.

The minutes pass. The Ironsides are losing ground, only a few yards, but losing. An exultant cry from the guards, then a louder cry, swelling to a triumphant yell as one of Rupert's subalterns, striking at Cromwell, wounds him deeply in the neck. He reels, and but for Ralph would have fallen from his saddle.

"My God! have they killed thee, father?"

"Nay, man," with a grim smile, "a stroke i' the flesh, a little blood. Lead thou the men; Whalley is dead. I'll ride to the rear and bring up the reserve."

He bound a handkerchief round the wound and wheeled his horse, and between him and the Cavaliers closed in a line of men which not the hottest of the Life Guards could pierce.

Yet the line was weakening, bending. One more rush, and Rupert would break through. Ralph saw it, and a fury came upon him. Were his men, the best in all the army, to be beaten back by these Cavaliers? He raised himself in the stirrups with a look upon his face that his men had never seen, and his sword was like a feather in his hands. With one sweep he cut down two of the guards who were pressing upon him, and then, turning in his saddle, he cried out: —

"Men, lads of my old troop, Cromwell's struck. Shall

they not pay for this? Then *charge*, for the love of God!"

A shout hoarse and inarticulate as the growl of a wounded lion, and then Ralph dug his spurs into his horse, the maddened beast sprang forward, and behind him there came three score troopers, bursting like a thunderbolt upon the exultant Cavaliers, and fighting as men possessed. The excitement spread through the regiment. Blows were rained upon them from the Life Guards' heavy swords, but they gave back two for one. In vain the Prince called upon his men to "drive those dogs to hell." They gained ground fast, the advance of the guards was stayed, and with one mighty heave and strain their line was broken, and the famous regiment rent in twain. But now beyond them two more regiments were forming for the charge, Grandison's reserve. The wearied Ironsides saw it and grimly closed their ranks once more; but ere they met them there came the glad sound of squadrons advancing from the right, and down at a swinging gallop came Leslie and his Scots. It was just in time.

The minutes pass, but now the scene has changed.

Backwards to right, to left, the scattered Royalists reel beneath the stroke. "God and the king!" grows faint; "God with us!" rends the air. Soon it became a rout, and northwards and eastwards the broken squadrons fled for their lives. A short and fierce pursuit, and then the trumpet sounded the recall.

One struggle was now over; a good breathing space was gained. The Ironsides returned slowly and unwillingly. They long to do unto these haughty Cavaliers what Rupert has so often done to others: hack and slay until hardly one remained alive. But the trumpet called them, and though revenge was sweet, discipline came first. So back they came, and fell quietly into rank; then cheered as through the wreaths of cannon smoke which hid the battle of the centre and right wing three horsemen galloped up: Cromwell, Manchester, and Sir Thomas Fairfax.

Cromwell, though very pale, was himself again, his mien erect, his voice strong and decisive, his eyes roving round the field and seizing every point. Manchester looked dazed and half stunned; Fairfax was badly wounded in the face. Not a man who saw the leaders but knew that, be their proper rank what it might, Cromwell was commanding now.

"Our right wing hath given way," he said to Ralph; "our centre be mostly driven from the field, Lord Fairfax and Lord Leven fled. Ye have the men in hand? Good. Then we make eastwards. Close there to the left. Steady at the trot!"

Across the moor they rode from west to east, towards York, over the ground where but an hour ago had been the Royalists' centre, which now was well in the heart of the Parliamentary position, carrying all before it. The moor was a mass of churned filth, slippery with blood, cumbered with bodies of dead and dying men, with artillery waggons, and the guns from which the gunners fled as the mass of horsemen swept upon them, solid squares of steel and iron. Past them the Ironsides rode without a glance to right or left, past stragglers, who had fallen out of rank, some from fear, some to plunder helpless comrades, on to where the battle is raging hottest, where Newcastle's white-coats are driving all before them. Now they are abreast of the position, and every trooper tightens rein, expecting to hear the order come to wheel and prepare to charge. But no order comes. Cromwell seems unconscious of the death-struggle that goes so bitterly against his friends. The men are amazed, and Ralph, unable to contain himself, cries out:—

"Shall we not strike them, sir? Our foot seem in a parlous state."

"Hold thy peace," was the stern rejoinder. "Thou

knowest naught. Forward, I say, forward! There be other work to do."

Forward they went, perplexed, but confident; Cromwell leading, with stern and quiet face, the face of the man who *knew*.

Most puzzled of all was Ralph; then, of a sudden, the truth flashed across him. Goring, with the cavalry of the left wing which had crushed Fairfax — he it is whom Cromwell seeks, knowing that should the "king's old horse" return while he was charging the white-coats he would be caught between two fires. And now, in the gathering gloom, they see horsemen approaching them, a large body of men riding fast. At sight of the Ironsides rapidly forming for the charge, these Cavaliers pause and hesitate. They have not expected this; they are taken by surprise. In vain do their leaders, Lucas, Urry, and Goring himself, tear up and down the ranks, shouting, cursing, imploring them to close. They advance readily enough to fight, for they are brave men, but their lines are ill-dressed, the squadrons in disorder. Then from the Parliamentary ranks come the words of command, and the Ironsides sweep upon them, every horse in hand, every squadron in its place.

" Charge! "

They shout no battle-cry; they keep their breath for blows. A fierce, mad rush of Cavaliers, a furious pounding hand to hand, and the "king's old horse" are hurled backwards, and thrown into irretrievable confusion. A panic quickly follows, and then away they go, pursued by the Ironsides, across the moor, over Atterwick Dyke, never drawing rein until they reach the gates of York. Meantimes the Ironsides rally, and now the white-coats, which three Scotch regiments still hold at bay, feel the weight of Cromwell's charge on flank and rear, and by ten of the clock, the battle of Marston Moor was won.

CHAPTER XLIV

THE day after the battle. There had been a council of war at Cromwell's quarters, but it was over, and Ralph, appointed that day colonel of the regiment, stood before his commander leaning on his sword.

"Thou askest much, too much," Cromwell was saying, with a curious hesitancy and uneasiness of tone. "Yet I say not that I'll deny thee. Nay, go if thou wilt, but be not too long away. I can't do without thee, Ralph; there be too much on our hands."

"I will wait for a better opportunity," Ralph answered. "Think no more of the matter."

Cromwell began to pace the room.

"If 'twould do thee a service, I'd insist upon it. I desire nothing but thy welfare."

"Your pardon, sir," was the blunt rejoinder; "that be not the truth."

"I say thy welfare," Cromwell repeated, raising his voice, "to see her whom you love, but may never possess ——"

"Never?"

They faced one another, Cromwell stern, yet troubled, Ralph dark and passionate.

"Son," Cromwell said, with an infinite sadness in his voice, "be sure that this denial of what thy soul craveth for be bitter to me, nigh as bitter as it is to thee. Indeed, since the death of our dear lad, it hath weighed upon my heart like lead. I cannot rid me of it. Every moment that I am at leisure I do pray to God to guide me, but the way is dark. I am as a child wandering in a wilderness, that knoweth not which way to turn, and so goeth round and round in a weary circle. I love thee, Ralph; I love thee so that even thine unbelief would not cause me now to withhold my consent to thy union with Rachel; but I have sworn to Hepworth that while thou holdest thy present heresy I'd keep thee separate from her. I took this oath in God's presence, my hand upon His holy book. Oliver knew not this."

Ralph drew a long, slow breath, and his head drooped. When he raised it his face was grey, as if ten years had passed over it.

"Then, indeed, sir, we may say farewell to all hope of happiness. I knew not this either. We have determined that against your wish we'll never marry. I will not take more of your leisure," moving towards the door; "I must write to her; you shall read the letter. My darling, my poor darling!"

His voice dropped to a whisper, but Cromwell caught the words. Ralph went to the door, and then looked back. He longed for a sign of sympathy and feeling, but Cromwell's face, turned partly away from him, was stern and inflexible.

"Be this religion?" Ralph muttered with a sudden bitterness. Then standing erect, he said, "May God have mercy, father, upon us both."

He was passing out, when Cromwell beckoned to him.

"Hither, I say, hither!" the words uttered in a low, strained voice.

Ralph came back wondering; Cromwell's mouth was set like steel, the whole face expressive of the sternest resolution, yet in his eyes there was a curious light.

"Give me thy hand, and look into my face. So! Aye, indeed, thou art like him. Thou art what he might have been; when first I saw thee I said so: thou hast proved it since. I mean not Oliver, but Robert, whom thou never saw, the dearest of all — of all. He died before his manhood came. May thou never know the bitterness of losing thy firstborn. I reproached God for it, but He was merciful unto me and sent thee. While thou wast speaking my mind went back over the two years that we have been together. Boy, thou hast thy faults — God be thanked for it, I'd be no fit companion for thee else — but thou hast been faithful, truthful, with a courage few possess. Why hast thou given me such service? I have been hard to thee always and unjust, yet never hast thou failed me, not even when, in my blindness, I'd have cut thee from my side. Why? Yet answer not," holding up his hand, "I know the reason: 'tis the power of loving that is in thee, that is it; and when that be in a man — I say *a man* — then doth he become a true disciple of our Lord, who died for love of men. Thou art one whom He would have loved. I say thou art!" with a sudden change of tone, as if he had been contradicted, "and being such, be worthy of the best. Lad, I love thee very dear, and as thou turned away in thy deep despair a whisper came — verily it came from heaven — that were I worthy of the love which thou hast given me I should allow *naught* to stand 'tween thy happiness and hers. I swore an oath once, but it was in ignorance, in blindness. I deplore thine unbelief, but, by the God that made me, Ralph, thou art a better man than I. So thou shalt go home to-morrow, and take my love and greetings to Rachel, and a letter to Hepworth. Beshrew me, Ralph, that man loveth thee now full well, yet he will dispute us to the last. Let him do his worst. I have ne'er failed yet to find a means to compass what my conscience saith is right, so have no fears. I have found guidance. The Lord Himself hath spoken, and my mind's at rest. 'Those whom God hath joined let no man put asunder.' Amen, amen."

THE END.

By WILLIAM BLACK

By Sir WALTER BESANT

IN DEACON'S ORDERS, and Other Stories. 12mo, Cloth, Ornamental, $1 25.

BEYOND THE DREAMS OF AVARICE, Illustrated. 12mo, Cloth, $1 50.

ARMOREL OF LYONESSE. Illustrated. 12mo, Cloth, $1 25; 8vo, Paper, 50 cents.

ALL SORTS AND CONDITIONS OF MEN. Illustrated. 12mo, Cloth, $1 25; 8vo, Paper, 50 cents.

GASPARD DE COLIGNY. 16mo, Cloth, 30 cents.

CHILDREN OF GIBEON. 12mo, Cloth, $1 25; 8vo, Paper, 50 cents.

FIFTY YEARS AGO. Illustrated. 8vo, Cloth, $2 50.

HERR PAULUS. 8vo, Paper, 35 cents.

FOR FAITH AND FREEDOM. Illustrated. 12mo, Cloth, $1 25; 8vo, Paper, 50 cents.

LONDON. Illustrated. 8vo, Cloth, Ornamental, $3 00.

ST. KATHARINE'S BY THE TOWER. Illustrated. 12mo, Cloth, $1 25; 8vo, Paper, 50 cents.

THE BELL OF ST. PAUL'S. 8vo, Paper, 35 cents.

THE IVORY GATE. 12mo, Cloth, $1 25.

THE REBEL QUEEN. Illustrated. 12mo, Cloth, $1 50.

THE WORLD WENT VERY WELL THEN. Illustrated. 12mo, Cloth, $1 25.

THE INNER HOUSE. 8vo, Paper, 30 cents.

VERBENA CAMELLIA STEPHANOTIS. 8vo, Paper, 50 cents.

HARPER & BROTHERS, Publishers

NEW YORK AND LONDON

☞ *Any of the above works will be sent by mail, postage prepaid, to any part of the United States, Canada, or Mexico, on receipt of the price.*

By S. R. CROCKETT

THE RED AXE. A Novel. Illustrated by FRANK RICHARDS.

Mr. Crockett can always be depended upon for a good story, and his many admirers will not be disappointed by "The Red Axe," which is an uncommonly strong novel of adventure.—*Brooklyn Standard-Union.*

Not only will his faithful readers be satisfied by "The Red Axe," but it is likely to add numerous new friends to his constituency.—*Philadelphia Press.*

LOCHINVAR. A Novel. Illustrated by T. DE THULSTRUP.

Admirers of S. R. Crockett will find occasion for neither surprise nor disappointment in his new story, "Lochinvar." It is just what we might expect of him after the assurance his other writings have given of the stability of his capacity for fine romantic fiction. He gives every indication that he is in the plenitude of his powers and graces as a constructionist and narrator.—*Washington Times.*

THE GRAY MAN. A Novel. Illustrated by SEYMOUR LUCAS, R.A.

A strong book, . . . masterly in its portrayals of character and historic events.—*Boston Congregationalist.*

Unquestionably a vigorous and thoroughly engrossing tale; one that adds to Crockett's fame.— *Chicago Standard.*

Post 8vo, Cloth, Ornamental, $1 50 per volume.

HARPER & BROTHERS, PUBLISHERS
NEW YORK AND LONDON

☞ *Any of the above works will be sent by mail, postage prepaid, to any part of the United States, Canada, or Mexico, on receipt of the price.*

By HENRY SETON MERRIMAN

RODEN'S CORNER. A Novel. With Illustrations by T. DE THULSTRUP. Post 8vo, Cloth, Ornamental, $1 75.

An extremely interesting and well-written novel.—*Spectator*, London.

A story that is far too interesting to lay down until the last page is turned.—*St. James's Gazette*, London.

He handles it with vigor, and maintains in this new field the reputation gained by his former novels.—*Outlook*, N. Y.

THE SOWERS. A Novel. Post 8vo, Cloth, Ornamental, $1 25.

"The Sowers," for subtlety of plot, for brilliancy of dialogue, and for epigrammatic analysis of character, is one of the cleverest books of the season.—*Churchman*, N. Y.

There have been few such good novels for years.—*Illustrated London News*.

The book is strong, epigrammatic, and logical.—*Critic*, N. Y.

A story of absorbing interest from the first page to the last.—*Scotsman*, Edinburgh.

WITH EDGED TOOLS. A Novel. Post 8vo, Cloth, Ornamental, $1 25.

Mr. Merriman is so original, and has such a nice knack of putting things together, that he keeps up the interest on every page. . . . The story ought to be one of the successful romances of the season.—*N. Y. Times*.

A remarkable novel. It is long since we have read so good a novel as this.—*N. Y. Mail and Express*.

FROM ONE GENERATION TO ANOTHER. A Novel. Post 8vo, Cloth, Ornamental, $1 25.

A book of unusual force. It contains a remarkably acute study of a selfish and silly woman—one almost perfect in construction.—*N. Y. Tribune*.

We have no hesitation in recommending it as a decidedly good and entertaining novel.—*Spectator*, London.

THE PHANTOM FUTURE. A Novel. Post 8vo, Cloth, $1 25.

To those who relish a minute and searching analysis of character, and who appreciate refinement and purity of style, we may recommend "The Phantom Future." . . . A charming story.—*N. Y. Sun*.

HARPER & BROTHERS, Publishers
NEW YORK AND LONDON

www.ingramcontent.com/pod-product-compliance
Lightning Source LLC
Chambersburg PA
CBHW030816110726
47900CB00006B/1643